EAST WIND

EAST WIND

BY

Julie Ellis

ARBOR HOUSE

NEW YORK

For Peggy and Fred McFeeters—
dear friends in good times and bad

Acknowledgments

I would like to express my deep thanks to the staffs of the various divisions of the New York Public Library, and especially to Nancy Krumholtz of the Jewish Division. My thanks, too, to the librarians at the Mid-Manhattan Branch, the Lincoln Center Branch and to Mr. Green of the Epiphany Branch.

My gratitude to the staff of the YIVO Institute of Jewish Research and to the librarians at the Museum of the City of New York, the Jewish Museum, the New York Historical Society, the British Museum in London and the Bradley Museum in Columbus, Georgia.

My thanks, also, to the Hong Kong Tourist Association, the office staff of Congregation Shearith Israel in New York City, to Rabbi A. Stanley Dreyfus of the Union of American Hebrew Congregations and to my dear friends Florence and Edgar Fink and Barbara and Hy Brett for being my "Information Bureau for Jewish Traditions" on many occasions.

My thanks to my son Richard for research on my behalf at the various libraries of Columbia University and to my daughter Susan for an able assist in research and copy editing.

CHAPTER

ONE

I N A THIRD floor bedroom of the Gomez house on Manhattan's Central Park West—fast becoming a favored residential neighborhood in this year of 1906—raven-haired sixteen-year-old Constance Levy sat in a slipper chair drawn up before a tall, narrow, lace-curtained window and gazed out on the overcast late afternoon.

Her slender shoulders were hunched beneath the delicate gray voile of her shirtwaist, her hands clasped tightly in her lap, white knuckles framing long, tapered fingers. Her blue eyes mirrored inconsolable grief. Framing her delicate upturned nose and gentle mouth was an expression worn by a parade of sleepless nights.

Eight days earlier Constance stood with family friends Thomas and Esther Gomez beside her mother's grave in the Cypress Hills Cemetery in Brooklyn—where members of Congregation Shearith Israel were always buried—and watched while the simple coffin was lowered into the earth. *How could she go on living without Mama?*

"Constance—" Esther Gomez's rich voice echoed in the hallway, "we'll be sitting down to dinner in about fifteen minutes."

"Yes, ma'am," Constance replied. Each meal was torture. The very thought of food nauseated her. But three times a day she sat obediently at the table and made a show of eating because she knew that loving Mrs. Gomez would worry if she didn't.

Constance rose to her feet and crossed to the large mid-Victorian wardrobe dominating the bedroom. She stared at the small, fragile reflection in the mirror. How could she look the same when she felt so different? When her life was in chaos? She didn't even know where she would live next week. How long could she expect the Gomezes to care for her?

Her thoughts darted backward, four years to the day. The Spanish-American War was finally over. Mama received the letter from the War Department, telling them that Papa—Captain Nathan Levy— was dead, that he had died of a fever on the ship that was bringing his regiment home. Mama had been so brave. Grieving for Papa, she had vowed to raise Constance—their only child—as though Papa was still alive. But in less than a year, they had had to move from their little row house on Henderson Place along East End Avenue between Eighty-sixth and Eighty-seventh Streets to a drab two-room flat on West Eighteenth Street.

Haunted by her memories of the squalid poverty in London's East End, Mama had feared the day when the money would run out, and they would be forced to move to the Lower East Side. Until Papa's death, they had lived so well. Not like the Nathans and Hendricks and Lazaruses, maybe—but well.

The widow's pension Mama received from the government was tiny, and Mama was too proud to accept help from the always charitable Sephardic community. She earned a little extra money by giving piano lessons to children of several families of Congregation Shearith Israel. One by one Mama's treasures disappeared.

Now Constance woke up every morning expecting to hear Mama's voice calling her to breakfast—only to realize that she would never hear her voice again. Sometimes she felt like she couldn't bear the hurt much longer. But she must be brave, she told herself, like Mama.

Papa and Mama had come to America from London right after their marriage seventeen years earlier. Mama was not Sephardic; she had been born in Russia and brought to London as a baby. Orphaned as a small child, she grew up in London's Norwood Jewish Orphanage.

If Papa had not died, Mama would still be alive. Constance felt a wave of self-reproach. She should not have let Mama go out in that terrible rainstorm three weeks ago. Of course she had insisted, because they needed the money. And the silver teapot *had* brought in a little something from the pawnbroker's shop. But she had been soaked to the skin. Four days later the doctor pronounced her ill with pneumonia. *Mama was only thirty-three years old. How could God let her die?*

Suddenly Constance felt as though she were suffocating in the pleasant little bedroom. The air seemed heavy, the walls threatened to close in around her. She had to get out. She felt like *she* was dying, thinking these same thoughts over and over. She hurried into the hall and walked to the narrow, carpeted stairs. But just outside the English Regency dining room, Constance froze. Mr. Gomez's voice drifted from the small family sitting room.

"All right, I'll tell Constance tonight." He sounded unhappy but firm. "I suppose we can't delay any longer."

"But to send that sweet child halfway round the world to live with her aunt and uncle . . ." Mrs. Gomez protested. "Why can't she live here with us? We have plenty of room, now that the girls are gone. I enjoy having her here and Hong Kong is a world away."

Constance felt cold shock move through her body. Her mouth was dry; her head was spinning. She was to go to Hong Kong to live with Papa's brother and his wife? But they were strangers. She'd never even seen them. Mama had told her that Uncle Lionel had come to New York on business once, but that was before she was born. Every year, on Rosh Hashanah, a letter arrived from him and Aunt Rebecca, and on Hanukkah some Chinese tea or a length of silk or a piece of white jade would come in a big box wrapped in brown paper.

"It's what Deborah wished." Mr. Gomez sighed. "On her deathbed she told me we were to send Constance to Nathan's brother and his wife in Hong Kong. How can I not do what her mother asked?"

"Suppose they don't want to take her in?" Mrs. Gomez sounded anxious.

"They wouldn't dare." His tone was rough. "How could they, after what they did to her father?"

Constance whirled around and stumbled back into the bedroom. She couldn't believe it . . . Mama wanted her to live in Hong Kong with Uncle Lionel and Aunt Rebecca—but what if when she arrived they refused to take her into their home?

And what did Mr. Gomez mean when he said, "They wouldn't dare. How could they, after what they did to her father?" What could Uncle Lionel and Aunt Rebecca have done to Papa to make Mr. Gomez so furious?

A rush of pride flooded Constance. Her father had been a great

11

man, the best. She would protect his memory. She would go to Hong Kong to live with Uncle Lionel and Aunt Rebecca—and she would find out what this mysterious thing was that they did to Papa. Suddenly the thought of moving into a new world didn't seem so terrifying. She was going to make her father proud. And Mama too.

Constance sat again in the slipper chair by the window. The image of her father sprang to life in her memory. She hoped it would always be like that. Papa had lost his mother when he was ten. It was heartless of his father to give him over into the hands of Papa's brother Lionel, fourteen years his senior and newly married, just so he could run off and live in Hong Kong. Four years later, when he fell ill, he summoned Lionel to his side and Papa was shipped off to boarding school, which he hated. Her throat tightening, Constance remembered the night Papa had told her and Mama about how lonely he'd been. Uncle Lionel and his wife had liked Hong Kong. They remained there after his father died. Why hadn't Papa gone to Hong Kong to live with them? Instead, fresh out of college, he had married Mama and come to America.

Before Papa died everything had been so lovely. Constance's eyes softened as she remembered summers at Manhattan Beach, a trip to Saratoga, picnics in Central Park amid the patchwork of autumn leaves. They shared so much love and laughter, the three of them.

She should have gone to work instead of going to school. She'd been twelve years old. Some of her friends were working—sewing in factories on the Lower East Side or as "cash girls" in department stores. She should have helped Mama instead of depending on her for everything.

Why couldn't they turn back the clock and live these last four years again? She would take care of Mama. It would be different.

Now Constance dreaded going down to dinner. But she had to face Mr. and Mrs. Gomez. She left her bedroom. Downstairs, as she stood under the arch of the entrance of the dining room, she saw that they had already taken their seats at the rosewood dining table.

Tonight as always they tried to make Constance feel comfortable. But an air of tension hung over the room. Constance ate in silence, her eyes on her plate. Mr. and Mrs. Gomez kept glancing at each other between Esther's strained attempts at conversation. Maybe they were going to wait until after dinner to tell her the news, Constance thought. Would this meal ever end?

At last the three of them retired to the parlor across the hall for tea, as they did every night. Constance remembered the times she'd sat here with Mama. Tears filled her eyes. Mama had loved this elegant room with its Persian rug, tasseled satin draperies, the tufted satin-covered rosewood furniture, the ebony inlaid tables.

Mr. Gomez cleared his throat. He looked imploringly at his wife for a moment, but Esther kept her eyes on the delicate Sevres teacup in her hand.

Constance fought the panic building inside her.

"It was your mother's wish, Constance, that you be sent to live with your Uncle Lionel and Aunt Rebecca in Hong Kong. I've arranged for you to travel with Mr. and Mrs. Hirsch, who have been home on sabbatical for a year. He's with one of the export firms in Shanghai. He and his wife will take you there and put you on the boat for Hong Kong."

Constance leaned forward. "Has my uncle agreed to have me live with him?" Maybe if they didn't like her they'd send her back . . .

"He knows about your mother's death and he knows you're scheduled to arrive on September eighteenth. Of course he'll be there to meet you, child. You musn't worry."

Constance couldn't share his conviction. She tried to remember something about her uncle and aunt. They had no children, she knew that. Uncle Lionel was in the export business. He and Aunt Rebecca were active in the circle revolving around the Ohel Leah Synagogue —they'd written Papa about it once or twice.

"You'll enjoy the social life in the British Crown Colony, Constance. There's a fine Jewish community there. Hong Kong has become quite a city. It has grown to a population of over 300,000."

"When must I go?" Constance spoke softly. The thought of leaving New York, the only home she had ever known, for a city where there probably weren't many people who spoke English was terrifying.

"In four days. You will meet Mr. and Mrs. Hirsch at dinner here tomorrow night. And you will travel with them by steamship to Liverpool, then to London for a few days, where Mr. Hirsch has some business." Constance's eyes widened. Papa's and Mama's London! "From London you'll travel to Marseilles, where you'll board a *Messagerie Maritime de France* steamer. It'll be quite an adventure, Constance. You'll go by way of Alexandria, Port Said, Bombay, Saigon, then up to Yokohama and down to Shanghai."

"And you'll be a guest of Mr. and Mrs. Hirsch at their house in

13

Shanghai for several days, until your boat for Hong Kong is scheduled to leave," Mrs. Gomez added. "They'll make sure to put you on the boat that will arrive at the time your uncle expects you."

"You've heard from Uncle Lionel?" Constance asked. She still wasn't convinced that Uncle Lionel and Aunt Rebecca were ready to take her in.

"There hasn't been time yet, dear. But the letter telling him of your arrival will be in his hands within a few days. He'll be there, I promise," Mr. Gomez said. "After all, he's your father's brother—he wouldn't leave you stranded."

I wonder . . . Constance thought.

"Mr. and Mrs. Gomez, before I leave I'd like to visit the cemetery one more time." How sad that she must go to live so far from where Mama lay buried.

"I'll go with you," Mrs. Gomez offered.

"May I go alone?" This would be her last farewell.

"Of course, my dear." Esther Gomez smiled. "John will take you in the Studebaker."

The next morning Constance went to the Cypress Hills Cemetery. Along the way she stared at every passing street. Would she ever see New York again? Would Uncle Lionel be there to meet her? What would she do if she were left alone in a strange city in the Far East?

Constance clutched at her purse. She hadn't even thought about money. Where could she work? She wasn't trained to do anything. The few dollars given to her by Mr. Gomez from the sale of the furnishings of the apartment wouldn't go far. Mr. Gomez insisted that it would be enough to pay for her passage to the British Crown Colony. But she would have no money to take her back to America . . .

Mama had been so brave when the money began to run out. How often she had denied herself just so she could make pretty dresses for Constance. She would secretly sketch dresses on display in Lord & Taylor's windows. Then they would go home, and Mama would work late into the night copying them. She remembered Mama haggling with the pushcart vendors on Hester Street, making sure she got the most for every dollar.

But Mama couldn't hide her anguish as one prized possession after another was sold to pay the bills. The piano lessons just weren't enough after Papa died.

As the Studebaker approached the cemetery, Constance began to

14

tremble. She felt like she was going through the funeral all over again. Though the day was pleasantly warm, she shivered. She heard the rabbi's voice entoning the last line of the kaddish . . .

"*Oseh shalom bimeromav, hu yaaseh shalom aleinu veal kol Yisrael, veimeru: amein.*" May he who causes peace to reign in the high heavens, let peace descend on us, on all Israel, and all the world, and let us say Amen. The words are beautiful, Constance thought in wonder. Why didn't I ever notice before?

It was here as she stood in the Cypress Hills Cemetery beside her mother's grave that Constance felt the first stirrings of her faith. Most of her life she had thought of herself only as an American. Now Constance Levy knew she was more. She was a Jew.

CHAPTER
TWO

THE SUN SHONE brightly on the International Settlement of Shanghai, making the residents feel as if they were living in a Turkish bath, even with the new electric fans. For endless summer weeks the temperature never dropped below 80°F, even at night.

When Ben Franks first brought his bride to the British settlement on the banks of the Whangpoo River fifty-four years ago, the Bund had yet to become one of the most handsome boulevards in the world. Today the Franks's *hong*—the Chinese name for a mercantile establishment—was one of the few originals still remaining on this handsome, bustling street.

The Franks's hong had a three-acre compound enclosed by a wall, with the most important building the simple dwelling house, built with solid walls and a verandah running around both the first and second floors. In a spacious upstairs bedroom facing the river, Sam Stone stood beside the four-poster bed and methodically packed his belongings in the portmanteau that had been Grandma Franks's going-away present to him.

Sam's English-style clothes, all bought at Lane, Crawford & Company on Nanking Road since he had first come to the Franks home almost four years ago, were to travel in the portmanteau. Once again

Sam wore the baggy cotton trousers and Chinese coolie jacket, the attire he had worn when he first arrived in Shanghai.

At twenty Sam was tall and slender, with tawny hair, lightly tanned skin, hazel eyes, and sharp features. Born Samuel Shih—the clan name bestowed on his family by the Chinese centuries ago—he had Anglicized his name at the urging of Mr. Franks, his sponsor since he had been brought from Kaifeng, the beautiful ancient capital of Hunan Province.

As he snapped shut the portmanteau and lifted it from the bed he thought about going home. It had been too long already. He had been brought to Shanghai on a special mission, along with seventeen other Jews from what was known as the "orphan colony of Jews"—a colony that had dwindled since its founding in the twelfth century to a population of barely two hundred.

The visitors from Kaifeng were taught Hebrew and English, and learned about their Jewish heritage. Since most Kaifeng Jews were now poor shopkeepers—though in earlier centuries they had been rich and important—they were also taught a trade before returning to Kaifeng.

Sam remembered how the Society for the Rescue of the Chinese Jews had been formed in Shanghai six years ago. He'd come to Shanghai with the others from Kaifeng in 1902, but within two years the project was suspended. Mr. Franks had explained how the Jews in Europe and America were too concerned about the plight of millions of Jews fleeing pogroms in Russia and eastern Europe to support a colony of less than two hundred Jews in Kaifeng. How grateful he had been when Mr. Franks insisted that his own family would continue to sponsor his education. At the same time he was learning the real estate business.

For the last ten months he had been working as an interpreter, both in the family hong and in Mr. Franks's real estate firm. He smiled, remembering the money he would be carrying home. And the white jade *chai* suspended from a gold chain that he had commissioned to be designed for him at the shop of Hung Chong on Nanking Road. A present for his grandmother.

It was his duty to return to Kaifeng and try to bring Judaism back into the lives of those in the colony. It had been selfish of him to delay this long. He closed his eyes and tried to imagine what it would be like back in Kaifeng. There was the house—little more than a hut—sitting just beyond the brick arches that framed Jewish Colony

17

Lane. It was difficult to imagine being part of that old world again, where he had felt so much more a part of his Chinese surroundings . . . thought like them, dressed like them, spoke the same language, ate the same food, attended the same schools. Now he felt more British than Chinese. He had even started to think in English.

But it was when Sam realized that Grandma Franks—whom he loved as his own grandmother—cherished hopes that he would someday marry pretty fifteen-year-old Rose, her favorite great-grandchild, that Sam realized he must leave Shanghai. He could not let Grandma Franks believe he would one day marry Rose. She was just a younger sister to him. Delightful, yes—but that was all. For four years he had been part of the Franks family. When he gave her a brotherly farewell kiss on the cheek last night, he noticed the look in her eyes. Yes, it was time he left Shanghai.

With a final glance around the bedroom Sam got ready to go downstairs to say good-by to Grandma Franks. He had said all his other farewells last night. Portmanteau in hand, feeling strange in his old Chinese attire, Sam walked downstairs.

She was in the dining room, having one of her endless cups of China tea, and the morning sun beat in through the three French windows facing south. The servants had taken up the carpets early in May, as they did every summer, and polished the floors to a luminous brown. The dining room was Sam's favorite room in the house, with its solid English mahogany furniture that blended comfortably with four Cantonese blackwood marble-topped *teapoys*. On the sideboard sat a pair of blue and white Nanking vases and between them a Chinese enameled porcelain punch bowl, painted with plum blossoms on an orange ground.

"You're making *hamin,*" he said tenderly, smelling the aromas that drifted into the dining room from the kitchen behind the house. An Indian-style *cholent* prepared with duck or chicken, rice, onion, ground coconut, and all flavored with turmeric and raw eggs, *hamin* was so special that Grandma Franks always insisted on supervising its preparation herself. "I'll remember it when I'm back in Kaifeng."

Small rounded Grandma Franks lifted her smiling face to Sam's.

"You tell your grandma how I make this," she ordered with mock sternness. "You have watched me often enough," she chuckled. It was Grandma Franks who had talked him into staying in Shanghai those first months when he had been so homesick. She gazed at Sam, and they both realized that this might be the last time they saw each

18

other. "She'll be so proud of all your learning."

Sam smiled, remembering. He saw himself as a small boy, sitting at his grandmother's feet while she wove exotic tales of centuries long past when the Jews, summoned to Peking to advise the Imperial Army, had been honored by the Empress Dowager of the Wei Dynasty. "It saddened my grandmother that Hebrew is hardly known among our people anymore, though we observe some holidays and abstain from eating pork," he said. "She's sad that the synagogue, which was built in 1163 and restored through the centuries, is little more than rubble now." He remembered when his grandmother took him to see the solitary tablet, standing up from the earth, that told him about the arrival of Jews in China during the Dynasty of Han, between the years of 200 B.C. and A.D. 226.

Grandma Franks spoke. "You remember to tell her that one of the scrolls from the synagogue at Kaifeng is safe in the museum of Hong Kong. I have heard," she added, "that it is to be presented by the city authorities to the Ohel Leah Synagogue there."

"I'll remember," Sam promised gently. As he bent down to kiss her, she drew him into her arms with touching urgency. He remembered how Grandma Franks had said that at her age each day was a gift. As she lay her head on her pillow at night, she asked herself if she would have the gift of yet another day. Her voice muffled in Sam's shoulder, she spoke fiercely.

"Remember always, Sam, that you are a Jew. Whatever comes, we will survive."

SAM left Foochow Road wharf in "Top Sea"—Shanghai—to travel to Kaifeng on a triple-deck steamer. He traveled deck class to save money. The ship swung from the turbulent Whangpoo into The River, the natives' name for the Great Yangtze. As it steamed northwest on the seven-hundred-mile river journey, Sam was oblivious to the picturesque fishing villages, the Chinese junks sailing upriver under large-ribbed sails, and the occasional appearance of great walled cities sternly guarded by high towers and ponderous gates. He was thinking about his old life in Kaifeng. What was going to happen to him?

Sam kept to himself, though despite his white skin his Chinese dress and knowledge of both Mandarin and Cantonese spared him the stigma of being a foreigner. So much of what his grandmother

19

had taught him as a boy had taken on new meaning through his Hebrew studies in Shanghai. Like her, Sam was frustrated that there were those in the colony who had abandoned their faith. Some were marrying Chinese or Mohammedans and forgetting they were Jews. It infuriated him. But it also strengthened his own faith. Whatever happened, he was a Jew. For life.

Though he would sorely miss Shanghai, Sam began to look ahead. He was anxious to see his family—he'd heard so little from them since he'd left. But he hadn't forgotten them. But all of Hunan Province was violently anti-foreign. At a moment's notice the peaceful city of Kaifeng could become a caldron of violence. What if they were in danger?

When Tsai Yuan-pei arrived in Shanghai he founded the China Education Society to camouflage his demands for the overthrow of the corrupt rule of the Manchus. The secret revolutionary activities began to spread rapidly. Although Sam was caught up in his new British life, he instinctively responded to the struggle of the Chinese people. At the age of fifteen—like his schoolmates—he had cut off his queue as a sign of rebellion against the old ways.

THE journey to Kaifeng seemed endless. But at last Sam was once again walking through the streets of the beautiful old city, making his way to Jewish Colony Lane. He couldn't believe how shabby the houses looked—had it always been that way?

He paused for a moment before his own two-room house. He thought about the white jade *chai* in his portmanteau. Surely Grandma would be happy when she saw it. He opened the door and stepped inside.

At first his sister Leah did not recognize him—after all, when he left he had been just a boy. And now he had returned a man. For a long moment she regarded him warily. Then she recognized him.

"Sam!"

She embraced him in a rush of Chinese. Sam tried to understand her—he was out of practice. She was telling him about the unrest in the countryside, the hardships of those in the cities.

"We were sure you were dead," she said breathlessly. "We'd heard nothing in almost a year."

"I sent letters. They probably didn't go through. I've heard nothing from you for months."

20

"Only Grandmother believed you were still alive . . ." Leah's smile faded. "Sam, much has happened since you went away—" She paused. And instantly Sam knew.

"Our grandmother?"

"She died six months ago," Leah said gently. "It was an easy death. She went to sleep one night and never woke up again."

Sam knew he should have expected it. If only he had come home sooner . . . Now only Leah and his parents were left. His two older brothers had taken Chinese wives, his sister Rachel had married a Mohammedan, accepting his religion. At least Sarah had married Joseph, a Jew. So, Sam thought. It is only Leah, and Sarah and myself who have remained true to our faith. And, of course, Grandmother.

Though she had been dead six months, Sam sat *shiva* for his grandmother. Afterwards he tried to convince others in the colony to return to their Jewish traditions. Didn't they see how important it was? They didn't. Sam was told to give up.

It seemed like there was no place for Sam in Kaifeng. Maybe he could return to Hong Kong—but not Shanghai, where he would become part of the life of the Franks family again. Despite his love for them, he knew he would bring only disappointment and pain to Grandma Franks and young Rose.

He would travel to Shanghai, he decided, taking the boat from there to Hong Kong. If he were older and wiser, perhaps he could have succeeded in his mission in Kaifeng. But he knew now that it was not within his power to bring his people back within the fold of Judaism. It was a knowledge that at once saddened and inspired him. Someday, he vowed, I *will* teach the ones I love what being a Jew really means. *I will.*

CHAPTER
THREE

CONSTANCE FOUND HERSELF growing fond of Mr. and Mrs. Hirsch. She respected their compassion for the Chinese—a feeling which prompted them to teach her about the oppression of the Chinese—under the corrupt Manchu government the Chinese had suffered at the hands of the imperialist soldiers.

And they had every reason to hate the foreign capitalists whose only interest was to make money off cheap labor. The Chinese worked ten to sixteen hours a day for thirty cents or less. But countless revolutionary societies threatened to change that.

"Within five or ten years," Mr. Hirsch predicted, "the people will arise and overthrow the government of the Manchus."

There were already signs of progress in opium trade. The government had just issued an Imperial decree demanding that opium be abolished within ten years. Efforts were already under way to close the opium dens in Hong Kong.

Mr. Hirsch, a tea-man, spent a great deal of time aboard ship with other *chasees*—men skilled in tea. Mrs. Hirsch happily settled in to the luxurious existence.

Gradually Constance began to enjoy herself. She loved their brief stays in foreign ports of call. When they sailed through the Suez Canal, she remembered Papa's story of how Disraeli had bought the

Suez Canal for Queen Victoria with Rothschild money.

But as the trip drew to a close, Constance again began to worry. What would happen in Hong Kong? Did Uncle Lionel know she would be arriving in the Crown Colony? Did he know when she would arrive? Would she be welcomed into her uncle's house?

The China coast would soon be in sight, and Mrs. Hirsch asked Constance to join her on deck.

"This is a sight you will always remember," Mrs. Hirsch said. "Look at the ocean. That saffron and chocolate you see coloring the water comes from the Yangtze River. For centuries the river has been bringing down earth from Keangsu Province to drop on the sea floor. Large areas of land where natives now grow rice and cotton and wheat were known generations ago as 'The Sea.' The river robs the west to enrich the east. Sometimes—like now—when the sea is especially calm the blue of the Pacific refuses to blend with the yellow from the river." Mrs. Hirsch leaned against the railing. "Look Constance. See the line from Pacific blue to Yangtze yellow?"

For the moment Constance had forgotten all her fears. Mrs. Hirsch explained that since the ship would be unable to make the journey up the Whangpoo River—which rushed up like a mill race to reach the Yangtze shore—they would drop anchor off the Chinese village of Woosung, twelve miles from the International Settlement. There they would be transferred from the ship to the tug which was to carry them up the river.

Constance watched the water swirling beneath them. Soon she would be in Shanghai—one of the great cities of the world . . .

The river was crowded with junks, gaily painted hooded sampans, big P&O boats, foreign-rigged schooners and men-of-war. For a moment Constance wanted to stay here with Mr. and Mrs. Hirsch.

But in three days she would be on yet another ship traveling to Hong Kong. I guess I should be grateful that someone is willing to take me in, she thought. But Mr. Gomez's cryptic words still bothered her . . . *"They wouldn't dare. How could they, after what they did to her father?"*

How could she live with them, knowing that in some dark way they had mistreated Papa? Papa had always spoken kindly of Uncle Lionel—maybe Mr. Gomez was wrong . . .

MRS. Hirsch crammed Constance's three days in Shanghai with sightseeing. They walked along the Bund, pausing to visit the beautiful Public Garden, where people gathered in the summer to hear the town band. Across from the Public Garden they saw the British Consulate compound. They walked through the Renaissance-style Masonic Hall, the long-established business house of the Jardine Matheson tong at the corner of Peking Road, the fine buildings of the *Daily News,* the new Russo-Chinese Bank, the Tudor-style Customs House with its 110-foot four-faced clock.

There was a line-up of rickshas in front of the Shanghai Club that reminded Constance of the carriages in London. The Shanghai Club, Mrs. Hirsch explained, was the center of the social and business life of the International Settlement.

Mr. and Mrs. Hirsch took her to a Chinese restaurant for dinner where the food was superb. Mrs. Hirsch wanted to show her Shanghai at night.

"Shanghai lighted her streets even before London," Mrs. Hirsch said while Constance gazed in awe at the display of electric street lights around them. "The old city walls enclose over 300,000 people, and the suburbs and the Settlement add at least 700,000 more to the population."

"Twenty thousand of foreign nationalities," Mr. Hirsch added. "Shanghai is a truly cosmopolitan city."

The following day Mrs. Hirsch took Constance in a rubber-tired victoria to visit the Central District. The narrow, winding streets were jammed with traffic. Sightseers, coolies, silk-clad Chinese merchants, foreigners of every nation moved in a steady flow all around them, riding in carriages, bicycles, rickshas, wheelbarrowed vehicles, motorcars, and occasional sedan chairs.

Mrs. Hirsch and Constance stopped to visit the Chinese shops filled with inexpensive curios and then moved on to Foochow Road, off the Bund—known over the Empire as the Piccadilly of China—where people flocked to the opium shops and the Chinese tea houses.

On her last day in Shanghai Constance saw the Jewish Synagogue at 16 Peking Road and the Jewish Cemetery presented to the community by David Sassoon in 1862. Afterwards Mrs. Hirsch took her for a carriage ride along elegant Bubbling Well Road to see the beautiful villas shaded by tall trees lining both sides of the road. The old and the new reed-built Chinese cottages and farms sat next to magnificent foreign villas.

Constance was enthralled by the seemingly endless stream of carriages that traveled over Bubbling Well Road, where the crossings were guarded by Sikh policemen . . . the Chinese ricksha men and their Chinese barrows as they made a dash to cross the streets.

"It's always like this after four in the afternoon, dear, don't worry." Mrs. Hirsch chuckled. But she loved these outings, fashionable among the foreign ladies and wealthy Chinese.

Finally, the time came for Constance to leave the Hirsches. She tried to behave when she said good-by to them on the tender to Woosung, where she would board an Indo-China Steam Navigation Company ship for Hong Kong.

"I arranged for you to share a first-class cabin with a lady missionary traveling to Hong Kong," Mr. Hirsch said. "There are less than a dozen first-class cabins on these ships, and they're always much in demand."

Mr. Hirsch told her that the trip would bring her into Hong Kong on Friday morning. In three days . . . Constance looked around at the other passengers. Most of them were Chinese. But who was that man, dressed in coolie clothes? He was extraordinarily handsome. What a funny combination—his features and complexion were Caucasian, but he was dressed like a Chinese.

The young man turned his head. Their eyes met. Constance felt her cheeks flush, and she lowered her gaze. What was she doing staring at strange men? She forced her attention back to Mr. Hirsch, but she felt the strange young man watching her. Why was her heart suddenly pounding? She couldn't concentrate on what Mr. Hirsch was saying about the monetary system in Hong Kong.

As the tender approached Woosung, Mr. Hirsch pointed out her ship. It was far smaller than the oceangoing vessel that had brought them to China—but, he said, this was a journey along the coast. She was glad Mr. Hirsch had arranged for her to travel first-class. The other accommodations were shunned by foreigners.

Within half an hour Constance was standing alone at the railing of the upper deck. As she waved farewell to Mr. Hirsch, she felt the loneliness return. The lower deck was jammed with natives bound for Amoy, Swatow, Hong Kong, and Canton. They all looked like they had families to go to, Constance thought. Who am I going to?

Constance introduced herself to the rotund lady missionary who was sharing her cabin. Though she had traveled thousands of miles along the Chinese riverways to spread Christianity, she confessed to Constance that she was terrified of sailing over the China Sea, and she planned to remain in their cabin with her Bible throughout the trip.

Remembering that Mrs. Hirsch had said to shade her face from the hot subtropic sun, Constance decided to wear her bonnet. She remembered how proud of it Mama had been—it looked just like the stylish millinery they had seen in Saks Fifth Avenue. It was the last thing Mama had made for her . . .

A slight wind swept along the river. Constance reached a hand to her hat. Too late. It sailed away, rising and falling along the deck. As she darted after it, a tall young man in Chinese trousers and jacket appeared. It was the same young man she had noticed on the tender —here on the first-class deck.

He lunged forward, caught the ribbons of her hat and brought it over to her.

"Sharp winds come up during the hot months," he said in English. His admiring eyes took in her slim figure and pretty face.

"Thank you." She smiled, slightly out of breath. "I would hate to lose it." Why was he looking at her like that?

"Are you traveling to Hong Kong?" He made it seem so important.

"Yes." Constance felt uncomfortable under his stare . . . goodness, she thought, he must think I'm a ninny. Why was he dressed as a coolie?

"To live?" he pursued eagerly.

"Yes. I'm going to live in Hong Kong with my uncle and aunt." She hesitated. "I'm Constance Levy." Was it proper to talk to strangers onboard ship?

"I'm Sam Stone." He smiled. "I'm going to live in Hong Kong too."

"Have you ever been there?" Constance asked.

"No. For the last four years I've been in Shanghai. Studying mostly. Working for the past few months as an interpreter for the Franks Export Company."

"You speak Chinese?"

"I *am* Chinese," he said and laughed at her obvious confusion. "I mean I was born in China."

"Oh. So your family are missionaries." She had read about the English missionaries who lived with the Chinese.

"No, I'm Jewish. My people have lived in China for many centuries. Four years ago the Society for the Rescue of Chinese Jews brought me to Shanghai. That's where I learned to speak and read English."

Constance couldn't hide her astonishment. "Why, you speak it as though it were your native tongue."

"I have an ear for languages," he shrugged.

"Where did you live in China?"

Constance surprised herself. Usually she was so shy with strangers. But she was eager to learn more about the handsome young stranger who looked at her with this frankly admiring gaze. He seemed to be convinced that they would see each other in Hong Kong . . .

CONSTANCE spent every moment with Sam. Already she'd told him things she'd never told anyone. When Sam learned that she was Jewish, he told her about the history of the Jews in China, where they were known as the *Tiao-chin-chiao* or "the sect who plucked out the sinews"—an allusion to their adherence to the Mosaic command.

He told his grandmother's tales about the Jewish synagogues of earlier generations—constructed in the Chinese style of architecture but modified in the interior to accommodate the Jewish requirements. He told her, too, of the Scrolls containing the Law of Moses written in Hebrew—the Torah—which, during a period of terrible famine some fifty years ago, had to be sold for food for the Jewish Colony.

In China, Sam said with pride, the Jews were free to live as they pleased as long as they observed a minimum of Confucian rules.

"A Jew might worship the images of Confucius and the Emperor, but he understood there was no religious significance when this was performed wearing only the official hat. He satisfied the rules without betraying his own faith."

Apparently until a century ago Jews had lived in many of the important cities of China. In the Early and Middle Ages there were large numbers of Jews, many of them important and rich. Their sons went to Peking for their examinations for the third—or doctorate—degree. They were advisers to the emperors, honored by the ruling dynasties.

For the first time since her mother's death, Constance forgot the past. She was happy with Sam. They lived in their own world.

Her initial nervousness had faded, and now she wanted to share everything with him. They had led very different lives, yet they were one. Constance didn't dare give it a name . . .

On the morning they were to arrive in Hong Kong, she awoke early, as always, eager to see Sam. But tomorrow she would be in a bedroom in the home of her Uncle Lionel. Tomorrow morning she would not leave her cabin to find Sam waiting for her on deck.

27

Where would Sam be tomorrow morning in that huge strange city? Where would he live? He was sure he would find a job and a place to live, though he knew that living quarters in Hong Kong were scarce because of the steady influx of refugees from the mainland. When would she see him again?

Slowly, she began to pack. She heard the missionary stir. Now was not the time to listen to the old woman's complaints. Constance left the cabin and went up on deck. She hoped that in the glorious moment when the orange-red ball slowly lifted itself above the horizon she would be with Sam.

But Sam wasn't there. And instead of orange-red splendor, the sky was overcast, the sun hidden by clumps of gray. A slight breeze ruffled the early morning heat.

When Sam arrived on deck, he seemed strangely serious. She hoped it was because he was sad to see their time together coming to an end. He talked to her about the problems of China, the rebellion of the students and the young intellectuals against the Manchu tyranny. She sensed that he was torn between his Chinese ties and the foreign world that had engulfed him these past four years. But he seemed to feel more comfortable in the English world. He admitted that this was why he had rather extravagantly taken a first-class cabin. Thank God he had, Constance thought to herself. What if she had never met him?

"After 'early rice,' " he said with a chuckle, knowing that now she understood that "early rice" was—in timing if not in content—the Chinese equivalent of the English breakfast, "I'll go down to my cabin and change into my British clothes." He felt like he was saying farewell to his family at Kaifeng all over again. When would they see each other again?

"There'll be no beautiful sunrise this morning," she smiled. "I've come to expect it." Had they shared only two sunrises before this morning?

"Let's walk around the deck." His voice was brusque, but his hand at her elbow was gentle.

"Early rice" was served at 8 A.M. By nine Constance and Sam were heading for the deck again. There was an easy silence between them as they thought about what would happen in Hong Kong.

It was Sam who spoke first as they emerged on deck.

"We'll soon be approaching the harbor, Constance." His eyes swept from darkening sky to choppy sea to the surge of activity among the ship's crew, intent on reefing deck awnings, paying more cable.

"Are we in for a storm?" Constance felt a flutter of alarm. But they were so close to Hong Kong. Could they be in danger?

"The typhoon season isn't over until the end of October," Sam said, "but I've never known a typhoon to come up without hours of warning. The Meteorological Observatories in Shanghai and Hong Kong send red signals when a typhoon is five hundred miles away. When it moves within a three hundred–mile radius, the signals change to black. Then typhoon guns are sounded."

Constance followed his gaze to the lower deck. The natives were shouting at each other, moving around in clusters. A crew member shouted to them to take cover. Constance felt the wind pick up.

"We're in for a typhoon," Sam said grimly, reaching for Constance's hand. "Warning or not."

From below a crew member shouted, "You'd better go below. The way that wind's coming up, we could lose the upper deck!"

Constance vowed that she would not show Sam how scared she was. Her hand in his, she remembered the lines from a Kipling poem Papa had loved . . .

> The East Wind roared . . .
> Look—look well to your shipping,
> By the breathing of my mad typhoon
> I swept your close-packed Praya and beached
>   your best at Kowloon.

"We'll sail this out," Sam said as they hurried from the deck. Rain was attacking the rocking ship in a brown sheet. Constance heard Sam say that in a few minutes the wind would reach a hundred and fifty miles an hour.

Constance and Sam waited in the doorway while those ahead pushed into the already overcrowded room. She recoiled from the stench of perspiring bodies and old fish.

"Wait," Sam ordered and pulled her towards a storage closet. "We'll be more comfortable in here, and just as safe." The closet had no porthole, but they could breathe through the cracks in the door.

"We'd hardly open a porthole, anyway." Sam tried to sound cheerful. Constance stared at him. Wasn't he frightened?

He pulled together two wooden cartons and they sat down in the darkness. His arm closed around her waist and she dropped her head on his shoulder. Despite her fear, she was happy. If only they could stay like this forever . . .

Above, they could hear the captain shouting orders to the crew. These were experienced seamen, Constance told herself. Surely they'd sailed through other typhoons on the China Sea.

"We're almost at the passes of Hong Kong," Sam spoke softly. "We'll make it." He paused. "But God help the boat people in this. If there had been warning, the sampans and junks could have gone to the typhoon shelter."

"Are there lifeboats on this ship?" Constance asked, aware of the alarm in the voices of the crew. "I thought I saw them—"

"A lifeboat will be useless in that sea. The waves are washing up to the lower deck. Nothing is safe in a typhoon of this velocity. But we'll make it," Sam added quickly. "I have a deal with God—I have to learn to be a true Jew."

Huddled together in the oppressive heat of the storage closet, they heard the lady missionary praying for their safety over the cries of the other passengers.

"They're getting up more steam," Sam said after a few moments. "We're moving straight ahead now, into the harbor."

"Sam, tell me more about your grandmother," Constance said. "Tell me about the Jews who came to China from Persia and India." She mustn't think about what was happening out there, she thought —sampans and junks overturned by the typhoon, dumping their occupants into the churning sea . . .

"The word typhoon probably evolved from the Chinese 't'ai fung,' which means 'great wind,' " Sam said. For Constance he wanted to sound calm—but he too was frightened. Constance wasn't fooled; cradled in his arms she could hear the pounding of his heart.

"WE'RE in the harbor!" a voice on the upper deck yelled.

"Sam, let's go see!" Constance pushed the door wide to dart out onto the lower deck.

"Constance!" He was at her heels.

On deck they held each other in the flying rain and spray, clutching at the rail. On the ship's lower deck, most of the fittings had been smashed.

"We must go back!" Sam shouted. They stood transfixed as a ship inched past them, just yards away, dragging her anchors as though they were made of paper. For a moment it looked like the two ships might collide. Constance held her breath. Other vessels, dragged from their moorings in the harbor and driven by the wind, were crashing against everything in their path. The ship eased past them. Constance exhaled in relief.

There was devastation on all sides. Overturned sampans and lighters bounced among the waves. Small boats flew past, powerless against the crushing force of the swells.

"Constance, we can't stay on deck!" Sam said again, but she didn't hear him. Her wet hair clung to her head. Her dress was drenched. She was staring at a small boat as it was hurled like a clump of seaweed by the crest of a wave.

"Sam, look!" She pointed toward a Chinese woman in the boat. The woman was crying and swaying perilously, as she held a baby boy aloft.

"Sam?" Constance turned toward him.

"Constance, there's nothing we can do."

"But the baby—he'll die—"

Sam pulled her from the railing, but not before they spied dozens of people in the water, hanging on to wreckage and crying out for help. A moment later the small boat beside them smashed against a ship at its other side. They heard the screams of the occupants. Sobbing, she buried her face in his chest. He picked her up and carried her back to the upper deck.

At last it seemed the wind was letting up, and the ship managed to hold its course. The shrieks from the passengers began to die down as they realized the typhoon was moving past them. Cautiously Sam leaned forward and pushed the door of the closet slightly ajar.

"It's almost over."

"How long has it been?" Her body ached from being in one position for so long.

Sam pulled out his watch.

"It's eleven o'clock. It was mercifully short." Constance stared at him in disbelief and he smiled indulgently. "This one lasted only two hours. Usually they go on for eight to twelve hours." These two hours had seemed an eternity . . .

"Sam, those people in the water—the woman with the baby—will we ever be able to forget them?"

"Time will lessen the pain. But we won't ever completely forget them. How else does the world survive?"

Now Constance began to worry again about what lay ahead. When they arrived in Hong Kong, would Uncle Lionel be at the landing stage? How had the Crown Colony survived the typhoon? Was Uncle Lionel all right?

Sam took her hand. "Don't worry, Constance. I'll stay with you until your uncle arrives. Soon we'll know how the city fared, but I'm sure few lost their lives—it's the ships that take the beating in a storm like this."

As they stood on deck as the ship moved closer to shore, they could already see that fine foreign ships of many nations—the German ship *Petrach,* French torpedo destroyers *Fronde* and *Francisque,* the American sailing ship *S. P. Hitchcock*—had either been beached or badly damaged.

"Constance, look." Sam pointed to the Praya. Roofs had been lifted right off some of the godowns. Some wharves had been swept away. "I'm sure most of the godowns have been flooded."

A launch came forward to remove the passengers from the ship. The lady missionary kissed Constance good-by and wished her luck in her new home.

"It was weak of me to fear the sea," she said. "I'll never be afraid again. God means for me to carry on my work."

"As God means for me to become a real Jew," Sam added.

At last Constance and Sam were ashore, standing together in the middle of the chaos. There was shattered glass and tiles everywhere . . . overturned rickshas and sedan chairs . . . piles of wreckage. Already the military, the police and sanitary authorities and their crews were frantically working to turn over the wreckage, rescue the injured and move the dead to mortuaries.

Constance heard a man say triumphantly that the trams would be running again by noon despite the uprooted trees and branches strewn across the tracks. It was amazing how swiftly life could return to its normal routine, she thought.

And hadn't Mr. Hirsch said that the trams were the only way to get to the Peak, where Uncle Lionel and Aunt Rebecca had their summer house? Where was Uncle Lionel?

"Constance, don't look so worried," Sam chided. "I won't leave you here alone."

"Maybe my uncle never received Mr. Gomez's letter, Sam. Maybe he's been up at the Peak."

"His wife could be there," Sam said. "But your uncle couldn't leave

32

his business for more than a few days at a time. I'm sure he received the letter." Sam squinted, staring into the distance. "Will you recognize him?"

"I told you. I've never seen him. Only in old photographs."

Sam touched her arm and pointed.

"Could that be him there? He seems to be looking for someone."

Constance's eyes followed Sam's to a small, compact man with a neat, graying mustache dressed in unmistakably British summer whites.

"I don't know."

"Mr. Levy," Sam called out briskly. The man spun around to face them and focused on Constance.

"Constance?"

"Yes." Her voice was almost a whisper. Thank God. Uncle Lionel was here . . .

Lionel Levy walked towards them.

"Thank goodness. I was terrified of what might have happened to your ship. We haven't had a typhoon like that since 1874."

"We were brought ashore in a launch," Constance spoke shyly. Uncle Lionel seemed like a gentle man, genuinely concerned for her. Maybe Mr. Gomez was mistaken after all.

"We were approaching the harbor when the typhoon struck." She was distracted by the wary, disapproving look on her uncle's face as he looked at Sam. "Uncle Lionel, this is Sam Stone. We were passengers on the same ship."

"And you're Constance's uncle, Mr. Levy." Sam sensed that Constance was ill at ease. Why was Mr. Levy looking at him like that?

"I was standing by to make sure Constance found you." Constance watched the two men. What was this tension between them?

"Thank you for watching over my niece," Uncle Lionel said coolly. "It was unwise but I was one of the few who came down to the Praya during the typhoon. I was worried about Constance—and about my godown." For a moment his gaze shifted into the distance. "The front wall was blown down. It'll have to be totally rebuilt. I think it will be quite a while before the Colony is back to business as usual. And I'm afraid it will take fifteen years to restore the Public Gardens to their former beauty. The Victoria Recreation Club has been totally destroyed."

Uncle Lionel was obviously uncomfortable. He directed his conversation at Sam, but their eyes never met. Constance wondered why

—was it Sam's clothes? There hadn't been time for him to change into conventional English garb. *Did Uncle Lionel think that Sam was Eurasian?* Well—whatever it was Uncle Lionel was obviously not pleased that she had met Sam.

"I guess I'll be on my way now." Sam extended a hand to Mr. Levy. "It has been a pleasure to meet you, sir," he said. He turned and smiled. "Good-by, Constance."

"Good-by, Sam." For a moment their eyes locked. They had spent a lifetime together since they met four days ago. Sam picked up the portmanteau at his feet and walked away.

Constance watched until he disappeared among the crowds of workers and sightseers. Was he running out of her life because of Uncle Lionel's disapproval? But Uncle Lionel didn't even know him.

When will I see him again? There are hundreds of thousands of people in Hong Kong. How will I find him?

Somehow, I will . . .

CHAPTER

FOUR

CONSTANCE WAS OBLIVIOUS to the wails from clusters of Chinese huddled together at the water's edge. All she could think about was Sam.

"Thank God, the Peak was barely touched." She started at the sound of Uncle Lionel's voice. "We do have a typhoon cellar at the house up there, if it had been badly hit. But the loss among the boat people must amount to thousands."

"We saw them in the water," Constance whispered. "There was nothing we could do to help them."

"I saw many heroic efforts from the shore," Uncle Lionel remarked. "Despite the terrible wind and rain Europeans and Chinese together saved many of the natives whose boats were shattered against the Praya wall." He was trying to distract Constance from a procession transporting bodies recovered from nearby rubble. But it was too late. She had seen the covered stretchers.

Twenty yards away a pair of coolies chanted *"En ché! En ché! En ché!"* as they carried a sedan chair with colorful green canopy and wickerwork sides.

Unfamiliar aromas wafted toward them. This was the Far East. Alive and exotic and frightening . . .

"I'm sorry about this my dear, but we'll have to stay in the town

35

house tonight," Uncle Lionel said. "I'm sure the weather will turn beastly again, but the *punkah* fans will relieve the heat. In the morning I'll take you to the house on the Peak—it's much cooler up there."

Constance tried to digest all of what Uncle Lionel was saying. She wouldn't be in the city—but that was even further away from Sam. . . . When would they return to the house in town? When would they attend services at the Ohel Leah Synagogue, where she was sure to see him?

Uncle Lionel lifted a hand to an approaching coolie with a bamboo pole across his shoulder.

"Catchee me to piece ricksha," he ordered. Constance winced, remembering Sam's contempt for the pidgin English that the British used to communicate with the natives. "The sedan chairs are necessary to travel up the slopes, but the rickshas are fine for moving about town. They're faster and more comfortable."

The luggage coolie nodded affably, at the same time picking up Constance's portmanteau with a look of surprise at how light it was. When would her small trunk be brought ashore, she wondered nervously. But Uncle Lionel would take care of that.

Already she was learning to lean on Uncle Lionel. After all her suspicions . . . but she couldn't believe that this gentle man could have done Papa any harm.

Was it that Mr. Gomez—so warm and loving himself—had been upset that Papa had spent lonely years deprived of the presence of his sole remaining family, first at the boarding school and then at college which he'd hated because all the other students had homes to go to on holidays? Maybe Hong Kong hadn't been a good place to raise a growing child. In the best British families, it was the custom to send the children away to boarding schools at an early age. Mama had always hated that.

Constance was sure that when Uncle Lionel met Sam again, he would see what a fine man Sam was. It didn't matter that Victoria was such a big city—she knew they would find each other. They had to.

The rickshas—preceded by the luggage coolie trotting along with Constance's portmanteau slung over his shoulder—moved swiftly through the town's wide, handsome streets. Constance felt embarrassed to be sitting in a vehicle drawn by another human being. Didn't anyone else think it was unfair? From his ricksha next to hers, Uncle Lionel pointed out the Hong Kong Dispensary which offered information about the island, the Lane, Crawford & Company store, the Hong Kong Hotel, beneath which was an array of shops—including W. Brewer and Company, his favorite bookstore. With pride he pointed out the Clock Tower, a square granite structure rising eighty feet into the air, and the city's major landmark.

They passed endless shops, tall commercial buildings, huge sugar factories, battery after battery of army barracks. Then the scene changed to avenues of classical white mansions with elegant porticoes and colonnades and balconies, shaded by flame trees and yellow jasmine. Gazing along the pine-clad slopes towards the Peak Constance saw the pretty houses rising, tier upon tier, to the top. The roads leading uphill were narrow and winding and steep. She could see why they needed the electric tram—opened, Uncle Lionel said, in 1888.

"Our new summer house is right at the summit." Lionel followed her gaze. "The Peak is the highest point on the island—eighteen hundred feet above sea level. We built the house four years ago. It's close to the Governor's summer residence." Constance caught a certain dryness in his voice. "That pleases Rebecca no end."

"It must be beautiful up there."

"Since the tram went into operation, the Peak District has become the choice year-round residential area. Only Europeans are allowed to live there. Rebecca goes up on the first of May and remains until October first. In the course of the winter we go up for brief stays." He hesitated. "Rebecca's health is delicate. We don't do much socializing except for the synagogue. She enjoys the change in the weather at the Peak house." Constance listened carefully. Uncle Lionel talked about Aunt Rebecca like she was an invalid . . .

As they continued, Uncle Lionel told her about the Jewish community, which numbered about one hundred—mostly Sephardim from India and Persia who had become British citizens—and pointed out the Ohel Leah Synagogue, presented to the community six years ago by Sir Jacob Sassoon. He spoke with pride of the illustrious Jewish families in Hong Kong: the Sassoons, the Kadoories, the Hayims and Silases, and Ezras. Denzil Marcus Ezra was with the Sassoon company and was co-owner of the *China Press.* He talked about the seasonal activities in the Colony: racing, yachting, tennis and croquet. Many of the city's residents took part in or attended the performances of the Amateur Dramatic Club.

Though it seemed like a long time, it was only ten minutes before Constance stood with her uncle at the door of a tall white colonnaded

37

house, where an array of French windows opened out onto the wide stone verandah and green blinds had been let down over the arches to keep out the brightly blazing sun. Like the other mansions they passed, the house was brick, with a granite foundation and a flat roof that looked out over the harbor. Constance had known that Uncle Lionel was the owner of an export company, so she guessed he had money. But this opulence took her by surprise. Had Mama known how rich they were?

The heavy oak door creaked open and the *comprador*—the Levys' major-domo, in a long blue gown, white gaiters and thick shoes—bowed in welcome. He gestured to another servant to come forward for Constance's portmanteau.

"Li, tell Mai-ling there will be two for lunch," Uncle Lionel said. The *comprador* bowed.

Constance was taken upstairs by another smiling *comprador* to a large, square, high-ceilinged corner bedroom, where her portmanteau was being deposited on a low bench between two windows.

Constance stared at the *punkah* fan, which had started the minute she stepped in the room. In Shanghai Mrs. Hirsch had explained to her that the *punkahs* had been invented in India and were very popular in China. The *punkah* was a large rectangular bamboo frame swathed in cheesecloth and suspended from the ceiling by a cord. Another cord extended from the frame through a hole in the wall to the second floor verandah, where a servant pulled it back and forth to keep it moving. The idea of another human being working so hard just so she could feel cool . . . why, it was almost as bad as the Southerners' treatment of the slaves in the Civil War.

While the *amah* was unpacking her portmanteau, Constance looked around her room. The furniture was a pretty blend of the best of mid-Victorian and Oriental. The bed was a half-tester with two posts, a pale blue velvet canopy and side curtains to screen the head of the bed. A Chinese armchair, inlaid with mother-of-pearl, sat beside an exquisite oriental lacquered cabinet, decorated in gold on a black background. And she even had her own bathroom. The *amah* was putting Constance's clothes in a mahogany wardrobe—almost identical to the one in her bedroom at the Gomez house. Aunt Rebecca does have good taste, Constance thought. I wonder what she's like?

The *amah* followed Constance into the bathroom to adjust the shower water for her. As the gentle spray warmed her, Constance allowed her thoughts to drift back to Sam. She mustn't worry, he had said. He would soon find a job and a place to live. And he would attend Friday evening services at the synagogue . . . surely she would see him there. But not this Friday, she reminded herself. Luckily, there were only eleven days left in September. On October first Aunt Rebecca would be returning to the town house and from the way it sounds, she's probably very careful about following customs.

While Constance sat at the mahogany dressing table and brushed her hair, another servant arrived to tell her that lunch would be served whenever she was ready. Feeling guilty about keeping Uncle Lionel waiting, Constance jumped up and ran downstairs to join him in the dining room, where he sat in an overstuffed chair reading a book and smoking a pungent cigarette. The Chinese, Constance remembered, rolled their own, placing bits of strong, fine-cut tobacco on fragments of rice paper—or smoked bamboo-stemmed water-pipes—and a pinch of tobacco was enough for one long puff. Glancing up with a smile, Uncle Lionel put the book in his lap and stubbed out his cigarette.

"You look amazingly refreshed after your terrible ordeal, my dear." His eyes were kind.

"All those people on the small boats—" She shivered. "I won't forget them for a long time."

"Sit down and eat," he encouraged. "The food is like what we eat at home, though occasionally we do enjoy some special Chinese or Indian dishes."

Already servants in long white gowns were moving noiselessly around the table. It made Constance nervous. Why did they need so many servants? She had hoped to help her aunt around the house. Now it looked like she wouldn't be needed.

"Is Aunt Rebecca all right?" she asked.

"The phone lines are down, of course; but I have firsthand word that the only damage on the Peak was to the greenery." Uncle Lionel sighed. "Already your aunt has sent word that she's well. Except for her nerves. She suffers from an unusually sensitive nature."

After lunch Constance went upstairs to nap. As she stood at the head of the stairs, she heard a stranger's voice in the foyer.

"Lionel, how are you?"

"Elliot, I'm glad you came. I've been busy with my niece—" Uncle Lionel stood in the foyer.

"I gather she arrived safely, then."

39

"Yes, thank God. That was quite a storm we had there."

"I thought you'd like to know, sir," the young man was saying, "I've arranged for temporary cover for the wall that was blown down and assigned guards to watch against intruders. Tomorrow the men will begin to rebuild it."

"You've done well, Elliot. Thank you. I have to go up to the Peak in the morning but I'll be at the godown no later than ten. And Elliot," he added, "keep your eye out for something that might please Rebecca. She's bound to be upset after all this."

Constance went into her room and lay down. Thank goodness Uncle Lionel's company dealt in rice, sugar and Chinese antiques—not in opium. Some of the stories Sam had told her about the evils of this drug had shocked her. Apparently the Chinese had used it as medicine since the T'ang Dynasty but Emperor Tao-kwang—who ruled during the Opium War—called it "the flowing poison."

While poppies were grown in China, the opium was extracted in British-controlled India. By 1800, Sam told her, the government of China had passed edicts against smoking and importing opium. Not only did the addictive drug destroy those who smoked it, but the opium trade drained silver from the country's already depressed economy. Still opium smuggling flourished.

It was the Opium War of 1840 that led to the cession of Hong Kong Island to the British. The Manchu negotiator was discharged for shaming the Chinese government by ceding the island. The British negotiator Charles Eliot was ridiculed by the British for accepting what was then a barren, rocky, seemingly worthless island.

Fifteen years later a second opium war broke out between China and Great Britain—with France as its ally. Now opium cultivation was permitted in China. The import of the drug from India was legalized. Sam predicted the opium trade would be worth over five million pounds this year. The local government would earn over two million Hong Kong dollars in revenues from opium licenses and opium "divans" or smoking halls. But only weeks ago the Chinese government issued an Imperial decree aimed at abolishing opium within ten years. Sam hoped the British government, fueled by indignation at home, would decide to curtail the export of opium from India. Constance was glad that Sam's firm—like Uncle Lionel's—exported rice and sugar.

It was so hot here, she thought drowsily, worse even than in New

York in the summertime. Maybe I'll sleep after all. I'll dream of Sam . . .

When Constance woke an *amah* was standing in the doorway. "Dinner will be served downstairs whenever you are ready, miss."

THE following morning Constance woke up with a start. She had been dreaming that she was falling through space. The hot sun seeped through the blinds. Despite the *punkah* fan she was damp all over, the sheets clinging to her arms and legs. She gazed about her unfamiliar surroundings. This was not like the other mornings; Sam was not waiting on deck for her.

She lay motionless, trying to relive the magic of those days aboard ship before the typhoon struck . . . remembering the terror of those two hours when she and Sam took refuge in the storage closet . . . she closed her eyes and felt Sam's strong arms tighten around her. If only she were in his arms right now, she thought dreamily. But then, that would mean . . . she felt her cheeks flush. What was she thinking?

There was a faint knock at the door. Before she could remember how to ask who it was in Cantonese, a slight young Chinese girl bearing a tea tray walked in.

"I Sakota," the pretty young *amah* said shyly, waiting for Constance to sit up so that she could settle the tea tray on her lap. "I speak English . . . a little," she added with a giggle.

"Thank you, Sakota." Constance pushed herself up and took the tray. Now she remembered that Uncle Lionel had told the young man caller last night that he expected to return from the Peak by ten o'clock. So that meant he would have to leave early. "Please tell my uncle I'll be downstairs soon." Sakota looked confused. "You understand, Sakota?" she asked gently.

After a pause Sakota smiled. "I tell."

Constance gulped her tea as she dressed, and went downstairs to join Uncle Lionel at the breakfast table. Despite the heat, breakfast was a big meal—sausage, eggs, kippers and tea. The heat doesn't seem to affect their appetites, Constance thought as she watched Uncle Lionel stab a fifth sausage. It was still hard for her to relax and eat with the Chinese "boys" serving them. And it was so quiet. Her fork kept clanking against her plate.

41

"Did you sleep well, Constance?" Uncle Lionel asked.

"Yes, thank you." She certainly wasn't going to tell Uncle Lionel how badly she'd really slept.

"I hope you like your room?"

"It's lovely, Uncle Lionel. The whole house is so beautiful."

"British in the tropics are apt to live far more extravagantly than they would at home," Uncle Lionel said wryly. "It's a failing we can't seem to overcome."

They finished breakfast and left the house. In Uncle Lionel's private rickshas—with the pullers and pushers dressed in colorful uniforms—they were taken to the tram. As they waited at the station, Uncle Lionel explained that the front row seats were always reserved for the Governor and his staff.

As the tram carried them up the mountain it seemed like life in the city was back to normal—the majestic Sikh policemen in their crimson turbans were back on duty as bearers carried richly garbed mandarins in scarlet-curtained palanquins along the broad streets . . . ricksha coolies carried their foreign riders . . . clerks and agents sent briskly about their business. Above the normal sounds of a busy city was the hammering and sawing of workers as they repaired the damaged buildings and ships.

At each stop along the tram's ascent, Constance watched crews of Chinese removing debris, cutting down broken boughs, replanting small uprooted trees. The morning air was fragrant with the scent of the hibiscus and poinsettias which grew wild in the hills. The sky was a deep blue.

"Rebecca will enjoy your company," Uncle Lionel said as the chair coolies carried them from the station. "Often I have to leave her alone during the hot months."

A light fog blanketed the mountaintop. It was pretty, Constance thought, not like the drab brown fog in London that Mama had talked about.

The houses they were passing on the summit looked like mansions. At last they came to Uncle Lionel's house—a stately white brick front with narrow stone verandahs that ran across the front on both the first and second floors and verandahs at the back of the house that looked out over Victoria Harbor and the China Sea.

"Do you notice the difference in the weather?" Uncle Lionel asked.

"Oh, yes." Constance did feel a light breeze blowing.

"And imagine—we're only ten minutes from bustling Victoria. But you know, Constance, I think more than anything else it's the wonderful quiet up here that makes me happy."

Constance felt more relaxed. Uncle Lionel was so easy to be with . . . how bad could Aunt Rebecca be?

REBECCA Levy sat in a pillowed wicker armchair on a shaded portion of the verandah. She wore a cool white cotton frock and her dark hair was drawn tightly into a knot. As Constance and Uncle Lionel approached, she saw that her aunt was tall and angular. She must have been beautiful once, Constance thought, with such delicate features and those huge dark eyes. But now her face was lined, and her mouth was set in a slight grimace.

"You're looking quite well, my dear," Lionel said softly as he bent to touch his lips to her cheek.

"I was so worried about you, Lionel." Rebecca made no move toward him. "I didn't sleep a wink all night."

"Didn't Li arrive with my note?" Lionel asked. Constance stood by self-consciously. It didn't seem like Aunt Rebecca was very happy to see Uncle Lionel.

"You knew I wouldn't be satisfied until I saw you myself," she reproached. "I was afraid you were trying to spare me."

"Rebecca, this is Constance. Nathan's daughter." Uncle Lionel drew Constance close.

"This is your home now, my dear." Rebecca lifted her cheek toward Constance. "After all these years I still feel as though I'm living in exile." She tossed Uncle Lionel a pained look. "But at least up here on the Peak I miss those horrible hot months. Not that this is the joy that so many people think." Uncle Lionel seemed to suppress a sigh. Rebecca turned back toward him. "Lionel, you'll be staying up for a few days?"

"I'm sorry, Rebecca. It's just impossible. There's been a great deal of damage to the godown." He hesitated. "And I heard someone say we might be in for a smaller storm tonight. I'm afraid I have to get back to town."

"Well, if you must . . . when will you leave? And I had a special dinner planned to welcome Constance. I even thought we could have Elliot join us—"

"Rebecca, Elliot and I will both be tied up until late tonight," he interrupted. "Now that Constance is here, I'm afraid I have to return

43

to town immediately. Why don't you take her to the restaurant?" He turned to Constance. "We have a delightful restaurant here on the Peak. You'll enjoy it as much as Rebecca does, I'm sure."

Uncle Lionel left and Rebecca showed Constance to her bedroom, a large airy, high-ceilinged room filled with Oriental and mid-Victorian furniture. Yellow wallpaper etched with a pattern of white birds covered the walls, and a blue oriental rug lay on the floor.

"Aunt Rebecca, it's a beautiful room!"

That seemed to please her. "Well I'm glad you like it, my dear. Elliot Hardwicke helps me with the decorating. He's Lionel's assistant in the firm. A talented young man from a titled London family. Of course, being the youngest, he doesn't get the attention he deserves. They seem to have no respect for his artistic accomplishments. I've arranged for him to do several portraits for families here, and they've all been delighted. He's been like a son to Lionel and me in the eight years he's been in Victoria."

As her aunt chattered on, Constance realized that little was expected of her in the way of conversation beyond looking interested in what she was saying and uttering a sympathetic word or two during the pauses. She began to suspect that Uncle Lionel might enjoy his days and nights alone in the town house.

CLAD in his white linen suit—summer attire favored by foreign businessmen in Shanghai and Hong Kong—Sam left his modest flat in Kowloon—inhabited by working-class Europeans and only a short ride on the Star Ferry from Victoria—to keep his appointment with Mr. Telford of Telford & Latham Export Company. Sam knew about the company from their Shanghai branch, and that the company's operations were quite similar to those of the Franks's hong. After a brief interview yesterday morning with a member of the firm, they had set up an appointment for him with Patrick Telford.

Sam disembarked and walked briskly, shunning the services of the chair-coolies. In my British clothes I'm one of the "foreign devils," he thought in momentary amusement. Not until he had returned to Kaifeng had he fully realized how Anglicized he had become. It bothered him. But he had talked to Chinese students who, after returning from studying in Europe and America, had also felt alienated.

Slow down, Sam told himself. There was plenty of time. The air

44

here was so heavy. Could it possibly be hotter here than in Shanghai? It wouldn't do to arrive for his appointment looking like he had spent the morning working at the docks.

Sam felt his self-confidence evaporating. Of course he spoke Cantonese and English perfectly—but would one year of full-time employment with the Franks's hong be enough?

Within minutes of meeting Patrick Telford he knew it would. Telford was a tough Scotsman who had come to Hong Kong eighteen years ago with his bride and a little cash. But he was determined to make his fortune—and he did. Many people left Hong Kong and returned to London or Belfast or Glasgow after they made their money. Not Patrick Telford. He knew he would never leave.

"You were really born and raised as a Chinese?" Telford asked.

"I was, sir." Sam smiled. "Except that my family was not Buddhist"—as were ninety-five percent of the Chinese. "I spoke only Chinese, went to Chinese schools, wore Chinese clothes." As Sam spoke he reminded himself that despite all this the Jews of Kaifeng lived apart from the other Chinese. Even though some could no longer practice their religion, at least they knew they were Jews.

"You never spoke a word of English until four years ago?"

"It's just as I've told you," Sam said. He couldn't wait to tell Constance—already he had a place to live and he would be an interpreter for Telford & Latham Export Company. Surely he wouldn't have too much trouble finding her—Lionel Levy owned a major business establishment in Victoria.

"Well, Sam, I do believe you speak the King's English better than I do." Telford struck Sam as a kind, unpretentious man. He had risen above his origins but he had not forgotten them. "Stick with me. You'll do well."

Almost two hours later, after a complete tour of the offices and godown—and instructions to report for duty at 8 A.M. the following morning—Sam left Telford & Latham to find Lionel Levy. He had to admit that he was a little worried—had he been rude to leave Constance with no word about when they would see each other again? But her uncle had been almost rude to him and he'd wanted to get away. Levy acted like Constance had degraded herself by being with him. Maybe it was his Chinese coolie jacket—after all, a white man in Chinese clothes wasn't a common sight . . .

Since that first day on the boat Sam had known that he could happily spend the rest of his life with Constance. But he also realized that Lionel Levy probably wouldn't consider him the most promising of suitors. Why? he thought defensively, I was good enough for Grandma Franks's great-granddaughter . . . shouldn't I be able to court Constance?

Lionel kept Sam waiting for over half an hour before seeing him into his office.

"Yes, Mr. Stone?" He didn't ask Sam to sit down.

"I left Constance rather precipitately," Sam began. Why did he sound so stiff and formal? "I meant to ask if I might call on her. I'm sure she'd like to know that I have found employment." It had been a mistake to come here. Levy clearly wanted no part of him.

"My niece has gone to stay with my wife at our house on the Peak. I'll give her your message when she returns to the city. Thank you for being so kind to her on board ship," he added. So—Constance had talked about him. "My wife and I are most grateful."

"Thank you, sir."

Sam felt humiliated at the rebuff as he left the office. I guess I will always be a Chinese coolie to Mr. Levy, he thought bitterly. I'm Jewish, and speak English as well as he does . . . never mind that I have a college education . . .

In the brilliant sunlight Sam swore that Lionel Levy would not keep him away from Constance. She would return from the Peak, and somehow he would see her. He would make a name for himself in Victoria. He would build a life for Constance. Lionel Levy couldn't keep them apart forever . . .

CHAPTER
FIVE

EACH DAY AT the house on the Peak seemed interminable to Constance. She would sit on the verandah for hours, listening to Aunt Rebecca's tales of how the world had mistreated her. For a woman who didn't get out to see very many people, she was certainly full of local gossip; but Constance quickly learned that everything that happened in the British Crown Colony was quickly passed around.

The Colony was built around the same caste system that Mama had hated in England. The wholesale merchants and their clerks considered themselves above the retail merchants and their clerks . . . the government officials considered themselves above all the merchants. The community was divided into endless cliques. The people who lived in Hong Kong looked down on those who lived in Kowloon, just as the Londoners who lived in Belgravia looked down on those of Brixton.

The fog had settled in soon after Constance first arrived nine days before and still hadn't let up. It seemed like the house sat in the midst of one huge cloud, totally isolated from the rest of the world. After a few days in the house with Aunt Rebecca Constance felt like she had to get out—even if only to walk down the road. But it was so murky outside that she really couldn't stray far from the house. And the dampness seeped into everything—even the linens and clothes had to be stored in "hot cupboards." The servants were constantly wiping water from the walls, mopping up puddles on the yellow tiled floors.

"Sometimes we're living in the clouds for weeks on end," Aunt Rebecca was saying on the verandah one afternoon. "It's like being in prison, not being able to see twenty feet beyond the house. Sometimes I think Lionel uses the business as an excuse not to stay up here."

"At least it's cool," Constance offered. "The heat must be intolerable in town." Only twice since she'd arrived had Uncle Lionel come up to the house. He admitted the weather in town was grueling—too hot even for his weekly chess game—but he insisted that work at the hong demanded his presence in town. Constance wondered . . .

"It's just terrible how this dampness spoils absolutely everything. I keep telling Lionel he should stop bringing books up here, but of course he's not happy without something to read. I don't know why we've stayed here as long as we have—most people remain in the Colony for eight or ten years, then go back to England to live like human beings."

Constance wondered if Aunt Rebecca really wanted to leave or if this was just more of her complaining. What if they did move back to London? Of course they'd take her. And she would never see Sam again . . .

When would they return to the town house? Monday would be the first of October and Aunt Rebecca still hadn't said anything about going back to town.

She wondered if Sam had found a job. Had he looked for her at Friday services at the synagogue? Now another Friday would go by without her being there. She hoped he would realize that she wasn't in town—after all very few ladies in the Crown Colony remained in town during the hot summer months. She had to know.

"Aunt Rebecca, when will we leave here?"

"On Monday, of course. We always leave on October first. I thought Lionel told you that—but then his mind seems to be elsewhere these days."

"Mr. Gomez told me about the Ohel Leah Synagogue," Constance went on, her heart pounding. "He said it had been given to the Jewish community by the Sassoons."

Rebecca pursed her mouth.

48

"The Sassoons give themselves airs. They came to China some fifty-odd years ago, unable to speak a word of English. Now they're important British citizens—in one generation. Their children live in palaces in London and entertain like rajahs. They socialize with King Edward and his court. Well let me tell you, my dear, they don't earn their titles—they buy them."

"Sam—remember, the man I met on the boat—told me that in Shanghai the Sassoons are looked upon as the Rothschilds of the Far East." She felt uncomfortable talking about Sam to Aunt Rebecca. The first time she'd mentioned him Aunt Rebecca had harumphed and muttered something about a Chinese Jew.

Aunt Rebecca shook her head.

"The Rothschilds have been friends of kings for many generations. They're financiers. The Sassoons are nobodies. Merchants, like us. Even in India they were not quite accepted in European circles. It's absurd the way they are courted in England and Europe!"

"Well, I am looking forward to services at the synagogue." Constance felt like she was always trying to bring Aunt Rebecca's unpleasant conversations to an end.

"If I'm up to it after the move into town, we'll attend Friday evening services," Rebecca sniffed. Constance had to smile at this—after all, it wasn't as if with all those servants Aunt Rebecca would be lifting heavy boxes.

"Now, dear, be a good girl and fetch me that pillow, will you? My back is aching from this ghastly dampness . . ."

CONSTANCE thought Monday would never come . . . but it did and now she was in the same city as Sam. But she wondered why he hadn't dropped her a note. He could easily have found her address. Maybe he had forgotten her.

She offered to go on shopping expeditions for Aunt Rebecca, grateful for the opportunity to see Chung-Wan—the Central District along the Praya—and hoping all the time that she would bump into Sam. It was an exotic city filled with fascinating sights—the sampans with oars that nestled around the two dozen or more oceangoing steamers usually in port; and the colorful streets, teeming with bearers of scarlet-curtained palanquins swaying from their shoulders. Constance noticed that there were none of the automobiles becoming so popular in New York. But everywhere there were British soldiers and sailors, booted officers carrying swagger sticks.

Constance shopped at Lane, Crawford & Company on Queen's Road and Praya Central for Irish linen handkerchiefs. At Campbell Moore & Company, under the Hong Kong Hotel, she bought Aunt Rebecca a special English perfume. Constance knew it would shock her aunt if she knew how often she'd shunned the sedan chairs and rickshas, but she loved walking around the streets. And the street cars installed two years ago—used mainly by the working class.

She inspected the foreign postage stamps at the Hong Kong Stamp Depot, admired the windows of Volgtlander & Sons, dealers in diamonds, silver, and telescopes, wandered through the Central Market —three minutes from the landmark Tower Clock—which extended all the way from Queen's Road to the Praya, though the Levy servants made all food purchases. But she never saw Sam . . .

Constance was impressed by the New Victoria Hotel in Queen's Road Central, whose rooms were said to be the largest and coolest and most beautiful in the Far East. And she flinched each time she saw an Englishman flogging a coolie with cane or umbrella. But nobody else seemed to be shocked by such behavior.

She couldn't stop herself from looking for Sam's face in the crowds. He just had to be at the Ohel Leah Synagogue on Friday evening.

But on Friday Constance didn't even know if she was going to be at the services. Aunt Rebecca vacillated from hour to hour. It seemed the moment she'd said "Yes, we'll attend services," she changed her mind—"No, Constance, I'm not up to it." Finally she agreed to go, in spite of the heat, which of course was more than any human being should have to bear.

They rode in the carriage to the Ohel Leah Synagogue. Though this was a violation of the Jewish law, Rebecca insisted that she was too weak to walk. As they approached the white three-story synagogue, Constance admired its enormous dome and pagoda-like turrets, its spacious open balcony and arched portico. It was a beautiful building —a perfect place of worship.

Constance was shy as Uncle Lionel introduced her to an elderly couple who were fascinated that she had come from America. She answered their questions about life in New York, but she couldn't concentrate. Was Sam there? Surely he would have immediately tried to become part of the Jewish community—his Jewishness was his private treasure.

"Lionel, I'm not up to standing in this heat," Rebecca warned as Lionel waved to another arriving couple. He seemed to enjoy the synagogue socializing. "Constance and I will take our places in the balcony." She took Constance's arm.

Walking with Rebecca into the marble-floored synagogue, up the narrow flight of stairs leading to the balcony where the women sat during the services, Constance was almost afraid to look around. Would she see Sam among the men gathered on the lower floor?

Rebecca led her to the first row. Her heart pounding, Constance leaned over the edge and scanned the crowds below. Sam was not there. All this time, she'd been so sure . . . but wait—just as the service was about to begin she saw a tall, slight young man in a white linen suit walking down the aisle. She leaned forward, straining to catch his every movement . . .

"Constance, do lean back, child," Rebecca whispered.

But Constance barely heard. She hadn't been wrong. It was Sam. And how handsome he looked in his British clothes—even more so than she remembered. Just as he sat down, Sam turned and looked up to the balcony, his eyes searching the crowds for a face. Her face? Constance timidly lifted a hand. Rebecca stared at her niece. Sam smiled and started to wave back, but remembering where he was, quickly turned and sat down.

Constance didn't hear the services. It was all she could do not to run to the lower floor. Whenever he dared, Sam turned slightly and looked up toward her. Would the services never end?

Finally they were over and Constance and Aunt Rebecca joined Uncle Lionel below. Now that the ladies had returned from the Peak or visits to Tokyo or wherever they went for the hot months there was lots of summer gossip. Constance noticed that Sam was talking to two men. Why didn't he come over to her? Was it because of Uncle Lionel's rude behavior at the dock?

Sam was struggling to be polite. But he had to talk to Constance. He tried to keep an eye on her as he spoke. When the conversation dwindled he excused himself and pushed through the crowd. At last he was at her side. Constance was grateful that Aunt Rebecca was listening intently to two other well-dressed ladies. Shyly, she took Sam's hand as he spoke.

"I've been waiting for you to return." He seemed so happy to see her. "I was sure I'd find you here."

"Are things going well with you, Sam?" The crowd faded, and it

51

was as if they were completely alone, back on the deck of the ship.

"I have a position with Telford & Latham. And Mr. Telford has helped me find a flat within comfortable walking distance to the hong." He glanced at Uncle Lionel. "May I take you to Thomas's Grill Room for tiffin on Sunday?"

He wanted to see her . . . "I'd love that. What time can I expect you?"

"Constance!" Her aunt's sharp voice interrupted. "Tell your uncle I'm feeling tired. Let's go to the carriage."

"Yes, ma'am." She hesitated a moment. "First may I please introduce Sam Stone, who saved my life during the typhoon—"

"We're most grateful," Rebecca said icily, "but I'm really not feeling at all well in this heat. Tell your uncle that I'll be waiting in the carriage." She turned and walked away without a backward glance.

Constance stared after her. How could Aunt Rebecca have been so rude?

"I'll call for you Sunday," Sam said softly. And his eyes told her that no matter how her uncle and aunt felt about him, he would. "Please tell me where."

Constance gave Sam directions to the Levy house, then told Uncle Lionel that they had to leave. Sam began talking to a tall, gray-haired man. Across the room their eyes met. Yes, Constance thought, I was right to trust him.

On the ride home, Constance sat lost in her thoughts. Sunday seemed like a year away—how could she wait until then to see her beloved Sam? As Rebecca directed one of her monologues at Lionel, Constance wondered what she would wear for Sam—it had to be something pretty, of course, but proper, too . . .

At the house they sat in the family drawing room. Constance loved this room with its early-Victorian Grecian sofa upholstered in gold brocade near the fireplace and the pair of Gothic-style oak armchairs framed by the Coramandel screens and delicate Chinese cabinets.

Rebecca told the *comprador* to bring tea for Constance and herself and a glass of champagne for Lionel—a Friday night ritual, she explained.

"Oh, Constance I exchanged a few words with your shipboard companion," Lionel said casually while settling into one of the armchairs. "He seems to be doing rather well for himself."

"Oh, yes." Constance leaned forward. "He has a position with Telford & Latham."

Rebecca frowned.

"Is that the Chinese Jew you were telling me about, Lionel?"

"Actually he's quite well-spoken, Rebecca. Apparently he was a protégé of the Franks in Shanghai. And he has joined the congregation." Constance watched Uncle Lionel carefully. He was defending Sam—maybe he'd had a change of heart.

"He's taking me for tiffin at Thomas's Grill on Sunday," Constance said. Would they let her go?

Rebecca turned to Constance. "You accepted without asking our permission?"

"Well, it's the custom now," Constance stammered. "I mean, in New York—"

"Constance, you are not in New York." Rebecca brushed her skirt distractedly. "And it is most unseemly to dart about with young men when you are supposed to be in mourning."

Tears welled in Constance's eyes. "Mama would understand, Aunt Rebecca." She saw Uncle Lionel shift uneasily and she knew she was being disrespectful, but she had to see Sam . . . "It's only for tiffin. Please, Sam saved my life during the typhoon. And I—I just want to see him."

"Constance, the man's Chinese." She grimaced. "You may have been born in America, but your father was British. He would hardly approve of such an association."

"Sam is a Jew who happened to be born in China. And Papa wouldn't have minded—he trusted me." Constance tried to sound calm. Logical. But her heart was pounding and she felt flushed. Whatever happens, she thought fiercely, I will not let Aunt Rebecca keep me from seeing Sam.

"Rebecca, you know about the Jewish colony in Kaifeng," Lionel said. "There was much talk at the synagogue about it. I understand the scrolls brought from their ancient synagogue are in our City Hall and are going to be presented to Ohel Leah."

"I don't care!" Rebecca's voice was shrill. "I'm sure that man has some Chinese blood. How dare he try to pass himself off as one of us!"

"Rebecca, young Stone is being accepted at our synagogue," Lionel said sternly. "We can do no less."

Constance watched her aunt and uncle, thinking—but not daring to say it—that even if Sam did have Chinese blood she would still see him.

Rebecca sighed.

"All right, Constance. You may see him for tiffin at Thomas's Grill Room." Constance clapped her hands, smiling gratefully at Uncle Lionel. "But only for tiffin. Not for dinner. Not in the evening. It's fine with me if morals are being ignored in London because Edward's saintly mother is dead, or that American girls are given ridiculous freedoms. But in this family we will show respect for conventions."

"Thank you, Aunt Rebecca," Constance said demurely. It was time to be respectful—she'd pushed her luck to the limit today . . .

ON Sunday Constance changed her dress four times before she finally decided on the lilac flowered crepe de chine that Mama had copied from the one they'd seen in Lord and Taylor's window. Whenever she wore it, she felt close to Mama.

She went downstairs. Sam would be here in ten minutes. She hoped he wouldn't be late: already her dress was wrinkling.

The *comprador* entered. "A gentleman to see you miss." Constance jumped up and ran to him, thinking how horrified Aunt Rebecca would be at her unladylike behavior. Sam stood in front of the door, looking slightly ill at ease but happy—and so handsome . . .

"You look beautiful," he said softly, escorting her to a waiting carriage. Can he afford this? Constance wondered. She would order the least expensive item on the menu at Thomas's Grill Room, she told herself.

"Tell me about your position," Constance said as they sat in the carriage. She felt odd being out alone with a man—a man who, she had to admit, was a stranger to her in some ways. The girls at school always giggled and asked, *"What do you say to a strange young man?"* But this was *Sam,* who she had shared a lifetime with on that ship from Shanghai to Hong Kong. She didn't have to worry. "Are you happy with it?"

"It's a fine beginning," Sam said.

"Tell me what you do."

The trip passed quickly as Sam told Constance about his interview with Patrick Telford. The food at Thomas's Grill Room was delicious. But most of all Constance thought how happy she was with Sam, how she wanted to know everything about him . . . and wanted him to know her.

She could not bring herself to admit that she was in love with Sam

Stone, yet she knew she wanted him to be part of her life. For now, that was enough.

DESPITE Rebecca's tight-lipped disapproval Constance was able to see Sam on Friday evenings at the synagogue, where he was already making friends among the congregation, and on Sunday afternoons for tiffin. Twice a week—on Mondays and Thursdays—at exactly four in the afternoon, she went to W. Brewer and Company to shop for the latest mystery novels from America for Uncle Lionel. She loved wandering around the little store, talking to the clerks— and she especially loved those days when she secretly met Sam there.

He was working very hard at Telford & Latham. Constance loved to hear about how quickly he was moving up by making a good impression on his superiors. One Monday afternoon in the bookstore he told her that he had been given the keys to the hong.

"So that I can relieve Mr. Telford of the task of opening up in the morning."

"Sam, you'll be putting in longer hours."

"Yes, but Mr. Telford raised my salary." He grinned triumphantly.

Constance knew Sam was saving every cent, allowing himself only the extravagance of taking her to tiffin on Sunday.

"You're worth everything the firm pays you," she said with pride.

"I'm saving so that some day I'll be able to buy land. I know the time will come when property in Hong Kong will be worth a fortune. I plan to buy before the prices soar." Sam smiled. "Mr. Franks trained me well in real estate, Connie."

Lately he'd been calling her Connie all the time. Nobody but Papa and Mama had ever called her that. But when Sam said it, there was a look in his eyes that thrilled her, and the touch of his hand at her elbow gave her chills. But he respected her. He knew she was still in mourning for Mama. And she loved him all the more for his gentle patience.

After a few minutes Sam said he had to go back to the Telford hong. Constance took the books she had chosen for Uncle Lionel to the cashier, signed a chit, and went home. Why couldn't Aunt Rebecca ever invite Sam for dinner? She always had Elliot Hardwicke over. But he was the only one—Aunt Rebecca insisted it was all her nerves could stand, along with the Friday evenings at synagogue. She

55

talked for hours on the telephone every day, mostly talking to her friends about Elliot.

Walking upstairs to her bedroom, Constance heard Rebecca on the telephone. She was talking about Elliot again. "He's the youngest son of Sir Alfred Hardwicke, the London ship builder."

She must really like Elliot, Constance thought. He is charming and intelligent, I guess. And he does know a lot about the arts. But sometimes he makes me feel so unimportant. He always talks about his life in London—the art, the theater, the opera and the ballet . . . but he never asks about anybody else. When Aunt Rebecca told her that Elliot had done the painting of Victoria Harbor hanging over the fireplace, she had been surprised . . . it was a sensitive portrayal, at odds with Elliot's cool demeanor.

All he and Aunt Rebecca ever talked about was their wonderful London. Why did he stay in Hong Kong? When Aunt Rebecca nagged Uncle Lionel about selling the business and returning to England, Constance always became very nervous. But Uncle Lionel assured her that Aunt Rebecca always carried on like this when she was feeling bored with the local gossip.

Constance smiled to herself, remembering Uncle Lionel's constant response:

"Rebecca, this isn't the time."

She looked forward all week to Friday evenings, but Sundays were special because she and Sam could dawdle for hours over tiffin. On one delightfully cool and dry Sunday in mid-December, as they sat at their favorite table in Thomas's Grill Room, Sam was reviling the British Crown Colony's social caste system.

"Here every foreigner tries to live like a Rajah," he was saying. "A taipan must be carried in his own private sedan chair by two or four coolies. He must belong to the Jockey Club or the Hong Kong Club with its leather chairs and crystal chandeliers. His social standing in the Colony is based on these fripperies." Sam leaned forward earnestly, covering her hand with his. "Connie, what brings every foreigner to Hong Kong is greed. They come here expecting to make a fortune in a few years, and then to return to London or Paris or wherever they came from. All a Chinese means to them is cheap labor. Then they scream that the Chinese are constantly swindling them. How can they expect a man they treat no better than an animal not to fight back?"

"Sam, all foreigners are not like that."

"Too many are," he said in frustration. "I lived as a Chinese for the first sixteen years of my life. I know how they feel. Just because I wear British clothes and live among foreigners, I'm not blind." He released her hand. He seemed to be struggling with something. "You've seen only the beautiful streets and avenues of Victoria. You don't know the Chinese district. Let me show you."

They left the restaurant and headed west along Queen's Road to Tai Ping Shan, detouring first to walk along the Praya, by the water's edge. Here Sam pointed out workers—though it was Sunday—who were unloading large chests of Indian opium.

"Thousands of chests arrive each week," Sam said, "many of them to be reshipped to the mainland. But let's walk now to the Chinese District."

They heard a gong beating as they arrived in the district. "Look, Connie—it's a wedding procession," Sam explained. "Chinese style."

Constance turned to see the highly varnished bridal furniture, piles of quilts, and the requisite wedding geese being carried by colorfully dressed coolies.

"That's the bride?" Constance asked, staring at the scarlet-gowned young Chinese girl being carried in a sedan chair.

"Chinese brides wear red rather than white." He chuckled at her surprise. "To the Chinese white is for mourning."

"It's colorful," she said, admiring the graceful folds of the bridal gown. All at once she imagined herself in white, standing with Sam under the *chupah* in Ohel Leah Synagogue. How presumptuous of me, she thought with a smile. But something in Sam's eyes told her that his thoughts were there too.

After the wedding procession had passed, she and Sam made their way into the Chinese quarters. In Tai Ping Shan every second shop sold spirits to foreign sailors and soldiers. Chinese women who had fallen from repute spent their days and nights in ill-kept hotels and lodging houses, close to the music halls so that they could solicit the sailors and soldiers.

The streets were wide—as in the European part of Victoria—but dirty, clogged with a noisy, uncaring humanity. Constance tried to absorb everything as she and Sam walked past painted houses with gaudy signs announcing the owners' names and the wares they sold, past the squalid houses of the families who worked in the factories and on the docks. A cluster of children scurried behind them, begging for money. Constance was shocked, but Sam reached into his pocket and gave each of them a coin.

"This is Victoria, also," Sam said quietly. "These and the boat people—who live and die, generation after generation, on the sampans and junks—are the biggest part of the population. The British are a handful in comparison. Living like potentates on the sweat of the Chinese workers."

"Sam, may we please leave?" she whispered.

AS Constance started down the stairs on Tuesday evening, she could tell by the pitch of Aunt Rebecca's voice that something was wrong. Her aunt was in the family drawing room; dinner was being delayed.

"Lionel, you are wrong. Mrs. Cohen was not making idle gossip," Rebecca was saying. "She felt it her duty to tell me."

"I'm sure there's a reasonable explanation, Rebecca. Let's just ask Constance ourselves," Uncle Lionel said. Constance trembled. What had she done?

Slowly, she walked into the drawing room. Her aunt spun around to face her.

"You've been seeing that Chinese—that Sam Stone—behind our backs! And I have to hear it from strangers!"

"You know I have tiffin with him on Sundays," Constance said softly.

"Besides Sundays!" Rebecca barked.

"I've seen him at the bookstore."

"It isn't enough that I allow you to go out with him every Sunday for tiffin, and that you see him at the synagogue. You have to sneak around corners too!"

"I wasn't sneaking around corners." Constance drew herself up and tried to stop the tremor in her voice. "I go to Brewer's to pick out books for Uncle Lionel and—"

"You told him you'd be there. You arranged an assignation!"

"Rebecca," Uncle Lionel interrupted, "it's true that Constance goes to Brewer's twice a week to choose books for me. Give the girl a chance to speak."

"Lionel, you're too easy on her. You always have been. You don't know a young girl's mind as I do. She went there to meet him. And now everybody at the synagogue will know that Constance is pursuing the Chinese Jew. It's disgraceful. It's humiliating."

"Rebecca, you're—" Lionel's face was ashen. He clutched at his chest, gasping for breath, sank into a chair. "I—I think I'm having an attack of indigestion—" He leaned back in the chair.

"Lionel!" Rebecca threw herself at his feet. "Lionel, what's wrong?"

"Aunt Rebecca, send for the doctor," Constance said quietly. One of them had to stay in control.

Rebecca turned on her.

"You did this! You've made him ill with your wild ways!"

"Aunt Rebecca, give me the name of the doctor." The sight of Uncle Lionel terrified her. "I'll have Li send a chair to bring the doctor here." Please God, let the doctor be available. Uncle Lionel can't die.

"Dr. Arnold," Rebecca whispered, while Constance leaned forward to loosen Lionel's tightly buttoned collar and tie.

"Where does he live?"

"On Queen's Road." Rebecca frowned. "No, that was his old address. It's in the book on Lionel's desk in the study." Trembling, she hovered over her husband. "Lionel, what should I do?"

"I'll find the address and send Li for Dr. Arnold," Constance said. "Sakota will bring you the smelling salts."

"Lionel, you have to be all right," Rebecca sobbed. "I can't lose you! I can't!"

Within ten minutes Dr. Arnold was at the house, putting Uncle Lionel to bed. Rebecca and Constance waited anxiously in the drawing room. It was funny, Constance thought . . . even though Aunt Rebecca drove Uncle Lionel to distraction with her constant complaining she must really love him. And while they waited for the doctor to arrive, Lionel had clung to Rebecca's hand. What an odd kind of love . . .

Rebecca jumped to her feet as the graying, portly Dr. Arnold came into the room.

"Dr. Arnold, how bad is it?"

"He'll be fine, Mrs. Levy," Dr. Arnold said briskly. "I gave him an injection. He'll sleep now. It was a very mild heart attack." He pulled out a prescription pad and began to write. "Send over to the Hong Kong Dispensary and have this filled. He's to have one pill every four hours—unless he's sleeping. Don't wake him for the pills."

"When will you be back?" Rebecca asked.

"I'll stop by in the morning," he promised. "There's no need to worry. He'll be fine."

"I'll go right up to him," Rebecca said.

"Mrs. Levy, he's sleeping," Dr. Arnold said gently.

"I'll sit there until he wakes." Rebecca was back to her old self, Constance noticed. "I'll nurse him myself until he's well." For an instant she glared at Constance. "I assure you he won't be upset this way again."

Constance sat alone in the drawing room until Sakota pleaded with her to go to the dining table.

"Young Missy must eat." But Constance was too tired to eat, so she went up to her room.

CHAPTER

SIX

EXHAUSTED AFTER A long, restless night, Constance leaned against a mound of pillows and sipped her morning tea. She heard talking in the foyer downstairs and froze. Had Uncle Lionel taken a turn for the worse? Had Dr. Arnold been summoned again? It was too early for a routine house call.

Then she sighed in relief. It was Elliot Hardwicke. Aunt Rebecca must have sent word to him of Uncle Lionel's illness. She would probably ask him to take over for a while.

She strained to hear what they were saying. Aunt Rebecca sounded overwrought, and Elliot, as usual, calm.

"We'll carry on at the hong," Elliot was saying. "The important thing is for Mr. Levy to rest. Tell him he's not to worry about anything."

In a few minutes Elliot left. Apparently Uncle Lionel had spent a comfortable night. But Constance wanted to be downstairs when Dr. Arnold made his morning call to ask him herself. After all, maybe it was her fault—she wouldn't want Uncle Lionel to become an invalid . . .

"Sakota, my blue flowered frock, please," she said, still shy about being waited on.

While Sakota fumbled with the tiny buttons at the back of Constance's dress, Constance tried to steel herself to face her aunt this morning. She heard Dr. Arnold come upstairs, knock at the door, and enter her uncle's room. She hurried downstairs to wait for him to emerge. Let Dr. Arnold say that Uncle Lionel will be fine again.

She heard the door opening, and waited anxiously for Dr. Arnold to stop talking to her aunt and come downstairs again.

"Mr. Levy's doing well, Constance," Dr. Arnold said as he descended the stairs. "They were fortunate to have you in the house at the time of the attack. He'll be fine, don't worry."

Constance smiled.

"Oh thank you, doctor. We were so frightened."

"Three or four days in bed and he'll be as good as new. I trust Mrs. Levy will not make him into an invalid over this?"

"She's very upset." Constance suspected Aunt Rebecca would play the devoted wife with the fervor of Sarah Bernhardt.

"He'll do better if everybody around him remains calm." Dr. Arnold's smile was dry. He knew Aunt Rebecca very well. "I'll drop by again tomorrow morning."

Despite Dr. Arnold's news, Constance was nagged by guilt. But she felt relieved when she heard later that Lionel had eaten a poached egg. It looked like he was going to be all right after all.

For the rest of the day Constance roamed aimlessly around the house. She didn't dare go into her uncle's room with Aunt Rebecca sitting there. She ate alone in the dining room, hardly aware of the food, wishing Sam were here. But he had been the start of all this trouble, and now Rebecca would forever blame her.

While Constance sat at the dining room table, she heard Rebecca on the telephone in the study but she couldn't make out what she was saying. What was she telling her friends about Uncle Lionel's heart attack? She'll probably hint that the strain of taking care of his troublemaking niece was too much for him, Constance thought. Aunt Rebecca would certainly never tell the ladies about Sam.

On Thursday morning Constance woke up and remembered today she was to go to Brewer's. But maybe she wouldn't be allowed to go anymore. How would she tell Sam? He would worry if she didn't show up. But by now, he must have heard about Uncle Lionel's illness. So he'd understand if she didn't arrive.

After Dr. Arnold checked upon his patient he told Constance that Lionel was on the mend and in fact, did not even have to remain in bed for several weeks as Rebecca had been insisting. By Monday he could go downstairs, and later in the week he could work at the hong for a few hours a day.

Around three in the afternoon Rebecca sent a houseboy to summon Constance. Eager to see Uncle Lionel—yet dreading the confrontation with her aunt—Constance hurried to their bedroom. Aunt Rebecca wouldn't dare make a scene with Uncle Lionel in the room —would she? Constance knocked.

"Come in," Uncle Lionel called. He sounded remarkably cheerful.

Constance pushed open the door and entered. Uncle Lionel, dressed in a long gown with a coverlet lying across his lap, sat in an overstuffed armchair, Aunt Rebecca stood before the window with her back to Constance.

"Dr. Arnold tells me that your quick thinking is responsible for my fast recovery, my dear." His smile was warm.

"Well, I'm just glad you're feeling better, Uncle Lionel." She noticed that Aunt Rebecca didn't turn away from the window.

"Constance, would you mind doing me one more favor, now that I'm an invalid?" He winked. "How about making your regular trip to Brewer's . . . I hear there's a new mystery out by an American— the name escapes me at the moment—and it looks like I'm going to have plenty of time for reading this week. Just tell the clerk you want the new mystery set in Washington by the American writer everyone's talking about."

"Well—thank you, Uncle Lionel. I'll go right away." Constance couldn't believe her good fortune. She would see Sam . . .

She practically flew out of the house. Uncle Lionel liked Sam. He was on their side . . .

The day was cool and dry. Constance knew she would probably get to Brewer's before Sam did, but she couldn't slow down—she had so much to tell him. Breathless, she arrived at the bookstore and quickly looked around to see if any of Aunt Rebecca's friends were there. But I don't care if they are, she thought defiantly. What is wrong with me talking to Sam in a place of business?

She asked the clerk about the novel Uncle Lionel wanted and he showed her to the appropriate aisle. After finding the book, *A President's Murder,* she signed the chit. Where was Sam? Restless, she left the bookstore under the Hong Kong Hotel and climbed the stairs up to the street. Sam was coming towards her. Constance felt relieved —she thought he had forgotten . . . but what was wrong? He seemed anxious.

"Connie, I heard about your uncle. How is he?"

"He's fine, Sam." She wanted to tell the whole story, but it would only hurt him. "He even asked for a book today."

"I just heard about it this morning when I met Mr. Solomon on Pedder's Street." Sam looked so handsome when he was serious, Constance thought. But he seems distracted. "Connie, I can't stay long today." He checked his watch. "You know I want to, but—"

"You're busy at the hong," she said.

"I have some work to attend to." His eyes held hers. "Could we —do you think we could have tea at the Hong Kong Hotel in an hour and a half?" He spoke shyly. "By then I could leave for the day." To be able to leave the hong so early was a treat for Sam. He usually had to stay to close up at 8 P.M.

Constance hesitated only a moment.

"I'd like that, Sam." She would take the book back to the house for Uncle Lionel and then she would sneak out again. Only the servants would know she was gone. Aunt Rebecca didn't seem to care where she went anyway. "Shall I meet you at the entrance to the hotel?"

"At five-thirty." Constance sensed something special in the way he looked at her. She felt a flutter of excitement. "Don't worry, Connie. You won't be embarrassing your aunt. I promise."

"I'll be there, Sam." Of course she trusted him. No one on earth could keep her from having tea with him this afternoon. Something told her it was going to be a very important day . . .

Sam left to return to the hong. Constance went home and delivered the book to Uncle Lionel. From the look in his eyes she could tell he was enjoying this rest from Rebecca. As he read Aunt Rebecca talked and all he had to do was nod during the pauses to show that he was listening.

Upstairs, Constance looked through her wardrobe. What could she wear to tea at the Hong Kong Hotel? After all, the hotel was the center of social life in the Colony—all the important teas, dinners, and dances were held there. And she'd heard that the hotel's public rooms and taprooms were popular with European society.

She wished she had some new clothes. Uncle Lionel had told Aunt Rebecca to bring in a dressmaker but something always seemed to come up. But never mind, Constance told herself, I'll wear my most elegant dress, the lilac velvet Mama copied from a gown worn by Queen Alexandra. And she'd wear Mama's gray wool cape over it because later it would probably get cold.

By the time Constance left the house to walk to Pedder Street, the sun was disappearing behind Victoria Peak and the sky was streaked with long pink clouds. As she approached the hotel she saw Sam waiting outside. Constance overheard a passerby remark, "Why, that young man always looks as though he had just stepped out of a bandbox." It's true, she thought with pride.

Sam reached out and took her hand, squeezing hard, as he escorted her into the public room where tea was served. Constance was impressed by how elegant it was. On one side of the lofty room tall French windows opened onto a stone verandah which looked out over the harbor.

Chinese "boys" in flowing white gowns served them tea. They lingered over plates of small sandwiches, cookies, perfectly brewed tea, conscious only of each other. As always, Sam talked about his work at the hong. But today would be different. She could hear it in the way he spoke, see it in his eyes . . .

"Would you like to take a carriage ride along the Praya?" Sam asked. "It's beautiful at twilight. I won't keep you out too late."

"It sounds lovely." Constance couldn't help but think how horrified Aunt Rebecca would be if she knew Constance was alone in a carriage with a man at twilight.

When they stepped outside it was dusk. A single star glowed in the darkening sky. Lamps hanging from the ships at anchor lit the harbor. Sam signaled for a carriage and helped Constance inside. He gave the driver instructions and climbed in, settling in his seat next to her. Constance started at the gentle pressure of his thigh against hers.

As the carriage made its way toward the Praya, Sam spoke of his plans for the future. He was convinced that within twenty years, Hong Kong would become one of the world's greatest cities. And he meant to own a piece of it.

By the time the horses were trotting along the Praya, night had settled over the island. Lights glowed from the houses clinging to the steep slopes. Lanterns marked the sampans and junks in the water. The whole city looked like an enormous jewel.

"Connie—" Sam reached for her hand in the semi-darkness of the carriage. "I know I have no right yet to speak to you this way, when I'm not prepared to care for a wife properly; but . . . when I do rise to that position, will you marry me?" It was what she had been waiting for . . . and she knew now that it was all she wanted in the world . . . She lifted her face to his.

"Oh, yes, Sam. Yes!"

Their lips met. Sam's arms drew her close at first gently, and then crushing her against him as they kissed. She felt his heart hammering as she clung to him, dizzy from these delicious new feelings.

At last, reluctantly, Sam pulled away. His arms dropped to his sides. He was trembling—and so was she . . .

Sam spoke softly.

"I'll take you home, my love."

"We'll tell no one," Constance said shyly after a moment of silence. "Not until the proper time."

"No one," Sam agreed. As he took her hand, Constance thought of Aunt Rebecca and what she had said about Sam being part Chinese. What if she tried to stop them from marrying?

If I have to, Constance thought fiercely, I will defy Aunt Rebecca. Nothing else matters but me and Sam. Together.

Sam reached into a pocket of his vest and pulled out a piece of white jade hanging from a gold chain.

"Wear this for me, Connie. It's a *chai*. The Hebrew symbol for life. I had it made in Shanghai as a gift for my grandmother. She would want you to have it."

THE next morning, when Sam left his tiny flat, he was ready to fight the world for his future. And Constance would be at his side to share that future . . . His only regret was that his grandmother had not lived to meet Constance. As for the rest of his family—well, they were no longer a part of his life.

He walked briskly. It was a crisp, cool morning. Later in the day the warm sun would bring the tourists to the coral beaches of the island. Tomorrow, he told himself, he would put some more money in the bank to add to his savings. Constance was to be his wife; he had to be especially careful with money.

As he approached the walled-in hong, he reached for his ring of keys. First he would unlock the gate, then the godown so that the *comprador*—who would be there in ten minutes—could check in the coolies. Soon the shroffs—the men whose business it was to discover by touch the light dollars and the bad—the Chinese mercantile assistants, and the European clerks would all file into their offices at one side of the compound.

The sentry who went on duty at eight o'clock every night waved to him. Even he didn't have a key to the godown—only Sam and Mr. Telford did. Sam had learned early on that Mr. Telford didn't trust many of his employees.

"An uneventful night?" Sam asked.

"Nothing to report," the sentry said, smothering a yawn. "See you at eight."

Sam walked to the large, rectangular cement godown and put the key in the lock. He stopped short. The door was unlocked. Mr. Telford must have come in early. Cautiously, he opened the door and walked inside.

"Mr. Telford?" Why hadn't the sentry told him Mr. Telford was already in? "Mr. Telford?"

There was something different about the room. What was it? He looked around.

That was it—the blank wall across from him, hadn't there been sugar there yesterday? And it was to be exported tomorrow . . . Sam sat down on the floor, stunned. During the night thieves must have sneaked in, stolen the sugar, and shipped it out in junks.

But what about the sentry? How could he have gotten in? And why had he stayed around if he'd been part of the robbery? Sam broke into a sweat. The sentry couldn't have known anything. It must have happened between 5:30 P.M. and 8 P.M., while he was away and before the sentry arrived. My God, Sam thought, if I had been in the godown alone, as I usually am, I probably would have been killed. Meeting Constance saved my life.

But how had they gotten in? Only Mr. Telford and I have the keys.

He rushed to the telephone in his office. Damn it, he thought, why does it take all this cranking just to reach the operator?

At last he reached Mr. Telford at his home on the Peak. Telford clearly did not appreciate having his breakfast interrupted. Sam told him what had happened. Telford was furious.

"Call the police immediately. Or have you done that already?"

"My first thought was to phone you," Sam said. "Now I'll call the police." He hesitated. "Mr. Telford, how could this have happened?"

"I have no idea. But I didn't do it and you didn't do it, I'm sure of that. I trust my judgment of people. And I can't believe that fool of

67

a sentry was involved. He wouldn't have stuck around if he had been. What time did you leave the hong, Sam?"

"Five-thirty. Usually I'm there until eight. Except on Fridays."

"Thank God you did leave early," Telford said. "Those bastards probably would have thought nothing of doing away with you if they had to. Damn it, somebody must have stolen my keys. Hang on, let me take a look—"

In a few moments Telford was back on the line.

"Well, they're all here. How in God's name—but don't worry. We'll get to the bottom of this before the day is over. I'll be down in twenty minutes."

The next two hours dragged. While Sam sat in his small office a Detective Bailey questioned a stream of workers outside. Even the sentry had been brought back for questioning. Within minutes Sam knew that Bailey thought he was guilty. He made a point of telling the detective that he had spent the first sixteen years of his life in China.

"You speak the language as well as any Chinese," Bailey said. "You must have friends in the Chinese quarter."

"I have no Chinese friends in Hong Kong." Sam tried to stop his voice from shaking. Because of his position at the hong he wasn't allowed to socialize with Chinese. "In Kaifeng, yes. But not in Hong Kong."

"You connived with a Chinese gang;" Sam began to panic. Despite the color of my skin and my perfect English, he thought, I'm Chinese. And therefore guilty . . .

"You let them into the godown so they could steal the cargo before it could be shipped tomorrow!" Bailey snapped.

"I left early," Sam conceded. Please, don't let them ask where I went. I can't implicate Constance. "I was out of the hong by twenty minutes past five."

"But you never leave before eight!" Bailey shot back. Obviously he'd asked the workers about his schedule. "You were here to let them in, then left just before the sentry was due to arrive. He knew nothing about what had happened earlier. That's why he stayed the whole night, as always. He'd made his routine check of the doors and found everything locked."

"Last night I left at twenty minutes past five." Sam tried to sound calm. "Work was done for the day. The coolies had been dismissed. The others leave early." He paused. "But wait a minute—one of the clerks had worked late. He was talking to me as I locked the door. And the door was locked when the sentry came on duty." If it hadn't been, the guard was to phone Mr. Telford immediately.

"Then, Mr. Stone, how do you think the robbers got in?" Bailey spoke quietly. "There's no evidence of forced entry."

"I don't know," Sam said. "Unless they found a way to have a key made."

"To be used on a night when you just happened to leave early." Bailey smiled humorlessly. "Two nights before a big shipment was to leave."

"I told you I was away from the godown," Sam repeated, his voice rising. "I don't know how they got in."

"And may I ask who you were with between five-thirty and eight P.M.?"

Sam hesitated.

"A young lady."

"From shortly after five until eight?" he probed. "When the robbery took place—"

"Yes," Sam said wearily. He dreaded the next question.

"And I presume this young lady will be willing to testify to that?"

"I couldn't ask it of her." He turned away from Bailey.

"Enough of this, Mr. Stone. I'm afraid you'll have to come down to the jail with me."

There was a knock on the door and Patrick Telford stepped in.

"May I speak to Mr. Stone alone for a few minutes?"

"Why?" Bailey looked at him suspiciously.

"Mr. Stone works for me, Detective Bailey. I need information about the shipment that was supposed to go out tomorrow. Please. Give us five minutes. I'm sure the Captain Superintendent of Police would expect you to grant me this courtesy. Or must I phone him myself?"

Bailey glared at Telford.

"All right, five minutes, but that's all." He slammed the door behind him.

Telford took a seat across from Sam.

"There's no chance of buying off those two. Not after those two inspectors were suspended a couple of years ago."

"But Mr. Telford, I had nothing to do with the robbery. You believe me, don't you?" Sam knew he was pleading, but what choice did he have?

"Sam, you don't have to tell me that." Telford softened. "But you're simply going to have to tell the police the name of that young lady."

"I can't do that, sir. It would embarrass her family, and would make life intolerable for her."

Telford sighed.

"I tell you what," he said. "You go along with the detectives, I'll bring down a young lady who'll convince the police you spent the entire night with her—starting at five-thirty. All you have to do is pretend you know her. Her name is A-lu-te."

"Who is she?"

Telford chuckled.

"A deliciously beautiful young Eurasian, who bestows her favors among the most distinguished gentlemen of the Colony. For a high price."

"They'll accept her word?"

"Don't worry, Sam, she has friends in the highest places. They wouldn't dare question her testimony."

"But how can we be sure someone won't come forward and deny she was with me?"

"All right Sam, if you must know—she was with me last night," Telford said. "Until I left her to go home for breakfast. No one will challenge her story, I assure you. Now relax."

THE hours inched by as Sam sat in a cell in the jail waiting for Mr. Telford to arrive with A-lu-te. Outside he heard the bustling sounds of the city. It was Friday night, he realized. He wouldn't be going to the synagogue tonight, but neither would Constance, since her uncle lay ill. At least she wouldn't notice he wasn't there and worry.

Sam sighed. He still couldn't believe he was sitting in a jail cell, suspected of robbing the Telford & Latham godown. Was it just this morning he had been planning his future?

Finally at dusk Mr. Telford arrived with A-lu-te, an exquisite Eurasian girl who flung herself into Sam's arms, and held him embarrassingly close in front of the police. Detective Bailey seemed to have swallowed the story, so he was released. A-lu-te gave an enthusiastic performance as they left together, her arm linked through his. Outside the jail, while Mr. Telford talked to an old friend, A-lu-te told Sam that she would be delighted to visit his flat any time.

70

"Just send a coolie with word that Mr. Smith wishes to see me," she whispered, slipping a piece of paper into his hand. "I will come to you. It will be my pleasure," she added. He gathered that her services would be free. But he couldn't betray Constance . . .

CONSTANCE returned to her bedroom after breakfast on Saturday morning and settled down in a chair by the window to read the collection of short stories by the American O. Henry, which she had borrowed from the study. She was restless and couldn't concentrate on the book. If only she had dared to attend services alone last night —she could have seen Sam.

Her fingers caressed the ivory *chai* . . . when would Sam feel confident that he could support a wife? Now that they'd talked about it, she felt like she couldn't wait for the day to arrive. All she had now was the memory of those long, sweet moments in the darkness of the carriage . . . she had never imagined she could have such feelings.

Maybe if she went for a walk she'd feel better. Right now her bedroom seemed like a prison. Aunt Rebecca was still keeping her vigil at Uncle Lionel's bedside—which Constance knew wasn't exactly his first choice.

As she left her room, Constance heard Aunt Rebecca's voice. Uncle Lionel must be sleeping, she thought—that was the only time Aunt Rebecca made her "telephone visits," as she liked to call them.

"I never trusted the man," Rebecca's was saying indignantly. "But this I never imagined. He's a disgrace to the community!"

Who was incurring the wrath of the telephone circuit today, Constance wondered.

"I trust he'll never have the gall to set foot in the synagogue again. Not after this. Lionel always thinks I'm too harsh, but this time I was right."

Warning signals went off in Constance's mind. *Who* might not have the gall to set foot in the synagogue again?

"Constance?" Aunt Rebecca called out. It was the first time she had addressed Constance directly since Uncle Lionel's collapse.

"Yes," she said uncertainly, pausing at the entrance to the study. Her heart was pounding.

"Rowena, I'll call you later," Rebecca said into the telephone and hung up. "Constance, I must talk to you."

71

"Yes, ma'am." Constance walked into the study. Something was very wrong. She regarded Aunt Rebecca warily.

"Close the door, child," Rebecca ordered. "The servants don't have to know everything."

Constance turned to close the door, then faced her aunt again.

"Constance, Rowena Sassoon just called me." Her mouth tightened. "You know how reliable she is. She's the soul of integrity. Apparently your 'Chinese Jew'—a member of our congregation—was arrested yesterday morning. Telford & Latham was robbed."

Constance stared at her aunt in disbelief. Was she saying that Sam was guilty?

"Sam could not be responsible!" Her eyes flashed defiantly. "I'll never believe that, Aunt Rebecca." She must go to him. No matter what Aunt Rebecca said, she would help him.

"Oh, he was cleared of the robbery," Rebecca said, and then with a small look of triumph, "A girl came to the jail. A Eurasian prostitute with high connections. She told the police that Sam could not have been responsible because he had been with her all evening. Now Constance, don't look like that. What could we expect of a man raised among the Chinese? Imagine. And he expected to be welcomed into the Jewish community. Be thankful you found out the truth now, my dear."

"Perhaps Mrs. Sassoon was mistaken," Constance stammered. How could Sam have gone from her to that Eurasian girl? After everything he'd said?

"It's true. You'll read about it tomorrow in the *Gazette.*" Rebecca rearranged the folds of her skirt. "He was arrested and then released when that Eurasian prostitute admitted that he had spent the evening with her. Of course, the newspapers won't refer to her as a Eurasian prostitute, but everybody will know when they read her name. Now I'm sure you'll understand why you are never to see that man again, Constance. I absolutely forbid it."

"Aunt Rebecca, how can we be sure that—"

"When you read tomorrow's newspaper, you'll be sure!" Rebecca snapped. "He fooled a lot of people here in the Colony. But I knew he was a bad lot when Lionel told me about meeting him on the landing wharf. Dressed like a coolie. What could we expect? He was a coolie until that stupid society brought him to Shanghai. He'll always be a coolie."

The ring of the telephone startled both of them. Annoyed, Rebecca reached for the receiver.

"Hello? Oh yes, Elise, I just heard all about it. Yes, just terrible . . . what? Oh, I know, apparently he's part Chinese, so that does explain it . . . but to think we were receiving him into our congregation. A man who consorts with women like that. Honestly . . ."

Cold and trembling, too numb for tears, Constance turned away and slowly climbed the stairs. In a few minutes her whole world had been shattered. Two days ago Sam had told her he loved her. He wanted to marry her. And he had left her to go to that girl.

Aunt Rebecca didn't have to forbid her to see Sam again. She would never speak to him again. Ever.

CHAPTER
SEVEN

ON SUNDAY, AS usual, Sam appeared at the Levy house to take Constance to St. Thomas's Grill Room for tiffin. He couldn't wait to tell her the truth about the robbery—he had wanted to telephone her yesterday but her aunt's obvious hostility had made it impossible. Today only the servants would be at the house. Connie would hear what really happened . . .

He rang the silverplated doorbell and waited. Someday he would buy a house as grand as this for Constance . . .

The door opened. The *comprador* bowed politely and handed Sam an envelope.

"Miss Levy?" he asked, startled.

"Missy not wish to see you." The *comprador* bowed again and retreated behind the door.

Sam stared in disbelief as the door closed in his face. Now he opened the envelope.

Sam, I do not wish to see you again.
Constance.

But he had been cleared of the charges. Surely Constance wouldn't believe he was guilty? Dazed, he walked away from the house. What could he do?

He would write her. After what had happened in the carriage, how could she doubt his love? Damn it, he would make her believe him —he had to.

Back at his flat he noticed a copy of the Sunday *Gazette* lying on his kitchen table. The headline caught his eye . . . so that was it. The blasted story of his being cleared by A-lu-te's testimony! But why hadn't Constance given him a chance to explain? Surely she'd understand why he didn't want to tell the police that at the time of the robbery he was alone with her in a carriage . . . of course, earlier they had been at the Hong Kong Hotel for tea, but that wouldn't have been sufficient for an alibi. It would have made her life in the Crown Colony—and with Aunt Rebecca—impossible. Wouldn't she understand that?

With fresh determination Sam began his letter. Every word had to be just right. He could not divulge Mr. Telford's relationship with A-lu-te, yet he had to tell Constance that Telford had used A-lu-te to protect him.

Sam opened his heart to Constance in the letter. He even offered to arrange for her to talk to Mr. Telford if she doubted his word. As Sam sealed the letter, he felt optimistic that Constance would understand. How could she not, once she had read the truth?

CONSTANCE sat alone in her bedroom. Sakota left a lunch tray at her door, but the food went untouched. How could she think of food?

What a fool she had been to think she knew Sam—to be so confident in their love . . . and all the while he carried on a secret life with that woman. Her face flamed as she remembered those moments in the carriage when Sam had held her in his arms.

She closed her eyes and fought the tears. She was glad Mama was not alive to see her like this. But she would not cry for Sam. He wasn't worth it. She would teach herself to live without him. She would ignore him if she saw him at the synagogue. She would go to W. Brewer and Company to choose books for Uncle Lionel and not even look to see if he was there. She would never forgive him.

She went to the bathroom and splashed water on her face. Sakota must not see that she had been crying. No one must know how Sam had hurt her. Later she would go downstairs for dinner and she would pretend that she perfectly all right. She had survived Mama's death. She could survive this too.

She felt the *chai* burning her throat. She snatched it from her neck and dropped it into a drawer. Tomorrow she would put it into an envelope and have one of the servants return it to Sam.

Constance heard the doorbell. Was it Sam again? She had told Sakota that she didn't want to see anyone today. But Sakota knew —like all the house servants—that it was only Sam who visited her.

Constance crossed to the door. The *comprador* had brought something upstairs to Aunt Rebecca. She heard them talking in the hallway.

"You will have a boy return the letter to Mr. Stone," Rebecca was saying. "The address is on the envelope. Read it for the boy."

SAM couldn't believe Constance had returned his letter unopened. Was her aunt responsible? Maybe Mrs. Levy had ordered Constance not to see him again . . . no, Constance was strong. She would have fought to see him if she'd really wanted to.

He would wait a few days and try again. Once Constance had thought it over she'd realize she at least owned him a chance to explain. He would go to the bookstore tomorrow, he would make her listen to him.

ON Monday a coolie from the Levy household arrived at the hong with a bulging envelope for Sam. Even before he opened it, he knew what was inside. He cradled the *chai* in his hands, remembering those precious moments in the carriage with the woman who was to be his wife . . . what had happened to destroy their future together?

It seemed the afternoon would never come when he would meet Constance at the bookstore. He knew exactly when she would arrive.

But she didn't show up. He had to face the truth: Constance had not come because she knew he would try to see her. He would try again on Thursday. Surely by then Constance would be ready to give him a chance to explain.

It was unfair . . . he had done nothing wrong. But the newspaper story had been ugly, filled with innuendo, he had to admit. Maybe he would wonder if he read a story like that. But after he had declared his love for her . . .

Sam couldn't concentrate or work throughout Tuesday and Wednesday—couldn't sleep the long nights. On Thursday at four he hurried to W. Brewer's. Again, Constance wasn't there. She must have changed her schedule. Maybe she would be at the synagogue tomorrow night. He'd heard that Mr. Levy would be back at his business next week. And the Levys were always at Friday evening services. But what if the congregation shunned him after what had happened? He shrugged it off. Whatever happens, I must see Constance . . .

At Telford & Latham things returned to normal. No one seemed to hold the incident against him. Mr. Telford was still convinced that Sam was innocent, but Sam knew he wouldn't be satisfied until the thieves were caught.

Arriving at the synagogue on Friday evening Sam braced himself for the inevitable coolness of the congregation. He could imagine how the ladies had gossipped about the incident—it was probably the most titillating event of the year.

But within a few minutes of his arrival he realized that he was being received as though nothing had happened. He tried to relax and enjoy the service, remembering how in Shanghai he had had so enjoyed the comfort of reliving his Jewishness every Friday. But tonight all he could think of was Constance.

His eyes searched the crowd. Mr. Levy was not here. Neither was Constance. But it was still early; the services would not begin for another ten minutes. He stood near the entrance, straining to see every person who entered.

Minutes passed and the Levys did not appear.

Perhaps Mr. Levy was not yet well enough to come to the synagogue, Sam reasoned. If that were so, Mrs. Levy would certainly not want to leave him alone. And Constance would never come without them. Then a thought occurred to him. Would the Levys stop attending services just to avoid running into him?

The rabbi was taking his place at the *bimah.* The members of the congregation moved down the aisles to their seats.

"Bless ye the Lord who is to be blessed," intoned the Reader. The services had begun. And Constance was not going to be there.

SAM brooded the rest of the evening. Before going to bed he decided to write Constance once more. He would send the letter over to the Levy house tomorrow morning. Perhaps at last she would listen . . .

Again, Sam lay awake in bed, turning the events over and over in his mind. Finally, an hour before his usual waking time, he got up and dressed. The letter was all he could think about.

He left earlier than usual for the hong, feeling guilty for not attending Saturday morning services, but telling himself this was his business after all. It was not as though his absence at the synagogue would make the minyan short the required ten men—they always had enough.

Walking on this crisp December morning he vowed that if he could win Constance again they would marry early in the new year. If they had to they would defy her aunt. Somehow, they would manage. He loved Constance, needed her—and he couldn't take this loneliness much longer. He yearned to come home to a wife who would share his dreams, his frustrations—and he yearned for a woman in his bed at night . . .

At nine o'clock he sent a coolie to the Levy house with the letter. He trembled in anticipation of what lay ahead. This was the most important day in his life.

REBECCA wasn't really listening as Mai-Ling told her the menu for dinner. Upstairs Dr. Arnold was examining Lionel. Imagine—Lionel had insisted on coming down for dinner tonight. And Dr. Arnold had said that Lionel could go back to work on Monday—I'm the only one around here who seems to know what's good for Lionel, she thought in exasperation.

"Yes, Mai-Ling, I'm sure that will be fine," she said. She had to hear what Dr. Arnold was saying. She stood at the foot of the stairs, waiting for the sound of Dr. Arnold's voice. Ever since the heart attack, Rebecca thought, she'd been thinking about what it would be like to be left alone in the world. She couldn't imagine living without Lionel—he was, well, she supposed she must really love him.

She had to convince him to sell the business and take her back to England, where they could live a less trying life. She was tired of living in exile. She'd never felt at home here. Except for the servants, she was afraid of the Chinese. The turmoil on the mainland—the horrors of the Boxer rebellion six years ago—it frightened her. And if—as Lionel predicted—the peasants eventually succeeded in over-throwing the Manchus, what would happen to the British on Hong Kong, so close to the mainland? Yes, she thought, for her sanity and Lionel's health it was high time they left.

In England they could live comfortably in a small country house on what they would make selling the business. Just the two of them. Something had to be done with Constance. Arrogant little snip. She'd known from the start that girl would be trouble.

A door opened on the second floor. Rebecca took a step forward, dropping a hand on the post of the balustrade. Dr. Arnold looked calm. Lionel must have passed the examination, she thought with relief.

"Lionel's fine, Rebecca." Dr. Arnold said. "Looks like it's business as usual from now on."

"Dr. Arnold," Rebecca began, "I'd like to convince Lionel to sell the business and retire. I don't think he should be under this stress every day." Why did he look guarded? Couldn't the idiot understand she was just concerned about Lionel's health?

"I understand your concern but that's really not necessary, Rebecca," Dr. Arnold said with a knowing smile.

"Dr. Arnold, if you'll forgive me, you don't know Lionel the way I do," she pursued. "He drives himself. He never truly puts the business out of his mind. And the heat in the hot months takes a terrible toll."

"Then you must persuade him to relax his schedule during the summer," Dr. Arnold said. "I'm sure the business will survive if he spends a few more days up on the Peak." He pulled out his watch. "And now I have to be on my rounds. But rest assured, Rebecca. Lionel has had a complete recovery. He's an ox, that husband of yours. Give me a call if you have any further questions."

Rebecca sighed. "Thank you for your time, doctor. Can you see yourself out?"

"Yes, Rebecca. Remember, plenty of rest . . ." Rebecca heard the front door slam.

"Dr. Arnold says you're doing well," she told Lionel upstairs. "But I think he's making a mistake in letting you return to the hong on Monday."

"Rebecca, I can't expect Elliot to oversee the business forever. I'll admit, he's indispensable in handling the antiques, but he's hopeless with the rice and sugar exports. And while I enjoy the antiques, it's the rice and sugar that bring in the money. I'm afraid that Elliot's talents lie more in art."

"You should sell the business." Maybe sounding logical would work. "We could live so well back in England if we did, Lionel. And even Dr. Arnold said you shouldn't spend much time in town when it's so hot. You know it can't be good for you."

Lionel was startled by this. Rebecca seemed to want to go back to England soon—even in this summer. Well, he wasn't ready.

The doorbell rang. Rebecca frowned at the interruption—just when it looked like she was getting somewhere with Lionel. And she hated people pouring into the house unexpectedly. Wasn't it enough that they all saw each other at the synagogue and talked every day on the telephone? Elliot was the exception—he was like family. Thank goodness she had convinced Lionel long ago that entertaining at home was bad for her health.

From the top of the stairs she watched as Li took an envelope from a coolie at the door and brought it up to her. Rebecca stared at the envelope. It was addressed to Constance. From Sam Stone. How dare he? Didn't he understand that he would never again be received in this house?

She hesitated a moment, then tore the letter into little pieces. It would be wiser not to mention this to Constance. The little idiot was still mooning over that crook. Rebecca smiled. She had other plans for Lionel's niece.

WHEN his letter was not returned Sam's hopes rose. All day he waited for word from her. Alone in his flat at night he paced the floor, convinced that she would respond even though it was too late for a letter to be hand-delivered.

Sunday came and still no word. Sunday, Sam thought wearily—

this used to be a day of joy, when Constance and I would go to Thomas's Grill Room for tiffin . . .

That night Sam realized he was not going to hear from Constance. Maybe his letter hadn't convinced her. Maybe she'd just thrown it in the fireplace without reading it. How in God's name could she be so unfeeling? Hadn't she been in love with him just a few days ago? Well, he could be cruel too. He would repay her for the pain she'd caused him.

Frantically he searched all his pockets for the little piece of paper with A-lu-te's address on it. And there it was.

He scribbled her a brief note, giving his address and signing it "Mr. Smith." He found a coolie to deliver it for him. He would forget Constance. He couldn't waste his life moping over one girl. There were plenty of others.

Sam began tidying up for A-lu-te. He straightened the books on his shelves, washed yesterday's dishes, turned down the bedcovers in his tiny bedroom. Where the hell was she? Now that he had time to think he was getting nervous.

He had slept with only two women—each time at a brothel frequented by the boys at college in Shanghai. He remembered the flattering attention of the prostitutes, both knowing how inexperienced he was but telling him he was a wonderful lover. After he met Constance he had thought all that was behind him.

Sam paced. Though the evening was cool, he was warm in his tweed jacket. He pulled it off, removed his tie and opened the collar of his shirt. Damn it, he thought, I'll never get used to these British clothes.

If A-lu-te was busy or if she'd changed her mind why couldn't she at least send him word? He could go to Tai Ping Shan, have *samsu* at the bar—though he really didn't like the potent rice spirit—and then go on to one of the licensed brothels. But he knew he would never do that—he'd heard too many stories about men getting diseases in the brothels. A-lu-te, with her important clientele, was the safest choice.

At last he heard a sharp knock on the door. He hurried over and pulled the door wide open. There was A-lu-te in a magnificently embroidered black silk kimono. Her lustrous black hair was tied in a French knot held in place by jeweled pins. She carried a wicker basket in one slender hand.

"It was not easy for me to come here," she said resting a hand on his chest. "It was necessary to send away a rich taipan."

"I'm a poor taipan," he said pulling her inside. Somehow A-lu-te reminded him of Constance—maybe it was her diminutive figure and delicate beauty. But he must not think of Constance—not now, not ever . . .

"Handsome taipan," she whispered, sliding her hand beneath his shirt and caressing his chest. Her eyes told him that tonight was pleasure for her—not business. "I bring you present." She gave him the wicker basket.

"Thank you A-lu-te." For a moment he was embarrassed.

"You have glasses, yes?" She reached into the basket and brought out a bottle of prime champagne.

"Not glasses worthy of this but they'll do," he said eyeing the label. He knew more about Passover wine than vintage champagne —that was going to change. But now all he wanted was to take A-lu-te to bed. Enough of this talk. "Let me open the bottle."

"I have placed in the basket a corkscrew," she said. "See?"

"You're beautiful." His eyes fastened on the velvet skin between her breasts displayed by her parting kimono.

"I will be beautiful all evening," she said. "And exciting. First we will have the champagne." She giggled.

"No. Champagne later." Sam reached for A-lu-te.

Her mouth was warm, her lips parting instantly. Her small firm breasts pressed against his chest, crushing hard nipples into his flesh.

"A-lu-te—" All he wanted was to bury himself in this slender passionate body.

"You pour the champagne," she murmured, "and bring it into the bedroom. I will be waiting."

Light-headed with desire Sam picked up the bottle of champagne and the corkscrew and hurried into the kitchen. Tonight he would at last be satisfied. A-lu-te would quench the desire for Constance that had kept him awake night after night . . .

He walked into the bedroom. A-lu-te was lying against a mound of pillows, her naked flesh gleaming in the dim yellow light. Her dark hair was loose about her face and cascaded down her back.

"Sit here." She patted the edge of the bed.

He sat down and handed her a glass of champagne, lifting the other to his lips. He was shy and a little nervous. A-lu-te must sense his inexperience—after all, she had slept with many men . . . men who knew what to do with a woman. But he thought with pride, I am young and strong—not like the rich old men she is used to.

He pulled her to him and kissed her—at first gently, then, no longer able to restrain himself, crushing her against the pillows, his hands exploring the gentle mounds and hollows of her body. "Take off your clothes," she whispered. Urgently, he unbuttoned his shirt and removed his pants, leaving them in a heap on the floor. As he lowered himself beside her, his thighs trembled in excitement.

"Let me love you," she whispered.

Gently, she kissed his ankle, her mouth moving swiftly up his leg, lingering on his thigh . . . burrowing between his legs. His hands tightened around her shoulders. He couldn't wait any longer . . .

"A-lu-te!" He pulled her over onto her back.

"Not yet," she crooned. "Later it will be better." She pushed him down until his head rested between her slender thighs. "Love me, Sam."

Probing gently with his tongue, his hands caressed her breasts as she moaned in pleasure.

"Now, Sam. Now!" She tugged at his shoulders. He plunged into her.

Together they moved in frenzy, each absorbed in the powerful force gathering within . . . until at last, a shower of spasms shook A-lu-te, and then Sam.

He lay limp beside her. The instant the passion abated, his loneliness returned, and he realized that A-lu-te couldn't blot out the memory of Constance.

An hour or so passed. A-lu-te propped herself up on her elbows. "Sam, I will fix us tea, and afterwards we'll make love again." She giggled. "You are not old, like those rich important men."

Sam was confused—he had enjoyed A-lu-te, there was no denying that, but he felt guilty and he couldn't stop thinking of Constance. At dawn they finally slept.

From habit Sam awoke at his hour. A-lu-te lay sprawled at the edge of the bed, murmuring in her sleep. He rose swiftly, deciding not to wake her until he was dressed.

He hurried into the kitchen, put up water for their morning tea and brought down two cups and saucers. When he returned to the bedroom, A-lu-te was lying on her back talking agitatedly in her sleep.

"Be careful, Mikawa . . . to take those keys from Mr. Telford . . . Mikawa, I'm afraid," A-lu-te wailed. "I'm afraid . . ."

Sam stood immobile beside the bed. Now he understood. While Mr. Telford slept in her bed, Mikawa had borrowed the keys so that his gang could rob the hong. But why had she come to him tonight? For pleasure? Mikawa was her lover. "Get up, A-lu-te," Sam said roughly. "Get up and get out."

CHAPTER

EIGHT

CONSTANCE MOVED AROUND the Levy house like shadow, a quiet desperation haunting her face. Her nights were sleepless, filled with memories of Sam. Occasionally she would go to W. Brewer and Company to buy books for Uncle Lionel—but only when she was sure Sam would not be there. She'd even given up her morning walks along the Praya for fear of bumping into him.

Life was almost back to normal.

On Monday Uncle Lionel had gone to the hong for three hours, and each day he stayed a little longer. This morning he had told Aunt Rebecca that tonight they would go to the synagogue.

At first Constance had wanted to stay home. But she knew that eventually she would have to face Sam. At least at the synagogue she would be with her aunt and uncle. And there would be people all around them. They would say hello—and that would be that. Or would it? A small part of her still wanted to believe that he was innocent. But she knew that couldn't be true.

The day trickled by. At last they were in the carriage en route to the Ohel Leah Synagogue. While Rebecca poured out her nightly quota of complaints and Uncle Lionel offered an occasional soothing word, Constance gazed out the window at the star-splashed night

sky and tried to make sense of her feelings about Sam. If Telford &
Latham hadn't been robbed she would never have known about him
and that girl. She would still expect to marry him. Maybe it would
have been better that way . . .

Constance tried to look calm as they left the carriage to join those
who had already arrived. A cluster of people gathered around Uncle
Lionel and Aunt Rebecca, everyone asking how Lionel felt and com-
menting on his speedy recovery. She hovered at the edge of the circle.
Despite her determination to ignore Sam, she couldn't stop herself
from looking for his face in the crowd.

"Constance, let's go up to the balcony, shall we?" Constance followed Aunt Rebecca up the stairs.

As they took their usual seats, she glanced below. Sam was no-
where to be seen.

"Thank goodness that Chinese Jew isn't here." Constance couldn't
help noticing how pleased Aunt Rebecca sounded. "I knew he
wouldn't dare show his face here. Even if he did somehow manage
to clear himself of the robbery charge."

"Sam was cleared? How do you know?" So—maybe he was innocent . . .

"Mrs. Meyers told me. Apparently the thieves were identified, but
they evaded the police. Still, he can't worm his way out of consorting
with a notorious prostitute."

Constance felt hot color flood her face. Was that why he wasn't
here tonight—was he with that girl? The synagogue had meant so
much to him, he told her. But he had told her a lot of things. She
wished she'd stayed home tonight.

After services Rebecca seemed to want to mingle with the others
for a while. Lionel was delighted not to be rushed off to the carriage
and gathered with the men at one side of the portico, while the
women clustered across the room. The men talked about everything
from partridge hunting to the peasant uprisings in Kwangsi and in
Szechuan. While the women talked about their children, fashions
and food and always how they missed life in England.

"I'm hoping that I can persuade Lionel to retire and take me back
to England," Rebecca confided to her friend Elise. "I'm sure that if
a decent offer for the business comes along, he'll be willing to talk."

Constance listened, stunned. Aunt Rebecca was determined to persuade Uncle Lionel to return to England—and when she got determined about something she almost always got her way. She would

86

nag and whine until she wore him down. Constance couldn't bear the thought of leaving Hong Kong, but she didn't quite know why. Of course it wasn't Sam, it was just that—well, she'd come to like the exotic flavor of the Crown Colony.

On the way home Rebecca mentioned that she had invited Elliot to dinner the following night.

"He so misses London, Constance dear. And there are few people in the Colony who share his interests. It'll be good for him to be with someone close to his own age. Be pleasant to him, will you?"

Later that night, as Constance was getting ready for bed, Aunt Rebecca came in.

"Constance, I must talk to you alone." She closed the door behind her. Constance stiffened. Only a few days ago Aunt Rebecca wasn't even speaking to her and now she was going to confide in her . . .

"You know Lionel's birthday is in April?"

"You mentioned it at dinner last night." Constance tried to relax. Anything was better than having another harangue about Sam.

"I've decided on a present for him. I'm going to commission Elliot to paint your portrait. After all, child," she said creeping a bony arm around Constance's shoulders, "you are his only living relative. And Elliot's been so depressed lately. A commission will cheer him up. All you have to do is sit for Elliot. But remember, it's a secret—between the ladies of the house. Agreed?"

It took all of Constance's self-restraint not to recoil from Aunt Rebecca's embrace.

"When will I sit for him?" she asked. Actually, the prospect of having her portrait painted intrigued her—even if it did mean spending time with the priggish Elliot Hardwicke.

"Now that Lionel has completely recovered I'm sure he'll be playing chess on Tuesday nights again. That's when you and I will go to Elliot's house for the sittings."

Elliot was delighted at the prospect of painting Constance's portrait. He and Rebecca made elaborate plans to insure the secrecy of the project. Every Tuesday night after dinner, once Lionel had left for his chess game, Rebecca and Constance went to Elliot's small hillside house.

Constance was amazed by how beautiful Elliot's home was. She'd always thought that men who lived alone were messy—but here each piece of furniture had been carefully chosen; the windows were draped with the finest velvet, the walls were covered in silk; lacquered curio cabinets contained a collection of rare Chinese porcelain.

Not much was required of her beyond sitting while Elliot painted and talked to Aunt Rebecca—who pretended to be absorbed in the newest fashion magazine—about London theater and London society. It was all very boring to Constance, but the two of them never seemed to tire of their subject. At around ten o'clock Elliot would announce that he was finished, summon his handsome young houseboy Ch'en to bring tea and cakes, served on Japanese Imari porcelain dishes.

The next few weeks dragged by. There was nothing for Constance to do . . . there were so many servants that she couldn't even keep busy with housework. She actually began to look forward to her weekly sittings for Elliot and Sunday nights, when he came to the house for dinner. She still attended services on Friday nights, and her heart started pounding every time she arrived. In spite of herself, she always wondered, would Sam be here tonight?

Sam certainly hadn't tried very hard to win her back—he sent just that one letter. He never tried to phone her or call at the house again. He never even showed up at services, and he must have known she would be there. Maybe he had never really loved her . . .

Constance was amazed when Aunt Rebecca arranged for the two of them to socialize with the ladies of the synagogue after all those of years of begging off because of her "delicate nerves." Actually, Constance had to admit that Rebecca could be quite charming when it suited her.

Then it suddenly occurred to her—Aunt Rebecca was attending these daytime social affairs because she wanted the local ladies to know that Lionel Levy would be receptive to the right offer for Levy Export Company. She was using gossip to flush out a buyer. Constance hoped her little plan would fail.

JANUARY in Hong Kong was a month of perfect weather, but Constance didn't notice. There were moments when she wondered if it wouldn't have been better if she'd drowned in the typhoon—anything would be easier than living through this loneliness and anger.

Over and over she recalled the precious hours with Sam aboard the ship from Shanghai. Their tiffins at Thomas's Grill Room. The meetings in the bookstore. But the memories only freshened the pain.

She tried to bury herself in books. It didn't work. And the thought that Aunt Rebecca was waging a relentless campaign for them to return to England only made things worse—she'd be half a world away from Sam.

One Sunday night at dinner—under prodding from Rebecca—Elliot invited Constance to attend the annual pony races later in the month.

"It's one of the major events of the winter season," he said. "The jockeys are dressed in colors, breeches, and boots, just as though they were racing at Newmarket."

"Elliot," Rebecca teased, "Constance knows nothing of Newmarket. She grew up in America."

"I'd like to go," Constance said, annoyed at yet another one of her aunt's allusions to her "inferior" American upbringing. "I've never been to the races."

She still avoided leaving the house alone, afraid that she might bump into Sam. What if she saw him with that woman? But she knew she had to get out—she was becoming almost a recluse. At least Elliot was a gentleman.

The day of the races arrived. Elliot was in high spirits when he called for her. On the way to the racetrack he told her about racing, explaining that some of the rich merchants maintained stables of ponies, bred in Manchuria and other parts of northern China, solely for racing.

"The annual races are always heavily attended," he said. And I'm sure Governor Nathan will be there. The racing people predict that twenty or thirty thousand people will attend today."

He explained that the row of two-storied mat-sheds along the course were erected each year just before the races and were usually reserved in advance by government figures and wealthy colonists. They were made of bamboo, with thatched walls and roofs—and were built without a single nail. The upper story of each mat-shed —equipped with comfortable basket chairs—offered the best view as well as a private dressing room and bathroom. The lower floor was used for entertaining. A large mat-shed with thatched roof, verandahs and sun blinds served as grandstand for most of those attending. People came from as far away as Shanghai to watch the races.

The excitement of the crowd at Happy Valley was contagious. After the third race, local society—that included Constance and Elliot —was invited to the private mat-shed for lunch with the Governor and the hostess of the day. There was plenty of delicious food, and

Constance drank more than her share of the excellent champagne. It was all so much fun—being with a charming man, talking to pretty women in elegant clothes and a few handsome men who paid her compliments that made her blush . . . for a few hours she forgot about Sam Stone.

BACK at the Levy house Rebecca waited impatiently for Lionel to return from the hong. Where was he? She paced the verandah. When Elliot had picked up Constance he had pulled Rebecca aside and whispered that early this afternoon Lionel had a meeting with an American who was interested in buying Levy Export Company. Elliot was worried—the antique exporting was little more than a diversion for Lionel, and if the new buyer decided to give it up, what would he do? But Rebecca was thrilled—maybe she would finally be released from this miserable country.

Lionel appeared, as usual, she thought, not having the decency to explain his early arrival. Wasn't she his wife? Weren't husbands supposed to share everything with their wives? Rebecca ordered tea brought to them in the study.

"You're looking tired, dear. Are you sure you're all right?" Maybe he would tell her if she pressed a little. "How was your day?"

"Just fine, Rebecca."

Damn it. That didn't work. "Perhaps you should go upstairs and rest after your tea."

"I'm not tired, Rebecca." He was being unusually brusque, Rebecca thought, raising her eyebrows in reproach. "Actually, it hasn't been such a good day." Lionel paced the room. "I've had a most disconcerting meeting with an American who thinks I'm interested in selling the business."

"Did he offer a good price?"

"Rebecca, I told you I don't want to retire." He reached for a cigarette.

Rebecca grimaced. She hated cigarette smoke in the house. Lionel knew that. But he always forgot when he was upset.

"Lionel, how can you turn down a good offer? You should retire. Dr. Arnold says you are not to spend another summer in the Colony." Not exactly true, but it was worth a try.

"He did not say that, Rebecca. He simply suggested I spend more time on the Peak in the summer."

"Lionel, you've had one heart attack. Are you going to insist on having another before you admit it's time to retire?" She lifted a hand to her chest, and tried to look pained, as if she were short of breath. "And you wouldn't only be hurting yourself, you know. You'll push me into a nervous breakdown."

The last seemed to have an impact upon Lionel—not for himself, for her. Silently, she congratulated herself.

"Rebecca, I had a very mild heart attack. Dr. Arnold says I'm fine." He stubbed out his cigarette. "I think you're overreacting to the whole thing."

"Dr. Arnold says," she mimicked in contempt. "Do you think you're his only patient? Well, you're my only husband and I have no intention of becoming a widow in the near future. You must take care of yourself. For both of our sakes. Lionel I insist. Please. Let's go home—let's go back to England . . ."

WHEN Constance and Elliot returned from the races, Rebecca was reading the latest British society gossip in *The Queen*. Rebecca invited Elliot to stay for dinner, explaining that it would be late since Lionel had not yet returned from a business meeting. Constance noticed a look pass between Rebecca and Elliot and was instantly on guard. Was it something to do with selling the hong?

Rebecca signaled to Li to bring tea into the drawing room, adding that now there would be four for dinner. Constance couldn't understand why Rebecca seemed to reserve all her charm only for Elliot . . . she was a different woman altogether in his presence. This must be the woman Uncle Lionel fell in love with all those years ago, Constance thought.

"Constance, you're looking a little pale," Rebecca announced when they had finished their tea. "Why don't you go to your room and rest before dinner? I'll send Sakota up to help you dress later."

"Thank you, Aunt Rebecca. Actually, I am a little tired." Obviously Aunt Rebecca wanted to talk to Elliot alone. She needed a rest from these two anyway.

ELLIOT turned to Rebecca.

"Is Mr. Levy going to accept the offer from the American?"

"He's gone off to talk money again," Rebecca confided with a smile. "He said he didn't want to retire. But I think I convinced him that he must take care of his health. I don't think he knows what's best for him."

"So you'll be going home." Elliot sighed. "I'll miss you. And I'll probably have to look for another job."

"Elliot, don't panic. It'll take months for the sale to go through—all those legal papers and heaven knows what else. And Lionel hasn't even accepted the offer yet." But, I know he will, she thought.

"You know, Rebecca, when I first came to Hong Kong, I never dreamed I'd still be here eight years later. Almost nine . . ."

"I hate to leave you here, Elliot." Rebecca tried to hide her excitement. Now was the moment to set another campaign in motion—to free Lionel and herself of the responsibility for Constance. "Has it ever occurred to you that if you were married your parents might forget that unfortunate affair from your school days and welcome you back into the family?" How shortsighted of Mr. Hardwicke, to make Elliot pay a lifetime of penitence for a schoolboy's fall from grace . . .

Elliot looked startled.

"No I—I guess I never thought of that." He paused, seemed to be debating something. "No, we left my father behind when we moved into the twentieth century. He'll never forgive me."

"Elliot, you may be doing yourself a tremendous disservice not to consider marriage. Certainly your father would not expect you to raise your family in this colonial outpost. They would bring you into their shipyards in England. You would have the affluence that is rightfully yours."

Elliot seemed to be wavering.

"Rebecca, I don't know—"

"Just think how happy you would be back in London!" Rebecca plunged ahead. "The theater, the opera, the art exhibitions. Trips to Paris and Biarritz and Monte Carlo. The Channel no longer exists—people travel from London to the Continent the way we go from here to the Peak. But it would be important for you to choose the right kind of wife," she cautioned. "Someone young and pliable, so that you could live the kind of life you prefer . . . what about Constance? She admires you so—and she's young and pretty and properly reared." Rebecca carefully omitted the fact that Elliot's parents might not open their arms to a Jewish bride. Anyway, hadn't Constance Rothschild become Lady Battersea?

"But Rebecca, I—I don't feel prepared for marriage."

"Elliot, do be practical. With a wife—the right wife—you will be able to live the kind of life you deserve. Surrounded by beauty, the arts. In London. Why should you continue to live in exile?"

"You don't know my father." He shook his head slowly. "I've disgraced the family. They want no part of me."

"Elliot, your father has seven granddaughters. You said yourself that your mother writes often about how he wants a grandson." She leaned forward, armed with the last of her ammunition. "Your two brothers are both getting on in years . . . your older sister is forty, the two younger ones spinsters. Elliot, it is you—and Constance—who could supply them with a grandson. You're their last hope. Marriage will lend you eminent respectability. I'm willing to bet that if you marry Constance your father will invite you both to return to London. You'll be taken into the shipyards. Elliot, my dear, you'll begin to live again."

AT first Constance was bewildered by Elliot's sudden attentiveness. But he was charming, handsome and good company—and it was all very flattering after what had happened with Sam. She wondered what he wanted from her—and how she should respond . . .

Elliot took Constance to plays at the local dramatic society . . . he taught her to play lawn tennis . . . they went to see the yacht races. Wherever they went she still looked for Sam. Once she had seen him dashing from W. Brewer and Company. Once she had seen him striding down Queen's Road with a package tucked under his arm. Each time her heart pounded insanely when their eyes met. But he had always rushed on.

Constance worried about what was happening with Uncle Lionel's business. Neither Uncle Lionel nor Aunt Rebecca would tell her anything, but she knew that heavy negotiations were under way. Uncle Lionel's attorney—a Mr. Bradshaw—came over at least once a week and Aunt Rebecca was beginning to make cryptic noises about how long paperwork took.

Elliot finished Constance's portrait only days before Uncle Lionel's birthday. That same evening Lionel announced that his attorney would arrive later that evening with the last of the papers before he signed over the hong to the American firm. He promised Elliot that he would stay on with the new owners.

93

Even though Constance had prepared herself for the worst she was stunned by the news. What would become of her? And there was so little time left . . . Uncle Lionel said they would be ready to leave within three months.

Mr. Bradshaw arrived and disappeared into the study with Uncle Lionel. Constance couldn't sit another minute with Aunt Rebecca. She excused herself, saying she had a headache, and went to her room. Why did the thought of going back to England frighten her? There was nothing for her here. But she still hoped that Sam would try to see her . . . that he would tell her how much he loved her and how he'd never gone to that woman. And it must come from him. Because Mama had told her to remember always to be proud . . .

REBECCA summoned Li to bring champagne. Victory was almost hers—the sale of the hong was going through. There was just one more detail . . .

"Elliot, you must decide now," she said after Li had left. Elliot looked at her quizzically. "About marrying Constance. In three or four months we'll be on our way back to England."

For several minutes Elliot sat lost in thought.

"Suppose I do ask her. What if she doesn't want to marry me?"

"Don't be ridiculous. What girl wouldn't? She's very fond of you. And she so admires your talents. Of course she'll want to marry you. Why don't you talk to Lionel about it?" she urged. Rebecca herself wondered if Constance would be interested in marrying Elliot. She was just headstrong enough to say no. And it seemed that she was still mooning over that Chinese Jew, the little fool. But I'll fix that, Rebecca thought smugly. I'll convince her that she must marry Elliot . . . "Lionel would expect you to do the proper thing and ask for his permission, Elliot. Why don't you speak to him tonight?"

Rebecca turned as she heard Lionel and Bradshaw leave the study. From the tone of Bradshaw's voice it was clear that the negotiations were over. Within days the firm would be handed over to the new owners.

"Elliot, I'll leave you alone with Lionel," Rebecca whispered.

"Ask him tonight for Constance's hand in marriage. I promise, you won't regret it."

UPSTAIRS, Rebecca paced the bedroom in her nightgown. What if Elliot lost his courage? She couldn't bear the thought of carting that child back to England. Finally she heard Lionel's step on the stairs. She jumped into bed.

"Hello, dear. Did Elliot talk to you about Constance? Isn't it wonderful news?"

"You knew about this?" he said suspiciously.

"Of course I did. Elliot tells me everything. And I think it's a wonderful match. Constance is a lucky girl." She frowned in irritation. "I thought it was rather obvious that his intentions were serious. But then, you've been so preoccupied lately . . ."

"Do you really think Constance will want to marry him?" Lionel reached for a cigarette.

"Lionel, you know I forbid smoking in the bedroom!" This wasn't going as she'd planned it.

"I'm sorry, dear."

"What exactly did you say to Elliot?"

"I said I'd like to think about it. I had hoped—as I know Nathan would have—that Constance would marry within our faith."

"Don't be stupid. If a Rothschild can marry outside her faith, why not little Constance Levy?"

"I'll have to talk to Constance," he hedged. "Shouldn't she have a say in this?"

"This is a wonderful opportunity!" Rebecca was angry now. "She'll be marrying into a titled family. She'll be marrying a man who's charming and talented who will someday come into money. What more could she hope for? Let *me* talk to her, woman to woman."

"All right, dear, you talk to her." Lionel seemed relieved. "Just feel her out. If she seems receptive to the idea, then I'll tell Elliot he can ask her. I just don't want her to be forced into anything." Rebecca knew that Lionel had only relented to avoid a scene. How could she have married such an impractical man?

"Good. I'll discuss this with her in the morning. Now can you come to bed, Lionel? There's a draft in this room and you know how I hate the cold."

CONSTANCE had not finished dressing when Rebecca knocked and entered her bedroom.

"I have some special news, Constance."

"Yes, Aunt Rebecca?" Suddenly Constance had a wild hope—maybe they had changed their minds about leaving . . .

"Last night Lionel had a talk with Elliot. You know how proper Elliot is—and quite rightly so, I think. At any rate he asked for Lionel's permission to talk to you about marriage."

Constance stared.

"I—I never thought that—"

"Come now, Constance," Rebecca chided, "you've been seeing Elliot steadily for weeks."

"But there was never any indication that—I mean, he never said a word about—" And she had been thinking that all Elliot wanted was companionship!

"As I've said, he's asked permission to speak to you about marriage and of course Lionel complied. I thought it best that you be prepared before he approaches you." Constance noticed Aunt Rebecca sounded irritated—no doubt because she wasn't immediately thrilled by this proposal.

"But Aunt Rebecca, I'm not in love with Elliot." The words caught in her throat. She was still in love with Sam. That was it. She would never love anyone else.

"Constance, you read too many romantic novels. How many wives marry because they're in love? They need a home. A protector."

"But Elliot isn't Jewish," Constance whispered. How often she had dreamed of going to the synagogue with Sam and their children . . . of celebrating Passover and Hannukah as Mama and Papa had with her. And now something else was becoming clear to her—Aunt Rebecca was trying to get rid of her.

"Constance, don't be a fool. At the bank they won't ask if Elliot goes to synagogue or church. He comes from a fine family. He'll be able to provide for you. What kind of position could you find for yourself here in the Crown Colony?"

"But there must be something I can do." It was too much for Constance to grasp all at once. Aunt Rebecca actually planned on

96

leaving her behind in Hong Kong. She was being abandoned again. "Maybe I could be a governess."

"Nonsense. You're too young to be governess. You don't have enough education. And you're an American." Rebecca was scornful. "You know that a white woman has only one livelihood open to her."

Rebecca had set the stage for this confrontation weeks ago, when she deliberately told Constance about the plight of European women who, having been deserted or widowed by working-class husbands, survived only as prostitutes or by taking beachcombers as lovers.

When Rebecca's eyes met Constance's, they were triumphant. She had won again.

"Face facts, Constance. You have no choice except to marry Elliot."

Constance struggled to consider her options. She could challenge Aunt Rebecca. Uncle Lionel wouldn't dare leave her in Hong Kong, would he? But even if that worked, how could she live in their house in England knowing how much Aunt Rebecca hated her?

She could ask Uncle Lionel to pay for her return trip to New York, but he would probably insist that she live with them instead.

And what could she do in New York to support herself anyway? She was too proud to throw herself on the mercy of Mr. and Mrs. Gomez. Working in a Lower East Side sweatshop was little better than being in prison, Mama always said. A salesgirl in a shop or department store earned three dollars a week. All she could afford would be to share a bedroom in a cheap rooming house, skimping on food, never able to buy clothes. Terrified of losing her job—that was if she was lucky enough to find one. Aunt Rebecca was right—she had no choice.

"I'll listen to what Elliot has to say," Constance whispered.

"Good. I knew you were a sensible girl."

CHAPTER

NINE

ONSTANCE CONCENTRATED ON smiling throughout dinner on Sunday night as Elliot and Rebecca chattered about the splendor of the late April flowers on the island.

"My favorites, though, are the narcissi you cultivate indoors all through the cool months," Elliot declared. "Oh, Elliot, you are so right," Rebecca said, beaming. "The *shui hsien hua*," he explained to Constance. "Immortals of the water."

While Rebecca and Elliot discussed the efforts following the typhoon last September to restore the once-exquisite Public Gardens Constance felt wave of homesickness. A whole winter had passed without snow. She remembered how beautiful Central Park had been that snowy afternoon long ago when Papa and Mama had taken her there with her sled. Afterwards they'd come home and Mama had made hot chocolate with mounds of whipped cream.

She tried to shift her thoughts back to the table. Elliot was smiling but Constance noticed that he seemed strained. Maybe he was having second thoughts about his talk of marriage . . .

She glanced at Uncle Lionel. He seemed distracted tonight. But she'd sensed from the start that he didn't share Aunt Rebecca's enthusiasm for this marriage. What would Mama and Papa think?

She liked Elliot. But she had never thought of him as a husband. I love Sam. How can I marry Elliot? If only Mama hadn't died—would she have let this happen to me?

They left the dining table to have their tea in the drawing room. Li served fragrant jasmine tea in Rebecca's favorite Wedgewood cups. Constance sat next to Uncle Lionel on the sofa that flanked the fireplace. Rebecca and Elliot sat across from them in a pair of brocade armchairs.

When the conversation finally wavered Rebecca and Lionel went to the study. Elliot left his chair and sat next to Constance on the sofa. He cleared his throat before speaking.

"Constance, I've taken the liberty of speaking to your uncle. He's given me permission to speak to you of marriage."

"I'm flattered, Elliot," she dropped her gaze. "But are you sure? You—we—" She hesitated. "We've been good friends but—" Never once had Elliot indicated any romantic interest in her. And never once had she felt that heart-quickening flutter of desire that Sam had sparked in her . . . But marriage to Elliot was survival.

"I'm sure, Constance." He took her hand in his. "Will you marry me?"

"Yes," she whispered. His hand felt cool and limp in hers—not warm and demanding like Sam's.

"I promise you we'll have a good life," Elliot said, lifting her hand to his mouth. Thank goodness he didn't try to take her in his arms . . . "May I ask your aunt and uncle to come into the drawing room so that we may tell them?"

"Please do, Elliot."

So she would marry Elliot and live with him in his small, perfect house high on the slopes, Constance told herself. She would forget she ever knew Sam.

REBECCA took over all the arrangements. It would be a small civil ceremony performed in the Levy drawing room by a member of the British Consulate. Only Rebecca and Lionel would be present. In three weeks Constance would become Mrs. Elliot Hardwicke.

Constance moved through each day as if in a trance. Rebecca brought in a dressmaker and his team of assistants to prepare a bridal trousseau. Constance stood for hours while the dressmaker pinned and fitted the white silk wedding gown—all the while nurturing the hope that Sam would hear about the wedding and come to claim her.

She lay sleepless every night tormented by the same questions: Why hadn't Sam fought for her? Didn't he know she wouldn't have resisted? And the awful thought nagged at her—what if her pride was committing her to a life of loneliness and regret?

CONSTANCE soon realized that her marriage to Elliot was not traveling the usual telephone gossip circuit. Apparently Aunt Rebecca had abandoned this amusement. Now when Rebecca's friends called, Li was instructed to say that she was not free to talk. Soon they stopped calling. Rebecca was too busy to care—with the wedding as well as with her preparations for leaving the Colony. Already Uncle Lionel had met prospective buyers for both the town house and the house on the Peak.

They no longer went to services at the synagogue. Constance suspected Uncle Lionel was embarrassed to admit to other members of the Ohel Leah congregation that his niece was marrying out of their faith. It bothered Constance, too. Being Jewish was so much a part of her—how could she live with someone who didn't understand that? Did Sam know she was being married to a non-Jew? She hoped not.

The night before the wedding as she was getting ready for bed, Aunt Rebecca appeared at the door. She seemed nervous.

"Constance, please sit down." Rebecca lowered herself into a chair as Constance sat on the edge of the bed. "Your uncle feels that since your mother is not here I should be the one to prepare you for what will happen on your wedding night." Her eyes avoided Constance's. "You will, no doubt, be shocked to discover what your husband expects of you. It's often quite an unpleasant experience the first time. But a wife must accept this as her duty because it is the only way to keep her husband faithful." Rebecca took a deep breath.

"Aunt Rebecca, I know," Constance said, feeling Rebecca's embarrassment. "Mama already told me." Mama was a woman ahead of her time, she thought with pride.

The relief on Rebecca's face was plain.

"Well, then—there's no need to discuss this further." She rose to her feet. "Though it seems unseemly that your mother would have talked of such things before it was necessary."

ON this night before his wedding Elliot sat alone in his studio and poured himself a glass of the vintage champagne that was one of his small indulgences. The studio was where he went when he had to be alone because it was the one room in the house that none of the servants—not even Ch'en—would dare invade.

Why in God's name had he allowed Rebecca to push him into this marriage? He had no guarantee that Papa would bring him back to London and into the business. He could still hear his father's recriminations after that one incident. He'd been just a boy. Barely twenty. And in one foolish moment he had ruined his life. How could his marriage—nine years later—make a difference?

He downed the champagne. God, he hated this life in exile! Maybe it would be worth it if there was a chance to live in London again. He looked at the clock. In less than twelve hours he would be married. A husband. Tomorrow—after the wedding—he would write Papa.

Despite the coolness of the evening he was sweating. He poured himself another glass of champagne. If he and Constance did return to London, would his father try to make him like his two brothers? He would be willing to work in the family shipyards, but he would not abandon his painting. His art was his life.

He finished the last of the champagne and tried to imagine taking the wedding vows . . . eating at the sumptuous wedding feast . . . taking Constance to bed . . .

Elliot pulled on his jacket, and charged from the house into the warm night. The air was fragrant with the scent of flowers. Despite the champagne he was sober. He had one thought in mind as he strode toward Tai Ping Shan. European women were available at certain taverns on Queen's Road—high-class Eurasian whores, favored by men in important positions. On this night before his marriage Elliot would take a Chinese girl to bed—the kind of girl who catered to soldiers and sailors. And he would prove he was a man.

Only once before had he visited a brothel. Drunk on *samsu,* he had made a fool of himself. He blamed it on the *samsu.* But he mustn't think of that now.

As he stepped aside to avoid a cluster of boisterous sailors drunkenly weaving along the street he realized that his expensive British clothes set him apart from others roaming the area. What if he were robbed? Across the street he spied one of the well-known brothels, and he hurried to get safely inside.

Instantly Pearl realized this was not her usual client. She showed Elliot upstairs and introduced him to Ca-lu-a—her best girl—a delicate creature draped in a colorfully embroidered red silk kimono.

"Handsome gentleman," she said in a high, light voice, untying the sash around her slender waist as she came towards him. The kimono parted, displaying tiny golden breasts and long, narrow thighs.

"You understand English?" he demanded.

"Some."

"Show me how good you are. Make me want you, you damn little bitch."

ON Sunday afternoon, with Sakota fluttering around to help with hooks and buttons, Constance dressed for her wedding. At last she was standing in front of the cheval mirror in her simple white silk dress and delicately embroidered lace veil, ready to take her place beside Elliot in the flower-banked drawing room.

Tears filled her eyes. She had always imagined Sam standing next to her on the *bimah* at Ohel Leah Synagogue . . . Sam proclaiming his lifelong love for her before God . . . Now she must face her wedding night with a man she didn't love.

The thought of giving herself to Elliot embarrassed her. Mama had made the wedding night seem like such a beautiful event. It would have been beautiful with Sam, she thought, I know it would. Enough. But how can I think thoughts like this on my wedding day? I have made the choice and now I must live with it.

With Sakota at her heels Constance went downstairs and into the drawing room. Elliot was talking to the consulate official who was to marry them, while Uncle Lionel stood by, grim and silent. Rebecca was arranging flowers at the altar. Sakota took her place in the hall just outside the entrance, along with Mai-Ling and Li.

Constance went through the brief marriage ceremony as if in a dream. Surely this wasn't her in the white silk gown and wedding veil marrying a complete stranger . . . surely it wasn't her delicate hand that now wore the simple gold band . . . Images of Sam's ivory *chai* haunted her. What was she doing?

Elliot leaned forward and kissed her—an almost furtive brushing of his mouth against hers. A few simple words and she was Mrs. Elliot Hardwicke.

After the ceremony the four of them went to the dining room for dinner. Please God let it go on forever, Constance prayed, fighting panic. Already her luggage was at Elliot's house. Sakota had gone ahead to unpack her clothes and lay out the bridal nightgown and negligee.

At last dinner was over. Rebecca made a great show of saying good-by as if they'd been the best of friends. Uncle Lionel pulled her to him and squeezed her tightly, his embrace telling her what he could no longer say. She had planned for this to be such a happy day —showing her love and faith with Sam . . .

Elliot sat silently as they rode to the house. Who was this man sitting next to her? She wished she could invent something—any-thing—to avoid lying between the bridal sheets with Elliot.

"The hot weather is almost here," Elliot said crossly, helping her from her sedan chair. "I suppose I could call a houseboy to bring a *punkah* fan."

"There's a breeze coming up now, I—I'm not really too hot." All she needed was a houseboy outside their window on her wedding night.

The servants were all in their quarters for the night. Elliot showed Constance to her bedroom. Thank goodness I'll have my own bedroom, she thought. Elliot's is all the way at the other end of the hall.

He hovered nervously in the doorway. "I'll see about a bottle of champagne." He hesitated. "I won't be long."

She closed the door behind him and crossed to the bed, which had been turned down by Sakota. The drapes were drawn tightly across the tall narrow windows. She was to be completely alone. In this room. With Elliot.

Her white silk nightgown and the high-necked matching negligee had been laid across the foot of the bed. Her fingers trembling, she fumbled with the many tiny hooks and buttons. Please, she prayed, don't let me be standing here half naked when Elliot returns . . .

She had just buttoned the negligee at her throat when she heard Elliot's tentative knock on the door. She spun around, her heart thumping furiously. She tried to calm herself. After all, she had known Elliot for months. She liked him. Maybe everything would be all right.

"Come in," she called, her voice high and thin. A stranger's voice.

Elliot came in holding a bottle of champagne and two filled glasses.

"You were a beautiful bride, Constance," he said stiffly, handing her a glass.

"Thank you, Elliot."

"Do you like your room?"

"It's lovely."

"If you wish to make any changes, please do."

There was a moment of silence. Elliot cleared his throat and put down his glass.

"I'll undress in your bathroom. If you like, you may turn off the lamps."

"Yes," she whispered.

As the bathroom door closed Constance finished the last of her champagne in one gulp.

She climbed into bed and lay beneath the silken coverlet in the darkened room, her fingers clutching the folded-over border. At last Elliot emerged from the bathroom. She felt him sit on the edge of the bed.

"You're so lovely, Constance." He dropped a hand on her breast.

"Elliot, I want to be a good wife to you—I really do." Tears stung her eyes. She would be. It was her duty.

Elliot shoved her nightgown above her thighs with one hand while the other fondled her breasts.

"Take off that thing," he said roughly.

She pulled herself up and drew the soft white silk over her head. As she tossed it aside in the darkness she felt a chill despite the warmth of the evening.

He hovered above her, his breath ragged, and finally dropped on top of her. His skin was clammy and unyielding against hers. She felt something warm probe insistently between her thighs. He grunted as his hand tightened at her breast, and he thrust in frenzied movements between her thighs. Was this the way it was supposed to be? At last he collapsed on top of her sweating and cursing under his breath. What had she done wrong?

Elliot swung himself over onto his back. He lay still for only a moment before getting up and disappearing behind the closed bathroom door.

Tears spilled down Constance's cheeks. She had failed as a wife. Elliot was furious with her. It was not at all like Mama had promised it would be . . .

NAKED, his clothes over one arm, Elliot stalked down the night-darkened hall to his own room. He pushed the door wide and stopped. Lying sprawled across his bed was Ch'en—his dark eyes full of reproach.

"Why aren't you in your quarters, Ch'en?"

"You wish I leave?" he said with a mocking smile. "Come. Let Ch'en make you happy. Like always."

"Ch'en, what have I done?" Elliot groaned as he crossed to the bed.

"You try what you cannot do." Ch'en reached out and touched him. "See? Ch'en know how to please you."

CHAPTER

TEN

EVERY NIGHT CONSTANCE waited for Elliot to come to her bed—dreading his arrival yet determined to prove that she could be a wife to him. Elliot was a good husband, she conceded —generous, quick with compliments and eager to introduce her to new interests—Chinese and Indian cuisine, the opera, the ballet . . . but she was conscious of an impenetrable wall between them. They were strangers living in the same house. Why had Elliot married her?

With all the servants there wasn't much for her to do and she quickly became bored with her days. She remembered Sam's contempt for the slothful existences lived by most Europeans in Hong Kong: *"Even the lowest rank of soldier is coddled by coolies. A coolie brings him cocoa and biscuits in bed in the morning. A coolie shaves him. Coolies do the cooking and sweeping and cleaning in the barracks."*

Elliot was very generous too, coaxing her into buying pretty clothes and perfume. Constance couldn't help but feel that his insistence was a bit strident—as if he was trying to divert her from the strangeness of this marriage with a new dress or a string of pearls.

She was plagued by guilt over the parade of idle hours that faced her every day. There was no one else in the Colony who was her age.

And while she could have been accepted into the circle of women married to wholesale merchants, Elliot had long ago established himself as a loner. It seemed that Rebecca had been his only friend.

Ignoring the heat Constance passed the time browsing in the fine shops along Queen's Road, hoping—though she hated to admit it—that she might see Sam. Once a week she and Elliot had dinner with Uncle Lionel and Aunt Rebecca—always seemingly interminable meals with Rebecca gaily orchestrating discussions about how happy she was to be returning to England.

It was late in June that they were finally ready to leave. Trying not to cry in front of Aunt Rebecca, Constance realized how much she would miss Uncle Lionel. It seemed like a lifetime ago that she had first met him with Sam on the dock . . .

"Write to us, Constance," Uncle Lionel said. "Remember, mail travels much faster now that we have the Siberian Railway."

"I will, Uncle Lionel. I promise."

Her last friend was leaving her.

Now she was truly alone with Elliot. Why had he never socialized in the Colony? The only people she saw were the servants and shopkeepers and Elliot. And her nights were the loneliest of all . . .

If only she could start going to services again—but she didn't dare. If she saw Sam now in her unhappy new life—well, she just didn't know what would happen.

Instead of taking her usual nap one sultry August afternoon she left the house and went to W. Brewer's for a fresh supply of books. Books had become her companions at night when Elliot secluded himself in his studio after dinner.

Constance was feeling happy today. The streets were empty and she could walk at her own pace.

Suddenly she stopped dead. There he was. Sam—wearing the sun helmet that was *de rigueur* for gentlemen of the Colony—emerging from the book store with a package tucked under his arm. For an instant their eyes met. Constance quickly looked down, pretending not to recognize him and darted into the Stamp Depot. There was something in his eyes—a look of reproach that burned right through her—and told her that Sam had heard of her marriage.

Constance struggled to regain her composure as she waited in line to buy stamps. Sam had no way of knowing that hers was a sham of a marriage—why had his look shaken her so? What did her husband do for physical satisfaction? Did he—she shuddered at the thought—go to a Chinese or Eurasian girl like Sam had? She remembered what Aunt Rebecca had told her about the way to keep a husband faithful. But Elliot didn't seem to desire her.

After the encounter with Sam Constance pulled herself back into her shell, living each day as though she had no future. But she knew something had to change. She couldn't live like this forever . . .

Elliot waited anxiously for some word from his family about his marriage. At dinner one night he mentioned to Constance that he hoped his father would suggest that they move back to London so that he could work in the family shipyard business. Constance was stunned. Once again she faced leaving Hong Kong—and Sam—behind her forever. Would she ever feel like she had a home?

Four days later Elliot came home in a rage. Apparently the letter from his father had finally arrived, but it said nothing about their returning to England. Constance tried to hide her relief but she did feel sorry for Elliot. He had set so much store by this.

Usually gentle with the servants, tonight Elliot was impatient. After dinner, when they settled in the drawing room he declared he wasn't in the mood to paint. He commandeered a bottle of champagne and sat sulking in a corner chair.

"Why doesn't Papa ask me to come back home?" he smoldered. "I'm finally a respectable married man. I suppose if I had married a Rothschild, his reaction would have been different." Constance paled. So, Elliot's father resented that she was a Jew . . . Instantly Elliot was on his feet. "Constance, forgive me. I meant only that money seems to be the only thing he respects."

"I know." Constance tried to smile. Elliot was really a kind man. She could have done much worse in a husband. But if his father did not like the fact that she was a Jew, what did Elliot really think? Maybe that was why he never came to her bed. Mama certainly sheltered me from some cold ugly truths, she thought grimly.

A few days later another letter arrived from Lord Hardwicke. This one, Elliot admitted, must have been motivated by his mother's intervention.

"Papa is setting me up in business here in Hong Kong. He says he's studied the market, and Hong Kong is a logical place for a ship repair firm. It doesn't matter that I know nothing about the firm—and could care less. He's putting money into my account at the Hong Kong and Shanghai Bank and he's sending an engineer from his own shipyard—a man named Converse—to set up the Hardwicke Ship Repair Company on Hong Kong Island. Converse will be arriving with his wife in about three weeks. In the meantime I'm supposed to scout about for a likely location. Of course, I'm to wait till William Converse arrives before leasing, Father would hardly trust me to make that decision. He seems to forget that I've held a responsible position for years."

"You'll have to give notice at the firm, Elliot."

Elliot's laugh was harsh.

"Forget it. It was just a matter of time before they fired me anyway. The American owner never cared about the antiques division. And his son has taken over everything I used to do for your uncle."

ALMOST one year to the day after her own arrival in Hong Kong Constance had William and Olivia Converse to dinner. The British couple had arrived four days earlier and Elliot had reserved a room for them at the Mount Austin Hotel, close to Victoria Peak and only fifteen minutes from town by the tramway.

William Converse was a pleasant, spare man in his early forties. His wife Olivia was a jolly, slightly plump woman of the same age with a mischievous sense of humor and a strong loving nature. Their own two daughters were married and living in London, so they welcomed the adventure of living in Hong Kong. Constance liked them both instantly and she wondered if she had found a friend in Olivia. Her days—and nights—had been lonely for too long . . .

Constance was thrilled when Elliot asked her to help Olivia and William find a house and hoped that William and Olivia could help her make Elliot less of a recluse.

When Rosh Hashanah came Constance could no longer deny that she wanted—needed—to go to services at Ohel Leah Synagogue. She caught herself imagining how wonderful it would be to pray with the congregation—and, yes, to see Sam. But she just couldn't face him after their brief encounter last month. It hurt too much. So on Yom Kippur she would not be in the synagogue to say *Yizkor* for Mama . . .

To her joy Constance found that she could talk to Olivia Converse about being a Jew. But despite Olivia's encouragement, she stayed away from the synagogue.

William joined the primarily British Hong Kong Club which Elliot had always ignored. When William went there on Wednesday nights to play cribbage, Olivia visited with Constance. Olivia had little patience with the formality of social life in the Crown Colony.

"Honestly," she clucked, "ladies too lazy to pick up a phone sending 'chits' on every thought or question that comes to mind; with the cost of coolies so cheap they ignore the telephone. And do you know I've heard of ladies in the Colony who send a coolie to the library with the note requesting books—they're too lazy to pick their own books!"

Constance was embarrassed that Elliot closeted himself in the studio every time Olivia visited, but she knew Olivia was too polite to ever mention it. She longed to confide in another woman. Was it normal for a husband to avoid his wife's company after dinner every night?

Gradually it became tradition to have Olivia and William to dinner every Friday night. To Constance's relief Elliot always played the genial host to perfection on these nights, shunning the studio, and it pleased her that he too liked the Converses. Though he was bitterly disappointed that his family was prolonging what he saw as his exile in Hong Kong with the ship repair business, he made a conscious effort to absorb as much as he could of what William Converse said.

At one Friday evening dinner—which happened to be the fourth night of Hanukkah—Olivia confessed that she was feeling homesick now that the Christmas season was approaching. As she spoke Constance realized how much she missed Mama during the holidays.

"But I'll keep myself busy," Olivia was saying. "With both our daughters with child it looks like I'll be sewing for them through Christmas and into the new year."

"A boy this time, please God," William said good-naturedly. "My sons-in-law feel it's a reflection on their manhood if they don't produce sons."

Elliot smiled but his eyes were serious.

"My father would agree with that wholeheartedly. He has seven granddaughters and no grandsons."

"Well then," William said slyly, "it's up to you to change that situation, isn't it old boy?"

There was an awkward silence.

Constance lowered her eyes to her plate, her face hot. Elliot had not come to her bedroom since their wedding night. Once she had imagined carrying Sam's baby . . . giving him a son. But that could never be.

Mercifully Elliot changed the subject to the growing troubles on the mainland. Again Constance realized that she couldn't let herself think beyond each day in this strange marriage. It was sad to think she would never carry a child. Would she become a vain, bitter woman like Aunt Rebecca?

But maybe if she and Elliot had a child she could finally push Sam from her mind once and for all. If only it were possible . . . she would pour all her love into that child. Tenderly she imagined herself teaching her child above love and kindness and being a Jew. Why oh why didn't Elliot ever come to her bed? Maybe Olivia could help. But her pride always stopped her from confiding in her friend.

Tonight William and Olivia left the house earlier than usual. Olivia was fighting off a cold. After Elliot and Constance saw them to the door Elliot went to the studio.

Constance stared after him. He must be upset, she reasoned. That's always where he goes when something is bothering him. What had happened at dinner to disturb him? Then a thought occurred to her —maybe it was the talk about a grandson. Maybe he, too, was embarrassed about their separate nights . . .

Constance was drifting off to sleep when a brisk knock came at the door. Her heart pounding she reached for the robe at the foot of her bed. Who could it be? The servants were all in their own quarters at this hour.

"Constance?" It was Elliot.

"Yes," she called back, tying her robe about her waist as she walked to the door. Don't panic, she told herself. He is your husband. She managed a weak smile as she opened the door. Trying to erase from her mind the ugly memory of her wedding night. Tonight would be different. She wanted a child . . .

"I thought you might be asleep—" Elliot hovered in the doorway. He seemed hesitant, as if he hoped she would send him back to his own room. But she wouldn't. Not tonight. She would prove herself a wife to him.

"No." She felt flashes of hot and cold at the thought of Elliot's touch.

"Actually—I was reading," she stammered. Thank goodness O. Henry's *The Four Million* lay on her night table.

111

"You looked beautiful tonight, Constance." Elliot walked across the room and stood awkwardly next to the bed.

"Thank you, Elliot." Constance took a deep breath and let her robe drop to the floor. If they were ever to have a child, she had to encourage him.

"I'm so sorry, Constance. I've been a rotten husband." His voice was choked.

"No, Elliot." She slipped between the covers. "You've been a most considerate husband. Really, I—I appreciate what a gentlemen you've been until we got to know each other better. Please. Come to bed." She knew she was playing a role. Maybe he did too. But Elliot wanted to give his father a grandson. And she needed this child—to save her sanity . . . to help her forget about Sam.

"You're too good, Constance. I don't deserve you." Elliot reached to switch off the bedside lamp.

Now Elliot lay naked next to her in the darkness. Surely he must hear the pounding of her heart. Gingerly he pulled her into his arms. She tried not to stiffen as he left a trail of soft kisses on her throat. How different she would feel if this were Sam holding her in his arms. Pretend it's Sam.

"Are you all right?" Elliot asked as he lifted one leg across her slender thighs.

"Yes," she whispered.

He reached for her hand and brought it to him, showing her without words what he wanted. His own hand moved gently between her thighs. She lay absolutely still with her eyes closed. The only sound in the room was Elliot's labored breathing.

Then he raised himself above her in one swift movement was inside her. She cried out at the sharp stabbing feeling.

"Constance?" He paused.

"It's all right," she encouraged and tightened her arms about his shoulders.

Elliot and she would have a child. They would be a family.

NOW Elliot came to her bed often. Each time he made love to her, she had to fight the urge to recoil from his touch. She sensed too that Elliot felt no joy in their lovemaking. A child should be conceived in joy, that's what Mama had said.

By March Constance knew she was pregnant. Elliot was ecstatic

112

when she told him. They both felt relieved that he no longer had to visit her bed.

"I'll sew for you as I do for my two daughters," Olivia promised when Constance confided her news. "Why I think I'm making this baby my adopted grandchild."

"You know, Olivia, Elliot is convinced it'll be a boy."

"Constance don't you understand men? When the time comes he'll adore it whatever it is."

As she moved into her fourth month, Constance decided to ask Elliot if they could join Ohel Leah Synagogue again. Despite her trepidation at the thought of seeing Sam, she was convinced that a child followed its mother's religion. Whatever else happened, her baby would be raised a Jew . . .

Elliot agreed to let Constance go to Friday evening services as long as Olivia went along too. Although a member of St. John's, Olivia rarely attended services at the cathedral. Constance knew she could persuade her friend to go with her to Ohel Leah.

Friday evening came and Constance dressed in a flurry of anticipation. Whenever she thought about seeing Sam she felt a flutter of panic—but I will be with Olivia, she told herself. Sam wouldn't dare make a scene. And why should she feel guilty about carrying her husband's child? She mustn't forget that it was Sam who had left her for another woman that night so long ago . . .

She decided on a China silk dress—one of the few outfits she could still decently wear in public. She inspected her reflection anxiously in the full-length mirror. If she wrapped the lace scarf loosely around her waist nobody would know . . . especially not Sam . . .

When it was time to leave Constance was suddenly filled with doubts. After all, she had married outside her faith. Maybe the other members of the congregation would look down on her—would snub her . . . and suppose Sam confronted her?

"Olivia, maybe I shouldn't go," Constance said as they waited for the carriage.

"What's this?" Olivia chided good-naturedly. "Of course you should go, my dear. Didn't you just tell me how important it was that my adopted grandchild be raised a Jew? Why you've been looking forward to it for days. Don't worry about how you look—nobody will guess. This is one of the most beautiful times in a woman's life. So enjoy it until stuffy customs push you into retirement."

Constance was silent on the ride to the synagogue. Once the baby

113

was born she would be able to forget Sam. Nobody else would matter.

Why couldn't Mama be here to share this time with her? But if Mama were alive, she wouldn't be Elliot Hardwicke's wife . . . she would never have met Sam . . . and she wouldn't have the sweet memory of those days with him on the boat—the one time in her life when she was wonderfully, totally alive . . .

CHAPTER

ELEVEN

SAM LOCKED UP the hong and strode in the direction of the synagogue. He had been doing very well for himself at Telford & Latham—in addition to his full-time position, he was taking on side assignments as an interpreter. Just this morning he had deposited a healthy sum in his account at the Hong Kong and Shanghai Bank.

Soon he would be able to buy some property. He remembered the stories he'd heard from Mr. Franks, who seven years ago bought land from Chinese, who were eager to leave the island at low rates, and then resold it at a great profit.

Every day Sam worked himself so hard that at night he often fell asleep with all his clothes on, a book opened on his lap. But his nights were not restful. Even now, after all these months, he asked himself why he had not forced a confrontation with Constance. She still loved him. He had suspected it all along . . . but he had been sure when he saw her that afternoon on Pedder's Street.

As he approached the synagogue he stopped short. Could it be . . . ? Yes. It was Constance—and a lady he didn't know. They were walking into the synagogue. His mouth went dry. His steps quickened. So Constance was the wife of an Englishman—a man outside her faith—she loved him.

Hurrying into the synagogue Sam caught himself hoping that Constance's return to their Jewish world was a sign that she might return to him. Just as he had almost caught up with Constance and Olivia he was stopped by Mr. Seixas, who always hounded him with questions about his life in Kaifeng. It took every ounce of restraint for Sam to be gracious while his eyes followed Constance walking up the stairs to the balcony.

"I'm glad to see that pretty American girl returning to the congregation," Mr. Seixas was saying. He leaned forward. "My wife tells me that—the good Lord willing—she'll be bringing another member into the congregation soon. Of course she wants the child to follow her faith." Mr. Seixas was amused by Sam's uncomprehending stare. "She's in a family way, Sam. And when will you marry and enrich the congregation?"

Stunned, Sam left Mr. Seixas after two other men approached. Constance should be carrying his child. Had the Levys pushed her into this marriage to keep them apart? How could Constance have let them?

He had heard via the Crown Colony gossip circuit that Elliot Hardwicke was opening up a ship repair business with his father's help. At least this meant that Constance wouldn't be leaving Hong Kong. And with a child on the way she would return to her faith. He would see her at services every Friday . . .

Again he was drawn into a conversation and he struggled to be polite while inside he was in turmoil. He wouldn't let himself look up to the balcony—it was torture enough just knowing that Constance sat up there . . . a new life growing within her that he had not shared in creating . . .

For the next several weeks Sam didn't miss a Friday service. But he didn't try to speak to Constance either. She always arrived with the same companion, went directly up to the ladies' balcony, and left immediately after services. It was obvious that she didn't want to talk to him.

One Friday in July Constance did not appear at the synagugue. She must be concerned about how large she's getting, Sam thought. But to him she looked more beautiful than ever . . . Tenderness, anger and frustration welled up inside him. Maybe the stairs were too much for her now. Why had that stupid husband of hers allowed her to traipse about the city in this heat?

Several days later at W. Brewer's Sam met Lucienne, a lovely young Chinese girl who rebelled against the old rules for women by helping her father in his shop. When she met Sam her interest in the bookstore took on a new dimension . . .

Sam was lonely. While he had many friends within the synagogue community, there were few unattached young people. And Sam's exotic background coupled with his lack of financial stability cast him in a questionable light as a suitor for the few young ladies who were not yet married. With Lucienne in his arms Sam tried to banish Constance from his mind and his heart.

Sam signed up for classes in commerce at the Hong Kong Technical Institute. Every minute of his life must be occupied—any void, any pause—and he caught himself yearning for Constance. And more than ever he was determined to make a name for himself in Hong Kong's business world.

CONSTANCE waited impatiently for the baby to arrive. The expected date had come and gone and with each passing day, awkward from her size and suffering from the intense heat, she tried to calm Elliot's fears that a late baby was a sign of trouble.

Sakota hovered over her, insisting that she take long afternoon naps, bringing her endless cups of tea. Olivia was as always supportive and affectionate. Dr. Arnold was philosophical: the baby would come when it was ready.

One mid-October afternoon, while she and Olivia were sewing in her bedroom, Constance felt her first contraction. She tensed at the fierce pain that gripped her body, her hands folded over the hard mass moving within her belly.

"Constance—is this it?" Olivia looked at her intently.

"I don't know. I felt like just a funny little pain—" Constance managed a strained smile. Up until now she hadn't let herself think about the delivery—she'd concentrated only on the joy of having a child. "Well, all right. A sharp pain." Her eyes met Olivia's. "I'm not sure."

"Let's not jump to conclusions. With a first baby there's plenty of waiting. We'll time the pains." Olivia looked towards the French ormolu clock with Sevres china panels sitting on top of a Chinese lacquered cabinet.

"Livvy, you'll stay with me, won't you?"

"Of course I'll stay. Now let me tell you about my first delivery . . ."

When Constance gasped again, Olivia's eyes moved to the clock.

"Twelve minutes," she said. "This baby means business."

"Olivia—" Constance hesitated. "I—I feel damp."

"The water broke." Olivia was on her feet. "Sakota, help Missy into a nightgown. I'll send a chair to the shipyard to bring Elliot home."

"But it might be hours," Constance protested.

"Elliot will want to be here, I'm sure. Now just relax, you've got other things to think about."

Sakota helped Constance change into a soft cotton nightgown before she got into bed. Constance tried to prepare herself for the pains . . . tried to remember that soon she would be holding her baby. As each pain tore at her body she fought the urge to cry out.

"It's only seven minutes now." Olivia stood in the doorway. "Constance, let go. Give in to the pain—scream if you want. I'm calling Dr. Arnold."

"Olivia, come back . . ." Where was Mama?

"I'll be back. I promise."

While Constance tried to find a comfortable position against the mound of pillows, Sakota pressed a cool towel to her damp face. Already her nightgown was clinging to her.

The next contraction ripped at Constance with a vengeance that left her dazed.

"He's getting rough," she said to Sakota, trying to keep a sense of humor. Why had she said "he"? She would love a daughter just as much as a son.

Within an hour Constance was in hard labor. Just when she thought she couldn't bear any more, another contraction seized her. This was worse than anything Mama had described . . . Olivia changed the pillow slips while Sakota went for a fresh nightgown. The *punkah* fan provided little relief against the suffocating heat.

"I really didn't know it would be this bad," Constance gasped. A fresh cry broke from her. "No, please God, no . . ."

Sakota was sent downstairs to bring Dr. Arnold while Olivia stayed at Constance's side.

"How much longer?" she whispered.

"You'll forget this," Olivia soothed. "I promise—once you hold your baby in your arms, you'll forget."

It went on for hours. Finally, as morning light seeped in through the shades, Constance pushed one last time . . . and a soft but sturdy cry filled the room. Her daughter was placed in her arms—masses of dark hair surrounded delicate pink features.

"She's beautiful," Constance whispered. "My daughter, Diana Hardwicke."

ELLIOT couldn't hide his disappointment. But it pleased him that the baby was named after his mother. Maybe that would have some effect back in London . . .

In naming the baby Diana, Constance was also naming her for Mama—her English name had been Diana, her Hebrew name Deborah. Lying with the baby in her arms Constance imagined the rabbi reading the prayer at the naming ceremony:

"May He who blessed our father Abraham, Isaac, and Jacob, Sarah, Rebecca, Rachael and Leah, bless Deborah, daughter of Constance, who has given birth to a child and her daughter that was born to her a good fortune, and let her be called in Israel Deborah, the daughter of Constance. Amen."

"I'll send a cable to London." Elliot tried to smile as he watched his daughter in his wife's arms. "She's beautiful, like her mother."

So, Constance thought, Elliot still hopes that his parents will summon him back to London now that he has a wife and child . . . She couldn't imagine life so far away from Sam . . .

SAM heard about Diana's birth at Friday night's services and immediately he left the synagogue to buy a bottle of *samsu*—less expensive than brandy and infinitely more potent—at a grog shop on Sai Ying Pun. Tonight he was going to get stinking drunk. It was the best way he could think of to get used to the idea of Constance bearing another man's child.

When he arrived home, he was momentarily surprised to see he'd left the lights on. But then he remembered—Lucienne was supposed

119

to come over tonight. Sam cursed under his breath. He didn't want Lucienne tonight. He didn't want anyone. All he wanted was to get drunk and forget . . .

Lucienne greeted him at the door with a warm smile which faded when she saw the bottle of *samsu* tucked in the crook of his arm.

"Sam what is wrong? Let me cook for you. We will eat together. I will stay the night."

Wordlessly Sam reached for her. "Lucienne, I don't want to hurt you," he whispered, his body pressed against hers.

"You are good for me, Sam." She took the bottle of *samsu* from his arm and put it aside. "All I want is to make you happy."

"What happened to the girl who wanted to be a man so she could help overthrow the Manchus?" he teased.

"I want to be part of the revolution, yes," Lucienne said softly. "But first I want to be part of you."

Sam wavered. He needed a woman tonight . . .

"Sam, let us make love."

She had to stand on tiptoe to bring her mouth to his. Instantly his arms pulled her close.

"Wait," she whispered and drew him into the tiny bedroom filled with the scent of burning incense.

Gently she led Sam to the bed and removed his shoes. Lovingly she undressed him. She would blot out his unhappiness . . . he would think only of the pleasure of their lovemaking. As he lay back against the pillows and watched her remove her silken trousers and jacket, he knew he had to have her . . .

"Lucienne—" His voice was thick with desire.

"You are so impatient, my love."

Languidly, Sam stroked Lucienne's lean, golden body. When he could no longer restrain himself Sam tore into her with a force that took her breath away. In a frenzy he pressed deeper and deeper— trying to blot out of his mind forever the image of Constance . . . until at last he lay spent beside her.

"Sam," Lucienne said after a few minutes. "Let me live with you. I'll cook for you and make a home for you and make love to you. Please, Sam."

Sam knew he would be ostracized from European society if he lived openly with a Chinese girl. But he didn't believe in hiding things, and Lucienne, too, would be putting herself in a compromising position in her society by living with him . . . maybe she would be good for him . . .

FROM the beginning Sam made it clear to Lucienne that they must never have a child. He knew all too well how difficult it was for a child of mixed parentage in the Far East. A child of his own would just intensify his guilt over the assimilation he had deplored in his brothers and sisters, an assimilation that had been a mockery of his commitment to see the growth of a strong Jewish nation.

At the synagogue they had talked about the settlements in Eretz Israel—the beginning of what must someday become a Jewish homeland. Sam knew that now he must leave the synagogue. There would be no more talks about Eretz Israel . . . his life would be Telford & Latham, and the nights with Lucienne.

Through Lucienne he found himself being drawn back into China's problems. Like her, he prayed for an end to the Manchu Ch'ing Dynasty and the establishment of a republic. Then on November fourteenth the Emperor Kuang Hsu died. Rumors circulated throughout China—though no proof emerged to support it—that the vindictive Empress Dowager, Tz'u Hsi, had poisoned him. But she, too, died the day following the Emperor's death.

It seemed to many of the young revolutionaries who had long ago lost their parents' respect for the Dowager Empress who ruled over them by a Mandate of Heaven, that now—with an infant on the Dragon Throne and a weakling as a Regent, Sun Yat-sen's T'ung Meng Hui could bring about an overthrow of the Manchus. They waited, hoping for action. Sam worried about the future of his brothers and sisters in Kaifeng.

Lying sleepless far into a night while Lucienne slept at his side, Sam decided to start a new venture—he would set himself up as a part-time real estate operator. He wanted the money to buy land. He was tired of waiting. Sam Stone would own a piece of Hong Kong Island.

CONSTANCE allowed only Sakota to help with little Diana. She slept with her bedroom door open so she could hear any sound from the nursery. To her relief, Elliot had made no effort to return to her bed.

121

She knew Elliot adored Diana. But he was still waiting for word from home, trying to convince himself that his marriage and the birth of a child would be his passport back into the bosom of the family. But instinct told Constance that an eighth granddaughter was not likely to make Elliot's father have a change of heart.

At last a few days before Christmas a package from the elder Hardwickes arrived. It was an elaborate lace christening gown for the baby, accompanied by a letter from Mrs. Hardwicke. She was honored the baby was named after her . . . she was so happy for them . . . but that was all. It was clear that Elliot and his family were to remain in the Crown Colony.

Elliot paced the studio, his face crimson with rage.

"A christening gown!" he blazed. "Is that all my child means to them? If Diana had been a boy, you can be sure there would have been quite a different reception."

"Elliot, be reasonable. They did lay out money to set up the ship repair company." Again Constance felt that it was partly her fault—first they had been annoyed that Elliot had married a Jewess with no money . . . and now she had given Elliot a daughter when his heart had been set on a son.

Now Elliot withdrew from Constance. But he loved Diana, and he was always attentive to her. Every night, when he came home from the shipyard he went straight to the nursery.

One beautiful January morning, Li—who had joined the Hardwicke household when Lionel and Rebecca left for London—appeared in the nursery and announced that William Converse was waiting downstairs in the drawing room.

"Please bring us tea, Li," Constance instructed as she hurried from the nursery. What had brought William here in the middle of the day? Was Olivia sick?

She walked into the drawing room to find William admiring the narcissi on a table drenched in sunlight.

"Hello, William. Is Olivia all right?"

"Oh yes, she's fine. In fact, she'll be over soon. You know you can't keep her away from her adopted granddaughter."

"Thank goodness. Won't you sit down?" Constance smiled in relief. "Li is bringing us tea." What was William doing here, if everything at home was all right?

"Constance, I shouldn't burden you with this . . ."

"Please do." She leaned forward.

"It's about the shipyard. I know Lord Hardwicke expects me to be a bird dog and report everything to him. Well, I just can't do that. Elliot and you are like my own."

Constance tensed. "William, what's wrong? Is Elliot causing problems?"

"Well, I'm afraid he's neglecting the business. He deserts the office every morning around ten and doesn't return until late afternoon. I was worried so I followed him one day. He goes to the Praya to paint. Now Constance, you know I handle the supervision of the work and the hiring of employees. Elliot is supposed to take care of the billing and soliciting customers. The records are in a mess. I've never had a head for mathematics. And I bumble things whenever I come into contact with customers. I just don't know what to do. Believe me, Constance—the last thing I want to do is burden you with my problems. But now the business is suffering."

Li arrived with tea. Constance was shocked. She didn't even hear William talking about the latest news from his daughters in England. What was she going to do? Their financial security was at stake. If the business failed they would receive no help from Elliot's father. And she knew it would be futile to talk to Elliot—in his present mood he would only fly into a rage.

"William, would it be possible to hire a man to take care of these duties?"

"We would have to bring someone from London." William sighed. "Lord Hardwicke would be furious. And it would be yet another expense at a time when we're already showing a loss."

"Would it help if I came in to take care of some of the paperwork?" Whatever it took, she would not let the business fail . . . Diana must never know the poverty she and Mama had lived through after Papa's death . . . Mama selling whatever would bring a dollar . . . running to the Lower East Side to buy food from pushcarts . . . counting every penny . . .

"I could send out the bills and keep records of who has paid and who hasn't. I have no experience. I mean nobody would ever hire me to work in an office, but I was always good at figures in school. What do you think?"

William looked relieved.

"Would you come in for a couple hours each morning? And who knows, maybe you could even handle some of the selling. You have such a way with people, Constance. I could teach you how to present our services to the customer."

"Oh, William, I don't know." Constance wavered. She wondered if she was getting in over her head. "I've never done anything like this."

"Well, I'll train you." Now William was full of confidence. "You're quick. I'm sure you can learn the business like that." He snapped his fingers. "And it couldn't hurt business to have a beautiful woman selling."

"Well, all right, I'll give it a try." She had no choice. William, bless him, was right—he was hardly a salesman. And clearly Elliot was running away.

She would have to be the one to make the business work.

CHAPTER
TWELVE

SECOND THOUGHTS SLOWING her every step, Constance approached the low, small, rectangular building that was the office of Hardwicke Ship Repair Company. She knew that William was alone in the office; he had phoned to tell her that Elliot had already left for his painting session on the Praya. She hesitated, reached for the knob. Why did she feel guilty about coming here like this? She wasn't deceiving Elliot. She was just doing her best to help out the business . . .

William rose from behind the desk and came forward with a wide smile.

"Constance, you don't know how glad I am to see you." He pointed to a stack of papers on his desk. "Just sit there and I'll try to explain what needs to be done."

As Constance listened to William her apprehension faded. She could handle making out the bills, checking up on what each account owed the firm. After all, hadn't she helped Mama keep meticulous records of every cent earned and every cent spent?

"William, you need some kind of a book to enter all this in."

"A ledger. Ah—it's in my desk drawer. Apparently Elliot never got around to setting it up."

Constance took over the office work with an ease that surprised her. But she was nervous when she and William confronted Elliot with her daily presence at the office. For a terrifying moment she thought Elliot was angry as he stared at them in disbelief . . . but instead he burst out laughing and congratulated William for "inveigling" her into taking over the duties he hated.

Soon the two hours every morning became four or five hours every day. At intervals Constance left the office to return to the house to nurse Diana. Olivia made a point of dropping by each morning to look in on Diana and Sakota because she knew this made Constance feel less guilty about her absence.

At William's urging Constance began to make phone contact with their accounts. Now she was gearing herself to go out and call on new prospects. William never tired of her questions. She was amazed to discover how much she enjoyed the daily challenges of business. But most of all she loved meeting new people . . .

As time went on Elliot withdrew deeper into his private world. Constance saw him only at dinner. After dinner he went briefly to the nursery to sit with Diana, and then retreated to his studio.

Constance noticed too that he was drinking heavily. In Hong Kong there was a high incidence of alcoholism among all classes—due to the boredom and loneliness that seemed endemic to life in the Colony for those not wrapped up in careers or unable to center their lives around their clubs.

When Constance tried to tell Elliot how she admired his paintings, he shrugged off her compliments as if irritated. Nothing he painted pleased him. The studio was where he went every night to drink. She doubted that he actually did any painting there.

One night over dinner Elliot insisted that they build a larger house on the Peak.

"Come now, Constance, this house is much too small for us," he said as she stared at him in disbelief. "It was adequate when I was living alone but it's just not appropriate for a family."

"Elliot, I thought we had everything we needed here." There was no money for a new house . . .

"I want Diana to be raised just as I was." He looked into the distance. If we must be stranded on this godforsaken island I'm going to see to it that she grows up in proper surroundings. Of course we'll keep this house. I'll use it for my painting—or when the fog becomes too much on the Peak, we'll spend time here."

"But won't it be expensive?" If Elliot was thinking his parents would help she knew they were in for trouble . . .

"We'll use the business reserve fund." Constance flinched. "And it's crucial that we find the right piece of land. Of course it must have a perfect view—and it should be isolated from other houses. We don't want noise from the neighbors disturbing us . . ."

While Elliot elaborated on his plans for the new house, Constance tried to grasp the reality of the situation. This meant she would have to go out and find new business. Didn't Elliot know how risky it was to use their cash reserve?

William had explained to her that despite the fact that there would be months when the shipyard would be idle, they had to retain their workmen—or be caught short when business started up again. And they always had to keep a large inventory of supplies on hand because it took so long and they had to travel so far to get them. Just yesterday William had been talking about cabling for more supplies . . .

While William was not the best salesman he did know how customers should be approached, and he knew what their business had over their competitors. Constance knew now that she had to learn how to sell. She would talk to William about it this week. She had to succeed; their security—Diana's security—was more important than anything else . . .

It was during those long moments when she sat in a chair by the French doors of the nursery with Diana at her breast that she felt some of the happiness she had shared so long ago on the boat with Sam. For a fragment of time her world receded and she was at peace with herself—and with the course her life had taken . . .

But still Sam crept into her thoughts. Was he happy? What was he doing with his life? She knew he was still in the Colony because just last week—twice—she had seen him from a distance on her way to the shipyard. Diana's birth hadn't changed her feelings . . . her heart still pounded wildly at the sight of him. Would she ever get over him?

SAM'S bedroom was dark. Sheets of rain beat against the window panes. Lucienne lay sleepless beside Sam. Afraid to wake him. He needed his sleep. He worked so hard. Most men would complain, but Sam was always seeking out more work—as an interpreter and also selling real estate from his tiny office on Queen's Road.

She was so proud that Sam was now a landowner. He had bought a small piece of unclaimed property at an auction. She was proud, too, that he was to become a British citizen. But she lived every day with the hurtful truth—Sam loved someone else.

During the day, after she had cleaned up the flat and shopped for groceries, Lucienne tried to sleep. Lying in bed at night she wrestled with her feelings about the life she had chosen . . . not knowing that even though she could never fully possess him nothing would drive her from Sam's life as long as he wanted her. . . . Every morning she woke up afraid—sure that today Sam would tell her to leave because he loved another woman . . .

Lucienne stiffened as Sam stirred in his sleep. In a minute it would start.

"Constance, why?" Sam muttered. "Why didn't you answer my letters? You know I love you. How could you marry somebody else? How could you do that to us?"

It was the same every night. Lucienne slipped out from under the covers and crossed to the window. Why did Sam insist they not have a child? Maybe if she gave him a child, he would forget this woman —this Constance that he talked about night after night. What kind of woman would cause her Sam so much pain?

She would give Sam a baby. Then he would forget.

Lucienne returned to the bed. She slipped beneath the covers and gently stroked his shoulders, his back, kissing his neck. He groaned and drew her into his arms.

"Connie," he murmured. "Connie . . ."

She would pretend it was her he loved. She would make him want her. Her mouth parted as she continued kissing him, moving down his body.

Trembling but still half asleep, Sam turned over and gently pressed against her. Lucienne's arms tightened around him in encouragement as he entered her. At least now he belonged only to her. Tears spilled down her cheeks as she moved with him.

"Constance," Sam moaned again.

128

Lucienne rocked back and forth more fiercely. She would give Sam a child, and he would forget Constance. He would.

FOR weeks Lucienne interrupted Sam's sleep to make love. At last she was sure she had conceived. She wished she had someone to share her news with, but her family had long ago said that they wanted no part of her life. She had disgraced them, by living with a foreigner. There was no going back.

Terrified that he wouldn't be pleased, Lucienne shyly told Sam that she was carrying his child. For what seemed like the longest minute in her life he stood silently staring at her. Then he drew her into his arms.

"We will raise our child as a Jew. And when the time arrives, he will be properly educated. He'll be a British citizen."

"But what if it's a girl?" For an instant Lucienne worried that, like her own people, foreigners fostered a disrespect for female children. But hadn't the British in Hong Kong declared *mui tsai*—the Chinese custom of selling girl babies—illegal? Surely Sam would love their child whatever it was . . .

"Lucienne—if it's a girl," Sam promised with tender solemnity, "we will love her, raise her as a Jew, and see that she is properly educated."

CONSTANCE vacillated between happiness at being active and use-ful in the business, and guilt that she spent so much time away from Diana. But the child didn't seem to be suffering, she told herself. A winsome and happy infant, Diana got the attention of the entire Hardwicke household—even the servants spoiled her. Diana's hair, dark at birth, was now auburn-tinted, like that of Elliot's mother—but that wasn't enough to endear her to the august Mrs. Hardwicke. Constance comforted herself with the knowledge that Olivia went to the nursery every day—she was the most loving grandmother a child could have.

Early in June—while he was still looking for just the right piece of property on the Peak—Elliot insisted on moving the household to a rented house in the Peak District for the four worst months of the year. Constance reluctantly consented because Diana was already fretting about the heat. And Constance could get to the shipyard each day by tram.

The rented house belonged to a couple who were on sabbatical in London. The furnishings were the worst of mid-Victorian, every room overcrowded with bric-a-brac. But Elliot—usually so sensitive to his surroundings—seemed oblivious to the ugliness of the house. Despite the heat he began spending several nights a week in town. Constance suspected that he was working on a new painting.

Constance was now actively soliciting business, though still insecure about her capabilities despite William's encouragement. But as she snared jobs away from men old enough to be her grandfather, she began to take pride in her job—and felt the awakening of new feelings of self-confidence. She looked forward to going to the office even in the intense summer heat.

Late in July William urged her to take a week off.

"Constance, you're working yourself into a shadow. Stay up on the Peak for a week. I guarantee you'll come back refreshed. And anyway you know how slow things are in the summer."

"Well, all right, William. I'll take a week off but on one condition —you promise to let me know if anything special comes up and I'm needed."

"You'll know fast enough. We're beginning to show a decent profit. I wouldn't let anything jeopardize that. Not even your well-deserved vacation." William chuckled.

"Do you think I could persuade Olivia to come up to the Peak with me?"

"That's a capital idea. I'll encourage her. Maybe she'll stay for a couple of days. You know how she dotes on the little Princess. Sometimes I think she actually believes Diana is her real grandchild. But she won't last long—she's convinced that after a few days her old man will start leaving the house wearing mismatched socks."

Early Monday morning Olivia arrived on the Peak. Constance loved being with her dear friend—really her only friend, she sometimes thought. Olivia's warmth, her love for Diana, her generous spirit helped Constance fight the loneliness of life with the remote Elliot.

The time passed quickly. They spent lazy hours on the verandah, cut off from the rest of the world by the damp, pleasantly cool mist that whirled about them. Diana and Olivia played games by the hour.

Thursday evening William came with Elliot to pick Olivia up, but first the four of them had dinner. Constance had never seen Elliot so relaxed, and she actually caught herself feeling a gentle, affectionate love for him—not passion, certainly, but a serene, warm feeling. Maybe it was the magic of being up here on the Peak . . .

Two days later she received a call from William. Apparently they were going to lose one of their major accounts to another firm offering better terms.

"Constance, if we drop our prices, we'll barely be breaking even. But if the other ship lines hear that we've lost the Angus Lines, they might follow suit. I hate to tell you to lower our prices, but I just can't see any other way out."

Constance paused for a long moment. She knew what had to be done.

"William, I'm coming into town. We're going to keep Angus without lowering our prices. I'll just have to convince them that we're worth it. Hang on—I'll be there in an hour."

THE office was suffocating in the heat, and beads of perspiration dotted Constance's forehead. As William outlined the problem a sales campaign took shape in her mind and she felt excited. This was a real challenge—if she could keep Angus Lines as a customer, then the business could only grow . . .

Instinctively she knew that while it was crucial to maintain a professional business demeanor, a little youth and charm and beauty never hurt . . . and a new customer who at first was amused at being approached by a young woman was a real challenge to her—she became determined to convince him that Hardwicke shipyards delivered. As a result, lately she had won the respect of even the most old-fashioned men.

She arranged an appointment with Mr. Winslow for that afternoon. William convinced her that in this heat she ought to take a ricksha—something she still avoided since that first ride with Uncle Lionel when she had just stepped off the boat.

"You know, Constance, you're probably the only white woman walking around in this weather," William teased. "That alone ought to convince Winslow we're something special."

Twenty minutes after she'd met Mr. Winslow Constance knew they had the account. The courtly Mr. Winslow had agreed to meet with her mostly out of a politeness—and some curiosity. He'd heard about this woman who was making a name for herself in business circles. And he had to admit, he'd been skeptical. But she had surprised him with her sharp business sense—she had presented the facts skillfully, convincing him that it was actually to his advantage to spend more for the quality service that Hardwicke offered. Quite a woman, that Constance Hardwicke . . .

She returned to the office glowing with her triumph and reported every detail of the meeting to William.

"Constance, I don't know what we would have done without you."

"Don't be silly, William. You could have done it. Now, as long as I'm here, I might as well go through the mail. By the way, where's Elliot? Painting at the Praya?"

"I think he goes to the house now—Constance, I think he goes there to paint . . . and drink."

"What do you mean? Elliot's been drinking during the day?" Constance forgot the morning's triumph. "Well, what can I do about it?" She was tired of Elliot's weaknesses . . . "I'm afraid there's nothing you can do, Constance. That's something Elliot has to do for himself."

"Lord, it's hot." Constance pressed a linen handkerchief against her forehead.

"I think I'll go over to the house and shower before I return to the Peak. Maybe Elliot and I can go up together."

Usually Elliot appeared at the office late in the afternoon, and they went up to the Peak together. On the afternoons when he did not come to the office he stayed at the town house.

In the ricksha ride to the house, she tried to sort out her feelings, but all she could think about was stepping into a cool shower-bath. Standing in the foyer she noticed that the house was strangely still. Where were the servants? Though most of the staff had been taken up to the Peak, two houseboys and a cook remained at the town house.

A vague fear gripped her as she walked around the silent house. Had Elliot dismissed the servants for the day? Where was he? Of course—she forgot, he must be in the studio. He was probably painting and just forgot the time. How stupid of her to overreact—she must still be nervous after the meeting with Winslow . . .

She walked down the long, narrow hall that led to the studio. The door was ajar.

"Elliot?" She walked to the door and looked inside.

Elliot was there, but he hadn't heard her call him. He was lying naked, asleep on a bamboo mat, his arms wrapped around the slender naked young body of Ch'en, the house boy. An empty bottle of whiskey lay on its side next to them.

For a moment Constance stood in dumb shock, her mind refusing to grasp the meaning of the scene.

Then the shattering truth knocked the breath out of her and she grasped the wall to hold herself up. So this was why Elliot had been reluctant to make love to her—and all this time she had been blaming herself . . . Why had he married her? And the second ugly truth hit her in full force—he must have hoped she would be his passport to respectability, back to London . . .

Her mind reeling she flew up the stairs and into Elliot's bedroom. She had to find some proof, some tangible piece of evidence to confirm that what she'd just seen wasn't a horrible dream . . . deep in a wicker chest she found Elliot's anguished letters of long ago— written but never mailed—to a male teacher who, it seemed, he had been in love with. She also found a journal kept in his sixteenth year in which he agonized over the imprisonment of Oscar Wilde, filed with yellowed clippings from the London newspapers covering the Wilde trial.

For one electrifying moment Constance forgot her anger and saw clearly that the man she had married was committed—as she was— to a life with someone he didn't love. She almost felt sorry for him. But her shock and revulsion of what she had just seen returned . . . How could Elliot violate her this way? She broke down, deep sobs wracking her body. Why had she driven Sam away? She could have been married to Sam.

Slowly she walked into her own bedroom. She couldn't stay in this house tonight. But she couldn't go up to the Peak and face the servants either. Trembling and pale, she sat on the edge of her bed —the bed where Diana had been conceived—and tried to think clearly. She could not leave Elliot. But how would she raise Diana alone? She was still haunted by the memory of Mama trying to bring her up alone—it had been such a hard, lonely life for her.

For Diana's sake she must not fall apart. Elliot didn't know that she saw him with Ch'en. She would pretend that it had never happened. Her life would revolve around Diana.

I'll go to Olivia and say that I found Elliot disgustingly drunk. As much as I love her, how can I admit the truth? I'll ask if I can stay in their house tonight because I'm too upset to go to the Peak alone.

CONSTANCE was relieved to find Olivia alone when she arrived. She stammered an excuse about Elliot's drunkenness and asked if she could stay the night.

"Of course you can stay, my love," Olivia said. "Sit down and I'll have Wang fix us tea." For Olivia a pot of well-brewed China tea was the answer to every crisis.

Constance was too distraught to sit still. She left the sofa to gaze out the window. It was twilight. This horrible day was drawing to a close . . . Why had she married Elliot, knowing she didn't love him? But she mustn't think that way—Diana came from this marriage . . . And the thought alarmed her—Diana must never know about her father.

"Come have tea," Olivia said gently, walking into the room with the tea tray. Constance knew Olivia sensed that something far more serious than Elliot's drunkenness was on Constance's mind. Maybe she could tell Olivia the truth—she wanted desperately to share her pain with someone . . .

For a few moments they chattered pleasantly about the business, Diana—but Constance was in turmoil. If Mama were here she would tell her the truth. In Mama's absence, there was Olivia.

"Olivia, I have to tell you something—" Her voice was barely a whisper. "But you must promise me that you'll forget all about this afterwards . . ."

Haltingly, she told Olivia the whole story—walking into the studio and finding Elliot with Ch'en . . . and the letters in Elliot's room.

"Olivia, what will I do?" Her voice broke. "How do I go on living with Elliot?"

"You'll live with him and pretend you know nothing," Olivia said firmly. "For Diana's sake you'll pretend this is a normal marriage." Despite Olivia's apparent calm Constance could tell she was stunned. "Elliot is a considerate husband and a warm father. You must ignore his private demons—and be kind to him."

"But Olivia, I don't know if I can. Right now I wonder if I can even set foot in that house again. I'll never—" she shuddered—"never forget that scene. As long as I live."

"You may never forget but you can go on living." Olivia put down her teacup and drew Constance into her arms. "You can and you will."

CHAPTER

THIRTEEN

ONSTANCE WALKED THROUGH her days in the following weeks as if she were living someone else's life. She pretended—and sometimes almost believed—that she had never seen Elliot and Ch'en in the studio . . . She thanked God that she had the incessant demands of the business to distract her. And those demands had become all-consuming now that it was clear that she was the one who was running things.

Every night Constance left the stultifying heat of town for the cool release of the Peak, dreading the time when they must return to their home on the slope, now haunted by that ugly memory. Elliot came to the Peak two or three times a week, sat down with her for dinner and then secluded himself in the nursery with Diana until going to his room.

Constance spent every free moment—except when Elliot was at the house—with Diana. She reveled with pride in each new tooth, her first faltering steps . . .

Constance encouraged Olivia to come up with William to escape the heat. She and Olivia never again discussed Elliot's secret life.

Three nights before they were to leave the rented house, Elliot appeared for dinner.

"I've found the perfect site for us." He was in unusually high spirits. Constance stared at him uncomprehendingly.

"For the new house, Constance."

"Elliot, do you really think we should take on such an expense?" She had been hoping he'd forgotten about the project.

"Constance, we must think ahead. Since clearly this is to be our permanent home—" Fleetingly bitterness tightened his mouth into a thin line. "I mean for Diana to grow up surrounded by whatever comfort and beauty we can provide."

"But the house on the slope—"

"Is far too small," he shot back. His mouth relaxed. "We'll make this new house a masterpiece. Not a mansion," he added quickly, "but the kind of home my nieces know. I won't have Diana deprived."

Constance sat silently as Elliot elaborated on his plans for the house. Perhaps it would be best. Elliot could keep the smaller house as his studio, where he could live his secret life—there was less danger of Diana ever finding out about it that way. Somehow they would manage. She would talk to William about it.

William was uneasy about Elliot withdrawing such substantial sums of money from the bank for personal use, but Constance pointed out that business was going well. She had even asked him to investigate the possibility of their building small boats for sale in addition to their repair service.

For Constance the return to their own house was a traumatic experience, since she knew that within six months they would be leaving it forever. Elliot was totally caught up in the building plans and seemed to be drinking less.

Constance tried to tell herself that she could survive this half-life, but there were still those moments when she looked for Sam's face on Queen's Road or at W. Brewer. She saw only William, Olivia and Elliot, and she hadn't been to services at the synagogue since the late months of her pregnancy.

On a late afternoon, as Constance hurried to Campbell Moore to buy a bottle of perfume for Olivia's birthday, she saw Sam leaving W. Brewer. She paused, her heart pounding, her face hot with anticipation. In a moment Sam would turn and see her. Instead, he waved to someone approaching from across the street: a lovely Chinese girl, whose flowing blue satin dress couldn't quite conceal the fact that she was pregnant.

Dazed, Constance darted into Campbell Moore. Somehow she knew that the Chinese girl carried Sam's child.

SAM was distraught over the news that was coming out of Hunan in the summer of 1909. According to the newspapers, floods and draughts had ravaged the land, forcing the people to live on bark and grass roots. Landlords, greedy merchants, and foreign firms hoarded rice for profiteering. The price climbed from two thousand coppers a picul—a weight equal to 133.33 pounds—to nine thousand coppers. Fighting starvation the people pleaded with the Governor to force a lowering of the price of rice. Instead the Governor ordered the soldiers to shoot. Dozens were killed or wounded.

Sam didn't want to leave Lucienne in her pregnancy, but he had to find his family. He promised to stay only long enough to give them money to see them through the crisis. When he arrived in Kaifeng he discovered that Leah and Sarah—with Sarah's husband—had moved away from Jewish Colony Lane and nobody knew where they had gone. Sam left his Hong Kong address with the family next door in the slim hope that if any of the family should return to Jewish Colony Lane, they would let them know where he could be reached. With a sense of loss and frustration Sam made his way back to the Crown Colony.

"You won't go away again?" Lucienne asked, the fear showing in her eyes.

"No, Lucienne, I won't leave you alone. I promise. I'll be at your side when our baby is born."

He was especially tender to Lucienne as her pregnancy advanced because he knew she was sad that she could not share this time with her family. He, too, regretted that their child would never experience the love of grandparents, never know the joys of sharing life with a big, loving family. But their child would have everything he could give. He would see to that.

It was a cold foggy day late in December when Lucienne went into labor. On her instructions Sam waited until the pains were close together before sending a coolie to bring Dr. Newcomb. He sat at the edge of the bed and held Lucienne's tiny hand in his as she tried to hide the pain that clenched her swollen belly. Perspiration glistened on her forehead.

"What's taking Dr. Newcomb so long?" Sam asked anxiously. "I told him to come immediately."

"Sam, it is natural to feel pain when the baby wishes to enter the world." Her amber eyes glowed with love.

"We should have asked the rabbi to marry us," Sam repeated for the dozenth time. "For the baby's sake."

Lucienne shook her head.

"It would bring disgrace to you to marry me. Nor would my family be less displeased. They know I bear a child. Five months ago I made a trip to my sister's house. If they wished to take me back into the family, then they would have sent for me. It's all right, Sam. All I need is you."

Sam started at the rap on the door.

"Dr. Newcomb," he guessed and hurried from the bedroom into the sitting room.

"Hello, Sam, I've brought a nurse with me," Dr. Newcomb said briskly as a small, motherly Chinese woman in white followed him into the flat. "As you know, Lucienne will not have an easy time."

Sam frowned.

"Lucienne said nothing to me."

"It's common sense." Dr. Newcomb gestured to the nurse to go to Lucienne. "You don't have to be a doctor to know that—she's very small-boned and narrow. I told her this when she came to me a month ago."

"What can I do to help?" Sam tensed as he heard a wail from Lucienne in the bedroom.

"What the father always does." Dr. Newcomb paused in the bedroom doorway. "Wait."

Sam realized that Dr. Newcomb disapproved of his liaison with Lucienne. Anger welled in him. Who was he to make such a judgment? But thank God he was here. Why hadn't Lucienne told him this would be a difficult delivery? She probably didn't want to worry him . . .

For hours the nurse moved in and out of the bedroom. Despite her professional brusqueness, Sam sensed that she was sympathetic towards him.

Hours passed.

Sam paced, drenched in perspiration despite the coolness of the night. This had been going on too long. Maybe he shouldn't have let

Lucienne become pregnant. Every time he heard her strangled scream pierce the stillness he cursed himself for his selfishness. At a particularly anguished scream he rushed to the bedroom door and threw it open.

"Get out," the doctor ordered. He retreated.

Then there was only silence. Sam stood immobile. Hopeful. Waiting for the sound of a baby's cry. Nothing. The door opened. Pale and solemn the nurse stood before him.

"Dr. Newcomb say for you to come in."

Sam strode past her into the room. Lucienne lay still, her face drained of blood. Her eyes closed.

"I'm sorry," the doctor said awkwardly. "We've lost her."

"Lucienne!" Sam hovered over the bed. "Lucienne!"

"Sam, listen to me. We could save the child."

Sam blinked in disbelief.

"You tell me she—she's dead—" It couldn't be true. Sweet loving Lucienne. Dead.

"We can try to take the baby from her."

"How?" Sam tried to focus on what the doctor was saying.

"Surgically."

"Cut her open?"

"To save your baby, yes, I'd have to cut her open." Dr. Newcomb was already reaching into his black bag.

"I won't have her cut up!" Sam yelled, furious. How dare he? Wasn't it bad enough that she was dead? Did he want to tear her apart too?

"Think of the baby, Sam. Do you want to stand by and let it die?"

His words hit Sam hard. He took a deep breath. Lucienne would want the baby to live. He spoke in a whisper.

"Go ahead."

While Sam stood at the window, staring out at the early dawn, Dr. Newcomb lifted the baby from Lucienne. Sam swung around at the first faint cry. Numb and disbelieving he stood by while the doctor covered Lucienne's body and the nurse cleaned up his daughter.

"The nurse will stay until you make arrangements for the baby's care," Dr. Newcomb said. "Will her mother's family take her in?"

"No," Sam told him. "My daughter—Emilie—will stay with me."

It was the name Lucienne and he had chosen, named for Sam's grandmother.

Sam sent word immediately to Lucienne's family. Two brothers, cold and taciturn, came to claim her body. He thanked God they didn't try to take Emilie from him. She was all he had left . . .

Now, more than ever, he wished that he could bring himself to face the congregation at Ohel Leah Synagogue. But he couldn't. The first Friday night after a girl child is born, the father would be called to the Torah to say the Torah blessing before the reading of the Torah prayer. At home alone he would say the blessing.

IN the spring Elliot announced that the new brick granite house was ready. For several weeks he had been making trips to nearby Canton and Macao to buy antiques—armchairs inlaid with mother-of-pearl, lacquered cabinets, coromandel screens. Constance was alarmed by his extravagance but Elliot insisted that with his expertise they were getting exquisite furniture at a fraction of what it would cost to have the furniture shipped from England.

Once they had moved into their elegant new home, Constance realized that Elliot's time would be divided between the two houses. He came to the Peak because he adored Diana. He amused himself by sketching her as she played, promising Olivia that he would give her a portrait of Diana for Christmas. He no longer made any pretense about taking part in the business. He arranged with the bank for Constance to sign all checks.

Each time Constance read about the troubles on the mainland, she thought about Sam . . . surely he would be worried about his family in Kaifeng. And she wondered about the child carried by that young Chinese girl . . . it must have born by now. Sam's child. She should have been carrying his child.

Why was it always so easy to see mistakes after they were made? Why had she refused to see Sam on that awful Sunday? Why had she allowed Aunt Rebecca to return his letter unopened? She had been so foolish. Sam had too much respect for his future wife to expect liberties—but he was a man. He had needs.

Now that she was older, she could recognize those needs in herself.

All she had known with Sam was one kiss in the carriage that night long ago . . . was it wanton of her to lie awake in the dark and wish that she were lying in his arms?

Late in May, when the heat was already driving residents of the Colony to cooler climates, Constance invited Olivia and William to the house on the Peak to spend Saturday night dinner and Sunday with her. Elliot had fallen into a pattern of spending Saturday on the Peak and Sunday at the town house.

After dinner the four of them went out to sit on the verandah in the cool evening mist. Mai-Ling, who had come to work for the Hardwickes some months earlier, brought them cups of fragrant jasmine tea.

"Elliot, Constance—William and I have come to an important decision." Olivia smiled as she exchanged a brief glance with her husband. "We've decided to spend our later years in Hong Kong."

"You mean never to return to London?" Elliot looked shocked.

"When William retires we'll go to London for two months every three years to see our daughters, and at intervals they'll visit us." Olivia was obviously happy with their decision.

"Good God, I can't imagine anybody choosing to live here," Elliot said bitterly.

"We like the climate," William pointed out. "The long months of warmth. I'll admit the summer is hot, but we welcome the respites. And it really doesn't bother us as it does so many of the British. No —Olivia and I are truly happy here." He patted his wife's hand affectionately. Olivia smiled.

"That's why we've decided to look about for a small plot of land before prices rise." Constance thought of Sam. Hadn't he said he was sure that in time property in Hong Kong would be worth a fortune? Olivia continued, "Of course we won't build right away. Maybe in five or ten years we'll be able to put up a small cottage. But I'll feel better if we have that patch of land waiting for us."

"You know land on the Peak is going fast," Elliot warned. "And it's already very expensive."

"Then we'll look on the slopes," Olivia said cheerfully, refusing to let Elliot's negative tone deflate her enthusiasm. "I'm going to see a real estate man on Wednesday afternoon. He has two pieces of land to show me. Would you be able to go with me, Constance? I'd feel better having a second opinion." She chuckled. "William seems to think one piece of land is no different from another unless it borders a river. As far as we know, there's not one river on the island."

"I'd love to, Olivia. I'll arrange to take some time off Wednesday afternoon," Constance promised. "And afterwards we'll have tea at the Hong Kong Hotel."

AT precisely three o'clock on Wednesday Olivia—wearing British walking shoes and carrying the obligatory parasol—arrived at the shipyard.

"I'll be just a few minutes," Constance promised as she finished off a letter to a new customer.

"Oh, take your time. I don't mind collapsing here for a while." Olivia plopped into a chair beneath the electric fan affixed to the ceiling. "I don't care what terrible things people say about electric fans, I think you were brilliant to order them from that mail order house in the States." She wrinkled her brow in concentration. "What is its name?"

"Sears, Roebuck in Chicago," Constance said, reaching for an envelope for her letter.

"Constance, you must think it's strange that William and I are willing to live so far away from our daughters."

"No I don't," Constance said. Too quickly. But it was just that she could never imagine being away from Diana—even when she got married and herself became a mother . . . But Olivia and William held a very special place in her life; she was glad they were going to be staying on in the Colony.

"You know, when the girls were small, I never left them—even for a day." She chuckled. "We certainly didn't belong to the wealthy class of British who kept their children at arm's length. But Betsy was born lame—without the use of her left hand." She smiled at Constance's look of astonishment. "I never talk about it because Betsy has learned to ignore it, and I'm proud of her for that. But when we're together, I instinctively want to make things easier for her—and of course that's wrong. And Anne—" Her face softened. "Anne's one of the New Women, determined to be free to do whatever men do."

"I guess I'm one of the New Women too," Constance said wryly. What would Mama have thought about that? "After all, how many women do you know who run a business?"

"You don't insist on going up in balloons and tearing around in a motorcar at terrifying speeds like my Annie. I worry about her. No

143

matter how I try, I always manage to say the wrong thing to Annie. So I've learned that we can be close at a distance. When we see one another for a few weeks at a time, I enjoy them all over again. William and I have our own lives to live. We like it here. And you're my adopted daughter and Diana my adopted grandchild. So if I make a nuisance of myself, you let me know. Not that it will do you any good."

"You could never be a nuisance. I'm so happy you're going to stay here. I—I don't really know how I would have survived without you." Her eyes misting, Constance leaned forward and hugged her dear friend.

"All right now," Olivia said with mock sternness, "let's stop being sentimental fools and go on with our business."

They left the shipyard to walk—despite the heat—to the real estate broker's office.

"I trust this young man instinctively," Olivia said as they approached the tiny storefront carrying the sign Victoria Real Estate. "I chose this afternoon because he runs the business only on a part-time basis."

Constance followed Olivia into the office. A man emerged from behind a screen. Her mouth went dry. Sam.

"Good afternoon, Mrs. Converse." Sam was clearly shaken. He tried to focus on Olivia.

"I've brought a young friend along with me." Constance interrupted.

"Olivia, Sam and I know each other." Her smile was tentative. "How are you, Sam?"

"Well." He was ashen. "And you?"

"The same." Olivia stood between them, staring from one to the other. She must know, thought Constance. It must be obvious . . .

"You have a daughter." Sam made it a statement. He must have heard at the synagogue.

"Yes." Her voice barely above a whisper. "Diana." She hesitated. "And you?"

He appeared startled by the question.

"I have a daughter also. Emilie. Her mother was Chinese." *Was,* Sam said. "She died when Emilie was born."

"I'm so sorry, Sam." She felt strangely guilty that she had survived childbirth and Emilie's mother had not.

"You're looking beautiful, as always." He tore his gaze from Constance and reached for his sun helmet. "Would you ladies like to see the property now? I have a carriage waiting."

CONSTANCE was grateful that Olivia kept up a steady stream of conversation as they rode to the first of the two parcels of land. Over and over her mind tried to grasp what her heart could not . . . she was riding in a carriage with Sam . . . the last time she had been in a carriage with Sam, he had asked her to marry him.

The carriage pulled up before an expanse of land shaded by an avenue of pines. Sam got out and extended a hand to help Olivia down. When he reached his hand towards Constance she hesitated, her heart pounding. She placed her hand in his. It was just as warm and soft and exciting as it had been a lifetime ago in the carriage . . .

For a few minutes Sam pointed out the assets of the property, admitting that water would be a problem.

"However, I'm sure that new reservoirs will have been developed by the time you plan to build," he reassured Olivia.

"Could I just wander around for a few minutes?" Olivia asked. "I'd like to get a feel for the view."

Panic brushed Constance. She and Sam would be left alone. The instant Olivia was out of earshot Sam turned towards her.

"Constance, I've never stopped thinking about you. Why didn't you give me a chance to explain? I wrote to tell you that Mr. Telford sent that girl to the police in an effort to clear me. Of course I couldn't tell them I'd been riding in a carriage with you at the time of the robbery. When you didn't answer my second letter, I had such hopes—"

"What second letter?" Constance was bewildered. "There was only one. Aunt Rebecca returned it to you."

"I wrote again, Connie—" A shiver of pleasure shot through her. Only Papa and Sam called her Connie . . . the two men she most loved. "—some time after that first letter. I couldn't believe you could cut me off that way." He reached for her hand, squeezing until it hurt.

"I never received the second letter," she said after a moment. "I— I'd hoped you'd write again—" All at once she understood and churned with fury. "Aunt Rebecca must have destroyed it!"

"Why did you marry Elliot Hardwicke?"

"Aunt Rebecca pushed me into it. She and Uncle Lionel were

returning to England and she made it pretty clear I wouldn't be welcome in their home. I was afraid of being abandoned in Hong Kong."

"You don't love Hardwicke, do you?"

"No. Nor does he love me." The old bitterness crept into her voice. But she couldn't tell Sam Elliot's secret . . . "Elliot's parents shipped him to the Colony years ago after he got himself into a scrape when he was at school in London. He hoped that marriage would restore him to the bosom of his family. Unfortunately for him, they still don't seem to be interested."

"Connie, I must see you," Sam said urgently. Out of the corner of his eye he saw Olivia walking towards them.

"Sam, I can't—" But her eyes told him she would.

"Tomorrow," he said. "At a tea house at the edge of the Chinese district. No one will recognize us there."

"We shouldn't . . . " But her heart sang.

"We have to talk." He reached into his jacket, pulled out a notebook and scribbled an address. "Tomorrow at four?"

"Just this once," she whispered. How could she deny herself this?

"Mr. Stone, I think this land is ideal," Olivia called out as she approached them. "I'll have to show it to my husband, of course, but you can consider it a sale."

146

CHAPTER

FOURTEEN

ONSTANCE WOKE UP after a night of troubled sleep to see Sakota hovering beside her bed holding a tea tray.

"Missy, is time," Sakota said apologetically. It was rare that Sakota had to wake her up. "Diana have her breakfast soon." Constance insisted on having breakfast with Diana every morning before going to the office.

"Thank you, Sakota. I'll be there in ten minutes."

Constance sipped at her tea, glad that this was one of the many times when Elliot was staying at the town house. She needed to be alone. In less than twelve hours she would be with Sam. Ever since seeing him yesterday she had been torturing herself—one moment convinced that it was wrong to see him, the next barely able to wait for the hour to arrive.

She finished her tea and dressed quickly. Nobody would see them at the tea house, Sam had said. It was at the edge of the Chinese district. And anyway, why shouldn't she see Sam? Her marriage was a fraud; Sam was free.

She lingered over breakfast with Diana wondering uncomfortably what she would do if seeing Sam led to a scandal. More than anything she must never disgrace Diana, so she must be discreet. Already Olivia suspected that there was something special between her and

147

Sam . . . but dear Olivia would wait for her to bring up the subject.

The day dragged by. Constance tried to focus on business but all she could think about was their meeting . . . How could she not see Sam? Since that first day on the ship at Shanghai, he had never been out of her thoughts. Let them have this one meeting. She would make him understand that they must never see each other again. But let them have today . . .

At last it was time to leave the shipyard. William didn't ask where she was going; she often went on personal errands during the business day. Sometimes she returned to the office; other times she went directly to the Peak.

Today she traveled by ricksha to the tea house. In spite of herself her heart leapt when she saw Sam waiting outside the tea house.

His eyes speaking for his heart, Sam reached up a hand to help her down from the ricksha.

"Connie, I couldn't sleep last night. I kept thinking about today." Constance blushed furiously. Still, after all this time just being with Sam left her tongue-tied . . .

Sam was well-known and respected at the tea house. He spoke not only Cantonese but the Mandarin dialect of the Chinese intellectuals. Had he come here with Emilie's mother? As though reading her mind, Sam spoke first after they'd been seated.

"I thought you would like this place. I've come here often since my first year in Hong Kong. Lucienne—that's Emilie's mother—liked it very much. I wasn't in love with her, but she filled a void in my life when I lost you." His hand reached across the table for hers. "Connie, nothing has changed for me. I love you—I want to marry you."

"Sam, I am married." She longed to throw herself into his arms. Why couldn't they be alone right now in some dark secret place where they could make love? "It's too late for us," she whispered. Was it?

"Divorce Hardwicke," Sam pleaded. "You told me he's not in love with you."

Tears filled her eyes, she shook her head.

"I can't do that, Sam. I can't do that to Diana."

"What about us? What about the rest of our lives?" He saw the resolve in her eyes and he loved her all the more for it. "We'll see each other," he said with confidence. "We'll find a way. Connie, I can't survive without seeing you. It was bad enough before, but now —knowing what your aunt did to us—" A thought occurred to him.

"At Friday evening services we can see each other. I've been going since Emilie was three weeks old. You'll come to services again?"

"Yes, Sam. I'll come." Sam was right. Let them salvage what they could of their lives. She paused. "Olivia really likes you. I'll ask her to invite you to dinner." Her face was luminous in anticipation. "Oh yes, Sam, we'll see each other . . . "

SELF-CONSCIOUS about attending services after her marriage to Elliot—a non-Jew—Constance asked Olivia to go with her to the synagogue. Later she would ask her to invite Sam to dinner. Haltingly she told Olivia everything . . . how she met Sam aboard the ship bound from Shanghai to Hong Kong . . . their growing love . . . their ultimate separation. Despair closed in around her.

"Olivia, how could I have ruined our lives this way?"

"You were a child then. Certainly no match for your aunt. But you know fate has a way of stepping in and changing our lives. Take each day as it comes for a while. See Sam at the synagogue. I'll invite the two of you to dinner here at the house. William will like Sam. We learned long ago not to invite Elliot for dinner. He always managed not to come."

"Oh will you, Olivia?"

"I'll invite Sam to dinner when we see him at the synagogue Friday evening. I promise. But how am I going to explain my regular attendance at the synagogue when even at St. John's Cathedral I appear only at the midnight candlelight service on Christmas Eve?"

On Friday night Constance appeared at the Converse house early. And earlier than necessary Constance suggested that they leave. She couldn't wait to see Sam. . . . But she tried to pretend it was just another evening as they rode through the streets pungent with the scent of flowers, the sky still a daylight summer purple. She fought to contain her doubts behind a tight smile . . . Why should she not see Sam, when it meant so much to both of them?

Constance and Olivia were among the first to arrive at the synagogue. Caught up in the miracle of sharing her world with Sam again, Constance murmured to Olivia that they should remain on the portico, where they would meet Sam before services began. Constance's thoughts drifted back to that first Friday evening almost four years ago when she had come to the synagogue in hopes of seeing Sam again after their separation on the dock . . .

Minutes after their arrival Constance spied Sam striding towards the synagogue.

"There's Sam." Constance had to restrain herself from running into his arms. If only she were Mrs. Sam Stone . . .

"Good evening, Sam," Olivia was cordial, giving no sign of knowing their secret.

Constance was quiet as Olivia and Sam made small talk. It was enough just to stand here close to Sam, to hear his voice . . . She saw his face light up when Olivia casually invited him for dinner on Sunday night.

If members of Ohel Leah Synagogue noticed that there was something between the two of them they would probably remember that she and Sam had survived the terrible typhoon of 1906 together.

Apparently Sam had been forgiven for his liaison with the Chinese girl. Mr. Seixas and others who stopped by to talk complimented Sam on his business successes and seemed to be glad that he had returned to the synagogue. Only now did she realize that he was an important man at Telford & Latham, and that his real estate venture had been going very well. In just four years Sam—not yet twenty-five—had earned the respect of the Jewish community.

EVERY week Constance waited eagerly for Friday night at the synagogue and Sunday dinner at the Converses with Sam along as a guest. Even the long days at the shipyard seemed less trying when she thought about seeing Sam . . .

Once she had arranged things so that Sam could see Diana—now almost two years old. As he held Diana in his arms tears filled her eyes. Why couldn't Diana be Sam's child? Once he brought Emilie to the Converse house for a brief visit before sending her home again with her *amah*. Both Constance and Olivia were entranced by the delicate-featured Emilie, whose golden face was surrounded by a mass of dark curling hair, so like her father's.

Sam was offered a small house on the slope for a very good price, so he decided to leave his flat. There were too many painful memories there for him . . . Constance knew that because of Emilie he wouldn't move to the Peak, which was reserved for white-skinned residents only.

She knew, too, that Sam was restless in their chaste relationship, —as was she. But what choice did they have? If residents of the Colony considered them anything other than friends . . . Constance shuddered at the thought of scandal touching Diana. But it was agony to make harmless conversation at the synagogue, with the Converses . . . and not be able to share her nights with him.

Every Sunday night after dinner at the Converses they went their separate ways. But one Sunday late in November as a rare winter rain drenched the island, Sam insisted that she accompany him in his carriage to the tramway that would take them to their separate homes.

"In this weather it'll be hard to find a carriage, Connie," he said firmly. "I have one waiting."

Constance wavered only an instant. To be alone with Sam even for the brief ride to the tram station was a precious gift. Her body trembled with the knowledge that there, in the darkness, Sam would surely take her in his arms . . . and for a little while they would leave behind the loneliness of the outside world.

"Thank you, Sam." The look in Olivia's eyes as they made their farewells told Constance to be careful.

Constance and Sam darted through the rain to the carriage. As soon as they sat down Sam pulled her into his arms, his lips meeting hers with an urgency as heartfelt and compelling as her own. The years slipped away and she was Constance Levy, listening to the pounding of Sam's heart as he pressed her against his slim, muscular body— Constance Levy, who was to be Mrs. Sam Stone . . .

At last, shaken and breathless, they pulled apart. In the carriage long ago Sam had kissed a girl. Now he held in his arms a woman.

"I'm a sort of caretaker for a house on the slopes," he said softly. "I have to look in on it once a week while the owners are staying in Paris. They've offered me the use of the house whenever I wish." His hand caressed her back. "Let me take you there tonight. Please, Connie."

"Sam, we can't."

"We can if we're discreet, Connie. It's torture to be in the same room with you and not take you in my arms. I've never loved anyone but you. I never will."

"Maybe, if we're careful . . . " Constance felt her resolve weaken. She hadn't meant for this to happen. But why should they deny

151

themselves? They weren't hurting anyone . . . "Oh, Sam, I love you."

Sam gave the driver different directions. He held her hand as he described the beautiful house belonging to the French couple, who would be away from the Colony for the next eight months. That meant . . . Don't, Constance told herself firmly. Don't even let yourself think that this is anything more than one very special night . . .

When they arrived Sam found the key and, opening the massive oak door with its silver knob, gently pressed her into the darkened foyer.

"The house is chilly," he said, turning on the lights. "I'll start a fire in the drawing room."

Sam took her hand and escorted her into a large, square, high-ceilinged drawing room dominated by a magnificent Waterford chandelier. He lighted a pair of wall sconces revealing graceful pieces from the Louis XV period in rosewood, amaranth and tulip. The chairs and loose-pillowed sofa were covered with damask and printed linen. Tables and commodes were decorated with marquetry and lacquering. On the tiled floor lay a silk Persian rug decorated in gold and silver thread with trees and bushes.

Constance stood beside the sofa gazing at the marble fireplace while Sam knelt and tried to start a fire. Something just didn't feel right. What was she doing here alone with Sam in a stranger's house? But she longed to lie in his arms—she couldn't fight it anymore.

Sam rose to his feet while flames wrapped themselves around the small chunks of wood in the grate.

"You're beautiful."

He drew her to him. She lifted her face to his, all misgivings falling away. So this was to be her wedding night—not that travesty with Elliot. Tonight with Sam would be a time to remember forever . . . A night of pleasure and tenderness and passion. She needed it so.

For a little while they were content just to stand lingering in anticipation of what was to come . . . when Sam reached for the buttons at the back of her frock, she was eager, and helped him.

"Oh Connie, I've dreamt about this," Sam whispered, pulling her down to the floor beside him.

He reached for pillows from the sofa to place beneath her head, then lowered himself above her. Long, graceful fingers touching. Lips touching. Constance closed her eyes and abandoned herself to feeling. It was her wedding night—with the man who was, in God's eyes, her true husband . . .

AS the weeks sped by Constance saw more of Sam than Elliot. In addition to the Friday night services and Sunday night dinners they occasionally met Olivia for tiffin at the Hong Kong Hotel or for some shopping. Constance loved every minute with Sam, wherever they were, whatever they did. And Olivia's unspoken approval of their love helped her through her dark moments of doubt.

There were times when Constance was frightened by her happiness. But whenever Sam brought up the subject of a divorce from Elliot, she put him off . . .

"Darling, let's just live for each day." The truth was, she didn't dare look into the future.

She and Sam worried about conditions on the mainland. He saw the approach of a full-scale revolution in China. Sun Yat-sen had been traveling through Europe and America to solicit support for the revolution. The Chinese were impatient to become a republic. Already coups had been attempted in Canton, Hangkow and even in the sacred city of Peking.

Elliot moved in and out of the house on the Peak only to spend time with Diana. He was always scrupulously polite to Constance, but she sensed a simmering unrest within him. What a mystery he was, this man she had married . . . Despite the secret life he shared with Ch'en, Elliot seemed a sad and lonely man, obsessed with this need to be accepted by his family.

Twice a year he received a polite but uncommunicative letter from his mother, inquiring about his wife and child. In March a letter from her announced the birth of yet another granddaughter. Elliot laughed bitterly.

"My God, my sister is almost forty-three years old and she and Gerald are still trying to present our father with a grandson."

THE conditions in China worsened. Ever since last April, when terrible anti-foreign riots took place in Chongsha, south of Kaifeng, peasants and young intellectuals had been poised on the brink of a massive rebellion. Now, a year later, word came to Hong Kong about the signing of a loan agreement with a four-power group of foreign

153

bankers for the construction of roads in China.

"We're going to see trouble on the mainland," Sam warned as they sat on the sofa in the drawing room of their "temporary" house. "In addition to more foreign bankers becoming involved in China's future, there's the new cabinet to be formed next month. Already people are saying that the majority of ministers will still be Manchus. Until the Manchu Ch'ing Dynasty is crushed, China can't breathe."

"Hush, Sam. You're not Chinese. Remember. You're a British Jew. You can breathe."

"You're right. I can. I can do more than that—" he grinned slyly, drawing her into his arms. "Stay the night, Connie."

"You know I can't stay overnight." How she wished she could . . . "Let's just be grateful for what we have."

Three weeks later Sam received a letter from his sister Leah. Along with their sister Sarah and Sarah's husband she had returned to the house on Jewish Colony Lane. Their situation was desperate. They had no money and it seemed that the revolution was imminent. She wrote that she feared for their lives.

Constance was shaken when Sam told her that he had to return to Kaifeng. Leah and Sarah wanted to somehow become part of the Jewish community at Shanghai. He would take them there, set them up in a small shop that would support them. And in Shanghai they would learn to speak English. They too would become British Jews.

"How long will you be gone?"

"It's hard to say. "I must first take them to Shanghai. The rebels make traveling dangerous. I'll ask the Franks to help me get them settled."

"Sam, why don't you bring them to Hong Kong?" Constance asked.

"They want to go to Shanghai." As he held her close she was afraid. What if Sam were injured? Or killed? "They feel kindly towards the Shanghai Jews because of the Society for the Rescue of Chinese Jews in Shanghai."

"What about Emilie?"

"She'll stay at the house with Jade and Chou. But I'm hoping you and Olivia will keep an eye on her."

"Of course we will," Constance said. How selfish of her to try to keep him here when his family was in danger . . . "I'll visit Emilie every day . . . Sam, be careful."

"I'll be fine, don't worry. Mr. Telford has given me four months'

154

leave. But with a little luck I'll be home long before that."

"It's dangerous traveling on the mainland now. Please, Sam, be careful."

"You know I will. I have two beautiful women waiting for me back home . . . I'll be carrying a lot of money so I'll have to take the slow, least-traveled routes to avoid the army and the rebels. Except for mail from Shanghai it's difficult to get letters through. Don't worry about me, Connie. I promise I'll come back to you."

Tonight their lovemaking was especially ardent. Afterwards Sam dozed at her side while she lay awake, still savoring the last moments of tenderness and desire. In a few minutes she must wake him, but please God, let me have just a little more time with this man . . .

SCARCELY a week after Sam's absence Constance awoke feeling queasy. She looked at the calendar. She and Sam had been so careful . . . she couldn't be pregnant. But in her heart she knew that she was . . .

Panic gripped her. What would she do? Elliot would know that this child was not his. This was Sam's child—if only she could hold her head high and tell the world . . .

Lying awake at night she tried to face the months ahead. She could not fall apart. She must think of Diana and the business. Desperately she tried to think of a way to avoid disgrace. There was one way . . . quickly she dismissed it. It was too horrible. But what choice did she have? She had to convince Elliot—quickly—that *they* should have another child—this time a son.

It was so deceitful—and the thought of those awkward nights of furtive groping with Elliot was almost more than she could bear. But the child she carried must enter the world as Elliot's child. No one —not even Sam—must ever know the truth.

She tried to formulate a plan. How could she get Elliot to return to her bed? How could she convince him that this time they would present his father with the coveted grandson?

She must. Somehow, she must.

CHAPTER
FIFTEEN

N OW THAT CONSTANCE actually wanted to see Elliot, he remained away from the Peak house for an entire week. Diana inquired plaintively about her father's absence. When he finally did arrive at the house on Wednesday evening—early enough to spend an hour with Diana before she was put to bed—he apologized for his absence.

"I was so involved in a painting," he explained as he and Constance sat in the drawing room waiting for Li to summon them to dinner. "I guess I lost track of time. Anyhow, I finished the painting."

"May I see it?"

"I ripped it to shreds," he said tersely. "It wasn't good enough."

"Elliot," she said with compassion, "you make impossible demands of yourself."

"I told you it wasn't good enough."

Constance glanced at the clock. It would be at least twenty minutes before Li announced dinner; now was the time to talk to Elliot. She took a deep breath.

"Did you answer your mother's letter yet, Elliot?" Her face was deceptively serene.

"No." He seemed taken aback. "There's no rush."

"I thought we might send her a photograph of Diana."

156

"Another granddaughter?" he jeered.

"Elliot—" She paused. Please God, don't make me do this . . . "It would make them terribly happy to have a grandson, wouldn't it?" Elliot stared at her.

"And it—it would be good for Diana to have a brother. Maybe—" she faltered, color edging her cheeks, "maybe we ought to consider trying to arrange that." Her eyes met his. Elliot had no way of knowing that she had discovered the truth about him and Ch'en but didn't he sometimes wonder why she wordlessly accepted his absence from her bed? Maybe he thought wives were grateful to be spared that side of marriage.

Elliot stood up and walked to the window. To present his father with a grandson would restore him to his father's good graces. It meant he could leave Hong Kong forever behind. He could live again in London. But to go to Constance's bed, night after night . . .

"There's no guarantee a second child will be a boy," Elliot said at last.

"I know," she said softly. "But it might be. A little brother for Diana." Or a little sister, please God . . . I don't want to have to leave Hong Kong. Whatever happened she would love this new baby as she loved Diana. *Sam's child.* She could have this piece of Sam forever . . .

"I suppose it would be good for Diana to have a playmate," Elliot conceded. There was a long silence and Constance could see the battle raging within him.

Li appeared in the doorway. Elliot turned in obvious relief. "Is dinner ready, Li? I'm famished."

Tonight Elliot would come to her bedroom, Constance told herself, fighting a wave of revulsion. She had to put out of her mind the night she saw him in the studio with Ch'en in his arms. She must think only of why she had to do this—and pray that God would forgive and understand . . .

WHEN eleven o'clock came and Elliot didn't appear Constance began to worry. Time was her mortal enemy—what if Elliot had decided he didn't want a son enough to come to her bed?

The knock on the door made her jump.

With a knot in her stomach, she reached to switch off her bedside lamp.

"Come in." She tried to sound sleepy.

The door opened. Elliot stalked into the darkness, swore as he stumbled against a chair.

"Are you all right?"

"I'm fine." Elliot's voice was harsh, his words slurred.

He stood beside the bed and removed his dressing gown. Then he slid beneath the covers. A cold foot brushed hers. Constance forced herself not to recoil from the stink of Irish whiskey on his breath.

Elliot made no attempt to kiss her. There would be no pretense tonight. They lay together in her bed to procreate, that was all. Elliot made no efforts to arouse her.

He brought her hand to him and showed her what he wanted. Gritting her teeth she obeyed. But he remained flaccid.

"God damn it!" he muttered, snatching her hand away. He lay silent on his back for an instant. Constance grew tense. He had forced himself to make love to her before Diana was born; why couldn't he do it now?

"Elliot?" She dropped a hand tentatively on his chest.

"Do you want another child?" he said roughly.

"You know I do," she whispered.

"Then excite me!" he ordered. "This way—" He reached for her shoulders and pulled her down until her head was resting between his thighs. "Kiss me, damn you!"

Startled, uncertain, she forced herself to obey. If it killed her she would bring him to passion. A wave of nausea gripped her and she wavered . . . "Keep going, damn it," Elliot muttered thickly. At last he had grown hard.

"Now!" he said and threw her across the bed.

She lay silent beneath him fighting tears of humiliation as he plunged into her harder and harder, his legs trembling with his frenzied movements.

At last, with a low moan he collapsed in a sweaty heap on top of her. Constance smiled grimly. Elliot would now believe the child she carried was his . . .

FOR the next four nights Elliot came to Constance's bed. For the next four nights she fought the humiliation, degradation and self-loathing that haunted her days . . .

On Sunday morning Elliot left before breakfast for the town house and Constance lay in the precious privacy of her bedroom, deliciously alone. She remembered that on Sundays at the town house all the Christian servants were given the day off. All except Ch'en.

CONSTANCE was alarmed by stories about the rioting on the mainland. China seemed on the brink of revolution. Where was Sam? She dreaded confronting him with her pregnancy. He had to believe she had conceived during his absence . . . that Elliot had wanted a second child . . . How could she refuse her husband? He would understand. And she debated about how soon she could tell Elliot that she was pregnant.

Constance waited for Elliot to return to the Peak house. A week went by. Ten days. His absence unnerved her. Had he abandoned hope of having a second child?

One night, just when Diana was again asking where he was, Elliot appeared in the doorway. He went directly to the nursery, telling Constance to allow Diana to stay awake until dinnertime. At the dinner table he was restless, taciturn, sharp with the servants.

Pale and strained, Constance couldn't wait for this dinner to be over. For a while Elliot would retreat to his room. When the servants had retired to their quarters behind the house, he would come to her bedroom.

She prepared for the night in dogged resolution. Just a few more nights and this madness would be over. She would tell Elliot that she was pregnant, and he would never come to her again.

While she sat at her dressing table brushing her hair, Elliot walked into the room without bothering to knock. He carried a bottle of champagne and two exquisite, fluted lead-crystal champagne glasses.

"Shall my lovely wife and I have some champagne together before a night of passion?" His sarcasm stung.

"Thank you." Guardedly she accepted a glass.

His dressing gown ties loosely about his waist, Elliot settled himself at the edge of the bed. All at once Constance understood why Elliot had brought the champagne—he hoped to make her relax so that she would be less reticent in her lovemaking . . . the things he asked her to do . . . she shuddered at the memory.

"Elliot, I—I suppose it's too early to be sure," she stammered, "but I think I'm pregnant."

"So quickly?" He, too, looked relieved.

"I can't be sure for another week or two, but I—I'm late. I'm never even a day late," she rushed on, color flooding her face.

"Then it's possible?"

"Oh, yes." She made a show of confidence.

"Then let's drink to our son!" His relief was plain as he held his glass out to hers. "May he spend his first birthday in London."

Elliot did not bother to linger in her bedroom. There was no need. They were beyond the point of pretending . . .

He was asleep when she left in the morning for the shipyard, gone from the house when she returned in the evening. She suspected that he had probably left for a private celebration—with Ch'en.

The following week Constance told Olivia that she was pregnant. "Elliot's just delighted. He's convinced it'll be a boy."

Constance could tell by the look in Olivia's eyes that she knew. But neither of them chose to acknowledge it.

"Well, I think it's wonderful news. And Diana needs a playmate. Does this mean that I'm going to be an adopted grandmother all over again?" Olivia smiled but her eyes were troubled.

Constance laughed.

"It certainly does. But we aren't going to tell Diana until it's closer to time. The baby will be her Hanukkah present. Elliot's Christmas present." There was a pause.

"What will you tell Sam?" Olivia asked softly.

"That while he was away Elliot exercised his marital rights. What else can I say?"

"My poor darling." Olivia reached to press one hand in hers.

"If it's a boy, Elliot's convinced his father will want him to return to London. Livvy, you know how much I want to stay here." Her voice shook.

"You know, Constance, I've learned in my grand old age that we waste a great deal of time worrying about things that never come to pass. Just pray that Diana has a little sister and leave the rest to God. Everything will work out, I'm sure of it."

AS the weeks flew by Constance once again immersed herself in the problems at the shipyard. Though Elliot had made tentative noises about coming into work on the days when she didn't feel up to it, she frankly didn't think they could afford to risk depending on Elliot now that they had expanded into building small craft as well as ships.

They needed her, and she was grateful for the distraction.

She was touched when Olivia arranged for Jade to bring tiny Emilie to visit Diana every day in the afternoon. Her envy of Lucienne had long since faded and Sam's little daughter had become very precious to her. These afternoon visits became a cherished ritual that helped Constance through the lonely months.

Once she got over the sleepiness of her first two months—she would doze off at her desk, only to be gently wakened by William—Constance felt fine physically. A seamstress had been brought in to devise dresses to hide her thickening waistline.

Elliot was in high spirits. He had written to his mother that Constance was pregnant again, that he was convinced this child would be a boy. He was back to his thoughtful, kind ways, pleading with her to spend less hours at the shipyard. Constance had come to think indulgently of him as another child. She didn't expect him to contribute to the business, and she never consulted him about any househould problems. He was a charming reclusive man who moved in and out of their daily lives, playing the indulgent father to Diana. It surprised her that after all the ugliness she felt only pity when she looked at him . . .

After almost nine weeks Constance finally learned that Olivia had received a letter from Sam, who was in Shanghai with his two sisters and brother-in-law and was setting them up in a small shop near the Bund. He wrote with great sorrow that Grandmother Frank, to whom he had written every Rosh Hashanah and Passover, had died a few weeks earlier. But he was grateful that she had lived to see the marriage of her favorite great-grandchild Rose to a fine, young Jew who had recently joined their community.

Exhilarated by the news that Sam was safe and would surely return to Hong Kong within two weeks, Constance steeled herself to tell him about her pregnancy.

As she wrestled with her guilt about having to lie to him, insomnia began to take its toll . . . her eyes were shadowed by faint crescents, she became jumpy, moody. The hours she spent at the shipyard dragged. Olivia was concerned.

"Constance, you must rest. What are you trying to do, take over all the shipping firms in Hong Kong singlehandedly? Think of the baby."

Constance smiled.

"I *am* thinking of the baby. The shipyard is our whole future and

161

I'm going to build it into an important industry." As Sam had vowed to create a real estate empire. For weeks now she had been trying to ignore the fact that Elliot would take them back to London if his father relented. She would face it when—if—she had to. "Sam says all of Europe is divided into two armed camps. He's convinced that not only will there be war in China but in Europe as well. Britain will need naval vessels. I mean for us to build them."

"Constance," Olivia shuddered, "don't even think about war."

"What I think doesn't matter. But if it does happen, I want us to be in a position to build destroyers."

"Won't that require more capital?"

"I've talked to the bank. They're willing to extend us a loan." She saw the shock in Olivia's eyes. "Not to build destroyers," she added quickly. "To finance a small pleasure yacht. We'll experiment on constructing a destroyer." She hesitated. "Would you be upset if I asked William to go to France—to Cherbourg—to look into the French models being built there now? He tells me they're much lighter and faster than the British or German destroyers."

"I think William would enjoy that," Olivia said slowly. "And if Annie hears he's coming to Cherbourg she can arrange to spend a few days with him."

"I suppose that means you'll go with him?" Constance couldn't imagine living the next few months without her dear friend . . .

"Constance, you're my third daughter," Olivia said gently. "I wouldn't consider leaving you at a time like this."

THREE months to the day after his departure Sam was back in Hong Kong. Not expecting to hear directly from him—they had agreed that he would never phone her either at the house or the office—Constance was startled to pick up the office phone and hear his voice.

"I'm home, Connie." She glowed just hearing his voice. It had been so long . . .

"You're all right?" she asked softly—wary even though she was alone in the office.

"I'm fine. When can I see you?"

"Come to Olivia's house for dinner." She hesitated. Surely Olivia wouldn't object. And William wouldn't be returning from Paris for another four days. "At seven?" She couldn't put it off any longer. Tonight she would tell him.

162

"I'll be there, my love. God, I've missed you!"

"I've missed you, too." Her voice caught. Tonight he would expect to make love to her . . . and tonight she must tell him that they could never be more than friends again . . .

"You've brought the children together," he said tenderly. "All Emilie chatters about is 'Di.' "

"It's good for both of them. Sam—" she whispered. "I love you."

Why must she go on and on hurting the ones she loved the most?

Earlier than usual Constance closed up the shipyard and left for the Converse house. She needed time alone with Olivia before facing Sam.

"Livvy, he'll be devastated," she said as they sat alone in the drawing room. "Maybe I should have just told him over the phone —maybe it would have been easier for both of us."

"Constance, you know you can't do it that way. You both have to face this thing. Together. You owe him that much."

Constance sighed.

"I know." Where would she find the strength to do this. What would Mama do?

"Darling, you'll still see Sam from time to time." Olivia knew it was meager encouragement.

"Olivia, I wonder . . . if I were Sam I'd never want to see me again."

"I'd hate to see Sam cut entirely out of your life," Olivia said slowly, and Constance stared at her in bewilderment. What was Olivia suggesting? "One aspect of your relationship must be over, but there's no reason you and Sam can't meet as friends." She paused. "The three of us will be friends."

"I don't know if I could stand it . . . and maybe Sam wouldn't accept it." But she wanted to believe he would.

"Life is a series of compromises. Wouldn't it be better to be able to see Sam occasionally than not at all?"

"But I don't know how Sam will feel—"

"Sam will take what can be salvaged—maybe not right away but in time. And, you know my dear," she chuckled, "as an adopted grandmother I have a vested interest in seeing Diana and Emilie—and the new baby—grow up together." Now Constance understood— Olivia meant for Sam to share in the life of their child . . . "God knows, it will be difficult for Emilie to grow up in the priggish Crown Colony—let her have Diana and the new baby as friends." This baby would be Emilie's half-sister or half-brother . . .

"Well, let's just wait and see how Sam reacts to all this, Livvy." Constance sighed. What if she couldn't convince him that this was Elliot's child? "It'll be such a shock for him. He'll look at me and he'll know. I'm sure of it." Constance lowered her eyes to her bulging waistline.

"So tell him quickly," Olivia urged. "The minute he arrives I'll leave you two alone. And I'll make sure the servants don't intrude."

WHEN the doorbell rang, Constance began to tremble. But she had to carry this off. She couldn't sacrifice Diana and the new baby to her love for Sam. She'd already been selfish enough in her life.

Constance crossed the room to gaze out the window while she listened to the sounds in the foyer. When Sam entered, her back was towards him.

"Connie!"

She turned from the window.

"Oh, Sam!" She held her arms out to him. He swept her into his arms. "Oh Sam, I've missed you so . . . I was afraid you might not come back."

"I missed you too. I hated delaying in Shanghai, you must know that—but I had to."

"Sam, we have to talk." He released her, sensing something different in her voice. She saw the look of shock—then joy—on his face when he glanced at her thickening waistline. Constance winced. She had to say it. Now. "Sam, it's not what you think. Elliot decided— only days after you left—that we should have another child." Her voice broke. "Sam, I didn't want it to be this way."

"It's my child!" He took her face between his hands and looked into her eyes for the truth.

"No, Sam. My husband's child. It was his right—I couldn't deny him."

"It's mine. You'll ask Elliot for a divorce. We'll be married."

"No. You were in China when I conceived. Sam, count the months." If only she could tell him it was his child . . . that he was more her husband than Elliot had ever been . . . "The baby will be born in January. He was conceived after you left me. I'll cherish the beautiful months we had together, Sam, because things can't be the same. But we'll see each other. Olivia and you and I—and the children. We'll be like a family."

"Why did I have to go away?" Sam was ashen. "If I'd stayed this wouldn't have happened."

"You had to go," Constance said tenderly. "And I love you for it. But it would have happened anyway. Elliot is my husband. It was his right to expect me to give him another child."

"I can't stay here and see you this way!" He paced the room. "Connie, I can't believe this is happening. Say it's not true." He searched her face, pleading with his eyes. Her heart breaking, Constance said softly, "It's true, my love. I wish to God it weren't . . . "

Sam's face darkened. He wheeled around, walked to the door and paused with his hand on the knob. "Connie—" his voice broke. And then he was gone.

Constance stood immobile, tears streaming down her cheeks. She heard the front door slam.

So this was it. She was alone. She had made her choice.

CHAPTER

SIXTEEN

ESPITE HER ADVANCING pregnancy, Constance continued to go to Friday services with Olivia, praying that she might gaze down from the women's balcony to see Sam. Just to *see* him would be enough. Once Olivia called to invite him to dinner and he said he would love to come—as long as he was the only guest.

Constance confided to the rabbi that, though she was married to a Christian, she wanted her children to be raised in the Jewish faith. If the child should be a boy, then he would be circumcised. She would face Elliot's objection later . . .

Late in September when the worst of the hot weather had finally passed, Constance let Elliot talk her into moving back to the town house until after the baby was born. She was very big with this pregnancy, and the stares she'd been getting on the tramway made her uncomfortable. Elliot would use the house on the Peak as his studio. Meaning that Ch'en would move in. Funny, the thought of Elliot and Ch'en no longer had the slightest effect on her . . .

Like all residents of Hong Kong Constance was now fully aware of the imminence of war in China. Now not only were the peasants and the intellectuals in revolt but also the gentry, who were threatened by the government takeover of the private railway lines. Hong

Kong's proximity to Canton evoked a great deal of concern among residents in the Colony.

The Hardwicke shipyard was thriving: the bank loan had come through and a small pleasure yacht—for which Constance had already negotiated a sale—was in work. The labor force of the firm had been doubled. William was jubilant.

"I look at you, Constance, knowing how young you are—a slip of a girl—and I marvel at what you've accomplished. You have a wise business head. The bank must have recognized this, or you would never have gotten that loan." Constance glowed with pride at his words. She was good—she knew it; and she thanked God she had the business to fill her days . . .

Constance heard about Sam through Olivia, who saw him regularly in spite of his attempts to avoid her. How could she have expected otherwise, Constance told herself. But she was happy for Sam when she learned that, with the retirement of Mr. Latham from the company, he had been promoted to a partnership.

Early in October the revolution was launched in the city of Wuchang. The rebels seized the city, then moved on to take Hankow and Hanyang. Open rebellion spread throughout the Chinese empire. In Hong Kong Chinese cut off their queues in a gesture of defiance to the Manchus. Two thousand years of Imperial rule in China was coming to an end.

The new young intellectuals, Sam told Olivia, expected the Republic to reform the old Confucian system and modernize China. Sam feared that the towering ambitions of many in the military would lead to a fight sparked by selfish aims to control and mold the old Empire.

Canton—barely ninety miles away from Hong Kong—was in chaos. Day after day there was fighting in the streets. Looting. Bystanders murdered. Olivia told Constance that Sam was worried about his sisters and brother-in-law in Shanghai, even though they were living in the International Settlement, wore European clothes, and were learning to speak English and Hebrew. Sam talked about their wish—to one day migrate to Israel, where Tel Aviv—the first all-Jewish city—was now over two years old and thriving.

Wealthy Chinese were fleeing the mainland, seeking refuge in Hong Kong. Olivia told Constance that Sam's real estate deals—in which he used his money to spread his holdings by buying options on land rather than making outright purchases—were the talk of the Colony. In this fashion he was tying up formidable tracts of land and reselling them at big profits in a soaring seller's market.

Like everyone living in the Colony Constance worried about the piracy flourishing in the waters around the island. A band of brigands set fire to a steamship, killing three hundred passengers. Residents feared that warlords preying on the south of China would cross into the Colony.

Olivia and William scolded Constance for working so late into her pregnancy, but Elliot was clearly relieved that no one was asking him to come back into the business.

Constance felt her first labor pains as she was getting ready to leave for the office on a morning in early December. She immediately sent a chair to fetch Olivia, and Sakota took Diana to the Converse house to remain there until after the delivery. Mai-Ling helped Constance into a nightgown. Having some experience as a midwife, Mai-Ling would stay with Constance throughout the delivery.

"Have you sent for Elliot?" Olivia asked once Constance was settled in bed and grimly timing her pains.

"Later." Constance clenched her teeth to silence the cry that welled in her throat. Now the fear she had been avoiding for months pushed its way into her thoughts. If the baby should be a boy, how would she make sure they remained in Hong Kong? "I've told Li to send a boy for Dr. Arnold, Livvy."

"He'll come quickly. The second one is much easier, dear. But Elliot will want to be here."

"I told you I'll send for him later." Constance knew she was being unreasonable. But she didn't want Elliot here—she wanted Sam . . . holding her hand while she fought to push their child into the world. "Livvy, do you think it's a girl?"

"If I knew do you think I'd be sitting here? Be patient." Olivia tried for a chuckle but her eyes were serious. She knew that Constance was facing a devastating possibility. Lord, she prayed, I hope she has the strength to see this thing through . . .

All at once the pains were coming one right after another.

"Not again!" Constance gasped. "I'll never go through this again."

"Well, it sounds like this baby won't keep us waiting too long," Dr. Arnold commented as he opened the door.

Constance clutched at the cloth Olivia had put into her hands. "The baby's coming!"

Dr. Arnold pushed aside the coverlet to check. "Soon, Constance —let's not get ahead of ourselves. Bear down for me, Constance. Come on, you can do it. He's coming head first. Now. Harder! Harder!"

"He?" Constance managed to ask between thrusts.

"Bear down a few more times and we'll know." Dr. Arnold encouraged. "A headful of tawny hair." Like Sam's, Constance thought fuzzily through the pain.

"Come on, Constance. One more . . . " Constance thought of Sam —if only he could be here . . . all the love and anger welled up within her and she gave one final push. In a daze she heard the first cry. And Dr. Arnold.

"It's a boy. You have a fine son, Constance."

"Adam," she whispered. "My son Adam."

Again, Elliot had chosen the baby's name. Adam if it should be a boy. Adam was her grandfather's name. Papa would have been pleased.

"Olivia," Constance whispered.

"Yes, dear?"

"Livvy, tell Elliot he can come now. He has his son. And Livvy— remind him the baby came five weeks early . . . "

Within forty minutes Elliot, grim and ashen, hurried into her bedroom.

"Was it bad?" His eyes were compassionate.

"It's always bad," Constance said wryly, "but now it's over, and we have a son." She looked towards the cradle where tiny Adam lay sleeping. How could she convince Elliot that their future lay here? The shipyard was thriving. If they could build destroyers that matched those of the French, they would make a fortune. "He's a big baby considering he's five weeks early." He was a tiny replica of Sam. The look on Olivia's face told her that. She had noticed this—but Constance prayed no one else would. It occurred to her that Elliot had never met Sam. If only Sam could be with his son now, holding him in his arms . . .

Elliot walked across to the cradle and gazed tenderly at the sleeping infant. He dropped to his haunches and caught one small finger in his.

"Poor little Adam," he murmured. "You'll never see London."

"What do you mean, Elliot?" Her blood turned to ice. What was wrong with the baby's eyes? "Elliot—what's wrong with my baby?"

"Constance, don't worry. His eyes are fine." Elliot pulled himself to his feet. "I just got a cable from London. My father is dead. He left me nothing. All we have is the shipyard." A vein throbbed at his temple. "We'll be on this godforsaken island forever."

"Elliot, we'll be all right." She tried to hide her joy. "The shipyard is in fine shape. I'm sorry that the children will never know their grandfather—"

"Forgive me if I don't mourn that bastard," Elliot hissed. "And if you'll excuse me I think I'll go fix myself a drink."

"Elliot!" But it was too late. She heard the front door slam.

FOR three days Constance waited for Elliot to appear at the town house—where she and the children were to stay for a month before returning to the Peak. Ever aware of his secret life with Ch'en, she couldn't bring herself to send for him. But she had to talk to him about Adam's circumcision—it had to be performed when Adam was eight days old.

When it became clear that Elliot might not show up before the eighth day, Constance arranged for the rabbi and the *mohel* to come to the town house. The thought of Adam's first rite as a Jew taking place in the synagogue—where she and Sam had shared so much—was more than she could bear . . . One night she dreamed of Sam holding his son in his arms after the circumcision while the *mohel* recited the traditional benedictions.

On the fourth afternoon, while Diana and Emilie hovered over Adam, Constance heard Elliot talking to Li at the door.

"Sakota, please take Diana and Emilie downstairs for hot cocoa." She must talk to Elliot about Adam's circumcision. What if he objected? In a long ivory velvet robe—a gift from Elliot after she had told him about her second pregnancy—Constance waited for him to come up to see Adam.

"Elliot, you don't look well," she scolded as he walked into her bedroom. It was true. He was drawn, with dark shadows underneath his eyes.

"I'm all right now." His smile enigmatic, he crossed to stand beside the cradle.

She paused. Now was the time.

"Elliot, I—I've been thinking about something very seriously. You

170

know that my religion is important to me . . . Well, I'd like to have Adam circumcised."

Elliot spun around with a look of distaste on his face. "Don't be ridiculous. It's barbaric."

"It's not barbaric!" Constance said with pride. "It has been practiced for centuries, not only by Jews but by Egyptians and Mohammedans and Abyssinians. Not just as a religious rite but as a health measure." She took a deep, determined breath. "Elliot, I want Adam to be circumcised."

She refused to flinch under Elliot's glare. Instinct told her if she held her ground Elliot would back down.

He shrugged.

"Well, all right, if it'll make you happy. But don't expect me to be a part of it. Frankly, I don't why you want to saddle Diana and Adam with the stigma of being Jewish."

"I'm Jewish," she shot back, stung. "I don't consider it a stigma."

"Nor do I," Elliot said calmly. "But this world is full of people who do. I'm not Jewish. My children could go through life as Christians."

"The children belong to the faith of their mother." How could she allow her children to be raised as other than Jews? Sam's son. "And anyway, when was the last time you attended church services, Elliot?"

"When I was at school, and I had to," he admitted. "Well—do as you see fit. I can see you have your mind set on it."

"Thank you Elliot. Will—will you be here for dinner?" Constance was eager to get the conversation on a different track before he had second thoughts. "Mai-Ling has been preparing a duck since yesterday."

"No. I'll play with Diana for a while and then go up to the Peak." He leaned over the crib again. "When Adam is a month old, I'll paint his portrait. You'd like that, wouldn't you?"

"Oh Elliot, yes." Constance was touched; what an odd man— one minute he seemed ready to lash out at her, the next eager to please . . .

"It won't be the best painting in the world, but you can hang it in the office to keep you company."

"I'd like that very much," she said softly.

Only minutes after Elliot had left the house, Olivia arrived for her afternoon visit. As she nursed Adam, Constance told her that Elliot

171

had agreed to Adam's circumcision. Her little victory today confirmed for her that she was the real head of this family—not a role that Constance assumed with any relish . . .

"Unofficially, of course, you're the children's godmother, Livvy," she said affectionately as she returned a sleepy Adam to his cradle. "But for the circumcision service a Jew must play this role. And the rabbi has said that the eldest Jew in the community—a Mr. Solis—will represent Adam's father, since Elliot is not Jewish." She paused as a daring idea took hold . . . "The godfather should be a—a close friend." She stammered in her excitement. "Olivia, do I dare ask Sam to be Adam's godfather?" Olivia's mouth dropped open in shock.

"Constance, how can you do that?"

"Everybody at the synagogue knows that we arrived here together. I told everyone how Sam saved my life on board the ship from Shanghai to Hong Kong. And I have no other real friend among the congregation. Oh Livvy, it would make me so happy!" Her eyes pleaded for acceptance.

"Constance, it—it's unwise."

"You said—all those months ago when Sam returned from Kaifeng—that the three of us should be friends. Let Adam grow up knowing Sam. Let Sam and you and I—and the three children—be a private family. If you ask Sam, he won't refuse me. In my heart I know he won't." Her face was glowing. "I know it's a compromise, but don't you think we deserve that much?"

There was a long pause as Olivia sat very still, her lips pressed together in a thin line.

"All right, Constance, I'll talk to Sam. But I don't know how he'll react. I'm not going to press him. And I know you don't want my opinion but I'm going to give it to you anyway: I think you're taking a big risk."

LATE that same evening Olivia phoned Constance. "Well, Sam was startled by your request, but he said he'll be happy to act as Adam's godfather. He's coming for dinner tomorrow night. After dinner I'll bring him over to the house to see the baby. Let Elliot begin to see Sam as a family friend."

"Elliot won't be here," Constance said. "He's back at the house on the Peak. Oh, Livvy, I can't wait to see Sam!"

172

"Constance, remember what I said—you and Sam are friends. That's all."

"I know. I'll be grateful for that."

AT Sakota's insistence Constance agreed to have dinner in bed; but after she had eaten she got up and dressed to receive Sam and Olivia. She couldn't keep the lilt out of her voice as she talked lovingly to Adam—as though he could understand the magnitude of this occasion. Sam would see his son . . .

An alarming thought struck her. What if Sam noticed—and it would be difficult not to—how much Adam resembled him? Would he make a scene? No, even if Sam did decide that Adam was his child, she was sure he wouldn't say anything to make their lives difficult —that's the kind of man he was.

Constance had already decided that the day after Adam's circumcision she would return to the office for the morning hours, and a week later she would resume her normal schedule. But as with Diana, she would interrupt her day to come home to nurse Adam.

As Constance went downstairs to the drawing room—for the first time since Adam's birth—she alternated between happy anticipation and fear . . . What if Sam changed his mind and didn't show up? It would be natural for him to have second thoughts about being Adam's godfather . . .

When she heard the bell, she restrained herself from rushing into the foyer. She had to be discreet about her true feelings no matter what . . . She waited impatiently for Olivia to bring Sam into the drawing room. Why must they dawdle in the hall?

Then she heard Olivia's voice. "Adam's a dear, sweet child. Already we can see that. Of course we're all a little prejudiced . . . "

Constance didn't hear the rest. Neither did Sam. The instant the door opened their eyes met. This time there could be no passionate embrace. But just to be in the same room with each other was enough. It had to be . . .

"Sam, I'm so glad you came." She hesitated, at first not trusting herself to extend a hand. Let him make the first move.

"I've missed you," Sam said. His eyes burned through her as he held out his hand.

"Constance, Sam has arranged to be at the circumcision," Olivia said.

Sam was still holding her hand. "It'll be early in the morning, I presume?"

"Yes," she whispered. "The preferred time." She fought to keep her voice steady. "Would you like to see Adam now?"

"I'd consider it an honor."

"He's in the cradle in my bedroom. Follow me."

As they went upstairs, Constance tried to think clearly. Did Sam still believe Adam was his child, as he had insisted when he first learned she was pregnant? Or had he come to believe that Elliot was the father? She had told him that the baby would arrive in late January; Adam had been born in early December.

Breathless as she arrived at the head of the stairs, she walked quickly to her bedroom door and pushed it open.

"In here, Sam," she whispered.

Olivia stood in the doorway. Constance walked beside Sam into the bedroom. She watched his face as he inspected tiny Adam as he lay sleeping in the cradle. With infinite tenderness he lifted the baby into his arms. There were tears of joy in his eyes when he turned to Constance.

Sam knew he held his son.

CHAPTER

SEVENTEEN

ONSTANCE AND SAM faced 1912 with an unspoken pact to center their lives around their businesses and the three children. Diana and Emilie were now inseparable, which brought Sam often into the Hardwicke home—occasionally even as a dinner guest—though only when Olivia and William were also present. On those rare occasions when he and Sam were thrown together, Elliot was polite but distant.

Constance told herself that hers was an endurable existence but all too often she lay awake at night in the loneliness of her bed, battling a yearning to lie in Sam's arms. Surely Sam must feel the same . . . but she would not let herself imagine how he dealt with his desires.

Once a week Constance went to dinner at the Converse house, where Sam was always a guest too. Once a week she invited Olivia and William, along with Sam, for dinner. She nurtured a defiant satisfaction in the knowledge that Sam was able to see Adam. On the nights they dined together, Olivia and Constance would sit and listen while William and Sam talked about the state of the world.

Sam prodded Constance into joining him in a private German class that met once a week. It was important that they be multilingual for business purposes, he insisted. Later they would study French and Italian.

Many of those in the Colony—like Sam and William—were concerned not only about revolution on the mainland but also about the war in the Balkans. Sam feared that at any moment all of Europe might erupt into war. Germany longed for expansion in Asia. France and Germany bickered over Morocco. England worried that Germany was amassing a navy and talking of taking over colonies.

"We're starting to work on a model destroyer," Constance confided to Sam over dinner one evening at the Converse house, "from the plans William was able to acquire in Cherbourg."

"The British won't let you sell to nations at war," Sam said.

"We know that," William said, "but we'd like to be ready when Britain does become involved." He sighed. "I'm afraid it's inevitable." Sam nodded in agreement.

Constance leaned forward. "Our finances are too tied up at present to do more than experiment," she said eagerly. "And there are problems. We hear that in France the model was left in the harbor and deteriorated. William is trying to figure out why."

As always when Constance and Sam were together, the conversation eventually turned to the children. When they finished dessert Olivia suggested they have tea in the drawing room.

"Connie, I hope you're planning on attending services this Friday," Sam said mysteriously while Olivia poured the Earl Grey tea for them in the Constance's favorite Sevres cups.

"Sam, you know Olivia and I are always there." She paused, waiting for him to elaborate.

"An elderly gentleman, who I think you'll be most interested in meeting, will also be there." Sam was obviously enjoying himself with this little mystery. "He has just returned to Hong Kong from Shanghai, where he knew Leah and Sarah and Joseph. Years ago he lived in Hong Kong. He remembers your uncle from his first days in the Colony. He says he knew your grandfather." Sam had been astonished to learn that Constance's grandfather had also lived in the Colony. She and Sam had shared so much, and yet they had never talked about her grandfather—she couldn't forget how cruel he had been to Papa.

"He knew Papa's father?" Constance felt a chill run through her.

"Mr. Mendez was quite fond of your grandfather and your uncle. He's anxious to meet you."

Constance tried to look pleased. "I'll be delighted to meet him."

"Constance, I didn't know your grandfather had lived here." Olivia turned to William. "He must have been one of the early settlers."

Constance's thoughts drifted to the past while the others talked. What did the appearance of Mr. Mendez mean?

ON Friday night Constance and Olivia arrived at the synagogue early, as they always did. Sam was already there, talking to a frail, white-haired old man.

"Constance," Sam called out ebulliently. He never called her Connie in front of strangers. When Constance and Olivia approached he turned to his companion. "Mr. Mendez, this is Constance Hardwicke, once Constance Levy. And Mrs. William Converse." Sam turned to Constance. "Mr. Mendez, who came to the Crown Colony from London when it was little more than a rock."

The old man's eyes lighted as he gazed at her.

"Why yes, you are Isaac Levy's granddaughter. And Lionel's niece. I can see the resemblance. You know, I was very fond of the two of them. Your grandfather was a fine man. It was miraculous the way he built the business from a little nothing into an important firm in the few short years left to him. But he always said, 'I'm building for my two boys.'" His eyes saddened. "I think he knew he had only a few years left on this earth, and nothing mattered except to provide for his sons."

Constance's mind was churning. He was an old man—maybe his memory was blurred. But now the words of Mr. Gomez from long ago—*"after what they did to papa"*—came back to her.

"My grandfather founded Levy Trading?" *Not Uncle Lionel?*

"Yes indeed. He started in a godown that was so small everybody wondered how he expected to conduct any business at all, but within a year he expanded. By the time he died he had expanded to what Lionel took over at his father's death. I was always sorry that Lionel could not persuade your father to join him in the business. After all, your grandfather had built Levy Trading for his two sons."

"Papa had moved to America. To New York." Constance sought to contain her excitement. So, half of Levy Trading had belonged to Papa. And Uncle Lionel had cheated him of his inheritance. "You

177

must come to have dinner with us one evening, Mr. Mendez." She was eager to know more about her grandfather. "Are you free on Saturday night?"

FOR months Constance watched while William and a special crew worked on the aluminum model destroyer whenever they could spare the time during the business day, all the while recalling that the French model, left in the harbor, had deteriorated. William was determined to make a destroyer that would last.

By the spring of 1913 the model was completed, though Constance was shocked at the investment of time and money involved. The boat was anchored in the harbor. If it proved seaworthy—they already knew that with its aluminum hull it would be fast—Constance would approach the British Admiralty, which was in the market for destroyers that could outdistance those of the Kaiser's navy.

Within three weeks William came to Constance with disturbing news.

"I don't understand it." He sighed in frustration. "I've been in regular contact with the French engineers. I thought we'd learned from their mistakes. They discovered that the aluminum hulls of their boats were attacked because the boats had been left in salt water beside wooden vessels with copper bottoms, and galvanic action took place between the two boats. But we've kept our model isolated from others. How could this have happened to our hulls?"

"Aluminum hulls are necessary for speed, William. There has to be a way to protect them." Constance again tried not to think about how much money they'd invested in their model—it must have been triple what they had originally anticipated. The bank had extended them additional loans, with first payments soon to be due. Had she in her inexperience taken on more than she could handle?

"There's only one possibility," William said after a moment of silence. "When the coolies cleaned the destroyer with soap and water, the water became alkaline."

"And that would cause deterioration?"

"Yes. But the boats have to be cleaned."

"What happens with the conventional steel boats?" Constance asked. "They've never deteriorated in the water. Is it because they're steel rather than aluminum—or is there another reason?" If they could sell destroyers to the British Admiralty, Hardwicke Shipyards

178

could expand by leaps, and Diana's and Adam's future would be secure. Whatever happened, they must never know the poverty that she and Mama had known after Papa died . . .

"What is it, William?" Why was he looking at her like that?

"Constance, you may have hit on the solution." He spoke excitedly. "Before the boat goes into the water, we'll paint it, as we would if it were of steel. Never mind that the hull is aluminum—we paint it! That *should* eliminate the deterioration in the water."

"How fast will you know?"

"It'll take a few weeks. That hull has to be replaced. And with the rising cost of aluminum it won't come cheap."

"Never mind. We'll do it." Constance's intuition told her this was right. "Replace the hull, paint it, and test. If it works, we'll contact the Admiralty."

Three evenings later Constance sat across the table from Sam at the Converse house. During the early courses, with servants moving in and out of the dining room, they talked about the children. Emilie loved being with Diana, and she had become a little mother to Adam. For Constance and Sam this was a special pleasure.

Next year Diana would enter the school for European children. A year later Emilie would begin her schooling. Sam was determined that she be admitted to the school for European children despite her Chinese blood, and Constance vowed to help him.

Constance and Sam had always objected to the caste system in the Colony. A wholesale merchant was welcome at the Hong Kong Club —but a retail merchant was not. Endless petty cliques socialized only within their own immediate circle. Constance loved Emilie as much as she loved Adam and Diana, and she worried about her future in this tightly governed world.

As always they left the dining room to have tea in the drawing room. Now that the servants were out of earshot, Constance told Sam about their problems with the destroyer. He realized that the shipyard was financially pinched and offered to help out.

"Sam, it's good of you to offer; but we couldn't accept." If a substantial amount of money from Sam's account suddenly went into the Hardwicke account, she was sure the entire Crown Colony would find out—and gossip. "I'll just have to work something out with the bank."

"If the destroyer can achieve the speed William expects, you'll be in a position to bargain for a big contract with the British government. The Hong Kong and Shanghai Bank will extend all the money you need," Sam pointed out.

"That's right," William said. "Let's get this model in shape to prove itself."

Again Constance went to the bank for an additional small loan. They hedged. Without consulting Elliot she offered to put up the Peak house as security. The bank agreed, though she had to get Elliot's signature on the papers. She returned immediately to the shipyard, and phoned Elliot at the town house.

Constance tensed at the sound of Ch'en's voice on the phone.

"Master painting," Ch'en reported. "Cannot disturb."

"Tell Mr. Hardwicke to call Mrs. Hardwicke at the Peak house this evening," she instructed. Damn. Just hearing his voice made her tremble . . .

Elliot called late that night while Constance was getting ready for bed. She could tell that he'd been drinking.

"I need your signature on some papers for the bank," she said warily. Despite his disinterest in the business he was aware that bank loans had financed their expansion into shipbuilding.

"Fine," Elliot said meanly. "Just put an X where I'm supposed to sign and send the papers over with a coolie in the morning."

"I'll send them over with a coolie right now," Constance said quickly. "Just sign at the X and give them back to the boy."

Constance waited anxiously for the papers to be returned. She doubted that Elliot would read them and object, but she wouldn't relax until she held them, signed, in her hands. As instructed, the boy brought the papers directly to her room. Constance sighed with relief. Elliot had signed.

At the beginning of May, as summer hovered over the island, William announced that the repaired destroyer had passed all tests. Constance could now approach the British Admiralty. Instinct told her to discuss this first with the local consular officers. Accordingly, through William's contact with his friend at the Consulate—who made a point of stressing that Constance was the daughter-in-law of the late Lord Hardwicke of London—she made an appointment to show the consular officers just how fast the destroyer could go.

At the same time she arranged for the local agent of Lloyd's of London to inspect the destroyer the following morning and to set a fee—bound to be shockingly high because of the typhoon season—for adequate coverage.

Hardwicke Shipyards—the company title had been changed two years ago—stood on the threshold of becoming as important as the London firm founded by Elliot's grandfather, which had since been sold to a competitive company.

The night before her meeting with the consular officers Constance invited Sam, Olivia and William to dinner at the Peak house. The dinner wasn't just a celebration of what she and William had accomplished; she wanted to spend tonight with Sam. In the morning he was leaving for Shanghai, where he would meet his sisters and brother-in-law before they left on the first lap of their journey to Tel Aviv.

"Connie, do you know there are now 85,000 Jews in Israel?" Sam had told her. "And with Leah, Sarah and Joseph," he added, grinning, "there will be 85,003."

She would not see Sam for two weeks. Tomorrow Jade would bring Emilie to stay at the Hardwicke house until his return.

"You've accomplished a miracle with the business," Sam told Constance over dinner.

"That's right," William added. "And if war breaks out in Europe, we'll be doing the British government a service. The Russo-Japanese War proved the importance of destroyers. Compared to warships they're inexpensive—an admiral might be afraid to take a daring action with a costly warship, but he could send out a flotilla of destroyers without breaking the Admiralty."

Constance turned to Sam. "Do you think the United States will become involved?"

He looked serious. "I doubt that any nation of consequence in the world will be able to avoid involvement. I'm afraid we're facing a war of world dimensions."

"Thank God Adam is a baby," Constance said passionately. But she was worried . . .

Sam was a British citizen—he would have to fight in a war involving Great Britain. Would Hong Kong be attacked? War was something that should not happen more than once in a lifetime! She would never forget the day the War Department telegram arrived telling Mama that Papa was dead—not on the battlefield, but from a fever he had contracted while fighting in Cuba. To lose Sam this way . . . She tried to shake the thought away.

"Hong Kong won't become a battlefield," Sam was saying. "Our greatest danger has been from the China mainland; but with all their internal troubles, they'll make no move against the island."

Without so much as a touch of his hand. Sam let Constance know how much he would miss her while he was gone. The fact that they could not make love seemed only to strengthen their feelings. Olivia was right, Constance thought—life is made up of a series of compromises. Let Sam and she be grateful not to be in each other's lives. And every day she thanked God for letting her bear his child . . .

Constance woke up the following morning instantly aware that Sam was at this moment heading for the ship that would carry him to Shanghai. His sisters and brother-in-law feared for their lives there. Sam agreed that they must leave for Israel before the world was torn apart by war and it would become impossible to emigrate to Israel.

It was a hot and humid morning—even on the Peak—and the air was almost sickeningly sweet with the blend of scents from the summer-lush gardens along the slopes. Constance knew that if she were going to get any work done today she would have to run the ceiling fan in her office.

Her thoughts kept returning to Sam. It was the beginning of the typhoon season, but today a brilliant sun was shining. In the past five years she had seen several typhoons but none to match that first one on her arrival in Hong Kong. Still, every year Constance worried. She would never forget the woman and her baby in that tiny little boat . . .

By the time she returned to the Peak house, exhausted from the heat, the sun was down and the sky overcast. After a visit with Diana, Adam and Emilie, Constance retired to her room for dinner on the balcony outside her door. At least on the Peak she could breathe.

But tonight sleep eluded her. As thoroughly awake as though it were the middle of the day, Constance tossed restlessly in her bed trying to quiet her fears about Sam. Thank goodness this wasn't one of the rare times Elliot decided to come to the Peak for dinner and stay the night . . .

Shortly before dawn, Constance slipped out from between the fog-dampened sheets, pulled on her robe and slippers, and went to look in on Diana and Emilie. The two little girls slept in a bedroom adjoining the nursery, where Sakota slept with Adam. Diana and Emilie were fast asleep. She tiptoed to the nursery; Adam clung to the teddy bear that Olivia had given him for his first birthday. He had kicked off the damp sheet. Constance went to the "hot cupboard" for a fresh one and brought it to his bed, feeling a surge of tenderness as she covered his tiny body.

On her way back to her own room Constance was all at once aware that a sharp wind was blowing. She turned around and hurried downstairs. In the heavy mists it was impossible to see if a typhoon warning signal had been posted. She telephoned the Meteorological Observatory, worried about the destroyer, which had been anchored along the Praya in preparation for tomorrow's inspection.

She couldn't get through. Others on the Peak must be bombarding the Observatory with calls. Already it seemed that the winds had reached gale force. Constance ran to the servants' quarters to make sure Li had the windows covered. When she opened the door she was hurled back, drenched, against the door. The rain was coming down in sheets.

"Missy go back," Li called. "We come take care windows."

"Thank you, Li."

Constance tried to tell herself that sharp winds and heavy rainfall did not necessarily mean a typhoon was coming. Wouldn't she have heard the typhoon gun by now? Just as she thought of it, the sound of the gun penetrated the night with eerie clarity.

Constance hurried again to the phone, this time to call William, who lived lower down on the slopes.

"I'm heading for the shipyard," he said. "And I'm bringing the houseboys with me. We're going to have to try to take the destroyer to a shelter."

"I'll come down, too," Constance said quickly.

"Constance, you can't make it down from the Peak in this. The tramway is sure to be out. Just look at it out there—trees are being snapped down like twigs . . . "

"God, William, it's not that bad up here," Constance gasped.

"It is below," William said grimly. "Stay there—"

Suddenly the phone was dead. The lines were down. Their destroyer was in danger. And their insurance hadn't yet taken effect. She just couldn't sit up here on the Peak and do nothing. Their entire future depended upon that destroyer. Without it they were lost.

She raced upstairs to her bedroom and dressed. It was as if time slipped away and she was back on the ship with Sam in 1906. Her heart was beating wildly. Disaster strikes so quickly—there was no way to know what havoc it would wreak in the Praya. The destroyer was virtually defenseless against typhoon winds.

Elliot was in the town house. Why hadn't she called him before the phone went dead and sent him to the shipyard? If he wasn't drunk he could help William.

"Missy, don't go to door!" Li warned as she came downstairs and crossed the foyer. "Big winds. Stay inside." The coolies and houseboys were now busy boarding up the windows. Li made sure the front door to the house was locked. "I make tea," he consoled, sensing Constance's fear. "Missy sit in drawing room."

"Thank you, Li." She knew Li was right. She couldn't go outside. She'd have to wait for the typhoon to be over. And pray that it didn't take with it the future of Hardwicke Shipyards.

THE typhoon raged for three hours. It woke the children but to them it was an exciting adventure. Constance paced her bedroom, haunted by the memories of being huddled in Sam's arms aboard that ship only a few knots from Victoria Harbor.

Constance knew that this wasn't as severe as the typhoon of 1906 but it was sure to bring destruction to the Praya. Why couldn't it have held off just one more day? By tomorrow morning an agent from Lloyd's would have completed his inspection and put through the insurance. It would be a blow to have to rebuild the destroyer, but without insurance it would be a devastating loss—if William hadn't been able to move the destroyer to a shelter.

Despite Li's and Mai-Ling's pleas to stay inside Constance went by chair to the tramway station, which was already back in operation. Along the way she saw the trees and shrubs that had been uprooted, the telephone wires that were already being repaired by emergency crews.

At the shipyard she found William—grim and pale—and the emergency crew he had assembled cleaning up debris. Elliot ran towards her.

"I came as soon as I realized what was happening," he told Constance. "Is everything all right up at the Peak?"

"We were barely touched."

"Were the children frightened?" It was the quiet, charming Elliot talking, the one who took her to the races a lifetime ago . . .

"They're fine, Elliot, really." She turned to William. "Is the destroyer all right?"

184

"Constance, it didn't have a chance. Another vessel smashed into her. I don't think we can salvage much of it."

"Well, what about the insurance?" Elliot asked.

"The man from Lloyd's was to come today."

"Good God. I suppose we're in pretty bad shape, then." Elliot's calm infuriated Constance.

"Yes we are in pretty bad shape. In fact, we're on the brink of ruin." Her voice was shrill. "Our whole future rode on that destroyer. We can't get another bank loan to rebuild." She wasn't going to tell him about mortgaging the Peak house. Not yet. They might be able to meet the bank payments on the loans she took out for the earlier expansion, but there was no way to repay this last loan without a large contract from the Admiralty.

"Well, there's no use trying to get money from my family," Elliot said, the old bitterness returning. "My mother put everything into my brothers' hands. They'll have no part of me."

Constance stood completely still, searching for a way to rebuild the destroyer. Their security—her children's future—hung in the balance. She would not let them suffer.

"Wait a minute—I think I know where to get the money." Elliot and William stared at her skeptically. "From my Uncle Lionel."

Elliot laughed.

"Are you mad? Mr. Levy will never advance you that kind of money. It must have cost you a small fortune to build that destroyer."

"The first one, yes," William agreed. "When we were experimenting. Now we know what to do."

"It's still a fortune," Elliot said stubbornly.

"We're gambling on enormous stakes, Elliot," Constance said. "We must raise enough cash to rush through another model. It's a lot of money, I'll admit, but I think my uncle will give us a loan." She felt a rush of confidence. In fact, I'm sure he will—because if he doesn't, I'll create such a scandal that he and Rebecca won't be able to live in England. I'll be leaving for London in twenty-four hours."

Olivia and William already knew about Mr. Mendez. Now, as briefly as possible, Constance told Elliot the story. He wasn't happy with any of it.

"I don't like this idea, Constance. What about the children? You'll be away at least a month."

"I'll ask Olivia if she and William will move into the Peak house until I return—" Her eyes swung to William.

185

"You know we will, Constance," William added.

"And, Elliot, I'll expect you to spend time with the children every day. Will you do that?"

"Yes, yes, I'll be there."

Constance smiled gratefully at him. She knew she could trust him. But he was obviously unsettled by the prospect of her going to the place he had for so long yearned to call home.

She turned to William. "I'll go by the route you followed when you went to France. I'll be in London in fifteen days, and I'll stay for three or four."

From London she would take a train to the village in Suffolk where Uncle Lionel and Aunt Rebecca had settled since his retirement. She would shame her uncle into loaning her the money. After all, it was rightfully Papa's. She would only ask for a loan; the money would be repaid.

Uncle Lionel wouldn't dare refuse her.

CHAPTER

EIGHTEEN

AT ONCE DREADING the separation from her children and wishing she could delay her departure until Sam returned from Shanghai, Constance forced herself to make the necessary arrangements to travel to London. She made reservations on the Trans-Siberian International Express, which connected the Far East with Western Europe, providing transportation from the Pacific to the Atlantic.

William insisted that she travel on the *Wagons-Lits* International, the only one of the three "fast" trains running each week between Shanghai and Moscow that lived up to its *trains de luxe* title. Only now did he confess to the hardships he had encountered in one of the two state-owned so-called luxury trains on his earlier trip to Paris. The *Wagons-Lits* International would get her to Shanghai in three hours, too little time to find Sam for even a few minutes together.

Arriving in Shanghai Constance boarded the ship that would make the forty-four hour voyage across the Yellow Sea to Dalny. The Southern Manchurian Company ship had spacious cabins and offered impeccable service. As the coastline of Shanghai receded, she stood on the deck and looked out at the long English buildings lining the river . . . remembering Sam's scorn for the foreigners who had taken the best of everything.

The trip to Dalny was pleasant, despite the heat, though already Constance missed Diana and Adam. Meals were festive occasions with twenty passengers from all over the world seated around the table. Constance got up to watch the sunrise every morning, and returned to the deck to witness the sunset.

At last they were almost there. A hilly coastline appeared . . . the earth was burgundy red and the waters an azure blue. After the health officers came aboard, the vessel was allowed to enter the harbor. Like several other passengers, Constance arranged to stay the night onboard ship. Tomorrow they would take the train from Dalny —the beautiful little city built, on orders from the Czar, in little more than a year as a terminus for the Express railway service—to Chang Chung, where they would connect with the real Trans-Siberian Railway.

Constance had expected to be bored and lonely during these days of traveling. By now she had grown to love the constant challenges and demands of the office, and she had to force herself to try to relax and enjoy lazy days spent just gazing out a train window.

She was pleased that at least she had been given a *coupe*—compartment—to herself in the spotless sleeping car, with a washbasin and adjoining bathroom. The food served in the dining car was excellent. The stations from Dalny to Chang Chung had both English and Japanese names—because they were traveling through territory now controlled by Japan.

At Chang Chung the next day the passengers en route for the West transferred to the real Trans-Siberian cars, and again Constance was given a *coupe* to herself, beautifully upholstered in velvet, the floor thickly carpeted, with an electric fan. This magnificent *train de luxe*— which had regular sleeping *coupes* and luxurious *cabins de luxe*—would carry them to Irkutsk, the capital of Siberia, where they would simply cross a platform to identical accommodations in which to continue their journey.

A train official in a handsome white uniform bound with gold escorted Constance to her *coupe*, telling her about the salon carriage, the *wagons-restaurant*, the bathtub in the baggage car, and the gymnasium with a stationary bicycle, dumbbells and an "exerciser." When it was time for dinner, Constance went to the dining car, where two clocks were on display, one providing the time in St. Petersburg and the other local time. After sitting down at an elegantly laid table, she noticed the piano at one end of the car and remembered how Mama

—whose parents had lived in a village near St. Petersburg—had spoken with pride of the Russians' love for music.

There were only three courses at dinner, including a vodka before the main course and a cordial afterwards. Constance didn't have much of an appetite because she was already getting nervous about the confrontation with Uncle Lionel. She had such loving memories of him that it pained her to think that there might be an ugly scene when she revealed the purpose of her trip.

She lingered over her cordial, unable to go back to her *coupe* and face the long, lonely night just yet . . .

"Mademoiselle," a deep voice startled her and she glanced up to see a handsome French army officer hovering above her. "Mademoiselle, I could not contain myself another moment. You are the most beautiful young lady I have seen on two continents. May I share your table?"

"Please, I think not," Constance stammered, but it was too late. He had already parked himself in the chair across from her.

"We have all these days ahead of us before we arrive at Paris." He leaned forward and whispered. "How better to spend our time than in each other's company?" He reached for her hand. She pulled it free, color staining her cheeks.

"Please I—I must ask you to leave." Frantically her eyes searched the room. Wasn't there anyone who could help? But they were all laughing and talking—lost in private conversations. Maybe if she just stood up and left . . .

"You will please do as the lady requests." A handsome tawny-haired, blue-eyed young man with an American accent stood by the table.

"As you wish," the Frenchman shrugged. *"Quel dommage."*

Constance practically hugged her rescuer in gratitude. "I can't thank you enough, sir—"

"The name's Field. Dr. David Field, and it's my pleasure. A woman traveling alone can't be too careful . . . would you like to join my wife Frances and myself at our table?"

"Why, Dr. Field, I'd love to."

THUS began a close friendship that lasted throughout the trip to London, where David and Frances planned to spend a week before returning to New York after David's yearlong tenure as a surgeon with the American Presbyterian Mission in Shanghai.

Constance was grateful for the companionship. But sometimes, as she sat alone with Frances in their elegant *cabin de luxe*—which had not only a brass bed, but also a drawing room and its own piano and library—she was embarrassed by Frances's confidences about her shaky marriage.

Frances was a wealthy spoiled New Yorker, and had at first anticipated an exotic first year of marriage in Shanghai. Unfortunately, reality didn't live up to her expectations . . .

"Constance, maybe it was that awful climate, I don't know. I was always flying into rages. I told David he'd have to take me back home —I just couldn't stand it there another minute."

The days passed pleasantly as the train moved westward, stopping occasionally at attractively painted wooden stations where Constance was overwhelmed with homesickness at the sight of barefoot little girls offering bunches of violets, bluebells, and tiger lilies. It was an enthralling journey across vast plains, past endless forests of white and yellow birch, beech and poplar.

Constance was fascinated by David's work in China. Clearly he was a dedicated physician, though he admitted that sometimes his ideas on surgery conflicted with those of his older, more traditional colleagues. In China he had found ways to prove his theories and learned methods not taught in American medical schools, which had become invaluable in his practice.

At Irkutsk Constance and the Fields crossed the platform to the new train that would carry them to Moscow and Warsaw and would connect with the Northern Express running between Warsaw and London. As the train sped across Siberia Constance remembered the stories Mama had told her about Russia . . . It was hard to believe that this country she was speeding across so luxuriously was the same land in which Mama's family lived in a tiny hut with a dirt floor —in daily terror that they would be killed during a pogrom.

As they approached Moscow, Constance tried to express her feelings to the Fields.

"I know," David said quietly as Frances looked on in confusion. "My grandfather emigrated from Russia in 1856 with his wife and their first child—my great-uncle Jacob. This was at the end of the reign of Nicholas I—a nightmare for all Jews." Constance stared at David in astonishment; she didn't know the Fields were Jewish. Hadn't he said he was attached to the Presbyterian Mission? "My grandfather was determined that his son would not be conscripted for the Czar's army at the age of eight. He had no intention of fighting for the Czar himself."

"Come now, David. Your grandfather fought for the Confederacy." Frances was obviously furious. So, Constance thought, the family had become assimilated . . .

"Constance," Frances smiled sweetly, "if you ever come to New York, you simply must visit us. Papa built us the most gorgeous house as a wedding present."

SIXTEEN-AND-A-HALF days after Constance left Shanghai she arrived in London. After exchanging addresses and warm farewells with Frances and David—who insisted on seeing her to her modest hotel on Russell Square—she was, once again, alone.

At the hotel she was given a pretty room with a fireplace, lilacs in a Burmese glass vase sitting on top of a mahogany chiffonier.

Though it was June, a maid had prepared a fire in the grate. Before going to bed, Constance sat before the cozy fire feeling like she was suspended in time. She was here in Mama's and Papa's London. Tears came to her eyes as she imagined Mama, laughing and pretty, walking beside Papa down the narrow streets . . .

She could remember only dimly the three fog-ridden days she had spent in London almost seven years ago, when she traveled with Mr. and Mrs. Hirsch to Shanghai. She had been too numb with grief then to enjoy the history-rich city around her. It seemed a lifetime had been crammed into the past seven years.

The next morning, after tea and a scone, Constance took a bus to Euston Station and boarded a train that would carry her to the village in Suffolk where Uncle Lionel and Aunt Rebecca lived. She had purposely not telephoned them ahead of time—instinct told her that taking them by surprise would be to her advantage . . .

Sitting on the train as it left the city for the lush and rolling English countryside, Constance was stricken with doubts. How could she convince Uncle Lionel and Aunt Rebecca she had proof that Papa had been cheated out of his inheritance? What if they didn't even remember Mr. Mendez? She had taken the precaution of talking to another elderly resident of the British Crown Colony who also attested that Levy Trading Company had been a prosperous firm before Uncle Lionel arrived in Hong Kong.

191

Papa must have known and confided this to Mr. Gomez. But Papa would not have fought over his father's estate. Anyway, he was doing so well in his own position; how was he to know that he would die, leaving Mama almost penniless? Leaving his only child orphaned at twelve?

She must be confident when she met Uncle Lionel and Aunt Rebecca, show them that she wouldn't hesitate a minute to take them into court to right this terrible wrong. How could Uncle Lionel have treated Papa—his brother—so badly? She had always thought he was such a kind man . . . but suddenly she understood; Uncle Lionel was no match for Aunt Rebecca. It must have been her greedy influence that pushed him into cheating Papa.

The train pulled to a stop at a tidy rural station. Constance found a taxi waiting to take her to the Levy's. Her throat tightened in fear as she stepped out of the taxi and stood in front of a fifteenth-century country manor house, surrounded by tall, old walnut trees and with a stone fence separating it from the country road.

A maid opened the door for her.

"Who is it, Alice?" Rebecca's imperious voice drifted to the foyer.

"A visitor, ma'am," Alice called back sullenly. Clearly Rebecca had endeared herself to her servants here in much the same manner as she had in the Colony. "A Mrs. Hardwicke to see you, madam."

There was a long silence.

"Show Mrs. Hardwicke into the drawing room. I'll be there directly."

WHEN the maid opened the door letting Constance into the drawing room she was astonished to see the photograph of Diana and Adam that she had sent Uncle Lionel sitting in a gold leaf frame on the mantelpiece. A wave of homesickness swept over her . . .

"Constance?" Lionel's voice cracked with surprise and pleasure.

"Uncle Lionel!" She rushed into his arms. "It's so good to see you!" And it was. If it weren't for Diana and Adam she would never do this to him . . .

"Is Elliot with you? And the children?"

"They're in the Colony," she stammered. Wasn't there some other way to do this?

"You're looking well." He was clearly puzzled by her presence.

"What brings you to England?" Rebecca asked from the doorway.

There was no pretense of welcome in her voice.

"Business," Constance said. "For the shipyard." True.

"You might have telephoned us from London, my dear." Lionel winced. "But I don't suppose Americans think of such niceties."

"Constance, you'll be staying with us, won't you?" Lionel asked, anxious to make her feel welcome. Constance saw Rebecca grimace.

"Thank you, Uncle Lionel, but I'm afraid I must return to London this afternoon." That seemed to please Rebecca. She strode into the room briskly.

"Oh dear, isn't that a pity . . . Lionel, aren't you going to ask the child to sit down? Honestly, where are your manners?"

"Oh, I'm sorry, Constance. Do sit down," Lionel drew her to the sofa. Rebecca sat stiffly across from them. "Tell us about how you are doing in the business." Lionel leaned forward eagerly. "I must say, from the little of it you mention—in between stories about Diana and Adam—it sounds like you're becoming quite the business-woman."

"Someone had to take over the shipyard," Constance said with a faint smile. "Elliot was neglecting the business. I mean—it's not that he meant to," she added quickly. "It's just that he's wrapped up in his painting."

"I never hear from Elliot," Rebecca said, her voice edged in re-proach. "What happened when his father died?"

"Elliot was disinherited. Of course, he has the shipyard. His father gave him that while he was alive. Since Diana was a baby I've run the shipyard with the help of the engineer Elliot's father sent from London." *Now,* she ordered herself, and her heart began to pound. *Now.*

"You run the shipyard?" Rebecca regarded her suspiciously.

"Yes, I run it," Constance shot back. "I've built it up from ship repair to ship building. We were in line for a contract with the British Admiralty when our model destroyer was wrecked in the typhoon last month. The insurance to cover its cost had not yet gone through. Now we must raise funds to rebuild the model."

"Surely you're not so naive as to expect Elliot's family to loan you the money?" Rebecca smiled demurely. "After his father disinherited him?"

"No, I don't expect them to loan us the money," Constance said quietly. "I expect Uncle Lionel to." Her eyes swung to Uncle Lionel.

Rebecca's voice was flat.

"You've wasted a trip."

"I think not," Constance pursued, her heart thumping. "After all, half of Levy Trading belonged to my father."

Constance watched the blood drain from Uncle Lionel's face. Rebecca jumped up, her hands clenched into fists.

"How do you have the gall to make such an insane accusation?"

"I've talked to men in the Colony who remember my grandfather. They told me that he built Levy Trading into a fine business before he died. Mr. Mendez said he couldn't understand why Papa never came out to Hong Kong to share in what his father had built up for his two sons."

"Louis Mendez?" Lionel asked. "The old fellow is still alive? We haven't seen him for nearly fifteen years."

"He returned from Shanghai after the revolution. And ready to testify if necessary." She tried to keep the quiver out of her voice.

Rebecca sat down stiffly on the edge of the chair.

"Constance, you are terribly misinformed and I—"

"Tell me how much you need," Lionel interrupted. "I will arrange to transfer the money into your Hong Kong account."

Rebecca, aghast, turned to her husband. "Lionel! Have you lost your mind?"

"No, Rebecca. I think I might just have found it. Come come, dear. We're getting on in years. It's time we put our house in order. I'll go with you into London, Constance. The money will not be a loan. It will be a settlement of a debt long past due."

CONSTANCE breezed through the return trip to Hong Kong, exhilarated by her success. Within four months the new model would be ready to demonstrate and they would get a contract from the Admiralty. Diana's and Adam's future would be secure.

But the new model took longer than Constance and William had estimated. An important shipment of materials was sunk by pirates, delaying the project seven weeks. Not until early January 1914 was the boat ready to be shown to the consular officers in Hong Kong.

Elliot—as titular owner of Hardwicke Shipyards—was to accompany Constance to the Praya to meet with the men from the consulate. When he did not appear at the office, William hurried to the house and found him fast asleep, a half-empty bottle of Scotch at his elbow.

194

Constance and William met with the officials. They were impressed with the performance of the destroyer and they wanted to begin negotiations with the Hardwicke Shipyards. Jubilant at their success, Constance, and William returned to the shipyard. Sam was pacing in the office.

"What happened?" he demanded. "I've been waiting here an hour—"

"They think it'll be an asset to the British Navy, that's what happened!" William could barely contain his excitement.

"Elliot promised that he'd go with us." Constance gave Sam a significant look. "But he couldn't make it." Sam would know what she meant . . .

"Constance, you'll have to talk to Elliot about making you legally responsible for the operation of the shipyard," Sam said. "The British Admiralty isn't some local operation that'll do business with a handshake. I think you should talk to him immediately."

Constance wasn't convinced.

"Do you think they'll do business with a woman?"

"Constance, my love," William chuckled, "England was ruled by a woman for over sixty years. I think they can accept you as head of a shipyard."

Negotiations dragged on for months, but they were all confident a sale would go through. On June fourteenth, 1914, the world was shocked by the assassination of Archduke Francis Ferdinand, heir to the thrones of Austria and Hungary, and of his wife Sophia. War seemed imminent. And many in the Colony were sure that Great Britain would become involved.

While Constance was eager to build the destroyers for Great Britain, it unnerved her to think that men would die on her boats. Though she had been a child when the United States fought in the Spanish-American War, she remembered Mama's scorn for those who thought of war as romantic and exciting. War meant death— Papa's death. War meant widows—Mama. And war meant orphans —herself.

On July twenty-eighth Austria-Hungary declared war on Serbia. By October thirtieth the Central Powers, which included Austria-Hungary, Germany, and the Ottoman Empire were at war with the Allies—Great Britain, France, Russia, Belgium, and Serbia. The month before the Allies had stopped the German advance at the First

Battle of the Marne, eliminating Germany's hopes for a speedy victory.

In Hong Kong Englishmen were rushing to volunteer for the British forces. Others joined the Hong Kong Volunteers. The shipyard lost half a dozen men to the British army. Sam wouldn't volunteer for service, would he? He couldn't leave Emilie alone, and he had his business that was so demanding—both the hong and his growing real estate domain. Mr. Telford was talking about resigning, selling out to Sam. No. She would not let herself think about Sam fighting in this war . . .

Sam was relieved that his sisters and brother-in-law left for Israel when they did. Since the outbreak of war immigration had ceased. But he worried about them incessantly. Palestine was serving the Turks—and their German allies—as the base for attacks upon the Suez Canal and Egypt. One early December evening when he came to Constance's house for dinner along with Olivia and William, he seemed particularly distracted.

"Sam, what's bothering you?" Constance asked softly while Olivia took William upstairs to visit Diana and Adam.

"Oh, Connie," he sighed. "It's what I hear from Israel. Word has come that seven hundred Jews who were nationals of enemy states have been deported to Egypt. Now there appears to be a mass exodus. I worry about what will happen to my sisters and Joseph. In Shanghai they became British citizens. To the Turks they're the enemy."

"Have you heard from your family?"

"It's difficult for letters to get through. Before the outbreak of the war, the Turks didn't bother the Jewish settlers. But things are different now."

"Sam, if they're sent to Egypt, they'll be safe in British hands." If only she knew what to say to comfort him . . . She started at the sound of someone at the door. Li was already hurrying on silken-quiet feet to respond to the caller. Who could it be?

"Li, please tell Mrs. Hardwicke to join me immediately in the studio." Elliot's voice, oddly urgent, drifted into the drawing room.

"Sam, please excuse me." Unnerved by Elliot's unexpected appearance—he had been here only yesterday—Constance rose to her feet and hurried across the pair of exquisite oriental rugs.

"Master wish to see in studio, Missy." Li met her at the entrance to the drawing room.

"Thank you, Li."

She walked down the hall to the studio. The door was ajar. "Elliot? What's happened?"

Elliot swung about to face her.

"Constance, I have decided to go back to London to volunteer for the British army." Constance stood completely still, stunned. Was he serious?

"Elliot, no! The children—" She stopped, seeing the determined look in his eyes.

"The children will do well without me." His smile was ironic. "Like other British children they'll survive if their father goes to fight for the British Empire. Someday Adam and Diana may boast about their father, who served in His Majesty's forces."

"Elliot, why are you doing this?" This wasn't like Elliot at all. "Why don't you join the Hong Kong Volunteers instead?" She felt desperate, unhinged. She knew that she wasn't in love with Elliot, but she felt a strong tie to him. And the children would bind them together forever.

"I plan to join the British Army. My brothers are too old. My father is dead. I'm the only Hardwicke in our branch of the family that can serve His Majesty. Just once the youngest, unwanted son will uphold family honor. I can't—I won't—deny myself that satisfaction."

"Well—when will you leave?" Constance stammered.

"By the end of the week. I want to spend some time with Diana and Adam first. You'll be safe here. It's not likely that the island will be attacked. And you have William to help you with the shipyard. You'll hardly miss me at all."

"I will miss you," she said softly. And she realized it was true. "The children will miss you. I'll pray this war ends swiftly, and you'll come back to us safely. Elliot, please. Be careful."

CHAPTER

NINETEEN

A T THE END of the week Constance, Diana and Adam saw Elliot off for England. An almost-six Diana was starry-eyed over her brave Papa going off to war, but Adam was too young to understand. Constance spared Diana a lecture on what war really meant—that many of those men on the boat wouldn't be coming home . . . Why destroy the little pockets of happiness in the world?

She returned to the Peak house sobered by her realization of all the responsibilities she must shoulder in Elliot's absence. And the children would miss him. Did she have enough love for both of them? He adored Diana, always spoiled her, and idolized Adam. She had always assumed that his reclusive nature and devotion to the children would keep him in the Colony.

But Constance knew it would have been useless to try to persuade him to stay once he had made up his mind. It would have been wrong, too. Elliot saw this war as an opportunity to prove himself—to at last be vindicated of the disgrace that had torn him from his family. She would not take this chance from him.

Knowing Constance would be depressed, Olivia phoned her at the office next morning and insisted she come to dinner. Without asking, Constance knew Sam would be there. She and William came directly from the office. The three of them were sitting in the drawing room discussing the island's diminishing labor force when Sam arrived.

Constance felt her heart leap at the sound of Sam's voice in the foyer. But she went cold with fear when he walked into the drawing room. He was wearing the uniform of the Hong Kong Volunteers.

"When did you volunteer?" Constance tried to conceal her alarm. Sam would be all right; the fighting would not involve the Colony.

"This morning," Sam said. His face was serious. "It's the very least I can do. And this way I can continue to run Telford & Latham and the real estate business." Sam paused. "I received a letter from Leah. Joseph was one of the people exiled to Egypt. He was accused of harboring Zionist sentiments."

"He'll be safe in Egypt, Sam," Constance said quietly.

"I'll sign up for the Volunteers if they'll have me," William said quietly. Only for an instant did Olivia's calm demeanor desert her. Constance suspected that William was acting on impulse. "We're going to see a lot of changes on the island," he warned. "Two more of our best workers are quitting to go into service. A lot of the Chinese are worrying that we're going to be attacked. I suspect we'll lose a substantial number of them."

Their whole world was changing, Constance thought uneasily, just when she had learned to cope with her own life another upheaval wrenched her back into confusion. But she had a job to do. She was building destroyers for the British Navy. Through war Hardwicke Shipyards would become a rich and powerful firm. And men would die.

All through dinner Constance felt Sam's eyes on her. He knew that Elliot had left yesterday for England; but surely he must understand that especially with Elliot in service they could share no more than what they had already allowed themselves.

When letters arrived telling Olivia that her daughters' husbands had both gone into service, she immediately joined a local war charity being formed in the Colony. Constance promised to help in her free time. She contrived ways to see Sam at every possible moment, always reminding herself that they must not overstep the boundaries they had set for themselves. But war had lent a fresh urgency to their love for each other.

In every household in the Colony the war became the main topic of conversation. The opening battles were over by early 1915: it seemed that there would be a stalemate. Six hundred miles of trenches crossed French soil from the Swiss border to the English Channel. Millions of soldiers lived in mud and filth, facing one another across a vast "no man's land."

Occasionally Sam received letters from his family in Israel. They lived in the crowded Egyptian barracks at Gabbari where the British gave the exiles shelter while the Jewish community of Egypt fed and clothed them. Joseph, like many others, was convinced that the Ottoman Empire would be defeated, that its lands in the Middle East would be wrenched from Turkish control. Jews in Israel were raising a claim to "reconstitute a national home in Palestine." Sam was ecstatic at such a prospect.

One Friday evening in March Constance attended services at Ohel Leah Synagogue alone—Olivia stayed home with a cold. Except for dinners at the Converse house this was her sole contact with anyone other than the workers at the shipyard, where she and William were fighting to stay on schedule despite the continuous loss of labor and the need to train new employees. As always Sam was waiting when she arrived.

"Where's Olivia?" he asked, genuinely concerned.

"She wanted to come, but William insisted she stay home. She has a terrible cold."

"I'll drive you home after services," Sam said. He had recently bought an automobile because he was convinced that useable roads would soon extend far up the slopes. "Oh, a bulletin from Emilie," he reported with a smile. "She informs me that she means to wait to start school until Adam can go with her."

"Next year she'll be ready for school." Constance was always self-conscious with Sam at public meetings even though she knew that no one suspected . . .

They were joined by several members of the congregation who were intrigued that a woman—a young and beautiful woman—was in the business of building destroyers for the British Admiralty. At the same time Constance could tell they were proud that a woman of their own community was so active in the war effort.

Sitting upstairs in the balcony during the services, she was conscious of Sam's eyes following her. Tonight Sam would drive her home . . . They would be alone in the car. But maybe he would drive someone else home, too—no, he wouldn't. Out of respect for the members of the congregation who were affronted by those who drove on the Sabbath, Sam always left his car a short distance from the synagogue; he would hesitate to offer to drive anyone else home.

At last the services were over. Tonight Sam chose not to dawdle over conversation; he hurried her out of the synagogue and to the car.

"Connie, I have to talk to you," he said as they approached the Daimler. "Please, let me take you to my house for tea before I drive you home."

"Sam, we shouldn't," she whispered. "We can't afford to have people talk."

"We must," he insisted. "I have things that must be said. There is something I must ask of you."

"All right, Sam. But just this once." There was something different in his tone—an urgency . . .

On the short drive to the house while they tried to chatter about innocuous topics—the children, the weather, the government—the question repeated itself in her mind: What was it that Sam wanted to ask her?

At the house Sam looked in briefly on Emilie. Both Emilie and her *amah,* who shared her room, were sound asleep. The servants were in their quarters behind the house.

"I'll fix tea for us," Sam said and grinned. "We won't tell the servants. Can't have the Master losing face."

"Let me help," Constance offered. She could tell that Sam was preparing himself for what he meant to ask her.

Over fragrant jasmine tea served in delicate Waterford cups Sam told her what he had been struggling with for weeks.

"Connie, I want to go to Egypt to join my brother-in-law. There are two men named Jabotinsky and Trumpeldor there, looking to form a Jewish legion to serve under the British in Palestine." His face was animated as he spoke. "This is the time when the roots of a Jewish state must be planted. I have to be part of that effort. But I can go only if you will take Emilie while I'm away." He reached for her hand in mute apology. "I know I'm asking you to take on a great responsibility—"

"Of course I'll take Emilie." Constance tried to contain her fears. Sam fighting in this awful war. But as with Elliot she knew that it would be wrong to stand in Sam's way. But what if he died in a strange land—away from Emilie, away from her?

"Sam, isn't there some other way for you to show your support? Why couldn't you send money to support the efforts to form a Jewish legion?" But she knew it was futile. What if she never saw him again?

201

"I have to go, my darling." He brought her hand to his lips. His eyes framed a question that made her tremble. "And when I come back, Connie, you'll divorce Elliot. How much longer must you play this charade with him? And you know that when this bloody war is over, Elliot will want to return to London. He'll have redeemed himself in his family's eyes. He's made it clear that he loathes Hong Kong." As deeply as she loved Sam, she had never told him the reason for Elliot's disgrace in the eyes of his family; yet she suspected that he somehow knew, had guessed, as had William. "Connie, a divorce won't bring shame on the children. The Victorian age is behind us. Elliot will agree to it. We can be married."

"Sam, if I could believe that could happen—"

"It will happen. We can't deny ourselves for the rest of our lives. Connie, I can't leave without knowing I can come back to Hong Kong and you. To you and my daughter and my son."

Constance was momentarily stunned. So he had known all along . . . she had suspected as much.

"You've always known about Adam, haven't you Sam?" she said softly.

"From the moment I saw him lying in that cradle. I never in my life felt such pride, such happiness. From our love our son was born."

"Sam, come home safely."

"I will. Because now I have something to come home to." He drew her into his arms. "In my heart you've always been my wife."

She knew she could not let Sam leave without their making love. Hand in hand they walked up the stairs and into his bedroom. This little while would be theirs alone. She stood immobile beside the bed while Sam drew the drapes tight against the night and then came to her.

"There'll only be one woman in my life," he told her, pulling her close. "You are that woman, Connie. I think I knew the first time we met on board the ship from Shanghai."

His mouth was warm and sweet and eager. She closed her eyes and abandoned herself to the feelings, murmuring faint reproach as his mouth withdrew from hers. Yet her lips curved in an expectant smile while he tenderly undressed her. One slender hand reached out to touch his shoulder as though to reassure herself that Sam was truly here.

"Connie, you're beautiful," he whispered as they lay side by side, bodies barely touching.

"Turn off the light," she whispered.

"Let me look at you another few moments." He ran his hand over her breasts. "Let me have this to remember."

"Sam, I love you." Why couldn't this moment last forever?

As her hand touched his hip, he groaned, no longer able to hide his excitement, and reached over to turn off the light. In the darkness he pulled her close. His mouth at her throat, his hands caressing her breasts. Her own hands gently pressing, searching . . . Soft sounds of passion welling in her throat as they moved against each other in growing urgency.

"Connie? he asked tentatively.

"Yes, darling, yes!"

FOUR days later, with Olivia at her side, Constance saw Sam off on the first lap of his journey to Egypt. Once again the one she loved was leaving her . . . The war took on a fresh horror for her. Occasionally she received brief letters from Elliot; she knew that he was frustrated at being tied to a desk job in London, but at least he was safe. Somehow she knew that Sam would be on the firing line.

From New York came another letter from David Field—signed "David and Frances." Constance was quite sure Frances had long ago forgotten their companion on the Trans-Siberian Railroad . . .

She always answered David's letters immediately, writing mostly about the children because he had seemed so interested in her family. When this latest letter arrived, Constance opened it with a sense of dread—she was sure that David was in some way going to get involved in the war. She was right; he had joined with the British, feeling his services as a doctor were needed.

Hong Kong continued to lose its citizenry. The year before, 72,296 people had fled the island and the pace didn't seem to be slowing. Constance spent long hours at the shipyards every day, determined to help in the British war effort though in her heart she hated killing for any cause. Inflation was rampant, the export trade brisk. And in Hong Kong and Kowloon, as if there was nothing extraordinary about these times, eighteen hundred flowering trees and shrubs, plus three hundred poincianas, were planted to add to the area's beauty.

"The war seems so far away here," Olivia said wistfully, as the two ate dinner at Constance's house on one of William's chess nights. "I think of Annie and Betsy in England with their families, trying to go on about their business as those awful Zeppelins attack. The husbands fighting in France. I can't imagine London with the street lamps covered with black paint, antiaircraft guns set up about the city. I know food is short, though Betsy and Annie both insist they're managing."

"Livvy, you're always sending them food packages," Constance reminded her tenderly.

"But they take forever to be delivered these days." Olivia sighed. "And I wonder how many arrive."

Letters from Sam were slow in coming, but Constance learned that he was now a part of the Zion Mule Corps, 650 strong. Though many Jews were insulted by Britain's arrogance at offering the Jews only this assignment, Sam agreed with Trumpeldor—and ultimately Jabotinsky capitulated—that it was important for the Jews to be involved with the British in any capacity in the fight against the Turks—even if it meant tending to the army mules on the Turkish front. The Zion Mule Corps was under the command of Irish-Protestant Colonel John Henry Patterson, whose devotion to Zionism earned Sam's deepest respect.

"Colonel Patterson," Sam wrote, "is a Bible-quoting Christian gentleman who has fervent Zionist beliefs. In the Bible God gave the Holy Land to Abraham. Therefore, as a Christian who believes in the Bible, Patterson also believes in Zionism. He feels that a Jewish homeland in no way conflicts with those Jews who have homes in friendly countries, but that a national home must be made available for those who face persecution and exile."

Elliot was relieved of duty in the War Department offices in London and joined an artillery division scheduled to leave shortly for France. The Allies had been shocked by the introduction of poison gas by the Germans, though it soon became clear that this new weapon of war would be little more than a nuisance.

Constance learned to live like other women whose loved ones were off fighting a war. She lived day by day, clinging to her sanity by focusing on the needs of her business and her children. Letters were the only source of hope—and they were few and far between. Elliot wrote terse notes laced with his distaste for the business of killing. Apparently his earlier zeal for proving himself to his family had disintegrated into disillusionment and fear. Constance's heart went out to him . . .

In June 1916 Constance got a letter from Sam saying that the Zion

Mule Corps had disbanded because they refused to serve in Ireland —even though they had performed with distinction in the nine-month siege on the Gallipoli Peninsula. Joseph was killed during the fifth month of the operation, which cost Great Britain two hundred fifty thousand casualties and ended in defeat. But Sam was philo-sophical about Joseph's death; it was a tragedy, yes—but it was an honor to die for a cause that Jews around the world supported. Constance was sure that Joseph's wife was less philosophical—as she would be—but that was the difference between men and women.

Sam was furious that the Zion Mule Corps had disbanded. But he had already signed up with another British unit, still clinging to the hope that Jabotinsky would persuade the British to establish a Jewish legion.

MONTHS became years. To the children, Elliot and Sam were war heroes—an image that Constance did her best to protect. And to her delight, Diana was already showing signs of having inherited Elliot's talent for painting. Largely through Constance's connections Emilie was at last admitted to the school for European children. But Con-stance moved through the days with a very small part of herself buried. When—if—they returned home safe she vowed that she would divorce Elliot. Sam was right—it was their turn for some happiness . . .

In the late spring of 1917 Prime Minister Lloyd George made the first overtures for the formation of a Jewish legion, though it wasn't until August that an official announcement appeared in the *London Gazette.* At that time Colonel Patterson, then in Ireland, was assigned commander of the "Jewish Regiment." The prospect of a new mili-tary unit to be called the Jewish Regiment upset many influential Jews—except for Chaim Weizmann and Lord Rothschild. The Jewish Regiment officially became known as the Royal Fusiliers, though everywhere they were referred to as the "Jewish legion."

Sam wrote that Patterson had arranged for the transfer of 120 veterans of the Zion Mule Corps—himself included—to the new legion. He had met a New York–born young Englishman named Jacob Epstein, who talked incessantly about one day becoming a sculptor, and both had just been recommended for a commission. He told her, too, about a young American woman—Golda Meir, from Milwaukee in the state of Wisconsin—who had fought to join the

Jewish legion but had been rejected because she was a woman.

On November second, 1917. Lord Balfour, the British Foreign Secretary, issued a letter to Lord Rothschild which pledged British support for "the establishment in Palestine of a National Home for the Jewish people." Wherever you are Sam, Constance thought, I share this joy with you . . .

ON November seventeenth, the Bolsheviks seized power in Russia. British and American newspapers insisted the Bolshevik reign couldn't last. The Allies were stunned when the new Russian government proceeded to withdraw from the war, freeing the Germans from Russian attack on the Eastern Front, and the world was shocked again the following year when word leaked out of Russia that the entire Russian royal family had been executed.

In November 1918 word flashed around the globe that the most terrible war the world had ever seen was over. Constance immediately reopened the town house and staffed it with servants. Before he left Elliot had shipped Ch'en off to the mainland and while Constance doubted that he would reappear in their lives, she suspected that Elliot would want to resume living in his private quarters. Until —if Sam was right—he decided to return to London.

Constance waited anxiously for word from Elliot and Sam. It was late December and Hong Kong was at its loveliest. Typhoon threats were past and the weather was mild and comfortable. With peace assured, a gentle euphoria permeated the Crown Colony.

One balmy Sunday morning Constance sat in a chair on the verandah while Diana struggled over a painting a dozen feet away. In the distance church bells rang.

"Mama, I hear a motorcar." A tall and slender Diana walked over to the window. The roads had showed some improvement in the past few years, but motorcars on the Peak were still rare.

Constance and Diana sat in silence, both thinking the same thought but not daring to say it . . . Constance rose to her feet as a British Army truck from the Hong Kong barracks pulled to a stop in front of the house. Puzzled, she watched while the driver jumped down and walked to the rear of the truck.

From the rear another man emerged and together they lifted out a wheelchair. They must have the wrong address, Constance thought in confusion. A face appeared. *Elliot.*

Constance stood absolutely still, watching the two men help Elliot, in his major's uniform, out of the truck and into the wheelchair.

"Elliot!" Numb, she left the verandah and hurried down the path. Dear God, this couldn't be happening . . . Why hadn't he written and told her? But she mustn't let him see her fear. "Elliot, why didn't you let us know you were coming home? We would have met you at the ship. Diana," she called, "your father's home!" As if he had just come back from buying the morning paper . . .

"You can go now." Tersely Elliot dismissed the soldiers after submitting to a kiss on the cheek from Constance.

The soldiers saluted and withdrew to the truck. Constance tried to think clearly. She wouldn't—couldn't—think about what this meant. Grimly she focused on the immediate problems . . . The coolies could maneuver the wheelchair up the steps to the verandah, but shouldn't Elliot's bedroom be moved to the lower floor? Would he need a nurse?

"It's been so long since we've heard from you, Elliot." Constance struggled to keep her voice light. "Diana, come welcome your father home."

Was Elliot going to be in a wheelchair forever? If so, how in God's name could she divorce him for Sam? She would have to spend the rest of her life with a cripple . . .

Shyly Diana approached her father.

"My God, how you've grown." Elliot spoke gently. "Diana, you're lovely. Like your mother."

"Diana," Constance said, "tell Papa about your painting."

While Elliot and Diana talked, Constance went into the house to summon help with the wheelchair. She mustn't let him see how upset she was. But how selfish of her not to think of his feelings. Maybe she should send for Dr. Arnold . . .

"Where's Adam?" Elliot asked Diana as Constance returned with two coolies.

"Oh, he's with Emilie out behind the house. He's teaching her to ride a bicycle. He's always with her." She sighed in exasperation.

"Who's Emilie?" Elliot looked puzzled.

"Emilie Stone," Diana said. "She lives with us. Ever since her father went to war."

"Sam Stone's daughter, Elliot," Constance explained, trying not to sound self-conscious. "There was no one else to take her in. She's a darling child."

"Fine. Well, I suppose I'll need a bedroom on the first floor. I don't want to be stuck upstairs. And we'll need a ramp so I can get this chair outside without having to call for help every ten minutes."

"I'll take care of it tomorrow, Elliot. Promise." Constance smiled.

"You always were so damned efficient." His smile was twisted. "My father would have welcomed a son like you." He paused. "Constance, I guess I should tell you now—I'll never get out of this chair." He waited for her reaction.

"Oh Elliot, I—I'm so sorry." She knew it wasn't enough. But what was there to say? She was sorry—for him, for herself, for Sam . . . She must not let him know that he had just destroyed two people's dreams. How awful it must be for him—to know that he would spend the rest of his life in a wheelchair. "We'll do everything we can to make you comfortable. Won't we, Diana?" She hesitated. "You never wrote a word about this." Hoping he couldn't detect the reproach in her voice.

"It happened nine days before the Armistice." He slammed a fist on the arm of his chair. "God, I go over and over it in my head. If only the war had ended ten days earlier . . . " He took a deep breath. "The doctors wanted to keep me in the hospital longer. But there was nothing else they could do for me. They knew it. I knew it. I told them I wanted to go home." At last Hong Kong was home, Constance thought. Had he finally washed England out of his life?

She signalled to the coolies and they pulled the chair upstairs. She saw Elliot wince in pain.

"Careful," she ordered sharply. "You mustn't jolt the Master."

First thing tomorrow she would arrange for ramps. Elliot must have some independence.

"You know, Elliot, this is wonderful weather for painting. We'll set up a place outdoors for you."

"Send in Adam." Elliot was brusque. "I'd like to see my son."

ON a Saturday in early January Sam was within hours of arriving at Hong Kong. At last. He had been frustrated by countless delays on the trip. But now that he stood on the deck of a steamer as it approached Victoria Harbor he was swamped with worries. He had been away for almost four years. Emilie will have turned nine last month; when he had left, she hadn't even started school. His face softened; bless Connie for arranging for Emilie to go to the school for

European children. Bless Connie for loving him.

There had been times when he feared he would not survive the war. And there were times when he didn't want to—when he held a dying comrade in his arms, when he learned that Joseph had been killed. He would never admit to Constance how disillusioned he had become with this war—with war in general. It was only the hope for a Jewish homeland that sustained him on the battlefield. That and the memory of Constance's promise to divorce Elliot and marry him when it was all over. Now, finally, they would begin to live. As Israel would live.

Even though Sam was exhausted he stayed on deck waiting for the first sight of Victoria Harbor. First he would see Connie, Emilie and Adam—his son. The thought of it filled him with pride. And Diana, who seemed almost his own because she was Connie's child. Tomorrow he would go to the hong.

He smiled. Frank Telford would be relieved to see him. Now Frank could retire. Telford & Latham would become Stone & Telford. And later he would resume his real estate activities. Yes, it was going to be a wonderful life . . .

The ship came into harbor early in the afternoon. The familiar beauty of the island, wrapped in sunlight, brought tears to his eyes. Nothing had changed. He should have written to tell Connie he was on his way home but he probably would have arrived before the letter. Now that he was really here he couldn't wait to hold Connie in his arms . . . to see his daughter and his son. Someday Adam would know . . .

On the Praya Sam—in his captain's uniform—swung his duffel bag over one shoulder and summoned a ricksha to take him to the tramway. It was a Saturday afternoon. Constance would be at the house. Almost dizzy with anticipation he gazed out the tramway window. Would Emilie remember him? And what about Adam and Diana, who called him "Uncle Sam"?

He left the tram station and walked to the Hardwicke house. New houses had been built in his absence. Brilliant red and green poinsettia were everywhere.

Tonight he would sleep in his own bed, in his own house. He would stand under a shower and feel clean for the first time in years. And he and Connie would talk about their new life. A shared life. Someday he would take his wife to Israel.

As he rounded a bend in the road the house appeared and an aching

209

tenderness suffused him. His walk became a run. From behind the house he heard the sound of children's voices.

There was Constance moving gracefully in a soft gray dress. He opened his mouth to call out to her, but the words froze in his throat. She was pushing someone—a man—in a wheelchair. Good God. *Elliot.* From the way she held her shoulders as she hovered over him, Sam could see that she was upset.

In a single moment all his hopes for the future were dashed. Constance didn't have to tell him; she couldn't divorce a husband who had been reduced to helplessness.

He paused. Maybe now wasn't the time for a visit after all. But he couldn't wait. He was home. He had come to the Hardwicke house to collect his child. That was all. Elliot wouldn't suspect.

"Hello there," he called out, and a pain shot through him as Constance turned to face him. Such delight on her face at the sound of his voice—and then anguish because she knew—as he knew—that their dream was dead.

"Sam, how wonderful to see you!" She rushed forward with her arms out.

"It's wonderful to be home." His eyes told her he understood.

"Elliot, Emilie's father is back." She was trying so hard to be casual.

Elliot turned the chair around to face Sam. His gaze trailed over Sam's uniform.

"Where were you?"

"Egypt and Palestine," Sam said. "And you?"

"The muddy trenches of France," Elliot said bitterly. "I caught a bullet in the side that traveled across to my spine at Aulnoye. Nine days before the Germans knew they had lost and asked for an armistice."

"God that's tough. I'm sorry." Sam was truly sorry for Elliot. But why did it have to happen?

"Sam, you'll hardly recognize Emilie." Constance's voice was unnaturally high. "She's so grown-up you won't believe it. And she's beautiful."

Elliot shifted slightly, grimacing in the effort. "Constance is always after me to do portraits of the children. She seems to think it's such a simple thing to do. But since the war I find I don't like to paint people. I prefer landscapes."

Constance tore her eyes from Sam's. "I'll get Emilie. And Diana and Adam too."

210

"I'm sure I won't recognize any of them." How could they stand here making small talk when their lives were crumbling around them? "Diana must be about ten now."

"Yes, she's a year older than Emilie. And Adam's eight." She hesitated.

"Well for God's sake go get them then," Elliot barked. "That's the trouble with women. They talk so damn much."

CHAPTER
TWENTY

ONSTANCE ACCEPTED THE long lovely gaps between life's occasional bursts of happiness. What choice did she have? But there were moments of weakness . . . when all she could think of was Sam and the life they would never share. She struggled to make Elliot a part of her family again, coaxing him to take pride in Diana's artistic talent, frustrated by his constant bitterness.

Constance would have enjoyed building some kind of social life, but Elliot didn't want to see anyone—certainly not her friends from the synagogue. With the war over she had written to David and Frances Field, but there had been no response. She hoped this was because they had changed addresses—she couldn't bear the thought of warm and friendly David Field being a war casualty.

Emilie had left to resume her life with her father, but she was constantly at the Hardwicke house, which provided a legitimate excuse for Sam's frequent presence. An enchanting little girl. She had become a sister to Diana and Adam and had earned a special niche in Constance's heart. In dark moments Constance berated herself for the secret that Adam and Emilie must never know—but all three children, in a dozen ways each day, made her life bearable.

On most nights—to Constance's guilty relief—Elliot dined alone in his room. She was unnerved by his nastiness towards the children. Before the war he had spoiled them, but now everything they said or did seemed wrong. Adam retreated behind a protective shell; Diana was bewildered and hurt. Constance found herself fighting with Elliot, begging him to stop using the children as his whipping post. Every day he painted in the garden, and every night he destroyed whatever he had created. Nothing seemed to satisfy him. In a few weeks Elliot had built an insurmountable wall between himself and his family.

Six months after his return Sam begged Constance to let him back into her life as her lover. Desperately she wanted him, needed him, but she refused. She was terrified of hurting Elliot, uncertain as to what form his wrath would take if he ever found out about the two of them . . . what if he tried to take away the children? She could never live with that loss, even for Sam. As it was now, Elliot's life consisted solely of painting, drinking and screaming at the servants. Diana's and Adam's avoidance of him only hurt him more, but he seemed unable to restrain his temper.

WITH the war over Hong Kong underwent profound social and economic changes. The island suffered from the dislocation of world trade, the loss of shipping, the shortage of many badly-needed commodities, particularly rice. Prices soared. Business concerns encountered intense commercial rivalry. With its lower labor costs and devalued currency, Japan became a formidable competitor.

Despite unceasing labor problems and strikes Constance was slowly building the shipyard into a major Far East business. At the same time Sam had expanded Stone & Telford and was rebuilding his real estate operation. Constance and Sam clung to the friendship that allowed them to see each other, tortured by the chasteness of their meetings.

The cinema became a popular diversion in Hong Kong. Cars were seen more frequently around the island. Diana and Emilie discovered American songs and ran around the house singing off-key renditions of *Blue Moon, April Showers,* and *Tea for Two.*

In 1922—shortly before Diana's fourteenth birthday—a seaman's strike paralyzed the harbor and spread to every branch of labor, even domestic servants. At the same time a serious recession rocked the island's economy. And in the midst of this chaos, Elliot made an announcement that threw Constance into panic. It was one of those rare mornings when because of the heat Constance went late to the shipyard. She was eating breakfast with Elliot in the garden.

"Constance, I want you to make inquiries about a school in England for the children," he said abruptly. "It's time we were all off this godforsaken island."

Constance paled as she stared at Elliot.

"But Elliot, they're happy here. They'd be miserable if we sent them to boarding school." How could he even think of sending Diana and Adam away from home? Adam had such a wonderful lively spirit—what would happen to that spirit in a cold, impersonal boarding school . . . and Diana, awkwardly tall for her age, blossoming into womanhood . . . They both needed the love and support of a sympathetic mother, a strong home life.

Elliot scowled. "Come now, Constance. Decent schooling is my children's birthright. I'm sure all their British cousins are in boarding schools." Brief, impersonal letters still arrived from London—twice a year. Letters which left him depressed for days afterward. "I expect my children to have the same advantages."

"But Elliot, they can have a fine education here." Constance steeled herself for a battle. To hell with their cousins! "They need to be with their family in their growing-up years. I know about the great British tradition of pushing aside the children. That's not the way Diana and Adam are going to be raised."

"Come off it, Constance. You're at the shipyard all day. You don't even see them."

Constance stared at him, stung by the sour hate in his voice.

"I see them every morning and every evening." Her voice shook in fury. "I spend every waking hour of Sundays with them. They know they have a mother. When they're upset, they come to me. I will not allow them to live halfway around the world from me."

Elliot looked amused.

"Come now, Constance. You don't really mean that."

"I mean it more than I've ever meant anything in my life." Elliot might be Master to the servants; but he wasn't her master. She would fight him all the way on this. "My father spent years at boarding school after his mother died. He hated every minute of it. He never forgot it. I will not let that happen to our children."

Elliot gave her a long, shrewd look. He sighed.

"All right, then. Have it your way. But I won't be responsible for any problems with them. You're the one—as you so maternally put it—who spends every waking hour of your precious Sundays with them."

It frightened Constance that the children might one day realize what a sham this marriage was.

"Please, Elliot. Let's not fight. Why don't you give Diana painting lessons? She's inherited your talent."

Elliot shrugged.

"Diana plays at painting. Later, if she's still interested, maybe I'll give her lessons." Briefly his eyes met Constance's. She was shocked at the pain she saw there. When he spoke his voice shook. "I've ruined your life, Constance."

"Elliot, don't be absurd." It frightened her to see him like this—but at the same time she pitied him. Who was this man—this child —she had married? "We have Diana and Adam, a thriving business, a beautiful home. We have much to be grateful for."

"Never mind—just—never mind." He sighed. "Where's Adam?" He never seems to be around."

"He's at Emilie's house," Constance said gently. "They're building a rock garden."

She knew that Sam encouraged these small adventures because they gave him a chance to be with Adam. And it warmed her heart that Adam loved being with his "Uncle Sam." Let Sam have this one pleasure . . .

AS Diana became a teenager her talent for painting became apparent even to a begrudging Elliot. Once amused and indulgent, however, he was now jealous and vindictive. For a while Constance stood by and watched him brutally and persistently tear down Diana's talent. But her frustration eventually gave way to anger, and the house became a battleground as Diana withdrew into her own world, painting only in the privacy of her room. She no longer shared her efforts even with Adam or her mother. For this Constance hated Elliot.

And there were serious problems at the shipyard. In 1925 a general strike and boycott hit Canton and quickly spread to Hong Kong. Actually it was a political movement that had arisen out of hostility towards the privileged status granted to foreigners. In Canton the

Kuomintang radical element organized a boycott of British and Japanese merchandise and vicious street fighting erupted between demonstrators and British and French troops.

Sam joined up with the Volunteer Corps, which had been mobilized to help the British troops cope with the emergency. Though the strike began to collapse, the boycott of British goods and shipping persisted, forcing many foreign merchants to borrow from the government in order to survive the crisis.

For Sam business was thriving. Frightened by the Kuomintang extremist elements, wealthy Chinese were fleeing from Canton and seeking fine homes in Hong Kong. Sam was becoming one of the wealthiest real estate entrepreneurs in Hong Kong. At the same time he struggled to improve the deteriorating housing situation for the soaring poverty-stricken Chinese population.

Constance knew that Emilie's security was what fueled Sam's near-obsessive drive to make his fortune. The life of a Eurasian— even a beautiful, intelligent girl like Emilie—could only be difficult. Among all the Jews in Hong Kong only one man had married a Chinese girl—and in so doing he had alienated himself from the Ohel Leah congregation. It was only the fact that Sam had made a name for himself, coupled with kind words from a few of Constance's more influential friends, that had made it possible for Emilie to attend the school for European children. But even with his growing influence Sam did not dare build a house for Emilie and himself on the Peak, still restricted to European residents. No, he would find a way to protect her from the ugliness in the world—he would make sure his riches bought her happiness . . .

IN the late spring of 1926 William suffered a heart attack and Dr. Arnold insisted that William return to the less enervating climate of England. The threat of losing her dearest friends was a devastating blow to Constance. Except for Sam, who knew and loved her better than Olivia?

It was Olivia who made her conscious of the special closeness between Adam and Emilie. Constance had always known that Adam enjoyed being Emilie's idol. Of course he didn't know that she was his half-sister, but she was his constant companion, to be teased, bullied and protected. Constance felt the disapproval in their limited social circle for Adam's choice of companion, but she never mentioned it to him.

Constance made every effort to help Olivia and William in the traumatic move.

"You'll come to see us of course," Olivia said firmly. "With the railroads improving every year there's no reason why you can't. And the children should see London." She was determined not to cry. Constance was like their third daughter. Diana, Adam, and Emilie were adopted grandchildren. "Here Diana is already going on eighteen, and Adam fifteen. It's time they saw London."

"And New York," Constance said, laughing. "Remember, their mother grew up in New York."

"We're not retiring to the country, you know," William said with a wink, dropping an arm around Olivia's shoulders. "They're not putting us out to pasture just yet. We'll be living right in London. While we will miss the beauty of Hong Kong, I think London will be an exciting change." But his eyes were wistful. Constance knew his affection for her and for the children was genuine.

It was Sam's idea to give a small farewell dinner party for the Converses. Just Constance and Elliot—if he could be persuaded to come, Diana, Adam and Emilie, and William's long-time friend from the consulate, Thomas Aiken, with his wife Eve.

Constance was appointed to take Emilie shopping for a special gown for the dinner party—her first grown-up gown. Emilie and Diana giggled incessantly as Emilie tried on dresses at the chic "Madam Shop"—a carbon copy of the new shops opening in Mayfair in London.

"Oh, Emilie, that's too utterly divine," Diana sighed as her dainty friend stood before the dressing room mirror in a green georgette evening frock fringed with narrow beaded strips of the same material, revealing much of her lean silk-stockinged legs and golden back. "But it'll have to be shortened."

"Diana!" Constance was shocked. "It's above her calf already."

"Mama, in Paris they're wearing dresses almost up to the knee," Diana said grandly. "Don't you ever look at the fashion magazines?"

"Well, I guess you have me there—I am usually busy looking at shipping magazines," Constance said ruefully. In truth, she had a natural sense of style that had earned her the reputation of being one of the best-dressed women in the Crown Colony.

"Mama, it has to be shortened or else Emilie will be the laughing-stock of the whole party. Mine too. Please?"

Constance laughed. "All right, all right. Now let's get out of here before I spend any more money . . . "

At last the night of Sam's dinner party arrived. Constance made a great show of enjoying herself, but she couldn't really celebrate the fact that Olivia and William would be gone in forty-eight hours. She knew she was being selfish, but it hurt too much. As she had anticipated, though he was fond of Olivia and William, Elliot made up an excuse and didn't attend.

With Diana and Adam in tow Constance climbed into the recently delivered Daimler, praying that Chou, the chauffeur, would drive carefully tonight. Diana and Adam were snipping at each other and tonight Constance was too distracted to stop him from careening through the narrow streets.

AS always Sam left his room and started downstairs to check on dinner preparations. With his efficient staff it was hardly necessary, but he had no one to share the early evening with and it helped him fight the loneliness that always threatened to submerge him as night came. At the top of the stairs he paused, then backtracked to Emilie's room. He knocked lightly.

"Ching-jin," she called out in the mandarin Chinese Sam had taught her.

Sam opened the door and stepped inside. He felt a surge of love for his truly beautiful daughter as his eyes swept over her.

"Do I look all right, Papa?" she turned around in front of him.

"My darling, you look beautiful." The pain returned as he thought for the hundredth time about her future. Where on this misguided earth could Emilie grow up into the happiness she deserved? "Like a cinema actress," he said, knowing nothing would please her more. So like Lucienne . . .

Emilie's amber eyes glowed.

"Will Adam think I'm beautiful?"

"Everyone will think so." But his smile was troubled. She would inherit a fortune when he died but would that be enough to blot out the faint gold of her skin?

"Papa, it's Adam I want to think I'm beautiful," she confided

218

shyly. "Do you think that my being two years older than he will stop him from falling in love with me when he grows up?"

Sam was white with shock. So that was it—he should have expected this, all the time they spent together . . .

His voice shook as he spoke.

"Emilie, Adam is like a brother to you." He tried to sound matter-of-fact. "You two have grown up together. Of course you love him —like a brother."

"No, Papa. I love Adam. Someday—if he'll have me—I will be his wife. Adam doesn't mind that my mother was Chinese," she said with pride.

"Emilie, no!" His world came crashing down around him. God, what terrible thing had he done to have to hurt his child like this? "You don't understand. I—I don't know how to tell you—"

"Tell me what, Papa?" She was composed, but he could see a stubbornness taking hold.

"I thought it would never be necessary for you to know." The knot in his stomach tightened. "Emilie," he said gently, "it's right that you should love Adam. As a brother." He paused. "Because Adam is your brother." He saw her eyes widen in disbelief. "Nobody in this world except his mother and myself know this. "I'm so sorry—but now you have to know, my darling." He flinched at the look in her eyes—a look of confusion, anger and sorrow that was burning a hole through his heart . . . "It's natural for you to love your brother," he repeated, stricken by her expression, "but the way our world is, you must never repeat what I've just told you. Not even to Adam."

"I won't tell him, Papa." Her voice—her face—were blank. "I won't tell anyone."

"Hurting you is the last thing in the world I would ever want to do—you know that don't you, Emilie?" He moved to take her in his arms, then stepped back. She was like a small ivory figurine, completely still and lifeless. He heard a car pull up in front of the house. "I'd better hurry downstairs. Some of our guests are arriving. Don't be long, Emilie." He tried a lighter mood. "I want to show off my gorgeous daughter." But as he walked down the stairs he knew that something was terribly wrong. I'll talk to her after the party, he thought, just to make sure she's all right.

Within a few minutes everyone at the party was in high spirits.

"Diana, you're a young lady," Sam said affectionately. "Emilie and you. Where have the years gone, Constance?" Behind his efforts at small talk was a gnawing concern about Emilie. He would have to tell Constance what had happened. Emilie was young—it would be natural for her to need some time to sort this out. Later she would understand.

"Where's Emilie?" Adam turned to Sam. Already he was almost as tall as his father and looked startlingly like him. Constance often wondered if anyone suspected their secret . . .

"She'll be down in a few minutes." Sam tried to sound casual. "I think she's putting on the finishing touches."

"Shall I go up and get her?" Diana asked.

"Come on, don't rush her," Constance protested tenderly. "Let her have all the time she needs. She's so excited about having her first grown-up evening dress. It's a very important occasion."

Conversation moved on. Now Sam was sweating, and by troubled glances from Constance he knew that she sensed something was wrong. At one side of the drawing room William and Thomas Aiken were reminiscing about their school days while Olivia and Diana listened. At the other, Eve Aiken and Constance were discussing the brilliant British playwright, Noel Coward, while Adam hovered around his mother and tried not to look self-conscious.

Sam frowned as the *comprador* appeared silently in the doorway to signal that dinner was ready. Where was Emilie? An agonized scream ripped through the festive atmosphere. Sam went cold with fear. The scream had come from upstairs. He dashed from the drawing room and up the stairs.

At the head of the stairs he saw Emilie's *amah*, Lotus Blossom, rocking to and fro. The door to her bedroom was wide open. Sam rushed inside.

Ashen, Emilie lay across the floor, her arms at her side. A large pair of scissors, jutting grotesquely out of her wrist, was covered with spurting blood, staining the green georgette frock with burgundy splotches.

"Emilie!" Sam dropped to his knees and frantically pressed his hands to her wrist, trying to stop the flow of blood. "Oh, my God! Oh, my God!"

"Papa, it hurts," she whispered. "Awful."

"You're going to be all right. Don't worry, everything's going to be all right," Sam gasped.

"No, Papa. I want to die. I don't want to live without Adam." She sighed—a long shuddering sigh. And then she lay still.

"Sam, you have to stop the bleeding!" Constance, chalk-white, hovered over them.

"It's too late." Sam said, his voice harsh with shock. He closed Emilie's eyes and drew the small, slender frame into his arms. "My daughter's dead, Connie. I've killed her."

CHAPTER
TWENTY-ONE

THE STUNNED GUESTS at what was to have been a gay farewell party for Olivia and William began shuffling quietly out of the house. Only Constance would stay. No one was allowed upstairs where Sam sat alone with his child in his arms. No one would intrude on these final horrible minutes as Sam struggled to find a reason—and at long last realized there wasn't one—for Emilie's death.

No one could understand why pretty, sweet young Emilie would want to take her own life. Only Sam and Constance knew why. And only they had to come to terms with it . . .

For Diana and Adam it was a pain that would stay with them forever. Emilie was the first person close to them to die.

"Was somebody mean to her at school?" Adam blustered. He would not cry—he was almost a man, and men did not cry. "If there was, I'll kill him!"

"It wasn't somebody at school, darling," Constance said. What could she possibly say to lessen the pain? "Emilie just couldn't face the life she saw ahead of her. We all loved her, but she knew that there's a cold world out there full of people who would look at her skin color and be cruel to her. For a little while," she soothed, holding

Diana close, "we had someone very special. Let's hold on to the happy memories."

Constance saw the last guests to the door. Now she had to go upstairs to Sam. He sat on the floor, blood stains on his jacket, Emilie's body still in his arms.

"Connie, I can't let her be buried in the Eurasian cemetery." His voice caught. The Eurasian cemetery had been set up at Mount Davis in 1890 as the "authorized Eurasian cemetery" and burial elsewhere was against the rules. "Emilie is my daughter. She was raised Jewish."

"She'll be buried in the Jewish cemetery," Constance promised. "We'll go together to make the arrangements. It'll be all right. I'll call Lotus Blossom to stay with Emilie while we're gone."

Constance summoned every bit of strength she had—and more—to see her through the next twenty-four hours. As a Jew Emilie's body had to be buried as soon as possible. To avoid getting the rabbi at the synagogue in trouble with the congregation for conducting a service for a Eurasian, Constance asked a sympathetic young rabbi, visiting from America, to officiate.

So, before the community knew what had happened, Emilie was laid to rest with a proper Jewish service, in the Jewish cemetery, with those who loved her at the graveside. Even Elliot had been there—somber and uneasy, but at least having temporarily forgotten his bitterness.

It was not the leave-taking that Olivia and William had planned at all. Sam blamed himself. There was nothing Constance could say to stop his bitter self-recrimination.

THE summer was long and hot. Sam tried to lose himself in his business. At last, in mid-August, Constance convinced him to come to their house on the Peak for a weekend of relief from the subtropic summer.

He arrived in time for dinner. Diana and Adam were happy to see their beloved "uncle." Emilie's death had somehow brought all of them closer together. Elliot made an effort and joined them at the dinner table, but he retreated to his room when the meal was over. Lately Constance had learned to be grateful for even token gestures of civility from her husband . . .

Adam talked Sam into a game of chess after dinner—an offer Sam

223

accepted, Constance knew, only out of love for his son. It worried her that Sam clung so tenaciously to his grief, and to his guilt. She, too, felt an agonizing responsibility for what had happened.

Saturday morning was one of those perfect days on the Peak, when the sun filtered through the mist, revealing a window of purple sky. The children were sleeping late as they always did on Saturdays. Elliot stayed up until dawn every day and slept till past noon.

Exhilarated by the beauty of the morning Constance asked to have breakfast served in the gazebo. At a table in the gazebo, surrounded by flowering shrubs and shade trees, Constance and Sam sat down to a hearty British breakfast.

Constance searched Sam's face for some sign of life behind the dull, hopeless eyes. When would he let go of his anger? She, too, had lain sleepless in her bed at night, filled with guilt over what had happened. But life must move ahead; Sam couldn't stay in the past forever.

Gently she took his hand. "Sam, you must stop torturing yourself. You have to learn to live again. Think of Adam. Let your love for him see you through this terrible time." Neither of them noticed Elliot wheeling himself along the path to the gazebo. "You have a son who feels very close to you. Find joy in Adam," she pleaded. "Let him help you."

ELLIOT backed up his wheelchair and turned around. His mouth was dry with shock. But why? Hadn't he suspected this for a long time? He could see it in the way they looked at each other. But he had never guessed that Adam was actually Sam's child. Waves of nausea rolled over him as he sat in his wheelchair.

Elliot spent the rest of the weekend alone in his room. Over and over he thought about the months before Adam was born. At first he had been enraged—but oddly now all he felt was a sad resignation. His life had been a failure. He could admit it now. His marriage was just one more mistake. He was truly sorry for Constance. She was a fine, decent woman . . . a loving mother to Diana and Adam . . . as good a wife as he had let her be. She could have walked out on him when he returned from the war. Other wives would have.

Somehow he knew that she and Sam were not having an affair

now. Christ, what she had shared with Sam Stone was far more of a marriage than what the two of them had.

On Monday, after a long, sleepless night Elliot left his suite. He had a houseboy set up his easel at the edge of the property, facing the magnificent view of harbor, sea, and sky, which he had—at last —come to cherish.

"I won't need you anymore this morning," Elliot told the houseboy, waving him away.

"No tea?" the houseboy asked. The master always had a pot of tea at his elbow when he painted.

"No tea. Get out," Elliot snapped, reaching for a paintbrush.

He made a half dozen strokes across the canvas, and glanced around to make sure he was alone. No one must ever guess the truth. He wheeled his chair close to the edge. It must look like an accident —he was so involved in his painting that he didn't realize how close he was to the edge.

His face set in determination, Elliot dropped the paintbrush and placed his hands on the wheels of the chair. He was going to give Constance her freedom. God, it was long past due.

He shut his eyes tightly and gave one final push. And in a blinding moment before the darkness came the thought took hold . . . I love you, Constance.

ELLIOT'S personal houseboy discovered his Master's crumpled body and the grotesquely twisted wheelchair in the ravine below the house. Again Constance steeled herself and gave Elliot a proper British burial in the European cemetery. A cable was sent off to his family, at Sam's urging addressed to his oldest brother—the current Lord Hardwicke—in the event that the shock was too much for his elderly mother. A cable of polite condolence was the family's response. Apparently even Elliot's death didn't interest them . . .

In her heart Constance knew that Elliot had killed himself. She made a point of accepting it as an accident for the sake of the children, telling them that at last their father was safe from pain. She hoped to God it was true.

As the weeks sped past, she tried to shrug off the guilt she felt at her relief to be free at last. Not that she had ever wished Elliot dead —she had often wondered what her life would be like without him, but she always quickly dismissed the thought. She had resented his temper, his moodiness—but they had shared a life . . . she would miss him.

Sam made it clear that he expected to marry her after a suitable period of mourning. He still grieved for Emilie; and he knew how deeply Elliot's death had shaken Constance. It was time for them to take whatever happiness they could.

"Connie, our time is coming," he said matter-of-factly as they shared a pot of tea in her office one late November afternoon. These days he often dropped in to spend a few moments with her whenever he was showing property nearby. He sipped his tea. "There's a quotation in the Bible that I like: 'To everything there is a season, and a time for every purpose under the heavens.' You'll be my wife at last."

"I guess I didn't expect it to happen like this," she faltered.

"Connie, let me take you to dinner tonight." Gently he turned her hand over in his and kissed the palm. She could see the love and hunger in his eyes and still—after all this time—it thrilled her . . . "We'll have dinner at the Hong Kong Hotel," he pursued. "Remember all the happy times we had there?"

"Sam, Diana and Adam will be expecting me home—" But she knew she would go with him. It had been too long since they spent time alone together.

"Call and explain you'll be tied up on business." He knew there were nights when she was at the shipyard till ten. "I'll pick you up here at seven."

Constance was annoyed with herself. She was a thirty-six-year-old woman—but now she felt lightheaded, nervous, like a carefree young girl . . . and all because she was going to spend an evening alone with the man she loved. She and Sam had agreed to wait out her year of mourning before marrying. They had said nothing yet to Diana and Adam about their plans. Tonight would be special . . .

She couldn't wait for seven o'clock to come. When Sam arrived—ten minutes early—Constance wished that she had gone home to change into something more elegant.

"Hungry?" he asked, crossing to the coat rack for her tweed cape—ordered from a shop on Bond Street in London.

"Famished." Could he hear her heart pounding as he draped the cape about her shoulders? She and Sam hadn't made love for twelve years. How had she endured all those years without him? She felt almost virginal.

While they sat at their favorite table in the hotel dining room, Constance thought back to their first night there. It was the night Sam had asked her to marry him. She could still hear his voice. *"I know I have no right yet to speak to you this way, when I'm not prepared to care for a wife properly; but when I do rise to that position, will you marry me?"*

"I remember the first time I brought you to this dining room," he said softly. "I knew then you were the only woman I'd ever love."

A Chinese "boy" dressed in a long, flowing gown appeared at the table to serve them. After they chose their dinner, Sam reached into his pocket and brought out a small box.

"Wear this for me, Connie," Sam said, handing her the box.

Without opening it she knew what was inside: the *chai* that she had long ago returned to him. But there was something else inside, too: a magnificent diamond ring surrounded by rubies.

With tears in her eyes she lifted the gold chain and turned so that Sam could fasten the *chai* around her throat.

"Sam, I can't wear the ring just yet. The children might be upset."

"Then wear it when we're alone. For me." He paused. "Connie, don't you think it's time Adam was told who his real father is?"

For the past several weeks Constance had been struggling with this problem. Especially now, with Emilie gone, Sam needed to be known —at least within the family—as Adam's father. And she wanted him to be. But there were Adam's feelings to consider. What if he was angry at them for deceiving him? At least she didn't have to worry that Adam was overly fond of Elliot—though Elliot had spoiled him dreadfully as a small boy, he hadn't been much of a father since coming home from the war and in fact Adam seemed to feel closer to his "Uncle Sam" anyway. Yes, she decided, he must know the truth . . .

"Sam, give me some time," she said softly. "Adam will know. I promise."

Sam smiled. "All right, my love. I've waited this long—I guess a few more months won't matter.

"Connie," he leaned forward and took her hand. "I want you to come home with me tonight. Say you will."

Constance felt a stab of fear. "But Sam—"

"There's no reason you shouldn't," he cut her off. "We're both free. If you're thinking of Elliot he's been dead four months."

227

"All right, Sam."

She didn't want to fight him anymore.

SHE leaned her head against Sam's shoulder as they drove out of the city and up the slope toward his house. Doubt tugged at her. What would their lovemaking be like after so many years? Ancient feelings from that horrible wedding night with Elliot taunted her. What if she could no longer satisfy Sam? But she trembled with desire for him . . . It would be all right. It had to be.

AT Sam's house the servants had all retired to their quarters.

He parked the Renault. Hand in hand he and Constance walked into the house and upstairs to his bedroom.

"Sam, could I take a shower?" she asked nervously. "It's just that I feel so dirty after a long day at the office."

"Go ahead." His eyes already made gentle love to her. "I'll bring up a bottle of champagne."

In Sam's luxurious marble-walled bathroom Constance took off her clothes and stepped into the shower. Had too many years passed for Sam and her? He was wealthy and handsome. Surely he could have his choice of much younger women.

As she stood under the warm, pounding spray she gazed at her body. Her breasts were still full and high, her waist slender, her legs long and firm. But could she respond with the passion that Sam remembered in her? She wasn't a young girl anymore . . .

Panic seized her. She had to get out of here. She just couldn't do this—not yet. But when? She imagined the disappointment in Sam's eyes when she told him she wanted to go home. She reached to turn off the spray, almost slipping in her haste. She pushed aside the curtain and stepped onto the plush rug next to the tub. If she dressed quickly she could meet him downstairs before he came up with the champagne and—

"Connie?" Sam opened the door. Under one arm was a bottle of champagne, in his hand were two glasses. His eyes swept over her body. "Connie, you're so beautiful." He set down the bottle and glasses and reached for a towel.

"You don't know how often I've imagined a moment like this," he

228

whispered, draping the towel around her shoulders and drawing her to him.

"Sam, you'll get wet," she laughed shakily.

"I'll be out of these clothes soon enough—"

His mouth was hard and impatient on hers. His hands fondled her damp breasts. The towel fell to the floor. The champagne was forgotten. Sam lifted her into his arms and carried her to bed.

Constance lay back against a mound of pillows while Sam undressed. He was slightly heavier but still lean and firm, broad of shoulders, flat in the stomach.

She closed her arms around his shoulders as he lowered himself above her.

For a moment she tensed, afraid that her body—so long denied love—would refuse him.

"Connie?" he said questioningly.

"Sam, I love you." She clutched at him.

And he slipped inside her. They moved together slowly, gently, and then faster, more demanding . . . It was going to be all right. It was going to be wonderful. She heard her own whimpers of pleasure, his groans of satisfaction as they clung together until finally they were suspended together in that one blissful powerful moment . . . and then at last they were quiet.

"It's like the very first time," Sam whispered, his mouth at her throat. They lay absolutely still, both knowing that in a little while they would make love again. Tonight a long hunger would be satisfied.

THREE weeks later Constance called Diana and Adam together to tell them the truth about Sam. Faltering but determined to finally be honest, she told them what her marriage to Elliot had really been like —omitting any mention of his homosexuality. There was no reason for them to know this, she reasoned . . . she still hadn't betrayed Elliot's secret even to Sam. Constance tried to ignore their stares of disbelief.

"Many girls marry for the same reason. Security for the future. I was sixteen and terrified of being stranded in Hong Kong. Your father—I mean—Elliot was terribly unhappy in the Colony. His family had exiled him here because of a boyhood indiscretion. He'd hoped marriage would reinstate him. It didn't."

"But you had children!" Diana said accusingly. Adam looked uncomfortable.

"We wanted children very much," Constance said. "And your father and I were so happy when you were born. But after that there was no more marriage between us. He was a bitter, tormented man. I would have given anything to make him happier. But there didn't seem to be anyone who could help him."

"What about me?" Adam asked shyly.

"Elliot always assumed you were his child. I managed that," she said awkwardly. "But your father knew from the moment he saw you—when you were only a few days old. You were lucky, Adam. You had two fathers who loved you very much."

She watched Adam's expression closely, hoping he wouldn't grow to hate her for this. But he seemed matter-of-fact. Almost pleased . . .

"Are you going to marry Uncle Sam?" Diana asked coldly.

Constance was disconcerted by Diana's hostility. Why was she reacting this way and not Adam? But she had always been more deeply involved with Elliot—maybe she felt that she had to protect him . . . If only this would help them be a family . . .

"Can I have Papa's studio?" Diana asked abruptly.

"Why yes, of course." Constance smiled, hoping for a response. Not a flicker.

In Diana's eyes Elliot had suddenly become a martyr. And Constance was the deceitful wife. But she would never tell Diana about the day she walked into the studio and discovered Elliot with Ch'en in his arms. Never.

IN the following weeks Constance became deeply troubled by Diana's resentment of her despite the delicious hours with Sam that made her feel young and passionate and carefree. She had always dreamed of her marriage to Sam as a happy, loving day, in the synagogue before the God that had watched Mama and Papa marry —but now, even when Sam simply came to visit, the air was fraught with tension as Diana acted barely civil. Adam, on the contrary, seemed devoted to his "new" father.

Constance wrote Olivia about the problem with Diana. Only Olivia knew the barren loneliness of the years she had spent as Elliot's wife. Only Olivia would understand why she felt she deserved this little bit of happiness . . . So why did she feel guilty? She was depriving Diana of nothing in admitting her love for Sam.

While Constance tried to divert herself from brooding over the problem by letting Sam bring her into his real estate operation, Olivia wrote and invited Diana to come visit them in London.

"Maybe Diana needs to spend some time away from you for a while," Olivia wrote. "To recognize herself as a person. I know how it pained you to see Elliot constantly tearing her down. We'll never know how deeply this scarred Diana."

Had *she* scarred Diana with her infidelity? But loving Sam had seemed so right—especially considering what a sham her marriage had been. And out of their love had come Adam—how could she ever regret that?

At the dinner table that night Constance said nothing of the invitation for Diana to visit London, only that she had received a letter from Olivia with much talk about the London theater, the shops and the exciting people. Olivia wrote too about how much she was enjoying her two daughters, their husbands, and the collective grandchildren. "Time has mellowed us all," she wrote. "Now it's difficult to believe that my relationship with the girls was ever anything less than perfect."

After dinner Adam excused himself to meet a friend to go to the cinema. Constance sat in the drawing room alone with Diana. While Diana hid behind one of London's latest fashion magazines Constance tried to concentrate on the newspaper, waiting for a phone call from Sam. She made a point of having dinner alone with the children several times a week so they didn't feel that Sam was taking up all her free time.

"Mama, I have to talk to you," Diana said abruptly, putting down her magazine.

"What is it, Diana?" She stiffened. Why did she always feel so defensive with Diana?

"I've decided I want to be a serious painter." She tossed her head defiantly.

"Well darling, I think that's wonderful! I've always had such faith in your talent."

"I'll have to study hard. Work hard. I realize it's a tremendous undertaking." Diana's words were tumbling over one another. "And I know exactly who I want to study with. He's in London. He's probably one of the finest teachers in Europe. Of course, he might not take me—"

"Of course he'll have you," Constance said automatically and then stopped dead. "London? But Diana, you're so young—"

"I'm eighteen."

"But to go off alone?" Another person she loved was leaving her. "Perhaps when you're twenty—" Maybe she could stall her . . . But in two years Adam would be going off to Oxford.

"No. I want to go now." Diana was perched on the edge of her chair, something in her eyes daring Constance to object. "Papa always wanted me to go to school in England. He was unhappy that you kept us here at home. If he were alive, he'd insist that I be allowed to go."

The phone rang in the study. Constance rose to her feet. Hesitated. She sensed Diana's anger that she was interrupting their discussion. The ringing stopped. Li must have answered it.

"Mama, I told you, I have to go to London to study with this man." Diana's voice was controlled but fierce. "I don't want to stay in the Colony. I don't want to stay in this house."

Li appeared in the doorway. "Phone for Madame. Mr. Stone."

"I'll be right there, Li." She turned to Diana. "We'll talk later. She hurried across the hall to the study. Feeling out of control. Maybe Sam could help . . .

She listened to his report of a meeting with a pair of German businessmen interested in investment in the Colony, trying to forget Diana's exasperation that she had gone to the phone. When would Diana come to realize that she was more than a mother? That she was also a woman with needs of her own?

"You're upset," Sam stopped in the middle of a sentence. "I can tell. Connie, what's bothering you?"

Haltingly she told him about Diana's plan.

"Let her go," he said quietly.

"Sam, she's just eighteen," Constance protested. "She's been so sheltered—"

"Let her go to London to study painting provided she stays with Olivia and William. I'm sure they would be delighted to have her for a while."

"Well, yes. In fact Olivia just wrote and invited her. She knew I was having problems with Diana." Constance paused. "But Sam, suppose Diana refuses?"

"Darling, you'll be paying her way. You can set the rules. She'll accept. And in London she'll come to realize what a wonderful mother she has."

Sam was right. But the thought of letting Diana go off to London —even to stay at Olivia and William's flat—somehow frightened her. Diana was so sensitive and headstrong. And these were such disturbing times . . . the girls with their dresses above their knees, their cigarettes, and their talk about "free love" . . . the drinking and the fast motorcars and the risqué plays and novels . . . And hadn't she just read something about the terrible traffic in England causing motorcar crashes? But she would listen to Sam and let her daughter go. She prayed it was the right thing to do . . .

DETERMINED not to soften, Constance faced Diana and laid out the conditions under which she would be allowed to go to London.

"Mama, that's archaic!" Diana stormed. "I'm a grown woman. Why do I have to live with Aunt Olivia and Uncle William? Don't you think I'm capable of taking care of myself?" Chameleon-like, she changed tactics . . . "I have an idea, Mama. I'll promise to have them over to dinner at my flat. Once a week." She smiled sweetly.

Constance smiled back. "No. You'll stay with Olivia and William. Or you stay in Hong Kong."

Diana sighed in exasperation.

"Oh all right. "But it'll be pretty humiliating to have to tell the other students that I live with family."

"You'll survive. And this is all assuming that this teacher accepts you."

"He already has," Diana confessed. "I wrote months ago and submitted some of my work. Mama—" All at once she was an eager little girl again. "He says I have real talent. He'll accept me as a private student."

Constance studied Diana. Tall, slender, beautiful. Possessing a rare talent that—she hoped—would not torment her as it had tormented her father.

"Then we'll have to set about making arrangements for your travel." Constance forced herself to sound cheerful. "When would you like to leave for London?"

CHAPTER

TWENTY-TWO

IANA WAS DISAPPOINTED that the Trans-Siberian Railroad had deteriorated to the extent that it was no longer used by Europeans returning home from the Crown Colony. She traveled mostly by ship to London, alternately enthralled, terrified, and excited about her future. She had enjoyed the rebellion, and even though she hadn't exactly emerged victorious, at least she was out of Hong Kong. Mama was so old-fashioned—insisting she wear her dresses below her knees when everybody knew that in London and Paris they were already over the knees. With the sewing skills she and Emilie had acquired a few years before, Diana had meticulously shortened most of her dresses and skirts as much as she dared—keeping in mind that Aunt Olivia and Uncle William were sure to be reporting to Mama regularly . . .

A lot of things that "The Bright Young People" took for granted shocked Mama. Like those marvelous books by Dr. Stopes, *Mother England*, and *Married Love*. She agreed with Dr. Stopes that contraception was better than abortion. And what was wrong with women smoking and drinking in public? If men could do it, why not women? But of course Mama insisted it was unfeminine and unhealthy.

Mama refused to talk about "companionate marriage," where you lived with a man for a while to see if it was going to be right before you went ahead and married him. Didn't that make more sense than what she had done—marrying Papa and finding out it was a terrible mistake for both of them?

Maybe Adam was right about Papa being sorry he married Mama because she was Jewish. Papa never went to church. But she didn't really think that was it at all. Mama was too busy with the shipyard to pay much attention to Papa. And she's the one who's worried about unfeminine behavior? That was more unfeminine than drinking and smoking in public. But there was no point in trying to convince Mama of that . . .

She still couldn't get used to the idea that Uncle Sam was Adam's father . . . that righteous, moral Mama had slept with Sam while she was married to Papa. Did Papa ever find out? Maybe that was why he was so nasty and horrible most of the time.

He was her father; she ought to be sorry that he died in that awful accident. She remembered the night she heard about it and she sat on the bed trying to cry. She hadn't been able to. She cried at the funeral; but she was really crying for herself, stuck in the Crown Colony where everybody was so stuffy.

Three days after her arrival in London, after she had met Mark Grant—the man who was to be her teacher—and had arranged for wickedly expensive lessons three afternoons a week, Diana decided to call on her grandmother. Every year there was a Christmas card from Lady Hardwicke; before she left Diana had scribbled down the address in the back of her diary. Maybe grandmother could help her understand Papa . . .

One thing she was going to find out was how the Hardwickes felt about Mama. Diana suspected that Mama was responsible for the alienation between Papa and his family. After all, it was pretty strange that when Mama went to London on business before the war, she didn't even bother to call on them. But that was going to change, Diana promised herself, standing in front of her mirror. She imagined the scene—the elegant Hardwickes would welcome her with open arms into their opulent drawing room and of course she would overwhelm them with her charm and poise . . .

She had to wear her longest dress, one that covered her knees. She suppressed a giggle. It was lucky she hadn't shortened everything in her closet. On board the ship she had taken up hems and plucked her eyebrows and snipped away at her hair until she looked just like the actresses in London.

"Aunt Olivia, I'm off to an art gallery." She paused at the entrance to the sitting room. Uncle William and Aunt Olivia were awfully sweet, though they lived in a completely different London from the one she meant to know. "Mr. Grant told me to look at some paintings."

"Diana, do you know how to get there?" Olivia asked. "Uncle William has a very helpful street guide."

"He gave it to me. I have it in my purse. Don't worry about me, I'll find it." She tapped her foot impatiently.

"Well then, enjoy yourself, dear."

"Thanks, Aunt Olivia . . . "

Feeling audaciously adventurous Diana looked for the house in Mayfair where her father's family had lived for four generations. At last she found it: an impressive six-story house with tall narrow windows, set back behind a low wall divided by a pair of gleaming black wrought iron gates. A regal mansion, Diana thought, just like I expected. But suddenly the dress she was wearing that had seemed so chic back in her bedroom seemed positively dowdy.

Trying to brush aside her nervousness she opened the gate and walked up the steps to the massive oak door. She was about to lift the highly polished silver knocker when she noticed the doorbell to the left. She pressed it, envisioning the reception awaiting her. The granddaughter the London Hardwickes had never seen. She remembered the rare occasions when her father had talked about his mother, who in younger days had the same auburn-tinted hair as she. He had never said much more than that about her . . .

The door opened. A man whom Diana presumed was the butler stared inquiringly at her.

"I'd like to see Lady Hardwicke, please," Diana's voice was crisp. "I'm her granddaughter, Diana Hardwicke."

After a barely perceptible pause the butler invited her into the huge, darkly paneled entrance hall above which hung a Waterford crystal chandelier.

"Please wait in here, Miss Hardwicke." The butler opened the door to what appeared to be a family sitting room. "I'll tell her Ladyship that you are here." Did he seem vaguely disturbed or was it her imagination?

Maybe she should have phoned before coming, she thought uneasily. But this was Papa's family; she wasn't visiting total strangers.

Finally she heard muted voices in the hall. Footsteps approaching.

She rose to her feet. This was a historic moment, to come face-to-face with her grandmother for the first time in her life.

The door opened. A woman with graying hair who somehow looked frumpy in spite of her elegant dress walked into the room. Her lined face was unsmiling, her gaze frosty.

"Edward said that a Miss Hardwicke had arrived." She was polite but clearly annoyed.

"I'm Diana," she introduced herself. "Elliot's daughter." She shouldn't have come here. "You—you're not my grandmother." Her heart was pounding.

"No, I'm Elliot's oldest sister." Papa's sister Alicia. She didn't ask Diana to sit down. "I'm sorry but my mother will be unable to see you. She's quite frail. She sees only her closest friends." Wasn't a grand-daughter close enough? "Do you plan to stay in London for long?"

"I'm living here. I came to study painting." She was trembling.

"Well—it was nice of you to call." Diana paused, realizing she was being dismissed. Alicia forced a smile. "My mother begs to be ex-cused. I hope you'll enjoy living in London."

"I—I'm sure I shall. Good-by," she said awkwardly. She wished she could say something terribly clever.

Diana left the house and walked out into the cool dampness of the March morning. Tears of humiliation blurred her vision. So much for Papa's family.

THOUGH Diana hadn't meant to tell Olivia and William about her visit to her father's ancestral home, she blurted out the misadventure halfway through dinner.

"I'm not surprised." Olivia said calmly. "They never forgave your father for some schoolboy indiscretion. They're narrow, shallow peo-ple. You can live a full life without being welcomed into that family."

"Diana, how do you like this Mr. Grant?" William asked. "Is he as fine a teacher as you expected?"

"He's wonderful." Diana tried to sound enthusiastic. "I'm so lucky that he accepted me."

The fiasco with her grandmother behind her, Diana told herself that she would concentrate on her painting. But through Mark Grant she was drawn into the fascinating new world of other art students. They all went to restaurants and theaters and public houses fre-quented by other artists writers and musicians. She was thrilled the first time someone pointed out a well-known painter arriving with a pair of beautiful models.

They went to the "Bohemian" clubs, where they were allowed to linger long past the hours when alcoholic beverages were legally served. They passed away hours dissecting the meaning of life and art. It was all very intoxicating . . .

DIANA was learning to adore American films. She read Michael Arlen and D. H. Lawrence and Aldous Huxley. She rode in fast cars and learned to smoke. She became best friends with Marilyn Meyers, another art student whose father had been knighted by Queen Victoria and who had her own flat in the new Devonshire House apartments on Piccadilly adjoining the Ritz Hotel.

Diana was thrilled when Clive Burton, whom she had met at the Princess Restaurant—which had four bands for dancing—began to pursue her. His father was somebody important in politics, Marilyn said, and his mother was a Christian Scientist. The autumn weekend when Marilyn went off to visit her parents and urged Diana to stay at her Devonshire House apartment, she knew she wouldn't refuse to allow Clive to "come in for a drink" after the theater. It was embarrassing to be the only virgin left in their group.

She and Clive went to the new Noel Coward play and loved it. Afterwards they went to a pub and he drove her home. He knew so much about the theater, he was very good-looking—everyone had a crush on him—very popular, he seemed to like her . . . she handed him the key to the apartment.

"Isn't it absurd how some journalists talk about Coward's plays being immoral?" Clive said as he unlocked the apartment door. "I could understand American journalists saying that—they're so provincial. But British journalists wouldn't dare say anything so foolish." He switched on the light. Diana felt a twinge of irritation. She loved Americans: their films, their novels, their music. Anyway Mama had been born in America; so that meant she was part American.

"Well I don't care what the critics say—I adore Noel Coward," Diana said airily. She was beginning to feel uncomfortable alone here with Clive.

"And I—" he reached for her, "adore you . . . "

She stiffened in his arms.

"Wouldn't you like a Manhattan?" It was the only drink she had learned to make—Marilyn had taught her.

"I'd like you." His lips were pressed gently at her throat and she remembered that book by F. Scott Fitzgerald where the girl talked about all the men she had kissed. Since she'd come to London, she must have kissed a dozen men. It hadn't been very exciting. Would it be fascinating to have Clive make love to her? She ought to know by now what it was like.

"Clive, you're tickling me." she squirmed as one hand tried to move underneath the V-neck of her dress.

He was ruffled. "Don't I excite you?"

"Oh, yes Clive, yes. It's just that—" How could she tell Clive Burton she was a virgin?

He reached for her hand.

"Let's go into the bedroom."

In Marilyn's bedroom, with its lemon-yellow walls and white leather furniture and a huge print of Van Gogh's *Sunflowers* hanging over the bed, Clive began to take off his clothes. Diana stood by uncertainly. It seemed so cold-blooded. Not the way Mama had described it . . .

Clive pulled off a sock and looked up at her.

"Well—what are you waiting for?"

"I'm enjoying looking at you." She hoped it sounded provocative.

"Stop wasting time." But she could tell he was pleased.

Slowly, she began to undress. When at last she was naked she stood by uncertainly. Was Clive supposed to make the first move? He pulled her down on the bed and began to kiss her. She tensed as his mouth moved to her breasts and a hand caressed that special place between her thighs. No one had ever touched her there before . . . Soon he'd know she was a virgin. How humiliating. Would he hate her for it?

His breath uneven, he raised himself above her. Diana tensed.

"Clive, I don't want to get pregnant." Now she wished she knew enough to carry condoms in her vanities like the other girls . . . for a fleeting moment he looked annoyed.

"Stop worrying. My wallet's right here by the bed."

As he reached for his wallet Diana tried to relax. She just hoped it wasn't going to hurt much. Laura, who knew everything, said it hurt just for a minute. Marilyn said you never forgot the pain—but

239

Marilyn was dramatic about everything . . . she guessed she could stand a little pain . . .

"Clive, turn out the lamp," she tried to sound sultry. If it hurt, she didn't want him to see her face. She should have had a doctor take care of this so Clive wouldn't have to know.

"Oh, so you're one of the romantics." He reached over and switched off the lamp. She felt something warm move between her legs. Then Clive's hand was fumbling down there, cold and rough, and suddenly she felt a sharp pain . . . Her arms closed around his shoulders, and soon she was moving with him. At last Clive groaned and, sweating, collapsed on top of her. Diana lay still. Afraid to move. That was it?

"You never did it before," Clive said with pride.

"Technically, no," she conceded. Thank goodness he wasn't annoyed. It would have been awful if he had laughed. He seemed to like it. But she certainly didn't think it was anything great. Was it her fault? Maybe she wasn't doing it right.

"At least you didn't bleed like a pig." He reached to switch on the lamp again. "There was this girl from the chorus of a musical last year —I thought she'd bleed to death."

Diana thought that sounded awfully cruel. Mama hadn't talked about it like that.

"Clive, that's crude."

"Just honest. Who'd expect a chorus girl to be a virgin? She went on to marry a Jew. He may have been a Rothschild," Clive said smugly, "but he was still a Jew."

Diana froze. She was Jewish. Marilyn was Jewish.

"You're lying in a Jewish bed," she told him, her eyes blazing, "with a Jewish girl."

"Hardwicke?" He lifted an eyebrow in disbelief.

"My father was a Hardwicke. My mother was a Levy. I think you'd better get out," she said coldly. "And I don't think I want to see you again."

WHEN Marilyn returned from visiting her family, Diana told her all about Clive and what had happened.

Marilyn was philosophical.

"Diana, Clive's not the only Englishman who's anti-Semitic. They forget what Jews have done for England. They forget about Disraeli.

They forget that without Disraeli and Baron Lionel Rothschild England wouldn't have the Suez Canal. My father told me about a certain British Lord who, though he has little taste for the Jews, admits that without them London would have no arts."

"Marilyn, I want to see the East End," Diana said urgently. That was where her grandparents lived before they moved to America. "That's the Jewish section of London, isn't it?"

"Part of the East End is Jewish, part is gentile."

"Show me the Jewish part."

Diana remembered the time when Adam had knocked down a classmate who was four inches taller and twenty pounds heavier than he because the boy had said something under his breath about "dirty Jews." Adam had learned to read Hebrew at classes at the synagogue and he had been *bar-mitzvahed.* To Diana synagogue was the place where she went with Mama on Friday nights if she couldn't think of any way to get out of it. It had been her "church," attended the way classmates attended St. John's Protestant Cathedral or the Roman Catholic Church or the Union Church—under protest.

She had grown up in a world of daydreaming, never thinking about being Jewish. She knew that Mama was Jewish and Papa wasn't. But somehow, when Clive had said that about the Jew something in her froze . . .

TOGETHER Diana and Marilyn walked through the lively streets of the Jewish East End. Here wages were low and unemployment on the rise, Marilyn said. Diana had never seen such poverty.

As they continued walking Marilyn explained that the East End was the home of the poor Jews and the newly arrived. East End Jews were hardworking and thrifty. Instead of moving away to fancier sections of London when they became less poverty-stricken, they used their money to buy better clothes, to travel, to upgrade their scale of dining. Many gentiles, overlooking the hordes of Jews living in poverty and seeing only those improving their lot, were jealous and bitter that these immigrants from foreign shores had so quickly elevated themselves.

As they pushed their way through the narrow, crowded streets in their smart expensive garb people noticed that they were obviously strangers to the area and stared.

Diana realized that she hadn't eaten for hours.

"Marilyn, let's stop somewhere for tea."

They walked into a small kosher restaurant that smelled like baking bread and after sitting down at one of the simple wooden tables ordered tea and hot apple strudel.

While they waited to be served and Marilyn chattered on about something, Diana noticed a handsome young man, dressed in clothes that looked more American than English, sitting across the room. It was clear that he didn't live in the East End.

"You have an admirer," Marilyn giggled. "Good-looking chap."

"Marilyn, be quiet," Diana hissed. "He'll hear you."

While they pretended to be engaged in fascinating conversation, it became obvious that Diana's admirer was trying to decide on an approach. He rose to his feet. Diana tried to concentrate on Marilyn. He hovered above them.

"Excuse me," he said smiling, "you're an American, aren't you? Didn't I meet you at a party on Long Island in June?"

"My mother was American," Diana told him, taking in his neatly-cropped dark hair, his eyes a startling blue in contrast to a golden tan. "But I've never been there." Her own smile was apologetic.

"You're from the South," Marilyn said.

"My bloody accent," he laughed. "Nails me every time. I'm Charlie Hendricks. From Columbus, Georgia."

"I'm Marilyn Meyers, and this is Diana Hardwicke. Would you like to join us?"

"I'd like nothing better." He slid into a chair next to Marilyn.

"What are you doing in the East End?" Diana asked.

He laughed.

"I'm staying with a great-aunt who lived here forty years ago. She always talked fondly about the East End—though you can be damn sure she wouldn't want to live here again—so I decided to take a look for myself." He was contemplative for a moment. "Back home I don't suppose there are much more than a hundred Jewish families."

"There are less in Hong Kong," Diana laughed. "That was where I was born. I lived there until a few months ago." Charlie Hendricks stared at her in surprise. She loved to see people's reactions when she told them about her background. "All this is very new to me," she admitted, gazing around the restaurant.

Charlie looked only at Diana as he spoke. "Sometimes we almost forgot we were Jewish. My folks went to the synagogue for the High Holidays, and we had matzos on the table during Passover. Matzos had to be ordered in advance from Hirsch's Grocery Store. Then I went away to school, and I came face to face with being Jewish. In the dormitories Jewish students roomed with other Jewish students, Christians with Christians. We were segregated by religion."

Diana and Marilyn spent the rest of the day with Charlie Hendricks. Diana was intrigued by his lilting Southern accent, by the way he crinkled his eyes when he laughed, by the disconcerting way he looked at her—as if he wanted to see right through to her soul. Before he said good night to them in Marilyn's flat, Diana knew she was in love with him.

CHAPTER

TWENTY-THREE

ONSTANCE ALLOWED HERSELF far more time than she needed to dress. But she wanted a few minutes to think before she went downstairs to join Sam beneath the *chupah* for the ceremony that would make them husband and wife. Today she felt like a young girl on the threshold of life. And yet here she was, thirty-seven years old—entranced as a sixteen-year-old at the prospect of marrying the only man she had ever loved. But there were moments when the pain from the past intruded on her happiness.

Last night she had written Diana to tell her that she and Sam were getting married today. They had waited even past the year of mourning just so that the worst heat of the summer would be over.

Constance knew it was absurdly romantic, but she wanted this— her real wedding day—to be perfect.

Would Diana ever forgive her? Sometimes she suspected hers and Sam's secret was more of a shock to Diana than Elliot's death. Adam seemed to have accepted Sam as his father with genuine pride; he was even eager for the day when Sam would legally adopt him. But not Diana . . .

Adam had been only three when the gentle, sensitive Elliot she had married went off to war. He remembered only the bitter, angry Elliot who returned. Diana had wanted desperately to be close to her father, and she had expected their painting to be a strong bond between them.

Constance felt the old anger return. Why couldn't Elliot have encouraged her? Diana had so much talent. She'd never be happy until that talent was satisfied. Maybe in London . . .

Diana wouldn't have wanted to come home for the wedding today. She probably would have been angry to be asked. Constance sighed. How she wished she could make this child understand! But she just couldn't seem to bridge the space between them. Wouldn't the passage of time only widen and deepen that space?

Olivia wrote that Diana was seeing a fine young man from the States. She suspected Diana was in love. And knowing that it would be important to Constance, she wrote that Charlie Hendricks was Jewish. Of course, Constance thought, Diana wouldn't dream of telling her mother any of this in the brief notes that she occasionally sent home . . .

She started at a light knock on her bedroom door.

"Mama—" Adam's voice. "Are you ready? It's time . . . "

DIANA and Charles walked hand in hand through St. James Park. It was a beautiful late October afternoon, the sun filtering through orange and red trees. But Diana didn't notice . . . all she could think about was the fact that by the end of the week Charlie would be leaving for home. He had already postponed going back three times. Now his father was insistent. Also, Charlie admitted he was running out of money.

"Why do you have to go home now?" Diana asked for what must have been the hundredth time. "Just when we're having such a wonderful time." When Charlie kissed her, she tingled all over. When he held her close she thought she would break in two; but they hadn't slept together yet and it bothered her. Hadn't she made it pretty obvious that she was dying to sleep with him? Of course she couldn't come right out and say it. But he must be able to tell she'd marry him tomorrow if he asked her. Marilyn said it was written all over her face . . . "At least, I thought you were having a wonderful time." She tried to look hurt.

"Listen, Diana, I have to go home and straighten some things out with my father." His expression was serious. "He expects me to go into his factory—seems to think I have a great future in the overall business."

"You'll write me, won't you?" She'd die if she never saw him again . . .

"You know I will." For a minute she thought he would kiss her right there in St. James Park.

"So, do you like living in Columbus?"

"It's a lot different from London or New York. Slower. Everything's less complicated. The biggest excitement is when a play comes into town at the Opera House—or when the Georgia–Auburn football game is played there."

Diana laughed.

"It sounds like Hong Kong. Except for the half million Chinese."

She would not let Charlie see how hurt she was that he was going back home without even talking about the possibility of them becoming engaged. Maybe London was just a big party for him. His college graduation present. He probably wouldn't write her even once. Well, maybe once. But then he would become involved with some Georgia girl and forget he ever knew Diana Hardwicke.

How could she live in London without him?

DESPITE the demands the shipyard made on her time, it was Constance's salvation. Caught up in the daily problems in her office she could push from her mind all her family worries—about Diana, so young and so far away from home, and now about Sam, overwhelmed with grief at the news that his sisters—Leah and Sarah—had been killed in an Arab attack on their village in Israel.

She tried to comfort him. But he blamed himself for having encouraged them to go to Israel. Night after night Constance would wake up to find only the imprint of his body on the sheets next to her. Sam would be prowling the house in anguish.

Late in December Sam decided he had to go to Kaifeng to try to find his two older brothers and his sister Rachel. Constance knew it was futile to try to persuade him to abandon the search, but she couldn't stop herself.

"Sam, the mainland is in chaos. The Kuomintang soldiers are everywhere."

"They're not hurting people. And I'll travel in Chinese dress so I don't stand out."

"But what about the business—"

"The hong can manage without me for three weeks. And you said you'll keep an eye on the real estate operations." He reached for her hand. "Connie, I won't be a fit husband until I at least try to find what's left of my family. I won't be able to live with myself." His eyes told her he was sorry for those nights she lay alone in bed—and she forgave him . . .

"Be careful, Sam." She would worry about him every minute he was away.

Two days later Sam left. Constance tried to forget that soon—in another two years—Adam, too, would be in London to begin his studies at Oxford. Thanks to the University Test Act of 1871, a large number of Jewish students were able to attend the prestigious university.

To add to her worries Diana had written with talk about studying art in America. Olivia suspected she was eager to go to America because the young man she'd known in London was now there. In some town in Georgia. Diana, of course, had no concept of how big the United States was.

Constance tried to convince herself Diana would soon abandon this idea, but she knew that her daughter was not ready to return to Hong Kong—and she feared that maybe she never would be. She decided to ignore Diana's talk about New York and the Art Students League for a while. At least in London Olivia could keep an eye on her.

At last, early in the new year, Sam returned from the mainland, exhausted and frustrated because he had discovered nothing about his brothers and sister.

Constance couldn't bear to see him so unhappy.

"Sam, you must stop torturing yourself. You have Adam and you have me. We're a family."

"Connie, without you and Adam I would be nothing. I know that. But why did Leah and Sarah have to die? Joseph died in battle; but they were just two good women leading quiet lives until the Arabs attacked the village. There has to be a Jewish homeland, Connie. We must have a place where we can live and thrive as a people." Constance shared this desire.

"There will be, Sam. In your lifetime there will be."

She had hoped that when Sam came home this time he would finally have put his pain behind him, but now the nights became even more frightening . . .

The first time it happened, she tried to tell him it didn't matter, that of course it would be all right. Now she didn't say anything. Every time Sam tried to make love to her he failed.

"Sam, it's all right," she whispered one warm April night as he sat at the edge of their bed with his head in his hands. "You're tired and upset. It's natural that—"

"Every time it's the same!" he exploded. "Connie, I feel like I'm not a man anymore."

"It'll be all right again, I know it will." It had to be. "Try to get some sleep."

She knew he lay sleepless until dawn while she pretended to be asleep. Sam was only forty-one. Men of his age still gave their wives children. Time would change things. She longed fiercely to make love to her husband again.

ON a lovely March afternoon, Diana waited impatiently for Marilyn outside the small tea shop that had become their special meeting place. For months she had been trying to persuade Marilyn to come to New York with her. Marilyn's family was wealthy—they would set her up in a flat in New York. But Marilyn kept hedging because she was—despite protests to the contrary—devoted to her large family. Mama knew that she and Marilyn were best friends. Naturally, if Marilyn went to New York Diana would go with her.

And now Diana had a special reason to go to New York. Charlie. In her purse was the letter from him, in which he said that he had finally convinced his father he would never be happy in the family business. In September Charlie would be coming up to New York to study journalism at Columbia.

The letter's casual tone infuriated her. Why couldn't he ever come out and say, "Diana, I love you"? She was sure he did. He was probably scared of being tied down to marriage—after all, he was only twenty-two. But in a few months he'd be in New York . . . She was determined to be there too.

At last Marilyn came charging into the tea shop out of breath as usual. Diana gazed with pride at her beautiful and chic friend. Whenever the two of them went out together, she couldn't help but notice how they attracted the stares of men . . . But of course the only man who mattered was Charlie. Even so, she and Marilyn dropped a lot of hints about their hectic sex lives because it was smart for a girl to pretend she knew something about men . . .

"You're late," Diana pretended to be angry. "And just when I'm bursting with news!"

As Diana outlined her plan about moving to New York she could tell that Marilyn would be happy to go with her. Her parents were trying to push her into a "suitable marriage" and she was anxious to be on her own.

"I'm sure we can manage it," Marilyn said with an elfin grin. "All I have to do is cry on Daddy's shoulder. But what about your mother? Didn't she give you a hard time about living in London?"

Diana was confident.

"If I tell her you're going with me and say I'll die if I can't go, she'll keep the checks coming. She feels guilty about having married Sam. Anyway, Mama knows I'll never live in the same house with them." Marilyn couldn't understand why Diana was so hostile towards her mother. It didn't sound like Mrs. Hardwicke was such a bad person —a little over-protective maybe, but weren't they all? Well, maybe some things were better buried in the family. She knew that as well as the next person . . .

IN three weeks Diana and Marilyn and a fleet of trunks were aboard the *Mauretania*, bound for New York. The girls were fascinated by this floating castle, with its main staircase paneled in French walnut, its Louis XVI writing room, its library paneled in gray sycamore with touches of gold and ivory, and bookcases exactly like those in the Trianon, its eighteenth-century main lounge and ballroom in the French motif, and its Verandah Cafe, a copy of the Old English Orangery at Hampton Court.

Marilyn's father used his New York City contacts to lease an apartment for the two girls in the Dakota Apartments, directly across from Central Park. Diana and Marilyn were thrilled with the romantic yellow-brick Renaissance building—its lofty gables, dormers, turrets, bay windows, and balconies. Diana imagined she was a princess living in a European chateau as she moved around the high-ceilinged rooms with parquet floors, mahogany wainscoting, and fireplaces and solid bronze hardware.

As soon as they arrived Diana signed up for classes at the Art Students League, while Marilyn made no bones about pursuing her primary interest—men. Marilyn swept Diana along on shopping sprees at B. Altman's, where they bought daringly short Chanel dresses and every kind of Dorothy Gray makeup in stock, and collapsed over tea at the Charleston garden.

In a long letter to Charlie, Diana tried to convince him to visit them in New York as soon as possible. She still couldn't believe that Columbus, Georgia, was a thousand miles away. In his response to her letter Charlie made it clear that it would probably be months before he would be able to come to New York. At first furious, Diana sank into a deep depression. In a blistering letter to Charlie she told him she never wanted to see him again if he didn't even think enough of her to run up to New York for one little visit . . .

Marilyn did her best to pull Diana out of her depression. She made sure the two of them were swept up into a flurry of parties. They led two lives—one revolving around the Art Students League and the other consisting of evenings at the theater and the best speakeasies, and weekends on Long Island with Marilyn's rich friends. It was all very entertaining—but it did not ease the ache caused by Mr. Charlie Hendricks . . .

They loved Fred and Adele Astaire in *Funny Face* and the new comedy called *Holiday* by Phillip Barry. They read the new collection of poems by Edna St. Vincent Millay and Stephen Vincent Benet's novel in verse, *John Brown's Body.*

Early in July they went to a movie party and saw the exciting new sound film, *The Lights of New York,* starring gorgeous Helene Costello.

"Wasn't that the cat's pajamas?" their host demanded as they emerged from the Strand, to be prodded into a pair of limousines waiting to take them to the Hotsy-Totsy, their host's favorite speakeasy.

After an hour at the speakeasy a guest in the party invited everyone out to his family's beach house on Long Island.

"Come on, guys, the folks are all away—Switzerland or something. It's hot as the devil here. Let's drive out and have ourselves a swim. There're plenty of bathing suits . . . " he winked. "If you're that old-fashioned."

They piled back into the limousines. Diana was exhilarated—what a treat to get out of this stuffy city in the first heat wave of the summer . . .

"Henry, faster!" their host barked at the chauffeur. "We want to get out there and swim!"

A scream rose in Diana's throat as she saw a car swing out onto the road ahead of them. The chauffeur jammed on the brakes, but not soon enough. She felt a bone crushing pressure on her chest. A searing pain.

And then—mercifully—oblivion.

WITHIN hours after the cable arrived telling her that Diana lay seriously injured in a Long Island hospital, Constance was on her way out of Hong Kong in a British Army plane. She had always been terrified of flying, but she had to get to New York—as fast as possible.

Sam had offered to go with her. But Constance had insisted that he stay in the Colony and keep the business going. It might be weeks before she could return. And they couldn't leave Adam alone.

As she sped towards her destination Constance pondered the past troubled months. Maybe her initial instinct had been right—maybe she should never have let Diana go to New York. Of course accidents can happen anywhere. But maybe if she'd been a better mother Diana would never have wanted to leave the Crown Colony . . .

What had happened to her marriage? Of course Sam loved her, as she loved him. How was she failing him that they could no longer share that love in bed? For months now he had been sleeping at the edge of their bed, shoulders tense, his back to her. No longer daring to even try to reach for her in the darkness.

At last she arrived in New York. After she had gone through customs, Constance recognized a pale Marilyn from Diana's description.

"Marilyn, how is she?" For days Constance had been imagining Diana in her hospital bed, crippled. Dying.

"She regained consciousness right after I cabled you. But the doctor is seeing her today. A surgeon who specializes in this kind of problem."

Constance barely noticed the porter taking her luggage.

"I want to see her. Immediately."

"She's been moved to a hospital right in the city, Mrs. Hardwicke. It's not far from the apartment. Let's drop off your luggage, then we'll take a taxi there."

"Marilyn—" she had to know . . . "Marilyn, this back injury—does it mean Diana can't walk?"

"Not yet. But the surgeon who saw her this morning is supposed to be great. Everything possible is being done, believe me." Constance stared ahead. Would it be enough?

IT seemed to take forever to deposit the luggage in the apartment. Constance noticed the changes in the city since she had left twenty-two years ago. She remembered the Gomez house, just a few blocks along Central Park West from the Dakota. Mr. and Mrs. Gomez were dead now. Marilyn tried to make small talk, but neither of them listened.

At last they were driving across town through the summer-green park to the hospital.

"Aside from the back injury how is Diana feeling?" Constance asked as they stood before the hospital.

"She's depressed," Marilyn admitted. "We all try to cheer her up. I'm hoping this new doctor will be able to help her."

Marilyn led her into the hospital and to the bank of elevators. They moved noiselessly to an upper floor, down an antiseptic-scented corridor to Diana's room.

"She's in here," Marilyn threw open the door to a room filled with flowers.

Diana lay in bed, her auburn-tinted hair rumpled and longer than Constance remembered, her wide blue eyes scared.

"Baby!" Constance walked over to the bed and tried to gather Diana in her arms. So young and afraid. "My sweet baby—"

"Mama, I can't walk," Diana whispered. Gone was the "Mother" that she had been using in her letters. "They don't know if I ever will."

"You will, my darling. I'll find the doctor who can make you walk." Her children would sustain her through anything; she must see them through every crisis . . .

"Marilyn and Freddie have been wonderful. Freddie is the boy whose car I was in when the accident happened. Along with Freddie's father they've handled everything. Freddie's father sent in a surgeon this morning." Diana paused, her eyes a mixture of hope and doubt. "He thinks he can help me. Something about an operation on my spine."

"Whatever it is, I'm sure he will."

"The other doctors on staff here disagree with him. I told him he'd have to talk to you, Mama. That you were coming today. I think you know him. He was all excited when he learned my name. He asked if my mother was Constance Hardwicke—"

"David!" Of all the doctors in New York, fate had brought David and her back together . . . "David Field!"

"Then you do know him?"

"Oh yes. I met him—and his wife—fifteen years ago on the Trans-Siberian Railroad—when I was on my way to London on business. We kept in touch until 1917. But I didn't hear from him after the war. I was afraid something had happened to him." Wonderful, kind David, after all this time . . .

"He wants you to call him as soon as you can. Mama—" Diana clung to her. "Do you think he can help me?"

"I have absolute faith in David." And she did. "He's a fine, dedicated surgeon. If he says he can help you, he will."

An hour later Constance sat with David in his Park Avenue office. Could it be fifteen years since she had seen him?

"Constance, you look beautiful," he said softly. "Just as I remembered you. And you know I think I knew who Diana was immediately. Except for her hair she's the image of you."

Constance smiled. "I don't know if that would please her as much as it does me. We've had our hard times together. But David—" she leaned forward—"will she be able to walk again?"

"There is an operation." David looked grave. "I've performed it twice with excellent results. But many of my colleagues disagree with me. They think it's too much of a gamble. My feeling is this—Diana is young and strong. And while I can't guarantee success, I think it's worth the gamble. I can't imagine a girl like Diana in a wheelchair for the rest of her life."

"If she were your daughter, David?"

"I'd operate immediately."

"Then do it, David. I trust you."

He seemed startled by the suddenness of her decision.

"Now, Constance, I want you to remember—if it fails it will take weeks for her to recover and she'll probably never walk again. I'm sorry to be so blunt but we all must face this possibility."

Constance was firm.

253

"Diana and I want you to operate. Please schedule it for as soon as possible."

TWO mornings later Constance was sitting with Marilyn in the waiting room of the surgery floor while David and a surgical team operated on Diana. It had been almost three hours. Every half hour or so Marilyn went for tea for both of them. They chatted about London, New York—anything but the possibility that the operation might be a failure. Constance wouldn't even think about it. How could she face Diana and tell her that she would never walk again? This time she just didn't have the strength. If only she hadn't let Diana come to New York . . .

Her thoughts turned to David . . . he had returned from a year as an army surgeon to find Frances in love with another man. They were divorced immediately. Frances remarried, was divorced again, and was about to marry for the third time. Poor David. He must be very lonely. But even on their trip together she had sensed their marriage was shaky. David deserved better. He had so much to offer a woman. Why hadn't he remarried?

Compulsively her eyes moved to the swinging doors. David and another doctor were emerging. She leapt to her feet. David was smiling.

"Constance, she's fine," he said, coming towards her. "She'll be on her feet and painting masterpieces in no time . . . "

"Oh, David!" Now she could cry. "I knew you'd see us through this. I knew."

Over dinner that night David told Constance that Diana could go home in three weeks—assuming there were no complications—and that she would probably be back on her feet and normally active in another three weeks.

Though she spent a great deal of time at the hospital with Diana, Constance made a point of leaving her alone with the hordes of friends who poured into her hospital room during visiting hours. It still hurt her that Diana never once asked about Sam or her marriage, that the deep affection Diana had once felt for Sam was now hostility.

David arranged for some free time every day and they either had lunch or a late dinner together. He talked mostly about his work— which was his consuming passion—but he wanted to know all about her life in the years since they had first met. She told him candidly about the emptiness of her first marriage, the triumphs at the ship-yard—and she was shy when she told him about Sam, so she talked mainly about Sam's commitment to Israel.

One Friday morning, two days before Diana was scheduled to leave the hospital, David called Constance at the Dakota.

"Constance, did I wake you? I always forget that people who aren't doctors sleep in the mornings."

"No, no I was awake," she lied, squinting at the clock. Five minutes past seven.

"Listen, I've managed to arrange for a long free evening like a regular person. I'm leaving the office at quarter to five and I'm not making any night rounds. It's going to be another one of those hot days that New York is so famous for. Anyway, I know a magnificent place for dinner up in northern Westchester. Unusual in decor, and the food is superb. Why don't we take a drive up there? It's a long haul, but the country's beautiful this time of year."

Constance didn't hesitate a moment. This was just what she needed . . .

"David, I'd love it." The oscillating fan sitting on the dresser in her bedroom did little to help the humidity that had already made her feel clammy and tired. "What time shall I expect you?"

CONSTANCE was surprised—and a little worried—by her anticipation of dinner with David. Of course she was flattered by his admiring gaze, his concern for her. And of course he had saved Diana—there was nothing wrong in having dinner with an old friend who had saved her daughter from life as a cripple . . .

Marilyn dashed into the apartment to change and to pack a valise.

"It's so awful in the city I decided to go to Southampton for the weekend. You don't mind, do you Mrs. Hardwicke?"

"Of course not. Enjoy the weekend, Marilyn. And make whoever is driving you be careful."

PROMPTLY at five David arrived at the Dakota. Constance was waiting. In minutes they were in David's sleek black Cord, heading out of the city. Since Diana's accident Constance had been afraid of motorcars. She tried to relax and enjoy herself . . .

With the windows rolled down and the city behind the warm summer air became bearable. David was in high spirits; Constance realized he was making a determined effort to charm her, and she was both flattered and touched.

The restaurant was situated in a charming house dating back to pre-Revolutionary days with the rooms of the lower floor set up as several small dining areas. Constance and David were led to a beautifully laid table set beside an open window. A gentle breeze ruffled the roses sitting on the table in a delicate vase. It was still early, and people were just beginning to arrive.

David was right. This was a special place. For the first time in weeks Constance felt safe, relaxed, lighthearted. Dinner was superb. David was warm, charming. This was the man who had made Diana walk again . . .

David seemed to be talking compulsively, as if to make up for all the lost years.

"You know, Constance, I suppose some would think I keep a harrowing schedule, but I really wouldn't have it any other way. Not until the day I retire. When the pressures get to me, I go to a little house I bought right after the war. That's how I discovered this place. It's about twelve miles above." His gaze was disconcertingly intense. "I've never shown a living soul the inside of that house. I'd like you to see it, Connie."

Constance started. Only her father and Sam had ever called her that. And she wondered about this invitation . . . but that was ridiculous, this was her old friend David . . .

"David, I'm flattered. Of course I'd love to see it." But her smile was uncertain.

"Let's go up there now. I'll get the check." He looked for their waiter.

Within twenty minutes they were standing in front of a small, simple house set in a clearing of a large wooded area, late summer sunlight spilling gold across the trees.

"I'll come up and paint it myself when it's a little cooler," David was saying. "Doesn't the air smell wonderful?"

"Oh yes. And there's a brook." Constance laughed. "I can hear it. You know, that's one of the things I've really missed in Hong Kong."

David unlocked and opened the door. Constance walked into a large room with a dark beamed ceiling and a huge stone fireplace. A wide black leather sofa, flanked by a pair of lounge chairs, stood in front of the fireplace. In one corner of the room was a heavy maple table, over which hung a Tiffany lamp.

"The kitchen's through the door there if you'd like more coffee. But I'm afraid it'll have to be black. I like to rough it up here." He smiled.

"No more coffee, thank you." Constance was enjoying the beautiful silence, the coolness of the room.

"On the other side," he indicated the arched opening to the right, "are my bedroom and studio." He laughed at her look of surprise. "Oh, I'm not a serious artist like Diana. But painting helps me relax. Come, I'll show you." He reached out a hand to her.

The studio was cluttered with canvases, some finished and some abandoned halfway through. But it was a pair of framed paintings on the far wall that held Constance's attention—gentle, lovingly detailed portraits of a startling-looking woman. It was her.

"David, they're—they're very good," she stammered.

"I'm glad you like them. But they're really only for me—I wanted to remember forever a very special encounter."

Her eyes met his. So, this was it . . . what she'd sensed but had been unwilling to admit. He'd even remembered the dress she had worn during that trip all those years ago. When she spoke, her voice shook.

"David, you're a very special person and I—"

He pulled her into his arms, his lips on hers warm and tender. She knew she should pull away—she loved Sam . . . but it had been so long since they had made love. David's arms tightened around her and she felt that old, familiar hunger . . .

"Stay with me tonight, Connie," he whispered.

"David, we shouldn't." How could she feel this way?

"Please. Let's just have this time together." He pressed against her. "Let me have this to remember. Ever since I met you I've known that you were the only woman in the world who meant a damn to me—"

CONSTANCE lay in the curve of David's arm and watched him sleep. She felt protective and sad and guilty all at once. If Sam had not come into her life, maybe she could have loved David. But she was Sam's wife, and one day, she knew, he would come back to her. Their marriage would be good again. She and David had both needed tonight. But it would never happen again. Surely David knew that . . .

"Connie—" He stirred.

"David, we—"

"Don't say a word." He pressed his lips to her throat. "Tonight, these few hours till morning will have to last me a lifetime."

Constance closed her eyes and abandoned herself to feeling. It had been so long . . .

IN the delicious country coolness of the early morning they dressed, neither tired though they had slept little. The road would be empty at this hour on a Saturday morning. They would be in the city before nine, even if they stopped off for breakfast.

Constance struggled with guilt as David drove towards the little country restaurant where they would have breakfast. She still couldn't believe it—for the first time in her life she had been unfaithful to Sam. The charade of a marriage to Elliot didn't count. No, since the day he asked her to marry him, she had been Mrs. Sam Stone, honest and true. Until now. How could she have been so weak?

CHAPTER
TWENTY-FOUR

IANA WAS THRILLED to be out of the hospital and in the apartment. She had almost forgotten those awful black days before the operation, the long nights as she lay awake imagining what it would be like never to walk again, assailed by memories of Papa in his wheelchair. It was over. She would stop being silly about Charlie. Forget Marilyn's advice about playing it cool . . . she would call him in Georgia. Surely if she was sweet and apologetic, he would forgive her for all the horrible things she'd said.

But she wouldn't phone him until Mama went back home. When was Mama leaving? She'd been back in the apartment almost a week. Didn't she realize that she planned on staying in New York? Being in the accident hadn't changed anything; it could have happened in London or even in the Crown Colony.

At last Constance announced that she had bought passage to England on the *Mauretania,* and that she would be staying in London for three days with Olivia and William before going back to the Colony. Before she left New York, she took Diana shopping at Altman's, where Diana found a fancy blue voile dress, and Saks, where they had fun trying on practically every hat in the store. That night Diana phoned Charlie's house in Columbus.

A Southern voice answered.

"The Hendricks residence."

"May I speak to Charlie, please?"

"Mist' Charlie is up in New Yawk. He's goin' to Columbia University up there."

"Thank you," Diana stammered, and hung up. Charlie was here. She'd go straight up to the school and find out where he was living.

At two o'clock the following afternoon Diana sat across from Charlie in a dark, wood-paneled restaurant. He listened intently—his face reflecting his concern—as she told him about her accident, her fears that she would never walk again, and how sorry she was that she had been hotheaded and stupid the last time they were together.

"Diana, I had to make my father understand I would never come into the business. I knew it would take months to get it through his head. I told you that. I'm the only son, so of course I was supposed to take over the business. Now he'll look for a son-in-law to fill the role." He grinned. "Luckily he has three daughters to help him out there."

"So you're serious about being a newspaperman?"

"You know, I think it's the only thing I've ever really wanted to do." It seemed to Diana that this was the first time he had opened up to her. "My mother's unhappy because she knows I won't try for a job in Columbus. But I could never earn the kind of money on the local newspaper that would let me live the way I like."

"So you think you're going to live in New York?" Diana probed. Wherever Charlie lived she would too. Eventually he would ask her to marry him. "Or maybe you'd like to live in London?" She'd loved London . . .

"I guess I'd like to live in a lot of places." Charlie grinned. "Even Hong Kong."

Diana couldn't imagine him in Hong Kong. She shrugged.

"It's not all that great."

"You're great," he said, reaching across the table for her hand. "I thought a lot about you while I was fighting with my father back home."

"I've thought about you." If only she had never slept with that creepy Clive Burton . . . but it would be different with Charlie—she had never been in love with Clive and she was in love with Charlie.

For the next four months Diana and Charlie spent every moment together. Diana decided to be honest with him: she told him all about

260

Clive, and he told her about the girl he had slept with when he was at the University of Georgia. Of course he hadn't been in love with her. They'd been at a house party, and he figured it was the sophisticated thing to do. It wasn't until the night before Thanksgiving—when Marilyn was spending the long weekend with friends—that Diana and Charlie finally slept together. They had made a pact not to go all the way until they were absolutely sure that this was the real thing.

First they had Thanksgiving dinner—Diana remembered her mother's reminiscences about Thanksgiving in New York with her Mama and Papa—at the Algonquin, because Charlie was intrigued by its reputation as a hangout for famous literary personalities. Then they went up to Diana's and Marilyn's apartment at the Dakota. Marilyn would be away until Sunday night.

At first they chatted nervously about the other people in the Algonquin dining room. Charlie thought everybody looked self-conscious because they thought they were supposed to be with their families and dripping sentiment about how thankful they were. Diana loved the idea of Thanksgiving and thought he was being too much of a cynic, though of course she didn't say so.

She offered to go out to the kitchen to make coffee for them, but Charlie clearly had another direction in mind. She didn't need a second invitation. She was a little nervous, though, about what it would be like to make love with Charlie . . . she would absolutely die if it were just like it had been with Clive.

But as she lay naked in Charlie's arms, she knew this would be different. She adored Charlie. She only hoped she would be able to please him. But soon she forgot her fears . . .

"You're something," Charlie whispered happily. "I knew you would be."

Charlie was serious about his classes at Columbia, but restless to move out into the newspaper world itself. And he still hedged about asking Diana to marry him. It was infuriating her, but she tried not to show it, convinced that he just needed time . . . Her own studies at the Art Students League were suffering because she made herself available to Charlie whenever he wanted her. They listened to George Gershwin as he played *An American in Paris,* laughed at the antics of the cartoon character, Mickey Mouse, in *Plant Crazy.* They dined at the Automat when their money was tight and at the Algonquin when one of them got a check from home. Diana even learned to cook so that they could have quiet dinners at the apartment.

Charlie's parents were unhappy that he was not coming home for the winter break. He was holed up in Diana's bedroom with his typewriter—he said he had no privacy in the dorm—working on an article about London's East End for an underground magazine. When word came through that the magazine was buying the article, Charlie celebrated by asking Diana to marry him.

After his initial reticence in asking her to marry him, Charlie now wanted to tell the world—but it was Diana who insisted they keep it a secret until the spring. His mother called early in February to talk about the wedding plans. Since Diana's family lived in Hong Kong, Mrs. Hendricks insisted that she and Mr. Hendricks arrange the wedding. They hoped that now that Charlie was taking on the responsibility of a wife he might reconsider coming into the family business.

In March Diana forced herself to sit down and write her mother that she was marrying Charlie Hendricks, "whom Aunt Olivia knows and likes," saying that of course she understood it would be impossible for her mother to come to the States for the May wedding, but that at some point in the future she would bring her new husband home to meet her mother and brother—she omitted mention of a stepfather.

She wrote, also, that Marilyn was returning to London—probably permanently—because of her mother's illness. Marilyn's father, always generous, complained that business in Great Britain continued to be bad; the recovery the country had hoped to see this year was apparently not happening. She would probably have to give up the apartment at the Dakota, which Charlie felt was beyond their means anyway.

By return mail she received a letter from Constance who tried her best to hide the hurt that Diana was sure—and sort of hoped—she felt at being excluded from her own daughter's wedding. As part of her wedding present, Constance wrote that Diana's allowance would continue for another year after her marriage . . .

"That should keep you at the Dakota, my love. I know how you feel about that crazy apartment."

When spring vacation at Columbia approached, Charlie told Diana that he had managed to get a writing assignment that would take him briefly to London.

"Don't worry, my fee will cover the costs for both of us, Di. But

262

we can't stay for more than three nights because I have to be back in New York for classes. Besides, we couldn't afford the hotel and meals for more than that."

"Oh, but Charlie, it would be wonderful to stay in London for a while. Maybe I could help out with the money." Diana had visions of a spring ocean voyage to England, night after night at the London theater . . .

"I go to school, remember, my sweet?" he clucked. "Are you trying to lead me astray?"

"I'm afraid I did that long ago, my darling."

THEY made reservations aboard the *Mauretania*, but this time they traveled third class. In London they booked themselves into a modest hotel in Russell Square. Within hours of their arrival Charlie was off to interview the subject of his article, so Diana phoned Olivia and asked if she could come over for tea.

Olivia was thrilled at the prospect of seeing Diana again. She had been expecting this marriage for a long time, and she insisted that Diana bring Charlie for dinner the next night.

"Diana, I just knew he was for you," she said happily as the two of them sat in her drawing room. "I know your mother can't wait to see him."

Diana paused.

"Well, Aunt Olivia, it won't be for a while. I mean I can't expect Mother to come to the States again. She was just here. So Charlie and I are going to be married in Georgia."

Olivia was shocked.

"You mean you're not going home for the wedding?"

"It's not practical, Aunt Olivia." She avoided Olivia's eyes.

"So you're going to deny your mother the joy of seeing her only daughter married?"

"Well—" Diana looked cornered. "It just wouldn't work out." She shouldn't have come here. "Anyway Mother's busy with the business and Sam—"

Olivia leaned forward. "Why don't we talk about your real reasons for not wanting your mother at the wedding? You know she would never be too busy to give you a wedding. Diana, I'm going to take advantage of my age and my love for both your mother and you. I think you're punishing your mother for her relationship with Sam."

Diana's face flamed with color and her rage—simmering beneath the surface for all these years—boiled over . . .

"Well, how could she have behaved that way? Having an affair with Sam behind my father's back. Letting him believe that Adam was his child!"

Olivia looked at her for a long moment.

"Diana, your father's dead. The truth can't hurt him anymore. Your mother was pushed into marrying him by her aunt. She was engaged to Sam, but your great-aunt made it appear that Sam was a philanderer. And of course," Olivia paused, "your aunt was unaware that your father was a homosexual."

Diana stared.

"What do you mean?"

"I mean that your father, knowing he could never be a real husband to your mother, married her with the hope of being welcomed back into his family. Your mother began the affair with Sam—whom she had never stopped loving—only after she discovered your father in bed with a young houseboy. But he never knew your mother was aware of his sexual inclinations."

"I don't believe it!"

"Darling, I'm sorry, but it's true." Olivia's voice was gentle. "Now I ask you—and I want you to think with your heart—what would you have done in your mother's position?"

"My mother told you this?" Diana whispered.

"She told only me. Not even Sam knows. She came to me after she caught your father with the houseboy. That was why your grandparents on your father's side shipped him off to Hong Kong. Apparently there was a hushed-up incident at school. The family was terrified of scandal. This wasn't long after the Oscar Wilde affair and—"

"Poor Papa." Diana stood up and paced the room. Even today muckraking journalists in Fleet Street wrote about how Freud, Jung and Havelock Ellis were responsible for the rise of all these elegant, prominent homosexuals . . . "To have been rejected by his own parents that way." Now her chilly reception at the Hardwicke house made sense.

"Yes—and now you are trying to reject your mother. Think about it, Diana. She was a young girl when William—in desperation—dragged her into the business. Almost singlehandedly she not only rescued it from failure but built it into one of the most important firms in the Far East. And she did it so that you and Adam could be

264

raised in the luxury you take for granted. From the beginning your mother has fought not for herself but for her children. If it were not for Adam and you, she would have divorced your father to marry Sam. But she wouldn't take the chance of losing you. And after the war, of course, there was no way she could divorce Elliot. Some women are born to give. Your mother is one of them."

Diana fought back tears.

"It's too late to change the wedding from Columbus to Hong Kong. But I'll take Charlie home to meet Mama as soon as possible." She hesitated, struggling for composure. "How can I thank you, Aunt Livvy?"

"Darling, be kind to your mother. And try to forgive." Olivia held out her arms. "That's all the thanks I need."

LATE in May, with the school year at an end, Diana and Charlie stepped on the train to Columbus. In the cavernous old railway station they were met by Charlie's mother and father and two of his sisters, all of whom were chattering excitedly about the wedding.

A flurry of letters between Mrs. Hendricks and Diana over the past several weeks had seen to the arrangement of the wedding. Bridesmaids and ushers had been chosen. Charlie's oldest sister—just home from Sophie Newcomb in New Orleans—was to be the maid of honor. His two younger sisters and cousins would be bridesmaids. Taking Constance's place would be Charlie's grandmother who would escort Diana to the *chupah*. The wedding and the reception would be held at the Ralston Hotel. As they drove to the Georgian house on upper Fourth Avenue where Charlie was born, Mrs. Hendricks pointed out the tall, dark-red brick Ralston.

"I'm surprised you didn't arrange for the wedding to be held at the Country Club," Charlie teased.

"I never set foot in that place," Mrs. Hendricks said sharply. She noticed Diana's confusion. "The Country Club," she explained, "to my knowledge numbers no Jewish families among its membership. I never attend any function held there, though Jews are received as guests." Was there a spot on earth where anti-Semitism did not cast its dark shadow? But Charlie had boasted that the *Columbus Ledger* had been active in getting rid of the city's Ku Klux Klan . . .

"Charlie and the girls attended parties at the Country Club during their high school years. Since then they've felt as I do. The Ralston

265

has beautiful facilities. I promise you, my dear, this wedding will be one of the loveliest the city has ever witnessed . . . "

For several days Diana was caught up in a round of parties given in her honor. She was delighted by the Southern charm and warmth of everyone she met, and comforted by the affection of Charlie's family.

At last the wedding day arrived—warm but not stifling as late May could be in Columbus. The sky a brilliant blue. At the Ralston Hotel in the room reserved for the wedding party, Diana stood in her pink chiffon-over-satin gown with its fashionable uneven hemline, wearing slippers to match, an imported French horsehair hat, and holding a bouquet of pink Briarcliff roses and lilies of the valley. Only now did she realize how much she missed her own family . . .

In the weeks since their trip to London, Diana had spent a great deal of time thinking about her life, the choices she had made, and trying to see herself honestly. She remembered her father's bitterness. His hostility. She remembered her mother's frenzied efforts to protect Adam and her from their father's temper. And she longed to tell her mother that she was sorry for not understanding.

The music that was to precede the ceremony jolted Diana back into the present. Miss Gertrude Chase was at the harp, Mr. Louis Chase on the organ, and Miss Louise Johnson on the violin. Diana remembered the funny stories Charlie had told her about the demanding spinster Miss Gertrude, who had taught him to play the piano at the Chase Conservatory. Shubert's "Serenade" would be first, then "At Dawning" and "I Love You Truly." The bridesmaids looked a little frantic but excited in their pastel gowns of crepe de chine with the same uneven hemlines, and carrying shephard crooks tied with tulle the same color as their gowns and showered with shasta daisies.

The opening chords of Mendelssohn's "Wedding March" were played, and the junior bridesmaids entered. As she went down the aisle, one thought turned over and over in her mind—Mama, I love you . . .

IN Hong Kong Constance buried herself in her work on the day of Diana's wedding. Sam was off in Canton on business, but he had promised to be home in time to take her out to dinner. He had been

266

very quiet when he left this morning. She could tell he was furious about Diana's decision. He knew how deeply it had hurt her. Adam was off with a friend at a golf match. Late in summer he would leave for England to get ready for Oxford. Adam, too, was hostile towards his sister for cutting herself off from them, but he kept his thoughts to himself, knowing his mother wouldn't hear a negative word spoken against Diana.

AFTER a brief honeymoon in the North Carolina mountains Diana and Charlie returned to the apartment at the Dakota. Diana sent Constance wedding photographs and dozens of snapshots taken during their honeymoon, but it did little to assuage her guilt. A dozen times she picked up her pen to write her mother about her true feelings; but the words wouldn't come. So she took refuge behind newsy, empty letters, telling herself her mother would understand.

With Charlie—and she knew that Sam and her mother, too, were deeply involved—she followed the fighting between Jews and Arabs that began at Jerusalem's Wailing Wall and had spread throughout Palestine. Eight American Jews were killed by the Arabs in the massacre at Hebron. Early in September she and Charlie pushed their way into Madison Square Garden to a meeting of twenty-five thousand Jews and gentiles and joined in the tumultuous roar of approval for a sympathetic telegram read on behalf of President Hoover.

Diana and Charlie lived very well, thanks to Constance's monthly checks and a little help from Charlie's parents who, Diana could tell, thought that Charlie would soon abandon this business of being a journalist and settle down to a responsible job.

Late in October 1929 America was rocked by the worst financial disaster in history. Everyone living in the United States was affected by the Wall Street Crash. Repercussions were felt around the world.

Charlie called home and learned that his father had suffered a mild heart attack after learning that all his stocks were worthless. Now his only concern was to meet obligations at the factory so they didn't lose the business. Charlie wondered if he should come home, but his mother convinced him to stay in New York and keep working.

But Charlie was finding it difficult to get assignments. Several of his markets had dried up. Diana and he were barely managing from month to month on the checks she still received from Constance, but they both knew that soon those too would stop. They began looking for jobs, but it was a tight market and they had a tough time finding positions to suit their skills.

Diana was shocked by the newspaper accounts of unemployment and poverty around the country. Senators were demanding action to check unemployment and attacked President Hoover's administration. The Communist Party staged unemployment demonstrations in Union Square. Bank rates fell to one-and-a-half percent, the lowest in the history of the Federal Reserve System. Bread lines and soup kitchens were springing up around the country.

At the end of April Diana realized that the next check from Constance would be the last. Of course if Mama knew they were in trouble she'd send something—but they were too proud for that. Somehow they'd manage . . . She was worried by the desperation she saw in Charlie's eyes, every time he returned from a futile job interview. Neither of them had ever thought that money would be a problem . . .

"Charlie, my mother knows an awful lot of business people," Diana said over dinner one blustery April evening. "Why don't I write and ask her if she has contacts her in New York that you could use?"

Charlie brightened. That's a great idea, Di. Tell her I'll work anywhere."

That night Diana wrote Constance, asking if she knew anyone who could help Charlie find a job—preferably on a newspaper. Diana wondered if Hong Kong's economy was in trouble too. But she had faith that whatever was happening in the Crown Colony her mother would survive . . .

Two weeks later a cablegram arrived.

JOB AVAILABLE HERE FOR CHARLIE STOP COME HOME IMMEDIATELY STOP CABLING FUNDS CARE YOUR BANK STOP CAN'T WAIT TO SEE YOU BOTH STOP MAMA

With mixed feelings Diana showed Charlie the cable. Of course she had overlooked the obvious—Mama would grab this opportunity to bring her back home. But once she had time to think about it she

268

was surprised by how much the idea of returning to the Crown Colony excited her . . .

"You notice Mama doesn't say what kind of a job," Diana pointed out.

"Diana, at this point I don't care. It's a job. Anyway I've always wanted to see the Far East," he chuckled. "Did I tell you that the new Madame Chiang Kai-shek went to school in Georgia? She speaks English with a Southern accent. Maybe I could interview her for the *Herald-Tribune*."

CHAPTER

TWENTY-FIVE

CONSTANCE COULDN'T BELIEVE that Diana had decided to take her up on her offer. She and Charlie and Adam—coming home from Oxford for the summer—would all arrive on the same day. Her children—back home at last. They would be a family again. And now when she and Sam made love it was like the first time . . .

Though Sam hadn't talked about it, she knew he missed the children too—Adam was his one grasp on immortality.

Sam had given up hope of ever finding his older brothers and sister Rachel; they had been swallowed up somewhere on the mainland of China—now controlled by Chiang Kai-shek and the Nationalists. In memory of Leah, Sarah and Joseph, every month Sam sent money to Israel—home now of one hundred sixty thousand Jews. Constance realized that Israel owned a part of Sam that she could never claim, but she shared his commitment to the new Jewish homeland . . .

Determined to keep her family together, Constance encouraged Sam in his ambition to become the most powerful real estate broker in the Far East. Money was the best way to serve Israel and he was at the same time building an empire for his son.

On Sam's advice, Constance was diversifying her own business. Both of them were uneasy about the world economy. As the depression took on global dimensions the trade in the Colony had dropped sharply and unemployment was skyrocketing. Already there was talk of the government creating jobs through road construction and other public works.

Together Sam and Constance plotted to make Diana's return permanent. They bought a floundering weekly newspaper in Hong Kong and reorganized it to cater not only to the Crown Colony residents but to the new English-educated Chinese elite, many of whom were active in the professions though still excluded from living on the Peak. Of course they intended to keep their financial control of the newspaper a secret, at least for now.

"It's enough that Diana and Charlie believe we used our influence to find a job for him," Constance said firmly. Nothing must spoil this reconciliation with Diana. She didn't know exactly how or why it had come about—but she planned to make it last. "We'll make it clear that Charlie will have to prove himself."

"Connie, relax." Sam's eyes were tender. "The way things are today I'm sure Charlie will work very hard to keep this job. And from what Diana says he sounds like a young man with a healthy dose of ambition."

"But, you know, Sam, I feel guilty that we're doing well when so much of the world is hurting."

"Connie, don't look for guilt. The children are coming home. Enjoy them." But already he was remembering that soon Adam would return to school . . .

CONSTANCE and Sam instantly liked Charlie. While the men talked far into the night about the depression in the States, the recession in Great Britain, the shortage of food in Russia, and the presence in Munich of a rabble-rouser named Adolph Hitler, who screamed about the "Jewish menace," Constance and Diana had warm, loving talks about the wedding and Diana's hopes for the future.

Constance was thrilled by the ease with which Diana and Charlie settled into life on the Peak in the house she and Sam bought them as their first anniversary present. She tried to hide her disappointment when Diana told her that she was no longer painting—all she wanted was to have a baby.

FOR Constance the next two years were good. Diana was home and happily married to a man she and Sam had grown to love as a son. Adam had decided that when he finished his studies at Oxford he would come into the real estate business with his father. When he was not worrying over the rumors filtering out of Germany about the growing power of Hitler and his National Socialist Party, Sam was engrossed in the plans for a new resort hotel in Hong Kong. Despite a floundering economy and Japanese hostilities in China, the wealthy of many nations were eager to acquire more wealth in the Far East. A hotel would prosper.

In order to finance the hotel without endangering his other holdings Sam had started corresponding with a German banking family. He insisted that Constance go with him when he was invited to Berlin to discuss the dealings in greater detail. It would be the honeymoon they never had . . . But Constance was ambivalent. Instinct told her this was not the time to leave Diana.

Constance was increasingly worried about Diana's depression over being unable to conceive. She seemed to have convinced herself that until she gave Charlie a child, she was not fully a wife.

"Something happened to me in that awful accident, Mama. I just know it. Why didn't Dr. Field tell me?"

"Because there's nothing wrong with you." Constance thought the real problem was that Diana had too much time on her hands—Charlie was tied up most nights at the newspaper. Maybe she could persuade Diana to resume her painting. "Dr. Field—"

"But Marilyn got married seven months after me. She has a darling little girl and she's already pregnant again. She—"

"Diana, this is not a race between you and Marilyn to see who can fill more cribs faster. When the time is right, you'll conceive." Constance hesitated when she saw how sad Diana looked. "Darling, will it make you feel better if I wrote Dr. Field to ask him about this? He wouldn't lie to me." She hadn't heard from David since New York. Since that night in Westchester . . . but for Diana she would do this.

"Oh yes, please Mama. Write Dr. Field. Ask him if he's keeping something from me."

While Sam continued negotiations with Berlin by mail, convinced that the time would come when they would go to Germany—Constance waited for a letter from David. She was sure Diana's fears were unfounded . . . Surely David would have told her if something had happened in that accident to prevent Diana from conceiving.

At last the letter from David arrived. He had been so happy to hear from her. Of course Diana had no cause to worry. She was a normal, healthy young woman. She just had to be patient . . .

Constance realized that David had made the letter sound like it came from a concerned friend—just in case she showed it to Diana. But Constance worried that the letter might not be enough to calm Diana's fears . . .

"I'm very excited about some findings in the research I've been doing since I last saw you. I've been invited to read a paper at the University of Berlin the first week in August. Every time I travel to Europe—which isn't often—I remember that journey on the Trans-Siberian Railway."

So, David would be in Berlin in August. Sam planned for them to be there in late July. Maybe Sam could postpone the meeting with the Rosenthals for a week or ten days. Even though she sent David a card at Rosh Hashanah every year, Constance had vowed she would never see him again after New York; but if they had dinner with David in Berlin and he reassured them—in Sam's presence—that Diana was able to conceive, then Diana would have to be convinced. Diana and Sam had become very close, and she was sure to take his word . . . Constance resolved to talk to Sam about this and then cable David.

IN their elegant and shockingly expensive suite at the Hotel Adlon on Unter den Linden, high above the petrol-scented avenue, Constance was nervous and excited as she dressed for dinner. She had expected to be too tired to go with Sam on his first meeting with Kurt and Leo Rosenthal, but despite her initial distaste for Berlin, she was fascinated by the somber grayish stucco, brick, and mortar buildings as they rode from the station to the hotel. She tried to forget that this was a country with five million unemployed, a city where the homes of thousands were mere tents set up in camps. She tried to forget what she had heard and read about Hitler and his Nazi Party.

She worried about her German, but Sam kept reminding her that the Rosenthal brothers spoke fluent English. One damp, sweltering late afternoon Sam had gone out for a walk along Unter den Linden. Constance told herself it was silly to be nervous . . . they were British tourists, safe from the insanity rippling through Germany. Like thousands of other tourists in this summer of 1932 they strolled through the streets, finding meager comfort in the knowledge that the American and British Embassies were close by.

Tomorrow she would call David at the Bristol Hotel and they would decide where to have dinner. Sam was looking forward to meeting this famous doctor who had helped Diana walk after many had given up hope. Constance tried to tell herself it would not be awkward to meet David again. They cared about each other too much to let what happened . . .

A somber and apprehensive Sam returned from his walk. He was shocked by the despairing faces of the people on the streets, depressed by the pervasive sense of desperation and decadence in this city—men and women trying to sell shoelaces, singing folksongs in courtyards. Begging. Young girls trying to sell themselves to anyone who would have them . . .

"Connie, we'll meet Kurt and Leo at Peltzer's. At Neue Wilhelm Strasse 5. The desk clerk says it's one of the best restaurants in town."

"Fine. I'm ready to leave whenever you are."

"Well, we have some time. Let's walk around for a while first."

As they strolled towards Peltzer's, Sam took Constance down some side streets. With his hand at her elbow, they walked past a trio of young boys hovering together conspiratorially over a cigarette, overheard a shabbily dressed pair of old men debating about what bets to place on the next day's races, and listened to a shopkeeper complaining about how he had to ring all coins so he wouldn't be cheated by counterfeiters . . .

Constance was unnerved by all the men in uniform. Stormtroopers. Brownshirts strutting in exaggeratedly wide brown trousers and dreary brown shirts. Pairs of officers rouged and powdered, walking arm in arm.

She had read about the nightclubs in Berlin like the Eldorado, where homosexuals met nightly and the Monocle, frequented by Berlin's lesbian population. Tourists flocked to both clubs. But the memory of Elliot still nudged her. Constance knew she would never visit these places . . .

Sam's voice startled her.

"Connie, it's time to meet the Rosenthals."

At Peltzer's they were shown to the table that had been reserved by Kurt Rosenthal. Kurt and his brother Leopold, two trim and dapper men in their early fifties, were already seated.

At a nearby table a group of Nazi chiefs were sitting back in their chairs talking loudly. Constance found their arrogance disgusting. Displayed conspicuously on the ample bosom of a middle-aged woman was a swastika. Constance looked away . . .

"May I suggest we speak in English?" Leo Rosenthal asked smiling at Constance. She suspected this was more a move of caution than courtesy.

After ordering for Constance and Sam and pointing out Julius Streicher, the widely disliked publisher of the pornographic Nuremburg weekly, and beautiful film star Leni Riefenstahl, Kurt asked Sam for more specific figures on the financing of the hotel. Keeping their voices low even though they were speaking in English, Kurt and Leo took turns reporting on what was happening in Germany— pausing each time their waiter hovered at the table.

Leo's face was grim as he spoke.

"In September almost two years ago the Nazi Party members came into the first session of the new Reichstag screeching *"Deutschland erwache. Juda verrocke."* Germany, awake! Judea perish! On Rosh Hashanah two years ago there was Jew-baiting on Kurfuerstendamm. Nazis smashed in the windows of the department stores, attacking anybody they suspected of being Jewish."

"Actually the Nazis are after the Jewish intellectuals," Kurt added. "They won't bother the important businessmen—they are necessary to the economy, which I don't have to tell you is in a deplorable state." He sighed. "Stock shares have fallen to shocking lows. City governments are defaulting on their bonds. The small storekeepers can't compete with the likes of the Tietz department stores. Unemployment soars. Bankrupts are committing suicide daily."

"We keep telling ourselves that Hindenburg—though he is already eighty-four and on the verge of senility—can control Hitler. In April he signed an emergency decree to disband Hitler's private armies, the

S.A. and the S.S. But in June he rescinded the order." Leo shook his head. "I don't know anymore."

"We have to believe Hindenburg," Kurt said sharply. "We cannot allow Hitler to win a majority."

"It's astounding to see monarchists, aristocratic men and women, fawning over this fanatic. They shut their ears to his tirades against the privileged classes. They fight to entertain the high-ranking Nazis." Leo's eyes were angry. "I was born in Berlin. My father and grandfather were born here. But I don't recognize my city any longer."

Constance and Sam were told that they were dining in a restaurant —and not at one of the Rosenthals' homes—because their families were on "extended vacations" in England. Constance and Sam knew not to probe. The Rosenthals scheduled conferences with Sam for the next two afternoons. Constance decided she would do some sightseeing. Tomorrow night they would be having dinner with David. It surprised her how much she was looking forward to it . . .

THE next morning—after calling David and arranging to meet for dinner—Constance and Sam visited the Old and New Museums and on the advice of a young American couple they met, ate a simple lunch and drank Rhine wine in the cellar of Lutter and Wegner, a charming old restaurant on Charlotten Strasse which, with low vaults and black ceilings, was famous as the scene of the opening of the opera *Tales of Hoffman.* Constance was intrigued by the photographs and framed inscriptions hanging on the walls—souvenirs of the great men and women who had been customers of the century-old restaurant. She got up from the table for a closer look.

"Why Sam, here's a photograph signed by Heinrich Heine. And one of Jenny Lind . . . "

After lunch Sam went on to meet Kurt and Leo Rosenthal and Constance looked for a present for Diana and Charlie in the shops of the fashionable section of the city. Laden with packages, she stumbled upon the umbrella-decked terrace of Doben's, and had a delicious "mocca"—coffee, heaped with whipped cream. Almost forgetting what was going on around her in this strange city . . .

As the afternoon drew to a close Constance started back to the Adlon Hotel. David would pick them up at their suite at seven, so there was plenty of time for her to soak in a warm tub before she had to get get dressed. She was glad David was taking them out of the city for dinner—it would be wonderful to leave behind the heat of Berlin for a night . . .

When Sam returned from his conference with the Rosenthals, Constance was stretched out on the bed, savoring her quiet moments and still tired from traipsing around the city.

"How was the meeting, Sam?"

"Fruitful," he said. But his face was serious. "For all their optimistic talk about this insanity not touching the important businessmen in Germany, Kurt and Leo are afraid of what lies ahead for the country. Particularly for the Jews."

DAVID was on time as usual. Only for a moment—when she introduced David to Sam—was Constance uncomfortable. But she knew immediately that the two men would like each other. So many times since New York she had wondered if she should tell Sam about David . . . but logic told her there was no reason. And now she was happy she had made that choice . . .

David asked about Diana, listening intently as Constance told him about her marriage and her fears that she would not conceive. When Sam asked David what the reaction had been to David's paper at the university, he launched into an enthusiastic report, though he admitted to some earlier reservations about coming to Berlin in its present precarious state. In the limousine David and Sam discussed America's reactions to Hitler.

"You know, Sam, what astonishes me is that most Americans dismiss the man as an agitator. They just don't take him seriously. Don't they realize he's a potential danger to the whole world?"

Sam nodded. "I know. It's incredible how blind people can be if they choose to. Here in Germany we have a paranoid sadist taking over, and the world tries to pretend he doesn't exist. And in Italy the people worship Mussolini, who caters only to the rich."

David was leaning forward in his seat, listening intently. "And in the Balkans and Poland, in Central Europe there's a powder keg that could blow up at any time—all while Russia plots to take over the world in the name of Communism—"

"Look there!" Sam interrupted, pointing out the window. "I hear that happens every night in Berlin."

A band of Nazi youths were painting swastikas on the side of a

277

building. The car moved past a paint-brushed sign reading We Want Hitler.

There was a moment of silence as the three of them pondered this ugly scene.

"David, where are you taking us?" Constance tried to lighten the atmosphere.

"To the Schildhorn," David said. "One of the men at the university told me it was not to be missed." Pulling his gaze from Constance, he turned to Sam. "After what you've seen in the last twenty-four hours, I suspect you're ready for some quiet and fresh air."

While they drove past the modern suburbs, Sam and David exchanged war experiences. Constance listened and suppressed a shudder. It sounded like they were gearing for another war. Inevitably the conversation returned to Hitler, Sam again despairing that the democracies refused to take him seriously. Only Winston Churchill voiced fears about what lay ahead if Hitler was not eliminated.

Constance was relieved when they arrived at a fragrant pinewood forest—the Grunewald. They left the limousine in a parking area and walked along the river to the restaurant. She felt miles away from Berlin and for a moment—just one—it seemed that all was right in her world . . .

AFTER a magnificent dinner, Constance, Sam and David rode back in the limousine to the Adlon. Sam invited David to join them for a drink in their suite, but David demurred. He had a busy day at the university tomorrow, and the following morning he would be on his way home.

Constance and Sam exchanged warm good-bys with David, who promised he would one day visit them in Hong Kong—predicting that within five years there would be commercial airline flights across the Atlantic and the Pacific.

"I like David Field," Sam announced, lying on the bed as Constance was washing her face in the bathroom. "He's bright, articulate, and compassionate." He hesitated a moment. "And he's in love with you." Constance froze, washcloth in hand. "Oh, I know nothing ever happened between David and you, but I imagine he's been in love with you since that trip on the Trans-Siberian Railway."

Constance snatched a towel and patted her face.

"Don't be ridiculous, Sam. David's in love with his work." She kept her voice steady as she came out of the bathroom.

"Believe me, Constance, a man can recognize these things in another man. But I'm not upset. Really. If anything happens to me, I know you'll have someone to turn to. David is a good man."

"Sam, I wish you'd stop being so melodramatic," Constance flared. "Honestly. You look in every corner and see tragedy."

CHAPTER
TWENTY-SIX

CONSTANCE AND SAM could not forget what they had seen in Berlin. Now, whenever Diana and Charlie came over for dinner, the four of them stayed up far into the night talking about the troubles in Germany. Charlie was the only optimist.

"I really think you're all overreacting. I mean, this man Hitler is insane," Charlie was saying as they sipped tea on the verandah on a mild early-November evening. "Didn't the Nazi Party lose two million votes in the election this week? They dropped from 230 to 196 seats in the new Reichstag. Another election or two and they'll be thrown out, I'm sure of it."

"But it's still the largest party in the Reichstag" Sam added. "I can see the handwriting on the wall. Back in August Kurt Rosenthal predicted that many Jews who were in a position to do so would start leaving Germany. He's sure that when Einstein leaves to teach in California next fall he won't return."

Constance was baffled.

"Well, why do Kurt and Leo stay?"

"Because, Connie, they want to be in Berlin to help other Jews if the need arises. And by God it will!" A vein was distended in Sam's forehead. "That's why Britain must eliminate these damn restrictions on immigration to Israel. There must be a space on this earth for Jews."

"Well, maybe this isn't the best time, but I have an announcement to make," Diana said softly.

There was a grim silence.

"I was going to wait until I was sure—"

"What is it, Diana?" Constance leaned forward, talk of Germany forgotten.

"Charlie, you won't be angry with me for blurting it out this way? But here I am with the three people closest to me in the world—and —well—I just have to say it."

"Honey, what is it?" Charlie reached for Diana's hand.

"I think I'm pregnant."

"Di, that's wonderful!" Charlie swept his wife into his arms while Constance exchanged a happy smile with Sam. In the midst of such horror in the world here was a tiny nugget of pleasure. Please, God, let it flourish . . .

DESPITE Diana's protests Charlie insisted that the delivery take place in the Peak hospital. The doctor suspected that she might be carrying twins and she was due to deliver in late May. In June Adam would return from Oxford with his degree. But Constance's joy at having both children home and a grandchild—or grandchildren—on the way was marred by the ominous rumblings from Germany.

On January thirtieth, 1933 Adolf Hitler had become Chancellor, gaining control of the police and the army. On April seventh a decree came through announcing that "Officials of non-Aryan origin are to retire." Artur Schnabel was cut off the air in the middle of a concert over Berlin radio. Conductor Bruno Walter was forbidden to give concerts in Germany. All Jews were ordered to wear the yellow badge indicating their faith.

Early in May Diana went into labor. She phoned her mother at the office in town.

"Mama, I think this is it. Wouldn't you know both Charlie and Sam are out of town?" Charlie had gone to the mainland to cover the latest Japanese hostilities against northern Chinese provinces. Sam was in Berlin again, finalizing the arrangements for the hotel. "The contractions are still pretty far apart, so I guess I shouldn't leave for the hospital yet."

"Don't worry. I'll be there in twenty minutes," Constance said. Twins might come faster . . .

"Mama—" she paused. "I guess I'm a little scared."

"Every woman is scared the first time, darling." She wasn't going to tell Diana it would be easy—but in 1933 there were ways doctors could make it easier. "Soon you'll forget about being afraid. Just think about holding your baby in your arms."

"But Mama, if I *am* carrying twins, do you think they'll be all right? They'll be so small."

Constance chuckled.

"Considering the size of you, I'd say that is not something you should worry about. Now let me get off the phone so I can come get you . . ."

Eight hours later, minutes before Charlie—panting from exertion, his face ashen—charged into the hospital, Diana gave birth to twins. A daughter Janet and a son Matthew. If only Sam were here . . .

"Write Dr. Field and tell him," Diana ordered, her eyes luminous as she lay back against the mound of pillows. "He was absolutely right."

THREE weeks before Constance and Sam expected Adam to arrive in the Colony, they received a letter from him saying that he wanted to go to London to live for a year after Oxford.

"Through a classmate I have a chance to work for a year in an architectural office. I think I could learn a great deal that will be useful in the business . . . "

Immediately Constance assumed the worst—that Adam, like so many young people who left the Colony to go to school, simply didn't want to return to the Far East, where the young and the old were definitely in the minority. Or maybe he had found a girl in England—Olivia hadn't said anything about a girl, but she didn't see him very often . . . Was she Jewish? Sam would take it very hard if his only child married out of the faith. As would she . . .

Constance tried to think beyond her disappointment as Sam read the letter and they waited in the drawing room for Li to announce dinner. Of course Adam was right to take the position. She could tell that Sam, too, was upset at the delay of Adam's homecoming, but he seemed proud that his son showed such resourcefulness.

"It'll be good for him, Connie," he said, putting the letter down on the coffee table. "He's using his head. It makes sense for him to come into the office as well prepared as possible."

"But Sam, remember—you have a large and capable staff. Don't put too much on Adam's shoulders right away."

Constance was worried about Sam. She suspected that he was becoming involved with Kurt and Leo Rosenthal in helping the Jews in Germany. When he returned from his last trip to Berlin he had been outraged about how difficult life had become for the German Jews—their shops were boycotted; placards reading "Germans, defend yourselves. Don't buy from Jews" were posted on their doors; Nazi youths invaded the libraries and burned all the books written by Jews. Sam had quoted Heine: "In whatever place they burn books, some day they will burn humans."

"Connie, I want the family to know how I run the business," Sam said. "Charlie, of course, is totally absorbed by the newspaper. But you and Adam should know about the business. Even Diana."

Constance was alarmed by this talk. It sounded like Sam expected to spend a great deal of time away from the Colony, and not because of the hotel—because of the Jews in Germany who would not or could not leave. Sam was convinced that Israel was their only refuge. Already many Jews who could leave Germany were rushing to Israel, some as "illegal" immigrants because of the British restrictions.

"Will Kurt and Leo be able to continue with the hotel?" Constance asked.

"God, I don't know . . . now it looks like they're running into some trouble with the financing. And Kurt is afraid the government may stop the next installment of money scheduled to be shipped into the corporate funds here."

"Then what will happen?"

"With business conditions what they are, we may have to hold up on the construction plans. But we have no real financial problems. We can weather any storm, Connie."

SUNDAY morning sunlight filtered through the drapes of the bed-sitter Adam had rented only three days earlier. He poured tea for two

283

and carried it to the bed where Peggy lay curled under a light coverlet against the morning chill . . . slender, dark-haired, blue-eyed Peggy, who stood barely taller than his shoulders . . . He was happy that for once they'd been able to spend the whole night together—her parents thought she was at her sister's flat.

He gave her a playful nudge. "You mean to sleep all day?"

"Not a chance. Darling, watch the tea—"

Adam put down the tea tray and sat at the edge of the bed. He had known Peggy six months, since her brother Roger—a classmate of his at Oxford—had brought him home for the Christmas holidays. By the time he and Roger returned to school Adam knew he was in love.

"My parents must have received my letter by now," he said, playing with her fingers.

"Oh, Adam. You're worried that they'll be upset, aren't you? Come on. They won't make you come home. You're a grown man, remember? They can't do that anymore." As always with Peggy, the words were tough but she said them with love.

Adam's face softened.

"You're right, I know. Anyway, they're great. They wouldn't do anything like that." But he remembered how upset Mama had been when Diana had gone off to London and then on to New York . . . "They'll miss me, of course." They'd worry that he was not returning to the Colony. "And of course they'd like you."

"Did you tell them about us?"

"Well—no, not yet. I just told them that I had this great opportunity to work in an architect's office."

"Wasn't it devious of me to have Roger persuade Father to hire you?" Peggy giggled. Adam had appreciated that—he knew that Peggy's parents would have practically started getting the wedding invitations engraved if Peggy herself had put in the request. He wasn't ready yet to make an official commitment.

"Well, you're a mighty devious woman." He reached for her teacup. "Get rid of that so I can make love to you."

"In broad daylight?" she said innocently.

"Why not? I want to make love to you every hour of the day." She laughed.

"I think you'd be pretty exhausted, my love . . . "

"You're deliciously warm," he slid a hand under the hem of her nightgown.

"Hot, darling. But we really shouldn't. I have to be dressed and out of here in less than an hour. I'm supposed to be going to church with Felicia this morning."

"You'll go to church," he promised. "After we make love. My delectable little *shiksa.*"

Later, after Peggy had left, Adam wandered through the East End. In the Crown Colony he had always been very conscious of his Jewishness, even though his friends had been an eclectic mixture of beliefs and backgrounds.

But it was at Oxford that he had found himself drawn to other Jews, recognizing the profound hopes they shared . . .

At Oxford Adam had been a member of the Jewish congregation, the Zionist Society—mainly out of respect for his father—and the Oxford University Jewish Society. He had written his mother and father—knowing how it would please them—that a Jew had opened Oxford's first coffee house and was said to have introduced coffee to England.

Like other Jews at the university he was worried about the activities of Sir Oswald Mosley and his group of black-shirted fascists. The Jewish section of the East End had recently been the scene of menacing demonstrations when the British fascists had marched through chanting, "The Yids! We've got to get rid of the Yids!"

Today Adam walked through the East End's narrow, crowded streets and tried to tell himself the Fascists would never make any real inroads in a city as civilized as London. This wasn't Germany, where that maniac Hitler was in power.

WHEN Sam set off on a trip to Istanbul early in February Constance suspected that this "business trip" was really made so that he could help move German Jews into Israel without British approval. These days Sam was unusually closed-mouthed about his activities, but Constance was not hurt by his silences—she knew this was his way of protecting her should the British ever discover his involvement. For weeks her joy in Janet and Matthew was dampened by her fears for Sam.

On the day that Sam returned from Istanbul, Constance received a letter from Adam. In barely three months—the end of May—Adam would marry a British girl in London. Her name was Peggy Gilbert.

Gilbert? Were there Jews named Gilbert? She was afraid to show the letter to Sam.

She waited until after dinner.

"He's coming home?" Sam asked eagerly, reaching for the letter.

"Yes. But first he wants us to come to London. For his wedding."

Sam's face lit up. He loved Diana's children, but Adam's child— well, Adam was his son . . . He scanned the letter eagerly.

"He doesn't say anything about the girl— Is she Jewish?"

"He says nothing about her family."

"We'll go to the wedding," Sam said with finality. "That way we can find out without having to ask."

"But can you get away from the business again? You were just—"

"Connie, Adam will be married with his parents there. The business will survive."

Constance wrote immediately to Adam that, of course, they would be coming to the wedding. She waited impatiently for his reply, hoping he would be more specific about Peggy's faith; Olivia hadn't known anything. But the letter that finally arrived was brief, because he was working long hours to absorb everything before he returned to Hong Kong with his bride. Apparently Peggy's parents had invited them to stay at their flat during the five days they would be in London but he had explained that they expected to stay with his Aunt Olivia and Uncle William.

Constance and Sam made a tacit pact not to discuss the problem of Peggy's faith. But both spent sleepless nights worrying—Constance, because she knew how much Adam's marrying outside the faith would hurt Sam; Sam, because he so desperately wanted a son who would fight for his people . . . At last the time came to leave for London. It was only on this journey that Sam broke down and confessed his sense of desolation that his grandchildren might not be Jews.

"Sam, they'll be our grandchildren; they'll be at least half-Jewish. In Germany," she said bitterly, "that makes them fully Jewish."

At last their train pulled into Victoria Station. Adam was waiting for them, his face glowing with love.

"Peggy meant to be here with me. She was upset that she couldn't come." He smiled triumphantly. "But the rabbi insisted she complete her studies before the wedding."

"Studies?" Sam was puzzled.

"Her conversion, Papa. There was a great deal to be done before she could be married as a Jewess. Did you think I wouldn't raise your grandchildren as Jews?" Wordlessly, Sam pulled his son into his arms.

In the taxi Adam explained that Peggy's parents—her mother a nonpracticing Anglican and her father an avowed agnostic—were less upset by Peggy's conversion than the fact that she would be living in Hong Kong.

"But I reminded them that people think nothing of traveling that far these days," Adam said cheerfully. "And it won't be a financial hardship for them like it is for Charlie's parents."

The twins were a year old; they were old enough to travel. Constance decided that she would give Diana and Charlie a trip back to Columbus, Georgia, for a month's stay. Let Charlie's parents, too, have the pleasure of seeing their first grandchildren.

Constance liked Peggy immediately—with her forthright nature and her boundless energy, she was a dynamo who would be quite a match for Adam. And she was touched that Adam and Peggy had arranged an orthodox ceremony. While the rabbi said the words that joined Adam and Peggy as husband and wife, she reached for Sam's hand. Today her world was full and rich . . .

CONSTANCE tried to tell herself that she should be happy. Diana and Charlie had returned from their trip to Georgia, the twins were a joy, Adam was married to a beautiful, delightfully independent girl who had insisted on coming into the real estate business with him —Sam boasted as much about Peggy's talent for dealing with people as he did about Adam's knowledge of real estate. But Constance was worried. Sam was becoming increasingly involved in covert missions on behalf of the Jews in Germany.

The Nuremberg Laws of September fifteenth, 1935 deprived Jews of citizenship, the right to hold public office and the right to work in the professions. Sam sat down with Constance to figure out how much money they could sent to support the establishment of Jewish schools in Germany, since most Jewish children were excluded from public education. He deplored the strict quotas set up by possible receptive countries.

The attention of many in the Crown Colony focused on the mainland. Since 1931, when they first invaded Manchuria and cut off three provinces from the rest of China, the Japanese had been on the offensive. In 1936 many feared the Japanese were plotting to take over all of China.

Constance was engrossed in the imminent birth of Adam's and Peggy's first child. Typically—and to everyone's consternation—Peggy blithely went to the office every day right up to her due date.

"Honestly, she'll have that baby at her desk," Constance fretted. But she understood Peggy's desire to keep busy. Hadn't she, too, clung to her desk at the shipyards before Adam was born? There were times when she caught herself wishing Diana had some of Peggy's spunk. Since becoming a mother Diana hadn't so much as touched a paintbrush . . .

In the late spring of 1936 Peggy and Adam presented her with a third grandchild—a daughter named Nadine for her maternal grandmother, but "the spittin' image," Charlie declared—and Adam agreed—of her paternal grandmother. Constance left the shipyards early two or three afternoons a week to visit Nadine before going home, making the supreme sacrifice so that Peggy could return to the office; she even let her borrow Sakota until they found an *amah* for Nadine.

The Japanese advance in China—accompanied by a mass influx of refugees in Hong Kong—disturbed Constance. Though Sam had long since abandoned any hope of finding his two older brothers and sister, he worried about what would happen to them as the Japanese pursued their bloody offensive. In July after fierce fighting they had occupied Peking and then Tientsin. In September they took Poting, which led to a week's rampage of murder, rape and looting by thirty thousand soldiers. Charlie was restless—tied to his desk while undeclared war ripped through China.

Then word ricocheted around the world that the Japanese had advanced on Shanghai in the heart of China. British experts guessed that Chiang Kai-shek's aim was to force foreign intervention.

The Chinese were being bombed by Japanese planes based on Formosa, shelled by naval guns on the Japanese warships in the Whangpoo. Suddenly the whole world realized what was happening in Shanghai.

Diana stopped by her mother's office on the second day of the battle of Shanghai.

"Mama, Charlie is impatient to cover the war in China. He's already cabled an American newspaper asking for an assignment."

"But what about the paper?"

"He's convinced it'll manage without him." Diana tried to sound confident. "He's determined to cover the war."

"Diana, talk to him. Isn't there anything you can say to stop him from doing this? What about the twins? Don't let him go looking for grief."

"Mama I can't stop him. It's his chance to become a full-fledged war correspondent and he's going to take it."

CHAPTER

TWENTY-SEVEN

I N THE PALE lamplight of their bedroom, the ceiling fan making a slight ripple in the stifling September heat, Diana lay in bed while Charlie showered. Would he notice that she wore her honeymoon nightgown? She remembered how much fun she and Mama had buying it at B. Altman's . . . how he'd admired the lacy neckline on their honeymoon . . . Tonight must be special for them. Tomorrow he was flying to Shanghai. She had to keep telling herself that Charlie's leaving had nothing to do with his feelings for her. He was a proud, brave man who believed in fighting for what he valued . . . She would not let herself think about the war correspondents who became casualties.

Charlie came out of the bathroom. "You're looking particularly beautiful tonight," he said, crossing to the bed. "I remember the first time you wore that—"

"Charlie, you'll be careful, will you?"

"I'll be fine." He pulled her into his arms. "But you can't miss an opportunity like this. Correspondents are flying out from London on chartered flights that cost their newspapers a small fortune. And here I am practically on the scene." Reaching across her to switch off the lamp, he felt the tension in her body. "Diana, stop worrying about me. I'm indestructible, remember?"

In the morning Diana drove Charlie to the Kai Tak airfield for his flight to Shanghai. Determined not to cry, she watched his plane take off and disappear behind the clouds. How would she live through the days—and nights—ahead without Charlie? When she got home she would dig out her paints and brushes. Maybe painting would distract her until he came back home . . .

Occasionally Charlie managed to get letters through to Diana. He was intrigued that Colonel Joseph Stilwell—whom he remembered from Fort Benning, Georgia—was a military attaché to the American Embassy in China, and loved being able to feed accurate information to the war correspondents.

"Honey, this is the easiest war in history to cover. While almost a million Japanese and Chinese fight in Shanghai, we spend most of our time in the untouched International Settlement. We go out each morning to drive behind the Chinese lines. We return to the Settlement for lunch, then drive to the Japanese lines in the afternoon. After dinner we write like hell on our copy, then rush to dispatch it at the telegraph office in the Settlement."

For three frustrating months the Chinese fought to return their position, each day's agony reported meticuously by the press. At last in November the Chinese—exhausted, starving, their numbers pitifully reduced—began to collapse.

Constance and Sam tried to hide from Diana the newspapers reporting the death of an English correspondent on November eleventh in the last hours of the Chinese defense. Diana found it, read it slowly, folded up the newspaper and put it aside.

"I'm sure Charlie's all right," she said softly.

Sam flared in his anxiety.

"When the hell are Britain and America going to pull their heads out of the sand and look at what they're doing? Japan is receiving most of its war materiel from the United States. British companies are supplying the Japanese in China. And the main concern of the British is that the Chinese resistance is killing trade in the area. That's what war always comes down to: dollars and cents . . . "

From Shanghai the Japanese advanced two hundred miles upriver to Nanking, the capital. The government was moved to Hankow. On December thirteenth Nanking fell. More than forty-two thousand civilians—men and women—were machine-gunned or used for bayonet or shooting practice. An American ship, the *U.S.S. Panay,* was bombed and sank. The American government—still unready for war—accepted Japan's apology.

Diana tried to isolate herself from the chaos in the world through painting and her children as the months limped along. Mussolini— whose forces had slaughtered Ethiopian troops—and Hitler were sending men and supplies to help Franco overthrow the Spanish government. Nazi conspirators assassinated the Austrian Chancellor, and in March German troops marched into and annexed Austria.

Diana was thankful to Peggy for inviting her and Constance to dinner a few times every week. Sam was often away on thinly disguised "business deals" that fooled no one in the family—they knew he was working to get Jews out of Germany and into Israel, and Adam had taken over as head of the family in his absence. Every time Charlie flew in from the war zone, Diana hoped he'd settle down at the newspaper. But every time he got back on the plane . . .

On a late October evening Diana and Peggy sat on the verandah and talked about their children while waiting for Adam and Constance to arrive for dinner. It had been over a year, Diana thought in frustration, since she had first gone with Charlie to see him off to Shanghai at the Kai Tak airfield. Would they ever be a family again?

Through the mist that settled down about the Peak they saw a car approach. It was Constance's Daimler. She screeched to a stop.

"Have you heard what's happened?" she called out, breathless as she ran up to them.

"No." All at once Diana's heart was pounding. "Is it Charlie—?"

"The Japanese are bombing Canton!" Pale and shaken, Constance leaned against one of the verandah columns. "They say it's terrible. The bombs are hitting the thickly populated areas of the poor. Demolishing everything."

"But—that's only ninety miles away." Peggy tried to sound calm. "What does that mean for us?"

"The Japanese wouldn't dare take on the British Empire," Constance said with what she hoped was conviction. "But those poor people in Canton . . ."

Diana began to panic. Charlie was out there somewhere. Near the fighting. Already two war correspondents had been killed in China. If only they had listened to Charlie's mother and settled in Georgia . . .

"What about the Chinese forces?" Peggy asked. "Is there a chance that they'll drive the Japanese out of the city?"

Constance sighed.

"I'm afraid not. Canton has practically no defenses. They were sure that the Japanese wouldn't dare attack so close to the Colony."

Diana shivered. And *they* were sure that Great Britain stood between the Japanese and the British Crown Colony. Had the world gone crazy? How could they be sure of anything? Why wasn't Charlie here instead of chasing down war stories? Weren't his wife and children more important than a damned newspaper story?

"There's Adam," Peggy said, hearing his car before they saw it emerge from the heavy Peak mists.

Adam pulled up behind the Daimler and hurried over to them.

"It's grim. Not only are the Japanese murdering thousands of defenseless civilians—they're blowing up almost every factory and modern building in Canton."

Peggy gasped.

"Well, Britain won't let them get away with this, will they?" Peggy said.

"I'm afraid they will, my love. They don't want to be dragged into a war without America's support."

"And if China falls into Japanese hands, what chance do we have here?" she asked quietly.

"It's as good as in Japanese hands right now. They hold every major city, every major port, the railroads. What chance does China have? As for us," Adam paused, "we're safe enough. For now."

MOST of the residents of the Colony believed that Japan was too involved in negotiating a settlement in China to consider an attack on Hong Kong. Although its population was heavily Chinese, the Colony was part of the British Empire. When Sam returned on the first night of Hanukkah after being away for nine weeks, Constance immediately sensed that he, too, was worried about Hong Kong's safety.

"God, Connie. It's all so frightening . . . At least when I went away to fight in the Great War, I knew that you were safe from the fighting. Now I can't even be sure of that."

"Sam, we can't run away." Now maybe Sam would stay home.

"Everything we've spent our lives building is here. It's chaotic, I know—but we have each other, the business, our family."

Sam smiled wryly.

"You know I thought after the last war I'd never have to fight again. Of course in China it seems like the fighting never stopped—but I really didn't think we'd see Europe like this again."

"Papa died in the Spanish-American War, Sam. Then we had to live through the awful Great War. How many wars in a lifetime? When will the world learn to live in peace?"

For the next few months Sam stayed in the colony. But he was disturbed by the presence of the Japanese just across the bay. Sometimes Constance woke up to find him standing absolutely still at the window, gazing out into the night.

Constance noticed, too, the little ways the war was changing their lives. The city was teeming with refugees from China. Restaurants were jammed. People lined up for the movies. Constance had to phone days in advance for an appointment at her beauty shop. Those who had once spent their free time devouring American film magazines and the latest issues of *True Confessions* now talked only about the progress of the war . . .

In May the British White Paper of 1939 was published, limiting Jewish immigration to Israel to another seventy-five thousand, at the rate of fifteen hundred a month. After that immigration would stop. Sam was outraged.

"The British are trying to appease the Arabs. Look at this! The Labor members in the House of Commons cry out against it. Churchill calls it a second Munich. And the Jews call it the 'Black Paper.' "

"Sam, I'm sure they'll rescind it. They'll have to. They know what's happening in Germany."

"They're playing politics, damn it!" He began to pace. Constance watched him, knowing what was coming . . . He stopped pacing and turned to face her. "Constance, I can't stay here and do nothing. I'm going to Israel. I'll offer my services to the Haganah." He smiled. "I'm not exactly a stranger to them."

"Sam, you've done enough. You're fifty-three years old. Leave the war to younger men."

"But I'm younger than some men of forty, and I've fought in Palestine; Connie, I have to go to help. They'll need me." She couldn't go through it again—those years of wondering if he would ever come back to her. She knew he loved her, but he was no longer her husband —he was married to Israel . . .

Within a week Sam was gone. Olivia wrote from England, begging Constance to bring her family to London. She and William feared the Japanese would attack Hong Kong. Peggy's parents urged them to come to London. David wrote asking her to move to New York.

"My country house is at your disposal for as long as you like. I'll help Diana and Adam and their families settle here. Connie, I'm worried about your safety . . . "

The months rolled by with no sign of trouble from the Japanese. But on September first, 1939, Hitler's troops moved into Poland and Austrian Jews were being driven into concentration camps. Another World War had started . . .

Emergency legislation was passed in Hong Kong to provide for censorship, requisitioning of ships and aircraft, and mining of the harbor approaches. The previous June the Colony had ordered conscription for male British subjects of European birth between the ages of eighteen and fifty-five. Now men between the ages of eighteen and forty-one who were fit for active service were enrolled in the Hong Kong Volunteer Defense Corps or the Hong Kong Naval Defense Force.

Four days after the invasion of Poland, Peggy and Adam came to the house for dinner. Constance knew instantly that she didn't want to hear what Adam was obviously bursting to tell her. He waited until they sat down at the table . . .

"Mama, I was at the Consulate this morning. I'm flying to London to join the RAF. Peggy's brother, Roger, is already in uniform."

"But Adam, what about Peggy and Nadine—how can you leave them?"

"Of course it will be hard to leave them. But England has to be defended. We'll be making it safer for you here in the Colony. Hitler has to be made to see that he can't grab the whole world by the throat." Constance looked at Adam with pride. This was Sam Stone's son . . .

"When will you leave?" She had to be strong. For Peggy. For Nadine. Her mind shot back to the day when—with Diana and Adam at her side—she had watched Elliot go off to London to enlist. She remembered how Elliot had come home. She remembered those who did not come home at all. "Can't you wait till the end of the year? Let us at least be a family for New Year's Eve."

"Mama, that's months away."

"Then stay till after Hanukkah." Just a few more weeks of knowing her son was safe . . .

"Hitler isn't going to wait till New Year's Eve or Hanukkah. I'm flying to England in a government transport day after tomorrow. Mama," he scolded, reaching for her, "don't look so stricken. I've been telling Peggy how wonderful and strong you were during the Great War. How you built destroyers for the British Navy. Don't make me look like a liar."

"How do you remember?" Her voice was thick with tears. "You were only three when the war started."

"I remember," Diana said unexpectedly. "I was six. I remember you used to tell Adam and Emilie and me how Papa and Sam were heroes. We never realized that people were dying in that war." Was there a hint of reproach in her voice?

"Diana, you wouldn't want Matthew and Janet to know, would you?" Peggy asked.

"They're eight. That's old enough to start learning the realities of life. Half of Charlie's conversation when he's home is about the brave soldiers who are dying in this war."

Diana looked pale and nervous. Constance suspected she was worried that Charlie might be drawn into the fighting.

"Come on, everyone," Adam chided, "I wish you all wouldn't look as though I were going off to be hanged. I expect to be taken out to dinner tonight and treated like a hero." He looked tenderly at the three women—wife, sister, mother. "It won't be easy on you with the businesses to run and the children to watch over, but I have great faith in the women of this family."

"Mama, let me know if I can help at the shipyard," Diana offered. "Everything seems to be running at the newspaper without a hitch."

"I'll be happy to put you to work, my darling. It looks like we women have a job to do."

CONSTANCE, Diana, and Peggy settled in to bleak days and long nights without their men—a life endured by women throughout the world. The occasional letters that arrived were read over and over, until the paper was worn, the ink smudged. They were frustrating letters—telling little about where the men were, what they were doing—and never mentioning coming home . . .

They did know that Sam was in Israel. That Adam was flying with the RAF. That almost daily the RAF was repelling German air assaults. Letters from Olivia told them about the blackouts, sandbags, gas-masks carried everywhere, and the frenzied efforts to provide safety for the people in London.

In the spring a letter arrived from Lionel Levy's solicitor. Lionel and Rebecca had died in a bombing attack, and Lionel had willed his estate to Constance. What remained after taxes would be placed in a London bank in her name.

Constance was deeply saddened by Lionel's death. He had been her one friend those first years in Hong Kong . . . She was touched by his generous spirit, glad that she had continued writing to him twice a year.

In May word came through that Peggy's brother, Roger, had been killed in action. Shattered, his parents left London and retired to the north of England. Peggy, who had always seemed so strong, clung to Constance for comfort. Both of them were haunted by the high casualty figures among the RAF, terrified of what that might mean for Adam . . . But neither Constance nor Diana nor Peggy even considered leaving the Colony.

LATE in June 1940 the Hong Kong Government announced that all European women and children had to be evacuated. They were to register on July second and be ready to sail for Manila on July fifth. There they would wait for ships to transport them to Australia. Constance called the family together at her house.

Diana and Peggy were indignant.

"Mama, they must be out of their minds," Diana declared. "I know several wives who're absolutely refusing to leave. I won't register."

Peggy nodded in agreement.

"She's right. Why this sudden panic? Everybody knows the Japanese can't afford to become involved in an attack on Hong Kong."

"And anyway I can't leave the Colony," Diana said. "I have to be here whenever Charlie flies home. And I just don't believe the children are really in danger."

"Nor do I," said Peggy. "And we're needed here. How can they order British women to leave when so many thousands of Chinese women and children—"

"All right, all right, you two!" Constance broke in. "We can stay.

I just spent an hour at Government House. The ruling specifically states that women who operate their own businesses, or are involved in defense activities are exempt. We're expected to register, but we don't have to leave."

"Thank God. They can't send all European women away," Peggy said wryly. "Every government office and commercial business in the Colony would be thrown into chaos."

Constance didn't laugh.

"Peggy, Diana, listen to me. If the Government ever proves to us that we are in real danger, we'll have to evacuate the children. There will be no discussion."

CONSTANCE, Diana and Peggy weren't the only women who refused to register. But on July fifth 1,779 of the 2,129 British women and children who had registered left for Manila on two *Empress* ships. On September second all Hong Kong schools for British children were closed. Mothers hastily organized private study groups. Amidst heated denials that an attack was imminent families began stockpiling food. Already air-raid wardens—men and women—were being trained for an emergency, and by November a massive program to build public shelters was under way.

Occasionally Charlie flew in from the fighting front in China. He, too, felt it had been unnecessary—so far—to evacuate the European women and children from Hong Kong. The Japanese were not yet ready to take on the British Empire.

It was late September and Charlie was back in the Colony on a three-day leave when word came through that the first peacetime American draft—the United States was still a neutral nation—had been passed by Congress and signed by President Roosevelt.

"What does that mean, Charlie?" All along Diana had taken comfort in the fact that Charlie was an American and therefore not subject to British conscription.

"It means that I have to report to the American Consulate and register for military service," he said gently. "But let's not panic, okay? As a married man with two kids I probably won't be called up right away."

"Charlie, it's bad enough you're covering the war as a correspondent." She knew correspondents always ran the risk of being killed or wounded. "I just don't want to see you in uniform."

"You know, Di, I've come pretty close to enlisting. I've talked about it with other correspondents. But the Ministry of Information keeps telling us we're an important part of the war effort. That's the only thing—except for you and the kids—that's stopped me."

"Oh Charlie, when will this be over?" Diana clung to him. She couldn't bear the thought of being alone again.

"I'm afraid it's going to get worse before it gets better, babe. I wish you'd take the kids and go home to Georgia. At least we can be pretty sure the war won't move over there."

"No. Whatever happens I want to be near you . . . "

THE confidence of the residents of Hong Kong that the Japanese would never attack was eroding. British wives and children were leaving for Australia and New Zealand, and even the Americans who had fled Shanghai for safety in the Crown Colony now felt vulnerable . . .

Constance was freshly aware of the inequities between the Chinese and the British. The little paper cups of ice cream which Janet and Matthew and Nadine bought in the small shops in the city cost more than an *amah* earned in a day. Most Chinese families lived in squalid housing, and refugees pouring into Hong Kong from the mainland slept on the sidewalks.

On November twenty-fifth the Government of the Colony issued a bulletin to the community that provided advice in case of attack and urged residents to avoid the urban areas. Constance meant to remain on the island but tried to convince Diana and Peggy to take the children and leave.

"But Mama, I can't leave now," Diana insisted. "Charlie could show up any day." She hesitated. "Let's talk about it again when he's here." Constance knew Diana was worried about Janet and Matthew, and if Charlie told her to leave, she would.

"I'm useful here," Peggy said stubbornly. "I feel I'm helping Adam." She hesitated. "When you go, Diana, I'd like you to take Nadine with you."

Peggy had moved in to take over the hong since the manager had left to join the fighting. Like other hongs in the area Stone & Telford sought to supply China with much-needed goods, but it was a clandestine arrangement. Behind the guise of ordering for the shipyard, Constance—like other firms on the island—bought up Chinese metals such as tungsten and malybdenum in order to prevent their falling into the hands of the Japanese.

Diana had to leave with the twins and Nadine, Constance told herself. The next time Charlie came home, she would discuss it with him. But she knew there was no chance of convincing Peggy to leave . . .

IT was a cool early December night on the Peak. Matthew and Janet were asleep. The servants had retired to their quarters. Diana sat alone on the verandah, too restless to read or listen to the radio. Outdoors she felt closer to Charlie; sometimes when the mist lifted she could see across the Bay to the mainland.

She heard a motorcar approach. Must be a neighbor returning from an evening at the cinema. People were always going to the cinema these days, probably to escape from the ugliness of reality.

A taxi appeared through the mists and swung into the driveway. Instantly she was on her feet.

"Charlie!" she called out joyously, running down the steps. "Oh, Charlie!"

He held her in his arms for a long, lingering kiss.

"What's happened in this damn city? It took twenty minutes to get a taxi."

"You'd have done better on the tram," she told him as they walked arm in arm up the steps to the house. "Are you hungry?"

"I can eat later," he said. "Right now I want a shower, fresh clothes, and you."

"Charlie, I've missed you so much. Sometimes it seemed like you'd never come home—" She moved into his arms as they stood in the foyer.

"Never come home! When I have a beautiful, sexy wife and two perfect kids waiting for me? You've got to be kidding." He kissed her again. "To the devil with the shower. I want to make love to my wife."

With the front door carefully locked Diana and Charlie went into their bedroom.

"Janet and Matthew okay?" he asked as they undressed in the soft lamplight of the bedroom.

"They're fine," she said. It had been so long . . . her body nearly cried out for him. "I'm fine. Or I will be in a little while," she amended with a shaky laugh.

"That's the worst part of this bloody war," Charlie said, pulling her down to the bed. "Being away from you."

With his free hand Charlie reached to switch off the lamp. They kissed, content for a few moments just to feel each other's bodies.

"God I've missed you," he whispered.

"What, no camp followers?" she teased.

"The only camp follower I want is you," Charlie told her, gently kissing her breasts. Knowing how this excited her . . .

"Oh, Charlie, I love you!"

DIANA lay wide awake in the darkness while Charlie went to shower. She knew that in a few minutes they would make love again. Somehow she would persuade him not to go back to the mainland. They would take the children and go to Australia until the war was over.

Much later, lying in the curve of his arm, she tried to figure out how to broach the subject. Just as she was finding the words, Charlie sat up. "My love, there's no other way to tell you this. I have a seven A.M. flight back to the mainland."

Diana stared at him, stunned.

"But Charlie, you've always stayed longer than this. You haven't seen the children."

"We'll wake them before I leave. Diana, I have to go." Gently he took her hand. "Honey, a few days ago I had a chance to fly with the crew of a Chinese combat plane. When the gunner was killed, I took over. Diana, I shot down a Japanese plane. And I felt happy. *I killed and I was happy.* That was when I knew I had to get into the fighting to end this war. It makes me sick that I was happy to kill. I'm going back to the States and I'm going to enlist in Columbus. I want you to take the twins and go to my parents. You'll be safe there." He hesitated. "And if Peggy is willing, take Nadine with you."

"She'll be willing," Diana said softly. Maybe Charlie would be put on some wartime duty in the States. With his experience as a war correspondent the army might give him a desk job in Washington. They could be a family there. "But it's useless to talk to Mama and Peggy—they're both determined to stay as long as possible."

"All right. But listen to me, Diana. This is December sixth. Back home it's still December fifth. In ten days—by December fifteenth—I want you to be gone from the Colony. I have to know that you and the kids are safe. Promise?"

"I promise. We'll leave by December tenth. Through Mama's connections I'm sure we can get reservations on an American ship sailing for New York." She knew the waters were treacherous, but surely they would be safe on an American ship . . . Diana snuggled closer. "With luck, Charlie, we can spend New Year's Eve together in Columbus."

CHAPTER
TWENTY-EIGHT

O N SUNDAY NIGHT Constance left her house for the five-minute drive to Diana's. Since Adam had left she and Peggy ate dinner every Sunday with Diana and twice a week she and Diana went to Peggy's for dinner. The other nights Constance ate alone in her office. She welcomed the demands of work.

As Constance opened the car door, she heard music. Diana was addicted to American songs and was constantly playing the radio. Tonight the plaintive strains of "I'll Never Smile Again" brought back special memories . . .

Diana walked out onto the verandah, her eyes luminous.

Constance knew instantly.

"Let me guess—Charlie's home."

"Well you're half right. He *was* home. Does it show that much?"

"It always shows." She put her arm around Diana. "But what do you mean he *was* home—that's an awfully quick visit."

"He had a flight out at seven A.M. Mama, he's going home to enlist."

Constance could see that Diana was trying to be brave.

"It was inevitable, my darling. We all just have to have faith that they will return to us. Thank God we have each other . . . " Matthew and Janet came running in, fighting over who was to be the first in their grandmother's arms.

"Daddy was here," Janet bubbled.

"He's going back to Georgia to enlist." Matthew's little face was serious.

"And we're going to Georgia to live until the war's over," Janet said breathlessly.

Constance's eyes shot to Diana for confirmation.

"It's true, Mama. I phoned you at home this morning to tell you, but Li said you had gone to the shipyard. Charlie wants us to live in Columbus until the war's over. We'll be taking Nadine with us."

Constance took a deep breath. When would her family be together?

"Well, I'll miss the four of you desperately. But Charlie's right. You'll be safe there."

Constance heard Peggy's car out front. Now they had to give her the news. It would be hard for her to send Nadine so far away, but Peggy was a realist.

Peggy's smile was warm as she approached, yet Constance noticed a certain tension in the way she held her shoulders.

"Hi everybody. Listen—I've been hearing rumors again about Japanese maneuvers on the mainland."

"That's been going on for several days," Constance said. She refused to let fresh fears spoil their time together. "I'm sure General Maltby has been taking precautions."

They sat down to dinner early because of Janet and Matthew. At five Nadine was already asleep. They cherished these dinners, even though the children and men were away. Despite her long hours at the hong Peggy somehow found time to read and was always telling them about her latest book . . .

"I've just finished a fascinating new novel by an American author. I'" lend it to you. It's called *For Whom the Bell Tolls* by Ernest Heming-..ay."

"Oh yes, I'd love to—" Diana said automatically, then paused. "No, I guess I won't have time. I promised Charlie we'd be out of here by the tenth . . . "

ON Monday morning Constance got up at six-thirty as usual and began her morning ritual before her long day at the shipyard. This was her only time to herself and she savored every moment—the hot shower . . . the hearty American breakfast brought to her room by Sakota . . . While she ate, Li popped in to talk about the day's household chores. When Sakota took away her breakfast tray, she settled down to do what she called her "cosmetic magic." Constance took a special pride in her appearance—at fifty-one she looked ten years younger and her figure was as slim and youthful as Diana's.

The shipyard was working on a destroyer for the British Admiralty. Many of their best workers were now on the battlefield and Constance was concerned about the inefficiency and slovenliness of the workers.

As she put on one of her favorite suits—made by a Chinese tailor—she remembered uneasily last night's orders recalling all service personnel to immediate duty. Lately local residents had been admitting that Hong Kong was underdefended—despite boasts to the contrary by the military.

Constance glanced at the French ormolu clock on top of the marble mantel. She was running late—it was almost eight A.M. on this December eighth morning. She started at the sound of an explosion. What was that? It had sounded awfully close . . . but it could be a military exercise at the garrison . . .

"Missy! Missy!" Sakota burst into the bedroom. "Missy, go see!" She pulled Constance by the arm to the window.

There was no military practice this morning. Constance and Sakota stood at the window and watched an air battle raging over Kai Tak airfield.

"Sakota, bring me the binoculars."

"I bring, Missy."

Constance lifted the binoculars to her eyes, adjusted them. A dozen bombers, protected by probably three times as many fighters, were diving over the airfield.

"Oh, my God!" It was a stunning scene—one RAF plane after another bursting into flames. The Japanese bombers were dropping to no more than sixty feet above their targets. Now they aimed for the eight or so civilian planes on the ground.

Shifting her gaze Constance could see Japanese troops crossing the Shum Chun River over temporary bridges. The British demolition troops must have destroyed the bridges in anticipation of an invasion. Probably within the last hour. It was hard to belive that all this had happened since those first quiet moments at sunrise . . .

Troops were crossing the bridges in droves. Constance fought panic. Surely British troops would stop them . . . Word must have gone out already to rush in reinforcements.

"The Japanese will come," Sakota whispered. "They will kill us." A small, cold hand crept to Constance's arm. "Missy, what we do?"

"We'll be all right up here on the Peak," Constance said with more confidence than she felt. "I'm sure the fighting won't move into the city—the British troops will hold them off." What was she thinking of? She had to phone Diana and Peggy. "Sakota, please see that bedrooms are ready for the children and their mothers. We'll sit out the fighting together." Sakota stood by helplessly, looking stricken. "It's all right, Sakota, We'll be fine."

"My mother," Sakota whispered. "She is old and alone in Kowloon."

Constance debated, staring at the action below.

"We'll bring your mother to the Peak. I'm sure it's all right to go to Kowloon for her. But go right away, Sakota, while the ferry is still running." Sakota scurried from the room.

Constance phoned Diana. Damm it. The line was busy. A moment later just as she picked up the phone again to call Peggy, it rang. Diana. She had been trying to reach Government House, to find out what was happening; but all the lines were jammed.

"Diana, bring the twins here—and stop off to pick up Peggy and Nadine. We'll stay here together."

"I'll bring food supplies. Mama, are you all right?" Diana was surprisingly calm. "I mean—we don't know how long this will last . . . "

Constance went downstairs to talk to the servants. Most of them were convinced that the British would drive back the Japanese before they could approach the island. Constance kept glancing out the window. Thank God no mists enveloped the Peak this morning. In the city everything seemed to be going on as usual. Maybe once Diana and Peggy arrived with the children she would go to the shipyard. Life couldn't stop because the Japanese had crossed the frontier. And she needed to keep busy . . .

Within forty minutes the house was filled with the sound of voices. Diana and Peggy refused to allow Constance to leave the

Peak until word came through that business was proceeding as normal. Peggy switched on the radio. A voice advised that the Governor was now operating under emergency powers. All food supplies were placed under government control. Residents must go to the Food Office and fill out necessary forms in order to receive food. A three-day allotment would be allowed. Those without money—mainly coolies, who wouldn't work until the fighting was over—would be fed at the public food kitchens being set up at various "safe areas."

Constance worried about how the fighting would affect the children. How sad that they had to witness the ugliness of war . . . but the only thing that seemed to interest them was the fact that school was closed for the day. When word came over the radio that the two battleships in port, the *Prince of Wales* and the *Repulse,* had been sunk, everyone was stunned. That meant that three of the four destroyers in charge of defending the island were absent from the water, two having sailed for Singapore hours before the attack.

Sakota returned to say that her mother was in the servants' quarters, and that most of those in Kowloon were packing up to move to safer areas. Many of the rice shops were closing—probably, Constance thought, because they anticipated an escalation in the price of rice.

By mid-afternoon Constance was restless. I think it's safe to go into the Central District." She had already talked to the shipyard manager; apparently only a skeleton crew was working. "I have some things to do at the shipyard."

"I'll go with you," Peggy said. She had spoken with the superintendent at the hong, who reported that no cargoes could be loaded or unloaded. Since the attack the harbor was strictly regulated. It was expected that at any moment all ships would be commandeered for naval defense. "I want to stop off at the bank."

Peggy and Constance exchanged a wary glance. If things got worse, they would need plenty of cash. But it wouldn't happen, Constance told herself. The British would get help to them somehow. But how? They couldn't get through the harbor now that the Japanese had sunk the *Prince of Wales* and the *Repulse* . . .

At dusk every household observed the previously ignored blackout ruling. Diana and Peggy put the children to bed, and the three women gathered around the radio. Word of the attack must have circulated around the world—they themselves had heard that the Japanese had struck Hong Kong, Pearl Harbor, the Philippines, and Malaya.

So, Constance thought nervously, Sam must know—he'd curse himself for not being here with her. In his last three letters he had pleaded with her to leave, but she had steadfastly refused. How could she walk out on the life they had built together? She was needed here. Their hong would help supply China with necessities.

David had written her once during the summer. He was now Colonel David Field, at a desk job in Washington. He was convinced the Japanese would attack Hong Kong. He'd urged her to take his apartment or the country house. Dear, sweet David. He would be so worried . . . And Adam flying only God knew where—he would worry. Charlie, probably still en route to Georgia, would be stunned to realize that December tenth was too late . . .

Within forty-eight hours Constance suspected that the fighting wasn't going to end anytime soon. Diana and Peggy instantly responded to a call for volunteers to help in the public food kitchens. Constance went to the shipyard—with the few workers who remained on the job—knowing that the destroyer they were working on was months from completion . . .

In four days the Japanese had taken the New Territories and Kowloon. In Hong Kong thousands were served at the public food kitchens every hour. Other Chinese bought their rice at government-fixed prices in the few rice stores the Government had ordered to remain open. The Europeans fared better, getting supplies from the major European stores. Their women crowded together in the Peak houses.

Billeting problems became serious. Housing in safe areas for families of the military and the defense was desparately needed. The Irish Jesuit Fathers and the students in the seminary volunteered to help transport the residents. Aware that drivers were urgently needed, Constance offered her services.

Air-raid signals were heard several times a day. Diana and Peggy confronted Constance.

"Mama, you must stop driving the transports," Diana insisted. "It's much too dangerous."

"But they need me. Too many drivers have already deserted.

Somebody has to move those people to a safe area."

"You've done your share," Peggy said firmly. "Let the students from the seminary carry on."

"No. As long as the ferries operate, I'm going to drive."

THE Japanese stepped up the bombing. The Jockey Club building was used as an emergency hospital, and additional facilities were set up at St. Albert's Convent and at St. Stephen's College at Stanley. Constance flinched at the whistle of every shell, shuddered at the thud when it hit. Civilians—mostly Chinese—filed docilely into shelters like the Gloucester Hotel corridors and public rooms. Everyone thanked God there was no night bombing. But on December fifteenth a curfew from seven-thirty P.M. to six-thirty A.M. went into effect.

Motorists without special permission were ordered to stay off the roads and had to relinquish their motorcars to the government. Servants began to desert the Peak houses. At Constance's house only Sakota and Li remained.

Remembering Charlie's colorful stories about the rebels in the War between the States, Diana suggested they hide their silver and priceless Chinese porcelains in the garden. Within each of them the cold fear that the Japanese could take the colony was fast becoming a reality . . .

On December twentieth the Japanese cut off the main reservoirs. The following day electricity and gas were cut off. The telephone service had been out for days. On the twenty-second one of the wives ventured from the house on the Peak to go to her flat in Happy Valley for more clothes for her two small children. She returned in near-hysteria. Two of her servants had been bayoneted and the children's *amah* had been raped by soldiers.

Determined not to absorb the panic around them, Constance, Diana and Peggy—along with the other English wives billeted in the house—went through the charade of Christmas Eve for their collective children, Hanukkah for the twins and Nadine.

"I never expected it would go on this long, Mama," Diana confided to Constance and Peggy as they searched the house for small presents for the children. On the mantel, for Matthew, Janet and Nadine was a menorah with lighted candles.

"We have to live day by day," Peggy said grimly.

"Li has been cooking a plum pudding for almost two weeks," Constance said. They didn't have to know yet that their food stocks would soon be depleted . . . "There'll be a fine dinner on Christmas day."

The women did their best to weave a festive mood for Christmas Eve dinner, cooked by Li on an improvised fireplace grill. After eating they moved into the drawing room for the opening of the presents. Sakota and Li passed around cups of hot chocolate for the children and eggnog for the women. It seemed almost peaceful in the house, as if this were just an ordinary day in an ordinary time . . .

Constance felt tears stinging her eyes as the children sang Christmas carols. Tonight the twins and Nadine were celebrating Hanukkah. The sweet young voices of all the children filled the drawing room.:

> *Silent night, holy night,*
> *All is calm, all is bright—*

Jews and Christians were one in their desire for peace.

"Where are our menfolk tonight?" Diana wondered aloud. "Charlie and Sam and Adam," she said softly. "Are they all right?"

Constance smiled.

"They are. I can feel it. They'll survive this war. Just as we'll survive this attack."

ON Christmas morning Constance stood at a window gazing through the binoculars that had become her steady companion. It appeared that the fighting had stopped.

"Are the Japs observing Christmas?" Diana asked Constance quietly from the door as she brought her a tray of tea.

"Hardly likely. But I have a feeling that something is going on—" She peered once again before handing Diana the binoculars.

Diana inspected the scene below.

"There's some activity at Japanese Military Quarters." The Japanese had taken over the Peninsula Hotel in Kowloon. "Do you suppose the Governor is discussing surrender?"

"Does he have any other choice?" Peggy came into the bedroom. "What's the point of killing off more British soldiers?"

By mid-afternoon the word came through. The Governor, Sir Mark Young, had surrendered to the Japanese.

"What happens now?" one of the young wives asked, holding her infant son.

"We wait here," Constance said quietly. "We wait and we pray that the Japanese are civilized."

CHAPTER

TWENTY-NINE

THE JAPANESE WERE in control of Hong Kong. Victory was theirs. The Japanese troops began a three-day leave, during which the Wanchai District was virtually turned over to them as a celebration grounds. They refused repeated requests from the British to bring in their wounded and dead. Everything was to wait until the Japanese fatalities had received the required rites.

Cremated in huge funeral pyres, ashes of the Japanese dead were removed with chopstick-like lengths of steel and deposited in small white caskets, to be shipped back to Japan. Memorial services were held on the cricket field and at various battle sites.

On December twenty-seventh the Japanese flag was raised in the Central District. Constance watched other buildings raise up the Japanese flag. On the following day a Victory Parade marched from Happy Valley to the Western District. All Europeans were ordered to remain indoors and threatened with execution if caught watching.

Feeling safe at the Peak house Constance and a group of wives stood at her bedroom window and took turns watching the parade through binoculars.

"Why can't we see a casualty list?" one of them demanded. "Why can't we see a list of the prisoners of war? Good God, it's uncivilized!"

"War is uncivilized," Peggy said from the doorway.

Somewhere in the house Diana was leading the children in an American songfest, their high little voices a poignant backdrop for the ominous events outside.

Row, row, row your boat
Gently down the stream—

Desperately, Constance tried to talk about something—anything— to fill the grim silence.

"There must be at least two thousand soldiers marching. Who's that officer on the white horse? He's somebody important if he's leading the parade."

Peggy squinted through the binoculars.

"That's Lieutenant General Sano."

The Chinese population had been provided with small flags and was instructed to wave them and cheer, though Constance noticed they did so with little enthusiasm. Overhead the Japanese Imperial Air Force performed aerial acrobatics as part of the display.

For the present—except during the Victory Parade—the Japanese seemed willing to let the Europeans move freely around the city. But everyone was ordered to bow to the Japanese sentries. Failure to comply brought a slap across the face. Constance's guests returned to their mid-level houses. Diana and Peggy and the children remained with her.

On January fourth an order came through for all British, Dutch, and American residents to report the next day at the Murray Parade Ground.

"Bring overnight bag," the mimeograph sheets and press reports stipulated.

Constance was relieved when word came through that residents on the Peak were not subject to this order; with Japanese approval, the Chief Justice had assumed responsibility for them. But word filtered through that those who did assemble at the Parade Ground had, after much confusion, been billeted in grimy waterfront hotels or cheap boarding houses in the Western District. On January twentieth and twenty-first they were sent to a hastily organized internment camp on the Stanley Peninsula.

For Constance time inched by. She kept up a cheerful facade despite tales that Sakota and Li brought back from the Central District of nurses—both Chinese and British—being raped and murdered,

Maryknoll fathers being brutally treated, and Chinese men and women used for bayonet or shooting practice by the soldiers. Several starving Chinese, trying to salvage a little rice spilled on the street, were shot and thrown into the harbor.

Constance was nervous each time Diana and Peggy left the house. She was worried about Diana, who was obviously distraught despite her efforts to appear calm. While Peggy was upset that now no mail could come through from Adam, she, too, managed to appear cheerful for the sake of the children.

On a late January afternoon Constance took up her now familiar position at the window to watch the activities below. Last week she had seen the endless cartons of merchandise being removed from the godown of Stone & Telford, as had been done to the other hongs.

Peggy walked in.

"What's happening today?"

"Oh, they're loading the motorcars. So far I've counted twenty-three ships with deck-loads of cars."

"When will they stop?"

"When they've moved everything that isn't nailed down." Constance couldn't keep the anger out of her voice. "Where's Li? It's chilly in here. I'd like a fire."

"He went down to the Central District for food." She hesitated. "There's no wood left for the fireplaces. No coal."

"Mrs. Anderson told me when she stopped by to borrow tea this morning that they're burning the chairs from the servants' quarters. Li will have to do the same." There was an easy silence between them.

"You know, Diana's terribly upset," Peggy said quietly.

"I know. I wish we could help."

"I wish I knew what was going to happen next," Peggy burst out. "I feel like we're living on the edge of a volcano."

"Peggy, the Chief Justice is sure we'll be able to remain here for a while. And there's food available at a price." Thank God Peggy had withdrawn that money from the bank—in large notes because they were easier to carry.

Vegetables were brought in by villagers early every morning, and stalls lined the streets. The stores had begun to reopen, but prices were highly inflated. Despite the apparent availability of food it was whispered around the Peak that two hundred people a day died of starvation.

Japanese officers were living in luxury in the Hong Kong Hotel. The Gloucester, renamed the Matsubara, catered to the very wealthy and served only Japanese food. Streets were being assigned Japanese names.

Late on a chilly afternoon Constance went to the door at the sound of the bell to discover an English-speaking Japanese major flanked by two lieutenants standing on the stoop.

Her heart pounding, she bowed and invited them inside. Her long years in the Orient had taught her the importance of politeness to both the Chinese and Japanese of good birth.

"Your Chinese servants have gone." The major must have assumed this since she had answered the door herself. "It's wise that they have left their British oppressors."

Constance almost smiled. She couldn't imagine Sakota and Li— outside looking for fuel—regarded her as a "British oppressor." But there was something chilling in the major's eyes . . .

The major turned to the two lieutenants and told them to remain outside.

"Would you like tea?" Constance asked as he walked into the foyer. Friendliness was the only approach.

He nodded.

"I am Major Yamamoto," he said stiffly.

"I'm Constance Stone."

The major took a notebook from his pocket.

"Please give the names of the occupants of this house." He sounded vaguely apologetic. "It is necessary for my report."

Constance gave him the names of Diana and Peggy and the children, praying Li and Sakota wouldn't return until he left. Sakota's mother never left the bedroom unless prodded by her daughter.

"If you'll excuse me, I'll prepare our tea." She hated having to treat this man as if he were a welcome guest in her home. "But first let me show you into the drawing room."

Constance seated the major and went to tell Diana and Peggy to stay out of sight with the children.

With tea tray in her hands Constance returned to the drawing room. Why was he here?

"You speak such beautiful English. She poured the tea in her Sevres china cups. "Where did you study it?"

"In the United States. At Columbia University in New York City."

They talked briefly about New York, and Constance actually

315

found herself enjoying the conversation. The major drained his cup and stood up.

"I am here to tell you that all occupants of this house must be ready to leave tomorrow morning at seven A.M. You may bring with you only one valise each. You are to be taken to the Stanley Internment Camp."

AFTER a long sleepless night Constance woke up at five A.M. It was a chilly, damp morning. She dressed in layers, wearing as much as possible so there would be space in her one valise for the essentials —soap, needles and thread, first-aid items, and a box of tea.

While Constance stood at her window, she heard Diana and Peggy's low voices. Last night, they had tearfully parted with Li, Sakota and Sakota's mother, all three of whom would seek refuge in a nearby village where they had relatives. The children were giggling as they were told to put on sweater over sweater, one more pair of socks. Didn't they understand what was happening? If only Sam were here . . . but she wouldn't think of him now. It tore her apart.

At five minutes to seven—acutely conscious of the Japanese insistence on punctuality—they were clustered in the foyer. At exactly seven o'clock a truck pulled up and they walked in grim silence towards it.

The camp accommodations consisted of the living quarters of the former prison officers and staff and their families, the prison officers' canteen, and other prison structures, as well as the adjacent buildings of St. Stephen's College.

By the time Constance and her family had arrived, the quarters were already overcrowded. They were taken to a prison officer's flat and down the flat's corridor to a single room fourteen feet by thirteen feet, already living quarters for two men and two women who were indignant at this fresh invasion. Constance noticed that there were only two cots, and she was relieved that she had insisted on bringing blankets.

"Mama, we're going to live here?" Janet whispered.

"Sssh." Diana clutched Janet's hand in hers while Constance held to Matthew's small hand, balled into a fist. "We must not make trouble."

"Come on. Let's put our blankets along this part of the wall." Constance refused to give the Japanese the satisfaction of seeing her fear. "Peggy, let Nadine sit with the twins—" she stopped. Peggy seemed frozen in shock, an arm clamped about Nadine's small shoulders. Constance felt the hostile silence of their predecessors in the small room.

"Mama," Nadine wailed, and lifted her face to Peggy. Peggy knelt down while Nadine whispered in her ear. She looked up, bewildered.

"She has to go to the bathroom."

One of the women leaning against the wall laughed.

"We've got one toilet for eighty people. She'll have to stand in line. Down the hall. That way," she gestured. "You'll see the line."

Peggy disappeared with Nadine. Constance stifled an impulse to follow them, to try to comfort them. Thank God Peggy had thought to pack a plate, a cup, and cutlery for each of them. The other people in the room kept empty tin cans nearby—that must be what they used for eating purposes.

They learned that the internment camp housed over twenty-five hundred people. The camp was dank and cold. The Japanese issued food rations every day, but the internees had to organize their own kitchen out of almost nothing. Food consisted of a bowl of rice, a spoonful of fish or meat, some vegetable and bread. They lined up twice a day, at ten in the morning and five in the afternoon, to receive their rations. Lining up for food and for hot water took as long as five hours a day. Water was available only for a few hours each day because of a lack of fuel to operate the pumps.

Constance tried to become friendly with the two men and two women who shared their room. At the end of the first week she gave up. Then she understood their reticence—they had discovered a trade "over the wire"—usually in the middle of the night—by which food could be bought at exorbitant prices from guards.

Constance noticed that Diana was pale and didn't have much of an appetite.

"Darling, you must eat," she said quietly as they stood in one of the interminable food lines.

"I can't. Mama, I might as well tell you. I'm pregnant."

Constance went cold with shock. Her grandchild—born in this place . . .

"When do you think the baby is due?"

"I figure September. If I weren't such a coward, I would get rid of it," she said fiercely.

"Diana, don't even say that. September is months away. We won't

317

be here. The British and Americans will have driven out the Japanese by then." She pulled her close. "You'll have this child. But you must eat. We have plenty of money—we'll buy food from the guards. I'll make a deal with them to bring in fruit and milk for you." The guards were greedy; they would be willing to take chances.

"Oh God, Mama, I could have been in Georgia to have Charlie's baby. If only we'd left earlier . . . "

Constance was determined to hide her worries about Diana's pregnancy. Somehow they would manage. A British Communal Council had been chosen from the internees to organize their lives in the camp. They had struggled to set up kitchens, had brought together the doctors and dentists and nurses among them to serve the internment community. Already Peggy had offered to organize a school group for the children in their own section of the camp and Diana had agreed to help. Are you listening, Sam? We will be a family again . . .

THEY had been in the camp almost a month when they had their first inspection.

One Japanese lieutenant walked in, followed by another person. He stopped dead at the sight of Constance.

"Madame Stone," he bowed.

"Major Yamamoto," she smiled in return.

He spoke briefly to the lieutenant, who proceeded to check the contents of the room, then turned again to Constance. He seemed puzzled. He gestured towards the two other women in the room.

"These two ladies cannot be your daughters."

"My daughters are teaching in the schoolroom. The three children are with them." She saw him wince as he tabulated the number of occupants in the room.

"I will find other quarters for you," he said quietly. "This can be arranged."

Her eyes widened in surprise.

"Well—thank you—that would be good of you."

Early the next morning Constance and her family were moved into a room of their own in a small cottage. Here there was one toilet for the twenty-eight people in the cottage. One of the men had built a grill across the fireplace in one of the rooms—originally a sitting room but now home to seven internees—where occasionally they brewed tea when they had fuel. There was no kitchen equipment.

Constance was even more surprised when Major Yamamoto began calling on them once a week, always bringing some small gift for the children. Milk, chocolates, jam. Maybe Nadine, Janet and Matthew reminded him of his own family in Japan . . .

A few days later four cots arrived. Diana set them up as improvised settees, draped them with their blankets by day.

Constance was outraged when someone in the cottage hinted that there was an ulterior motive behind the major's attentions.

"You're a beautiful woman, Mama," Diana said softly. "Of course the major admires you. But who cares what anybody says? His friendliness makes life a little easier for us." She smiled ruefully. "If anything can be easy in this insane place."

"I just wish we could hear from the men," Peggy said in frustration. "Why don't they lift this rotten censorship so we can get some mail?"

LATE in March five internees—one of them a woman—escaped from the camp. Immediately an additional roll call was scheduled for ten P.M. All internees were ordered to be in their quarters between eight P.M. and eight A.M., all lights to be out by eleven o'clock.

Peggy told Constance she was sure she'd heard the sounds of a radio in the room next door, occupied by five men. At midnight last night, aware that a guard was approaching, she knocked sharply on the wall between their rooms to alert them.

In their gratitude the two younger men—professors from the university—became friendly, reporting what little news they were able to pick up with the radio. The whole world knew that Hong Kong had been attacked and that thousands of Europeans were interned at the Stanley Camp and at other camps. The five people who had escaped in March had reached safety via Cape Collinson, aided by Chinese friends on the outside. Apparently, that same night a party of Americans—again including a woman—had escaped by boat to Macao. From now on it would be more difficult to escape.

The arrival of summer made life in the cottage almost unbearable. Suffocating heat blanketed the camp, and there were no electric fans, cooling drinks, or shower-baths to offer relief . . . Constance saved a cup of water every day to wash the faces of Matthew, Janet and Nadine, who played listlessly on the floor.

Constance often stood longingly at the window and stared out at the sea in the distance. Occasionally they were given beach privileges on Tweed Bay. For her the most demoralizing part of their internment was the lack of hygienic facilities. No one was able to wash properly, and with the sweltering temperatures the air was sour with the stench of sweat and stale clothing.

Early in July Major Yamamoto stopped by with milk for the children and a bag of fruit.

"I am being sent to Tokyo within a few days. I will not be able to see you again." He gazed around the room, his eyes softening at the sight of Nadine, who was playing with the tiny doll he had brought her on an earlier visit. "I wish that we might have been able to meet under different circumstances."

"We, too, major." Constance was genuinely sad to see the departure of her one friend among their captors.

Diana leaned forward.

"Would you—would you be able to mail a letter for me from Tokyo?" They had decided that the men were most likely to be in touch with Olivia and William, so a letter to London would be their contact point. "To friends in London," she added, embarrassed by her boldness.

The major was torn.

"It would not be permitted. Censorship would forbid this. I am sorry. But you are allowed ten word messages via Tokyo. Since May this has been allowed."

"We've sent them," Constance said harshly. "I'm sure they were never delivered."

DIANA'S baby was due soon. Constance shopped frenziedly "over the wire," forcing her to eat so she would be able to breast-feed the new baby. Constance and Peggy ate sparingly so that the children could go to bed with full stomachs. They were aware, too, that their cash was fast diminishing—and no one could guess how long they would be here . . .

The ban was lifted on packages and only a week after Major Yamamoto's departure they received a food parcel from Olivia and William.

Peggy was radiant. "They must have published the list of internees! That means the men know we're here."

"Now don't get carried away," Constance warned. It's possible that Olivia and William simply guessed we were here. And it may have been months since they sent it."

"Is there a letter?" Diana asked.

"If there was, it's been destroyed." Lovingly she put the tins of meat, biscuits, and tea on top of the valises they had stacked together to serve as a table. "Bless Olivia and William."

This one sign from the outside world was a potent morale-builder for weeks. By way of the secret radio in the next room they were able to get some news about the progress of the war. In the Pacific the Allies had faced a string of defeats—at Wake Island, Singapore, the Philippines, the Solomons, New Guinea; but now it sounded like there had been a reversal. At Midway American planes had destroyed four Japanese carriers. Now American marines were storming ashore at Guadalcanal.

"They're on their way to Tokyo," Bert—one of the owners of the radio set—murmured. "But don't spread the word around that we hear the news or we'll lose the radio. There's always some bastard ready to run to the Japanese."

EARLY in August Diana went into labor. Peggy kept the children out of the cottage until regulations ordered them indoors. If the baby had not been delivered by then, the children would visit next door. Bert went for the doctor minutes before curfew.

"If only Charlie knew . . ." Diana gasped between pains.

"Save your strength, my darling," Constance pleaded. She prayed this would not be a difficult delivery.

"I don't want the children to hear me," Diana said tightly. "They're too young to have to know—" Her voice broke off in a scream of anguish.

"It'll be over soon," Constance soothed. How different from Diana's last delivery in the hospital on the Peak.

Bert returned with Dr. Holsyoko, who was frustrated by the unsanitary surroundings. Constance was relieved that he spoke excellent English.

"Can't you give her something for the pain?" she asked impatiently as contractions wracked Diana's body at two minute intervals. "This is 1942. Women aren't supposed to suffer like they used to."

"This is the Stanley Internment Camp," Dr. Holsyoko snapped.

"We don't have the medication."

When Diana seemed too exhausted to cope any longer, the doctor announced that the head had appeared.

"Come on, girl," he coaxed. "You can do it. Just a few more pushes and it's over."

In minutes Diana lay limp and waxen while the doctor cleaned up her new son.

"His name will be Nathan," she said softly. "After my grandfather." Constance's eyes filled with tears. If only Sam were here to share this moment with her . . .

"And may he grow into as fine a man as his grandfather," she said tenderly.

Diana tried to sit up.

"He's to be circumcised."

Dr. Holsyoko looked startled.

"Why?" he blustered. "In an internment camp?"

"Because, Dr. Holsyoko," Constance said with pride, "Nathan is a Jew. He is to be circumcised on the eighth day. It is what his mother wants. And his father would want it too." There would be no *mohel,* but she would find a Jewish male somewhere in the camp to read the benediction in Charlie's name.

NATHAN was a joy to his family. Diana regained her strength slowly—common among the few women who gave birth in the camp —but she was able to nurse him. Constance was relieved, but she worried whether they would be able to buy milk if Diana's milk dried up.

They had a small celebration when Nathan reached seven weeks. Constance had been able to buy a loaf of bread minutes before the eight P.M. curfew, along with a tiny jar of jam. They each had a slice of bread with jam; the rest would be shared by the children over the next few days.

Morale in the camp was at a new low. Many found it impossible to adjust to the lack of privacy and having to hoard every scrap of food. Smokers who couldn't afford to buy cigarettes smoked pine-needles or sweet potato leaves or scoured the ground for butts. Ration cards had to be issued to prevent an internee from trying to get more than his allotted rations. While many were patient and helpful, others were hostile, interested only in improving their own situations.

Quarrels broke out. Ugly accusations were hurled. Petty thievery was rampant.

When Bert came into their room on a sultry late September evening, the look on his face told Constance this was not one of his casual visits.

"I have something to tell you," he said abruptly after checking to make sure the children were asleep. "I have plans for an escape."

Excitedly they clustered in a corner of the room and listened.

"You know what will happen if you're caught," Constance whispered.

"Edward and I can't take this life anymore."

Peggy was intrigued but skeptical.

"How will you get out?"

"Our garden is close to the fence—beside the dung heap that the guards avoid because of the stink. For almost three weeks, a little at a time, we've been digging a tunnel to the outside." He smiled at their looks of surprise. "Edward and I are engineers. We may have been tied up with school books for the last eight years, but we do know something practical. It's ready. All we have to do is climb through, dig another opening at the end, and we're free."

"When are you going?" Diana asked.

"Tomorrow night. At midnight," Bert said. "By then the guards usually let up on patrol. They get together for a smoke or a drink."

"Take the children with you," Diana pleaded, her face a mirror of hope. "Not the baby," she added quickly. "The twins and Nadine. They'll be quiet."

"Yes, do Bert. Please. Take Peggy too." Constance pressed. "She can handle the children. They'll be no trouble. If you make it to Macao, the British Consulate will take care of them."

"We would take all of you if we could," Bert said apologetically, "but it would be too dangerous. We figured one of you—"

"You go with them," Peggy told Constance. "The children and you."

"No. I'm going to stay with Diana and the baby. You're young, Peggy—you have your whole life ahead of you."

"It might look better if a woman is with us," Bert admitted. "But I worry about the children—"

"They'll do whatever Peggy says." Only God knew what lay ahead. At least let the children be saved. "If anybody sees two men,

323

and a woman, and three children, they'll never suspect you're internees escaping."

"Mama, you should have Chinese clothes. The Japanese want the Chinese to leave."

"We have clothes for three adults." Bert said. "Hidden in the tunnel."

"You'll need some money," Constance said quietly. "I can help."

"No, Mrs. Stone, you'll need the money here. We'll probably find villagers who will help us." Bert straightened up. "We'll leave at midnight tomorrow. I'll knock three times on the wall. Come out into the hall. And for God's sake be sure the twins and Nadine understand what they have to do."

CHAPTER

THIRTY

CONSTANCE LAY RIGID on her bed all night listening to the monotonous drizzle of the gentle rain. She listened anxiously for signs of wind, knowing that the threat of typhoon would force them to abandon their escape. But there was no wind.

She got up before daylight and used the bathroom. As she rinsed her hands in the ice-cold water she started at a rap on the door. Someone else wanted to use the bathroom. Silently she shuffled back into the room. It was time to wake Peggy, who was on kitchen duty in the mornings.

Every minute of this day would seem endless. Constance wondered if she could live through it. All her hopes for her future, her children's future, pinned on this one precarious moment . . . she shivered. Nothing would happen to them. They would not be caught.

After the morning lining-up for rations was finally over, Constance hurried to the college quarters of the clinic, where she had been assigned to work. She was pleased to see Diana making color sketches for the play being presented by internees next week—subject, of course, to Japanese censorship. A special committee of internees were trying to lift the morale in camp through entertainment and sports events.

At the clinic Constance heard that those with private gardens would have them confiscated within a day or two.

Constance cornered her informant.

"Why?"

"The gardens are to become communal property," he explained. "Whatever is grown will be used to supplement daily rations."

Thank God Bert had chosen tonight for the escape. Tomorrow might be too late. She couldn't wait for time to pass so that she could go back to the cottage and spend time with Peggy and the children before they left.

She took off her shoes—precious commodities now—and walked barefoot in the mud through the drizzling, steamy rain to their cottage. At the door she tried to wipe the mud from her feet with some leaves. As soon as she walked into the room, and saw their serious little faces she knew that the children had been briefed on what to do.

"I have something special for my precious little ones," she said with synthetic gaiety and reached into the pocket of her blouse for the small packet of chocolate she had managed to buy this morning. It had been ridiculously expensive, but it was such a small thing and gave her so much joy . . . Let the children leave here with the memory of a grandmother who loved them dearly.

Moments later Peggy walked in. Constance stiffened as she realized that she was limping.

"Peggy, what happened?"

"I fell in the mud." She was almost apologetic. Constance was always telling her to slow down . . . "I—I think I've sprained my ankle." She eased herself onto the corner of a cot.

Constance walked over to her.

"We'll have to get you to the hospital. They'll strap it. You'll be all right by tonight."

"Not a chance." Peggy slowly lifted her leg and extended it along the length of the cot. "Look how it has swollen already." The skin was blue and yellow, the ankle bulged. "It's agony just to stand. You'll have to take the children, Mama."

"They'll wait a day," Constance said and stopped dead. "My God, they can't wait." She explained about the gardens.

"You'll have to go, Mama," Diana said. Bert and Edward can't wait for Peggy's ankle to heal. This is our last chance."

BY eight o'clock all the people in the cottage were in their rooms. At ten o'clock the lights went out. At exactly midnight three light knocks on the wall told Constance that she and the children were to join Bert and Edward. She tried to keep the farewells restrained so the children wouldn't be upset. They had to believe this was an adventure, that soon they would all be reunited . . .

The rain had stopped, but the night sky was dark. Not a single star, not a trace of moonlight. They walked in silence. Nadine clung to one of Constance's hands, Janet to the other. Matthew held Nadine's other hand. At the dung heap Bert bent to brush aside the compost pile concealing the entrance to the tunnel. Edward reached inside and pulled out the hidden trousers and jackets.

In the darkness, the two men and Constance changed into the Chinese attire, rolling up their own clothes into a bundle to be left in the tunnel. Bert led the way through the narrow tunnel, just large enough to permit the entrance of one adult at a time. Matthew followed, then Janet and Nadine. Constance moved behind them.

At a whisper from Bert, they paused, huddled in the darkness until he had dug an opening for them to reemerge. He held out a warning hand until he was sure the guard was well beyond their site.

"Now," he whispered.

Holding on to the children, Constance followed the two men. Not knowing where they were headed but confident that Bert and Edward had a plan. They had often visited friends teaching at St. Stephen's; they knew the terrain. By daylight they would have to be pretty far from the camp. Their feet sucked into the mud as they struggled to move quickly.

"A boat will be waiting for us just ahead," Bert whispered. Constance was bathed in sweat, breathing heavily. Bert was carrying Nadine. "I arranged it through a minister from town."

They arrived at the designated spot. No boat was in sight.

"He was caught," Edward whispered tightly. "Now what the hell are we going to do?"

"The boat *is* here." Bert snapped. "Look over there. See the sampan?"

Two men emerged from the sampan to help them aboard. They crossed the water in silence to the village of Tong Fuk on Lantao Island. Here they were handed over to a pair of villagers, who hurried them into their home.

"It looks like we're going to be all right," Bert said as they gratefully accepted the rice and tea from their village hosts. He smiled reassuringly at Constance. "Somehow—from Macao—you'll make it to London with the children." He sat with Nadine on his lap, one arm around her.

On the following night a junk arrived to take them to Macao. The two men asked for help in joining British forces. Constance and the children were led by the Macao underground into Free China, and from there began the long journey to London by ship, rail, and plane.

A pale and gaunt Constance sat with the children on a plane in Lisbon that would take them to London. Several kind British officials had made their journey possible, and of course money had made the trip a little easier.

"It's seven o'clock now," she told the children. "By two we'll be in a taxi driving to your Aunt Olivia's flat." None of them had ever seen Olivia and William, but they had heard much about their adopted great-aunt and great-uncle.

Bert had told them that London had not been badly hit in the past few months, though the city did live constantly in the shadow of raids. What if Olivia and William had been injured? Or—she couldn't bear to think it—killed? But they had sent that package, if not recently, at some point . . . she couldn't believe that they weren't alive. And she prayed they had some news of Adam, Charlie and Sam . . .

True to Constance's prediction the four of them were in a taxi on their way to the Converse flat in Piccadilly shortly past two that afternoon. She gazed out the window, oblivious to the chatter of the children. They were here—they were truly in London. But it was not the London she remembered . . . Where houses and shops once stood, there were craters . . . a big department store was torn apart, its windows boarded up . . . It was a London ravaged by war.

The taxi deposited them before Olivia and William's building.

Trembling, Constance stepped out of the taxi with the children, approached the building, walked into the tiny foyer, and rang the Converse doorbell. In moments a buzzer sounded and Constance pressed the door open.

With the children thumping at her heels, and whispering excitedly, Constance led the way up the stairs, willing her aching legs to move faster. She didn't realize until now how weak and lightheaded the lack of food and sleep had left her . . .

At last they were on the right floor. A door opened. Olivia. At first she was frozen in place, open-mouthed in disbelief.

"I wasn't sure we'd really make it," Constance said, her voice shaking. She threw herself into Olivia's arms. "Oh, Livvy, I've waited so long—"

Olivia broke down, sobbing. The two women stood together in the hall holding each other, rocking back and forth, not saying anything because there was so much to say that words could never express it.

"Come inside," Olivia finally managed, her eyes sweeping over the children as they clustered around her jockeying shyly for the position closest to Constance. "Diana's twins," she recognized from photographs. "Adam's Nadine."

"Olivia, have you heard from Sam? From Adam and Charlie?"

"All three. As soon as they heard about Hong Kong, each wrote to me. It was always assumed that we would be the clearing station in case of trouble. Don't worry, they're all fine. Sam is somewhere in Israel, doing what he called his 'usual work.' I imagine with the censorship that was all he could say. From Adam's veiled insinuations I gather he's been flying missions over Dieppe. The Allies have been giving the Luftwaffe a devil of a time. He was here in London for a week's leave at the end of August."

"You saw Adam?" Her baby. "How was he?"

"Fine. I was startled at first. He hadn't changed a bit. Still the image of Sam."

"And Charlie? You said you heard from Charlie?"

"He's with the American forces in the Pacific. I wrote each of them and promised to follow up as soon as I could find out about you all."

"Olivia, when that package came, we went out of our minds with happiness . . . just to know that there was a world outside that horrible place—but also that you knew where we were."

"I must confess, I didn't really when I shipped it out. It was a shot in the dark. But William and I didn't dare allow ourselves to think anything other than internment had happened to you. Then in July the Americans from Stanley were repatriated. That was when I wrote the men and told them where you were for sure. Now let me put up some tea for us and some cocoa for the little ones. There's a tin of biscuits they might like, too. But my pots," she laughed. "All my beautiful pots went to the aluminum dump when Lord Beaverbrook —I think it was back in 1940—asked all housewives to contribute their aluminum for building planes."

"At Stanley," Constance told her quietly, "we cooked in tin cans. We used to pray that we wouldn't break the one plate and one cup for each that we had brought from home to the camp."

"Quite a change from the days of your beautiful Sevres china, isn't it, my child?" Olivia said softly.

Constance smiled.

"I must report to the Consulate first thing tomorrow. I've made a half dozen statements already about our experiences at Stanley, but I've been told to check with the Consulate here in London."

And then you'll have to register for ration coupons for the children and yourself. When I go shopping, I carry around a pound of paper," she said, laughing. "You should see William, standing in line with all the rich matrons from Mayfair for our sixpennyworth of gumdrops."

Olivia turned her attention to the children, eager to make them feel at home. She insisted that the four of them stay in the flat. While there were many problems, at least for now they were not suffering from the heavy bombing of the previous year.

"If only Diana and Peggy and Nathan were here," Constance said with tears in her eyes. "Charlie doesn't even know about his second son. God, war is horrible, Livvy."

Constance wrote to the three men and sent packages to Diana and Peggy, giving Olivia's return address, but confident that Diana would recognize her handwriting and realize they had arrived safely in London. She prayed the packages would be delivered. The thought of Diana, Peggy and Nathan left behind tormented her—but at least their lives weren't in danger . . .

CONSTANCE and the children settled into their new lives. After almost a year at Stanley they were all wonder-struck at the simplest of amenities—having a room of one's own, spending as much time as they wanted in the bathroom . . .

330

Constance slept on a cot in the sitting room. Olivia and William entertained the children with reminiscences about Diana and Adam that freshened Constance's growing need to see her family together. It was a disjointed, intoxicating, unreal time for everyone . . .

All three children were sent to school. Nadine's first school outside the camp. Constance volunteered as an aid at one of the army hospitals. Since she had to leave early every morning for the hospital, William took the children to and from school, though Matthew tried to convince them that at ten he was old enough to take them all there himself. When they came back to the flat at the end of the day Olivia always greeted them with cocoa and a biscuit.

Constance waited for letters from the men, knowing that they were sure to be slow in coming but still impatient. She continued to send packages to Diana and Peggy at the internment camp, heartbroken by rumors that conditions in the camp were growing worse as the war continued, and frustrated that she couldn't send more. A thought occurred to her . . . what if she wrote David at the Washington address he had given her, telling him what had happened to them since Hong Kong's fall, enclosing a check? America had so much. Maybe David could send packages from Washington to Diana and Peggy. Surely he would do this for her . . .

David responded with astonishing speed; she guessed that he had used his military connections to rush his letter through. He was very concerned about their welfare, and tried to be optimistic about the safety of Diana and Peggy and little Nathan. He had already shipped packages to Stanley. Was there anything he could send her in London?

In late January the air-raids began again. Despite allied victories Londoners suspected the worst was yet to come. In February Constance received her first letter from Sam. He wrote eloquently about the need for a Jewish homeland. Veiled hints—mention of Leo Rosenthal—told her he had been in Germany. How? When he had told her how much he missed her, it brought back the loneliness that she had pushed aside all this time. Life without Sam was hollow; it held no luster . . . but he had another love—another life—distinct from her . . . Israel. And she had come to accept this in him.

Two days after she heard from Sam, Constance got a letter from Adam. He was all right. He was happy that she and the children were in London, but worried about Peggy and Diana. She worried that there was no word from Charlie. Then, on the same March day, letters arrived from Charlie—somewhere in the Pacific—and from Diana.

The Japanese had just agreed that internees might write one letter a month of twenty-five words. Of the dozen packages Constance had mailed out, only one had arrived. Peggy and she and little Nathan were doing well, but food was in very short supply. She asked for powdered milk and a sketchpad. There wasn't room to say anything else. Constance nearly cried out in frustration at the end of the letter, haunted by Diana's simple plaint, "food is short." How would she survive another month before hearing from her again?

William prophesied trouble for London when he heard on the radio one evening in April that Berlin was being heavily bombed. For the past few weeks the Germans had been concentrating on daylight raids in the rural southern districts rather than on London.

"We're going to get it again."

Olivia looked up from her knitting.

"No, William. I think they have their hands busy with other things."

"How many missions before Adam will come home again?" Constance wondered aloud. Each time she heard that the RAF was dropping bombs on Berlin a chill moved through her. Had the Rosenthal brothers gotten out in time? Or were they in one of the concentration camps? Olivia sighed.

"Constance, you must stop worrying. Adam will be all right. That boy was marked for a long life. It's in the stars." Olivia had recently become devoted to astrology and she was always predicting someone's future with "it's right here in his horoscope."

London underwent a series of nightly air-raid alerts but it didn't appear that there would be a reatalation for the raids on Berlin. Weeks became months as London's skies remained free of enemy planes. Many Londoners were sure that the city would not be attacked again; despite the allied offensive in Europe, officials suspected otherwise.

A blanket wrapped around her shoulders, Diana sat hunched over her sketchpad one dark late afternoon and drew Nathan as he napped beside her on the one cot allowed them since the escape almost sixteen months ago. While the other cots had been confiscated as punishment, no one else had been moved into the room, for which she and Peggy were grateful.

They were not punished for the escape. Other internees had been crippled by torture as a reprisal for attempted escapes or suspicion of espionage. Diana had even heard of executions taking place on the beach outside the camp . . .

She started as the door opened. During these past sixteen months she had come to jump at any unexpected sound.

"Look!" It was Peggy, her face glowing as she charged into the room with a box wrapped in brown paper under her arm. "Another package from London!"

Her excitement was contagious. "Is there powdered milk?" Diana asked. Milk for the baby was an especially urgent need. He had started to walk so late, and sometimes he was so listless it frightened her. But no one had any energy. All the internees were painfully thin.

"There's powdered milk," Peggy said, the package unwrapped. "And tins of meat and cheese and tea. Oh God, did you ever think you could feel this way about food?"

"Peggy, when will the Allies reach the island?" Diana said in frustration. Since the American air-raid right after Mama got out with the children, and a subsequent one on Nathan's first birthday last August, air-raids were frequent. Internees had been killed in the Allied air-raids because at one point the camp was not marked by white crosses, as decreed by international convention. "Sometimes I wonder if they'll ever get here . . ."

"Soon." Peggy tried to sound convincing. "It has to be soon."

Diana wanted to believe her. But it had been so long.

"Well, soon or not, we'd better hide the food."

"First, Di, let's have a tin of that meat right now. For once we can go to sleep with full stomachs."

IN February London once again was a blitz city. Olivia and William had insisted on staying in London during earlier periods of heavy bombings, but now with the children to consider they accepted their daughter Anne's invitation to stay at their house in the country.

"The children have been through enough," Olivia told Constance. "They don't need to go through nights of sleeping in steel bunks on tube-station platforms. Anne has room for all of us."

"You go with the children, Livvy. I'll stay. I'm needed at the hospital. And I have to be here when the letters come." With God's help Adam would come one day. She lived for that moment.

William looked worried.

"I don't know, Constance. I don't like leaving you here."

"I have to stay." Constance smiled. "It's enough to know that the children will be safe with you."

ONCE they had left the empty flat was depressing and Constance began to remain for extra duty at the hospital. If she kept busy, she would have less time to worry. And somehow at the hospital she felt closer to the men. Letters came through so rarely and were always so brief. Occasionally she went out to the country for a day to see the children, but something always called her back to the city.

Each day, like thousands of others, Constance waited in line at the newsstand for the trucks to arrive with the latest editions of the newspapers. On June sixth fleets of Allied planes headed for the coast of Normandy. Londoners rejoiced that British soldiers were soon to be back on French soil, a retaliation for the horror of Dunkirk.

The battle of Normandy dominated every Londoner's thoughts and conversation. With the arrival of D-Day life in London began to return to normal. British and American uniforms had conspicuously thinned out, making the city more accessible. Restaurants and the cinemas were no longer crowded. Only the newsreel theaters were doing capacity business.

Constance was acutely aware of how close Adam was as he flew missions right across the Channel. Recently she had been receiving postcards from him—as if he were only off to the seashore for a few days. Anytime she met an RAF flier, bombardier or navigator in the hospital she asked about Adam. So far no one had heard of . . .

Now London was assaulted by "buzz bombs—" the first pilotless planes. Day and night sirens warned of a new attack by the robot bombs, considered to be more of a nuisance than a real threat.

Constance woke up on a Saturday morning late in June to the hum of the "doodlebugs." She lay still in bed listening intently to the noisy roar overhead, then sighed with relief as it faded off into the distance. Today she was off duty, but the prospect of spending the day in the flat—despite her exhaustion—was a depressing one.

Suddenly it occurred to her . . . she didn't have to stay away from the hospital—they were always short handed. She jumped out of bed, put up water for tea, and went into the bathroom, cheered by her decision. The men at the hospital needed her . . . and so many of the wounded were coming to them now straight from the battlefields.

When she arrived at the hospital she was told that ambulances had been delivering patients since dawn. Immediately she hurried to her ward.

The head nurse greeted her.

"Dearie, are we glad to see you. We're getting them straight from Normandy, and a lot of them are in bad shape."

For the next seven hours Constance worked without a break. At last, exhausted and famished, she asked to be relieved so that she could go for tea. On her way to the canteen set up for the aides, she paused to allow a nurse wheel a bed from the operating room across the hall into the ward next to her own station. A doctor was walking next to the bed, talking quietly to the nurse. Some of the patients were so young, she thought compassionately; the new National Service bill of January decreed that they be brought into service at seventeen and a half.

The doctor beside the bed made a motion to another doctor walking down the hall. But Constance didn't notice. Her eyes were riveted to the face of the young man on the bed.

"Adam," she whispered.

The doctor whirled around to face her.

"You know this patient?"

"My son. He's my son—" They were taking Adam into the ward. Why couldn't she move?

"Are you all right?"

Constance nodded.

"My son?" She looked up at the doctor.

"He's doing fine physically." She felt a gentle pressure at her elbow as he lead her into the ward. "Right now he's amnesiac, but we're confident he'll come out of it. We've had no identification on him other than that he was in the RAF, which, of course, we knew because of his uniform. He must have brought his plane down, then managed—despite his wounded leg—to take shelter in a nearby barn. Advancing Allied troops found him there. He doesn't remember anything."

"He's Major Adam Stone," Constance said, her strength returning. "But this amnesia—"

"How long have you been an aide here?" the doctor asked gently.

"Over a year and a half." If only David were here . . .

"Then you know how often these boys have temporary amnesia."

"May I stay with him?"

"He's sedated. He'll be out for hours."

"Please. I'd just like to sit with him. I haven't seen him since he left Hong Kong to enlist back in 1939." A jumble of feelings churned inside her . . . joy that finally Adam was here, out of the fighting . . . fear that the amnesia might be permanent. "I won't disturb him."

"How long have you been on duty?" the doctor asked.

"Seven hours," she said, "but—"

"Go to the canteen, have something to eat, then come back. I'll leave word that you may stay with him."

Constance went to the canteen and forced herself to eat. It was the only sensible thing to do; the doctor was right. But she had no intention of leaving the hospital until Adam woke up. He wouldn't recognize her and it hurt just to think that the joy of their reunion would be one-sided—but just to be able to reach out and touch him, to know that he was alive . . .

Barely aware of what she had eaten, she finished and returned to the ward.

The nurse nodded briskly as she entered.

"You'll let me know when he wakes?"

"The minute he wakes. I promise."

As she sat beside Adam her thoughts drifted back through the first years the day she realized she was carrying a second child—Sam's child—that bleak day in September, 1939, when Adam sat proudly at the dinner table and announced he was going to enlist . . . so much love and pain already in this young life . . .

The nurse looked in three hours later.

"Sleep's good for him," she smiled. "I'm going for tea. Would you like a cup?"

"Thank you, no."

Twenty minutes later Adam stirred. Constance moved to the edge of the chair, reminding herself she must not cry. Adam would not know her. Right now let it be enough that he was here.

He opened his eyes and looked at her. Nothing.

Constance rose to her feet and leaned over him.

"Would you like something?"

"A glass of water—" His voice oddly detached.

She gave him the water, fighting the urge to draw him into her arms. He was so much thinner than she remembered . . .

After sipping at the water for a moment, Adam handed the glass back to her and she put it on the table next to the bed.

"The nurse will want to know you're awake," she said softly.

DURING the next few days Constance went back and forth between Adam and her work on her ward, staying at the hospital for sixteen hours at a time. He didn't seem to think anything of it, assuming by her uniform that she was just another nurse's aide. The doctor assured her the leg wound was healing well. The infection had cleared up. But he was becoming less optimistic about the amnesia.

"We don't know much about it. You know that. It's just a matter of standing by and waiting."

The doctor had indicated that Adam would be hospitalized for at least a month. After that she could take him home with her. But what if he wouldn't go? Why would he leave the hospital with a total stranger?

Whenever Constance finished her duties in the adjoining ward, she would come into Adam's ward and sit by his bed. Often he didn't even wake up; and if he was awake, she pretended to be busy, changing his bedpan or refilling his water pitcher. He never asked her anything about herself—just stared quietly ahead, absently fingering his blanket.

Today he was sleeping. As usual, she offered to help the nurse on duty. Everyone working on the knew—and was sympathetic to—her situation.

Constance felt the by-now familiar tension in the ward as the shrill air-raid sirens sang overhead. There was one boy, no more than sixteen—how had he managed to get into uniform?—three beds away from Adam who always started whimpering at the sound of the sirens. This time the harsh whirr of a buzz bomb seemed to hover directly over the hospital.

"Please," the young boy cried out, his hands over his ears, "God save me—stop it . . . "

"It's all right," she said, moving to his side and taking his hand in hers. "Just a nasty doodlebug. It's probably a mile away by now."

She started at the sound of Adam's voice.

"Jaimie, what the hell's going on?" He sat bolt upright. "The tail's on fire!"

Constance rushed over to him.

"It's all right," she repeated, taking his hand. "A doodlebug, and it's gone now—"

Adam frowned, puzzled.

"I must have been dreaming—"

"A bad dream, Adam?" she remembered all the times she had said the very same thing to him when he woke up crying a. night . . .

He stared at her peculiarly.

"Adam? You called me Adam?" He searched her face. Suddenly a light broke through behind his eyes. "Mama! You're here!" He pulled her to him. "Mama, it was awful out there. The plane was on fire. I was hit in the leg. Jaimie and Doug were both finished—" He paused, still confused.

"Hush, darling, it's all over now." She rocked him in her arms. "You must rest and get well. Then you'll come home with me to Olivia's flat. We'll go up to see Nadine and the twins in Sussex and—" she hesitated, realizing that this rush of names was confusing him . . .

His voice was soft.

"Diana?"

"They're still in the internment camp. But darling, the way the war is going it's bound to be over soon. We'll be a family again."

Within three weeks Adam, on crutches, was settled in the flat. In another week they would go up to Sussex. While the Allies were scoring victories—one of which was the resoundingly uplifting liberation of Paris—Mr. Churchill warned against bringing the children back to London, urging parents to remove those still in the city. But the general feeling among the Allies was that the war was all but over.

Constance wanted to be happy, to celebrate the end of this war that had ripped open the world, torn her family from her . . . but no word came from Sam or Charlie. And the brief twenty-five word letters from Diana were only frustrating reminders of how far away she was. Until they were all united, how could she feel the war was over?

CHAPTER
THIRTY-ONE

SLOWLY ADAM WAS recovering. Constance prayed the war would
end before the doctors declared him fit to return to duty.
Autumn became winter. Adam discarded his crutches for a
cane. Like all the British they lived every day with the fear
that another catastrophe crouched behind every corner . . .

Germany's Battle of the Bulge came as a shock to the Allies. Many
people began sleeping in the tube shelters again, but Constance and
Adam stayed in the flat. At Manetta's, the Four Hundred, Mirabelle,
and the Stage Door Canteen the young danced the fearful nights
away.

In February, Churchill, Roosevelt and Stalin met at the Yalta Conference to prepare for the postwar period. On April fifteenth the
news of Roosevelt's death—at the moment the Allies were fifteen
miles from Berlin—richocheted around the world. Early in May the
war in Europe was over. Londoners roared into the streets in a tumultuous celebration. Bells pealed, planes roared over the city, the tugs
on the Thames whistled. But for Constance and Adam and millions
of others the celebration must wait until Japan, too, conceded defeat.

"We must find a furnished flat," Constance said on the morning
after V-E day. "Olivia and William will return to London now with
the children. Papa will surely join us in London." After all these years

he would come home to them. It didn't seem possible. "We'll need a flat for ourselves until we can go home again." It had been impossible to get a telephone call through to Sussex yesterday. Tonight she would try again. Perhaps Sam would phone them.

"All I can think about is the internment camp," Adam confessed, his eyes betraying his fears. "The Japs know the end of the war is in sight. How are they reacting? What will happen to Peggy and Diana and the baby?"

"Darling, we have to be patient." Constance would not let him see how frightened she, too, was for Diana, Peggy and little Nathan. "It won't be long now. It can't be."

ON August tenth in the Stanley Internment Camp the internees suspected something unusual was happening when all the technicians and their families were suddenly transferred to Ma Tau Chung Camp in Kowloon. They lived now in constant hope—despite the terrible conditions—that the long war was at last over.

On August fifteenth the canteen received their first supplies in months. Then free cigarettes were issued. Shortly afterwards every internee received a roll of toilet paper—a luxury quickly nicknamed "Victory rolls!" Rumors flashed around the camp that the fighting was over.

The Japanese military told them nothing but the English-language *Hong Kong News,* circulated around the camp, reported a cessation of hostilities. They were warned against any demonstrations—until the British arrived, the Japanese were still in control.

On August twenty-ninth Diana held three-year-old Nathan and tried to stop him from cowering at the buzz of the planes overhead.

"Nathan, they're not dropping bombs. They're bringing packages for us. Goodies, my precious," she said tenderly. Food and medicine, which they so desperately needed.

"Di, it's over!" Pale and thin, Peggy looked up at the planes. "It's really over!"

"Charlie's going to see his son." Tears of joy filled Diana's eyes. "Nathan, you're going to see your Daddy."

WITH Adam and Sam at her side while the children hung onto the rail of the ship, chattering and fidgeting in excitement, Constance watched the skyline of Hong Kong emerge through the morning fog. How she welcomed the familiarly oppressive September heat after all this time . . .

They were coming home. Tonight was the eve of Rosh Hashanah. She and Sam had prayed that they would be home—surrounded by children and grandchildren—for the New Year.

At last they were ashore, the children at once impatient to see their mothers but shy after the long separation.

"There's Diana and Charlie!" Sam waved furiously above the heads of others gathering on the deck. "That must be Nathan in her arms!"

"Mama!" Diana cried, pushing her way through the crowd, Peggy and Charlie at her heels.

"Adam!" Peggy called out.

In moments they were clustered together, everyone laughing and talking and crying at once.

"The children have grown so." Diana clung to the twins while Peggy stood silently, squeezing Nadine, tears running down her cheeks.

"Of course they've grown," Charlie chuckled. "Did you expect them to wait for you?"

"You're all so thin," Constance fretted. "But that'll soon change."

"Let's go home," Charlie urged. His eyes softened. "By the way, guess who came to us as soon as she heard that people were returning to their houses?"

Constance knew instantly.

"Sakota."

Diana laughed.

"That's right. She made it clear she was on loan to us only until you returned, Mama."

"What about Li?" Sam asked, gazing at Adam.

"Li died two years ago," Peggy said. "Very peacefully in his sleep, we heard. But you know as bad as times were, he and Sakota still delivered packages of rice to us at the camp."

"I think conditions will improve now for the Chinese in Hong Kong," Sam said. "The war brought out so much that needed to be told."

Constance knew the city would have to be almost totally rebuilt. Charlie—who had received permission to come straight to Hong Kong from Okinawa—told them that over seventy-two percent of the foreign communities had lost their homes and one hundred sixty thousand who once lived in flats were now homeless. A million Chinese had been driven away by the Japanese, reducing Hong Kong's population to six hundred thousand.

The fishing fleet was a shambles. Livestock had disappeared. Millions of trees, planted to stop erosion and to hold the runoff of the rainy season, had been cut down for firewood. Railroad and ferry lines were ravaged almost beyond repair. Ninety percent of the survivors were destitute; a few collaborators and black-market operators had made their fortunes.

"THANK God for the land," Sam said softly as they gathered around the dining table in Diana and Charlie's house for the pre–Rosh Hashanah dinner. "We know that will be returned to us by the government."

Charlie cleared his throat. "Quiet, everybody. The synagogue has not yet reopened. But we'll hold our own services here. We'll welcome the New Year in together. As a family."

"Charlie and I sent a New Year's cable to the family in Georgia," Diana added. "Next year we hope they'll be able to spend Rosh Hashanah with us here."

Sam sighed.

"What will be in Israel next year? The war is over in Europe and the Pacific, but no doors are open wide for the refugees of the most terrible war in history." His words reminded them of the horror of Auschwitz, Belsen, Buchenwald, and Dachau—they were still open wounds. "Six million Jews have died. Hundreds of thousands are emerging—more dead than alive—from concentration camps. The hope of a National Home kept them alive. Churchill was a man of compassion. Now we have a man in the British government, this Mr. Bevan—" Sam's voice trembled with rage—"who says the Jews from the concentration camps should not be sent to Palestine. They 'should return to their former homes and rebuild Europe.' To rebuild a continent that left them to die in crematoriums!"

"Sam, the situation will change," Constance said appeasingly. "The world will make demands."

Sam looked drained.

"The Haganah will make demands," he said. "Already they are

working with the IZL and Lehi to form a Jewish Resistance Movement. One war is over; another is beginning."

"Let's start the New Year with sweetness, shall we?" Peggy interrupted. She placed on the table a plate of *taiglach*—a concoction of dough baked and cooked in honey with candied fruits and nuts and formed into small pyramids. "Happy New Year, everybody."

"It'll take time," Constance said as they lifted their wineglasses in a toast to the New Year, "but the city will be rebuilt. Our businesses will be rebuilt." She knew she had to face the devastation of the looted godown, the shipyard and newspaper, stripped of all machinery and equipment. But Charlie had told her that much of the furniture from the Peak house had been held in warehouses by the Japanese. "People will return to the city. Businesses will start up again. Land will become valuable." She took a deep breath. "We won't be kept down."

EACH day brought new grief, with the news of someone else killed in the internment camp or shot down in the war. But as Constance had predicted, the city forged ahead. Within six months the British had restored the government of the Colony. Many British businessmen, including Sam, accepted temporary Government positions to speed recovery. Chinese were flocking back at the rate of one hundred thousand a month.

Like many others, Sam was impatient with the shortage of desperately needed building materials. Every night he regaled Constance with harangues about the Government's refusal to appropriate public funds to rebuild damaged property. Money was tight, but Sam and Constance rejoiced that their land was returned to them, certain that in time it would be worth a fortune again.

After a year Sam resigned from his government position to join Adam in the hong, now known as Stone & Stone. The real estate business became a family enterprise, with the women and men working together. Slowly Charlie was acquiring equipment to start up the newspaper again. Diana was planning an exhibit of her paintings.

Sam talked wistfully about the resort hotel he would complete one day. It would be a showplace on the beach for Hong Kong. Only the foundation and framework had been built before the troubles in

343

Berlin had put a hault to the operation. Sam made a determined effort to track down Kurt and Leo Rosenthal, who had saved dozens of lives in Berlin. Both had died in Buchenwald.

Constance tried to tell herself that Sam had come home to her, but she knew his heart remained in Israel. As their financial condition improved she hoped his obsession would be satisfied by the money they contributed to the cause—but in her heart she knew it was not enough.

"Connie, only when Israel is independent will I breathe freely."

It was a truth that still hurt . . .

On November 29, 1947 the United Nations Assembly recommended the partitioning of Palestine. There was to be an independent Jewish state.

But Sam was skeptical.

"We're accepting a compromise. And what will be the result? Instability. Friction. The Arabs—with four million square miles blessed with oil and water, begrudge Israel's less than eight thousand square miles, much of which is desert."

"Israel will become an independent state, Sam. That's what we've been praying for. Can't you be happy with that?"

By the beginning of 1948, at every family dinner the children— Matthew and Janet were fourteen, Nadine eleven, Nathan six— coaxed Sam into talking about his days with the Haganah, the time he parachuted into Germany. This was a family that cherished its heritage, Constance told herself with pride.

In the spring David wrote, asking if he could visit them when he came to Shanghai in October on a medical mission. Still sensitive about Sam's statement that David was in love with her—partly because she knew it was true—Constance immediately wrote back insisting that he be their guest. David was a wonderful friend . . .

The world was getting smaller, Constance mused. In the fall of 1946 Charlie's parents visited Hong Kong. Next year Diana and Charlie and the children would spend some time with them in America. And now David was coming to Hong Kong.

As the spring gave way to summer, Constance felt the restlessness in Sam. She tried to convince herself that if they could afford to finish bulding the hotel, he would be diverted from his worries about Israel. If current negotiations with an American firm for a vast tract of land in Kowloon went through—Sam's lease had ninety-one years to go

—it would provide them with money to move ahead with the hotel. Building materials were still scarce and prohibitively expensive, but Constance decided to push Sam into going ahead with the hotel after the Kowloon tract sale.

"Connie," Sam said thoughtfully over dinner one night, "I'd like to take you to Israel for a few days. You need a vacation. And I want us to see the first home for our people. Together."

"Sam, how can we leave now?" But the thought was exciting . . . To at last see Israel—to share Sam's dream with him . . . She knew from reports that at the moment there was a lull in the activity of the snipers who, for months, had made travel in Israel dangerous for a Jew.

"Connie, don't you see? There will always be something to stop us from going—and time is our enemy. If we wait we may miss this one chance to see our homeland. No. I insist. We'll take the time now." He paused.

"And soon Israel will declare itself a state. I want to be there when it happens."

Sam had always said that once Israel declared itself an independent state war with the Arab nations would be inevitable.

"It could be dangerous," Constance said carefully.

Sam shrugged.

"Living is dangerous. After what we've been through, would you be afraid to go to Israel?"

"No." Not when it meant so much to Sam . . .

"The actual time and place of the declaration is being kept a secret to ward off an air-raid," he continued. "The press and public will know only a few hours ahead of time. But word has come to me that we are to be in Tel Aviv on May fourteenth. The fifth of Iyar, 5708 on the Hebrew calendar. At midnight of that day the British mandate will expire. The last British soldier will leave Israel. We will be an independent state.

CONSTANCE and Sam arrived in Tel Aviv on May thirteenth. As representatives of Charlie's newspaper they received pass credentials that would guarantee them entry to the hall where the proclamation of the state of Israel would be officially made.

After they registered at the King David Hotel, they walked around

345

the wide boulevards of the surprisingly modern city. The sky was bright blue. From the friendly, bustling cafes drifted the rich smell of coffee. The streets were crowded, everyone talking at once—wondering when the proclamation would take place . . . Constance was filled with an overwhelming joy at being present for this historic occasion, anger at the suffering of the Jews through the ages—and most of all, a deep and abiding respect for Sam, this brave, loyal man who had given her God's two greatest gifts—his love, their shared heritage.

"Sam!" An astonished male voice interrupted them. "Sam Stone! I should have known you'd manage to be here today!"

"Maurice!" Sam threw his arms around a wiry, curly-haired man in his early forties. "God, when did I last see you? Was it our drop into Germany?"

Maurice laughed.

"It certainly was. I knew you'd make it back."

Constance stood by while the two men talked. Now she understood this closeness between Sam and the others of the Haganah. They were brothers, risking their lives for Mother Israel. Once she had thought of Israel as Sam's mistress. She had been wrong. Israel was his wife and mother, the very core of his being . . .

"Maurice, I'm sorry—I'm being unbelievably rude. This is Constance, my wife. Connie, Maurice and I escaped death together maybe fifty times."

"Your wife?" Maurice clucked. "She looks more like your daughter. Such a beautiful woman."

"She was in the internment camp in Hong Kong, Maurice," he continued proudly. "But she escaped, bringing out three of my grandchildren with her."

They ate dinner with Maurice at a cafe. When Maurice left, they didn't probe; both Constance and Sam knew he was here on official business.

They stayed up most of the night, reminiscing, talking about the future of Israel. Sam knew—as did all Jews in Israel—that soon the Arabs would attack. This proclamation would infuriate them. But she and Sam would leave on Saturday afternoon—before the trouble erupted.

Shortly after two P.M., as all correspondents had been instructed to do, Constance and Sam—with notebooks in hand—went to the appointed meeting place. It was a brilliantly sunny day, not a cloud in the sky. The blue and white flag of Israel was everywhere, and a hum of excitement ran through the throngs filling the streets. They were waiting to become a state. And they waited, too, for the Arabs to seek their revenge . . .

Taxis took Sam and Constance and the other correspondents to an area on Rothschild Boulevard, next to Herzl Street. Here they lined up in a roped-off area to have their credentials checked by Haganah military police. A decrepit plane dropped copies of the declaration of independence. Though no official word had been given—except to the two hundred invited guests—a crowd was already forming in front of the Tel Aviv Museum, where the ceremonies were to be held.

"Why was the museum chosen for such an important occasion?" Constance whispered to Sam.

"Probably because it is small enough to be guarded well."

After another wait they were led into the museum. In the main halls Israel's flag hung from the windows, which had been blacked out in the event of an air-raid. Behind the table where the members of the provisional government would soon take their places hung a large portrait of Theodor Herzl, whose book fifty-two years before had given birth to the modern Zionist movement. The jammed hall was airless and hot. But nobody cared.

At precisely four P.M. Ben-Gurion rose to his feet and rapped with a gavel. The ceremonies were beginning. Every person in the hall arose and sang *Hatikvah.*

For fifteen minutes, reading quietly and distinctly, Ben-Gurion read the declaration. The silence was broken only by the sound of weeping. Constance could feel that Sam was struggling to keep himself from breaking down. This day was truly God's day—Israel was a state. A refuge for a people who had roamed the earth for two thousand years . . .

When Ben-Gurion finished reading, he asked the members of the People's Council to rise and stand in line to sign the scroll that established the Jewish state. As they rose to take their places, Rabbi Fishman-Maimon repeated the Hebrew prayer of Thanksgiving:

"Blessed be Thou, O Lord our God, King of the Universe, who had kept us alive and made us endure and brought us to this day. Amen."

As the members signed the scroll, the Palestine Philharmonic orchestra, seated in the adjoining room, played *Hatikvah.* Every pair of eyes in the room was rivited to the signers. For them this moment would live forever . . .

When the signing had been completed, Ben-Gurion rapped again. *"The State of Israel is established."*

CONSTANCE and Sam wandered among the crowds, sharing in the triumph of the day. A dream had become reality. All around them there was laughter and singing. Nobody seemed to care that already air-raid protection tents were being set up in the streets.

Constance and Sam waited for a table in a street cafe—too excited to be hungry, but it gave them an excuse to sit and watch the celebrating crowds. Neither wanted to relinquish this moment—this was a night to be shared with all of Tel Aviv. A gentle breeze from the Mediterranean cooled the hot city.

They strolled along with the throngs until the early hours of the morning, stopping occasionally for tea. And then startling news rippled through the crowds. President Truman had recognized the new Jewish state. Instantly the streets and cafes were filled with Israelis dancing the Hora. It was almost dawn before the streets were finally cleared.

"ARE you glad we came?" Sam asked Constance as they prepared for bed.

"Oh Sam, yes."

"I think," Sam said slowly, "that this was the day of my life for which I was born. Nothing can ever compare with what happened here today. And you are the only woman in the world I would share it with, Connie."

"We have to be up early to pack, Sam," she said gently. "Come to bed."

THEY woke up early, packed and went down to breakfast.

"Connie, let's stay another day," Sam said as he sipped his coffee. "How can we leave in the midst of such joy? I want to savor it for just one more day."

"But we have our reservations—"

"We'll change them. I'll take care of it, Connie. Let me just walk for another day in this beautiful new state of Israel."

As always, Constance knew it was futile to argue with him once he'd made up his mind. He was drunk on Israel's triumph—as was she. She knew, too, that he felt a guilty to be leaving when war was surely imminent. But for too long Sam had fought Israel's battles . . . through two world wars he had struggled for this day. Surely he had proved himself a Jew . . .

Again they roamed through the city, stopping at cafes whenever they were tired. Feeling at one with everyone around them. And then as quickly as it began it was over. Planes swooped overhead. Enemy spitfires dived over the city. Across the street a girl screamed, her khaki slacks crimson with blood. A few feet away a man bellowed in pain.

"Sam!" Constance screamed, "Sam, let's get to a shelter!" Bombs were falling. Machine guns rattled. Where was Sam? "Oh, my God—"

He lay on the sidewalk beside her. Blood oozed from his chest. He was chalk-white, gasping for breath. She dropped to her knees beside him.

"They can't mow us down, Connie—We'll survive. Israel will survive—"

She held Sam's lifeless body in her arms, oblivious to the chaos around them. Hospital and military trucks were moving into the street. The planes were gone. Someone gently took his body from her. Sam had come home. He would lie in Israel forever.

TWO days later Constance stood at the rail of the ship that was to take her on the first lap of her ship-plane-rail journey back to Hong Kong. The outline of Tel Aviv was disappearing in the early purple dusk. She had buried Sam where his heart had belonged for so many years. There was peace in that.

She knew she had to bring order back into her life. One day soon she and Adam would build Sam's resort hotel on the beach. The Samuel Stone Hotel.

All the times before when Sam had gone away, she always knew he would come back. Since she was sixteen he had been her life. Now he was gone.

349

She hoped the memories would last forever—Sam asking her to marry him . . . Sam and Lucienne together on the street . . . Sam looking in her eyes as she told him she carried Elliot's son, and knowing the truth . . . Sam holding Adam in his arms for the first time . . . Good and bad times—they were all she had left.

She remembered something David had once said to her.

"Life is a series of rooms, Connie. We've just shared a small but very precious room."

Sam had shared many rooms in her life. There were rooms in his life she had never shared—but that didn't lessen the quality of their love. It was time she moved to other rooms.

She remembered Sam's last words: *"Israel will survive."*

She, too, would survive. Sam wished that for her.